THE PERFECT SISTER

Zoë Miller was born in Dublin, where she now lives with her husband. She began writing stories at an early age. Her writing career has also included freelance journalism and prize-winning short fiction. She has three children.

www.zoemillerauthor.com
@zoemillerauthor
Facebook.com/zoemillerauthor

PREVIOUSLY BY ZOË MILLER

The Visitor
A House Full of Secrets
Someone New
A Question of Betrayal
A Husband's Confession
The Compromise
A Family Scandal
Rival Passions
Sinful Deceptions
Guilty Secrets

THE PERFECT SISTER

Zoë Miller

HACHETTE
BOOKS
IRELAND

First published in Ireland in 2020 by HACHETTE BOOKS IRELAND
First published in paperback in 2021

1

Cataloguing in Publication Data is available from the British Library.

ISBN 9789781529385052

Typeset in Sabon by Bookends Publishing Services, Dublin

Printed and bound in Great Britain by Clays Ltd, Elcograf, S.p.A.

Hachette Books Ireland policy is to use papers that are natural, renewable
and recyclable products and made from wood grown in sustainable forests.
The logging and manufacturing processes are expected to conform to the
environmental regulations of the country of origin.

Hachette Books Ireland
8 Castlecourt Centre
Castleknock
Dublin 15, Ireland

A division of Hachette UK Ltd
Carmelite House, 50 Victoria Embankment, London EC4Y 0DZ

www.hachettebooksireland.ie

Dedicated to the wonderful bright stars who bring so much joy and love to our family –

Cruz, Tom, Lexi, J.P., Sophia, and Éabha, our newest little star, who arrived into our world in the middle of a global pandemic, a beacon of love and hope.

'May the dreams you hold dearest be those that come true.'

CHAPTER 1

Holly

ON A WET WEDNESDAY NIGHT IN FEBRUARY, the past I'd struggled in vain to put behind me detonated without mercy, exploding its dark menace across the living room of Rose Cottage.

It began as the most innocuous of moments. Luke was channel-hopping, searching for the post-match analysis of a soccer fixture. Then, in an instant that stopped my breath, the television screen was filled with an image of Liffey Gate. Despite the words of protest flapping inside me like caged birds, and the scalpel-sharp pain that sliced my stomach, I reached out and stilled Luke's hand on the remote control.

I think because he was so startled, he didn't object.

'Once heralded as the ultimate experience in dockland living,' the female reporter was saying, 'and brought to market in a blaze of high-octane, champagne-filled publicity, now, fifteen years later, a succession of fire-safety examinations have identified so many problems and lack of appropriate standards that the only option is demolition.'

Demolition? Icy fingers clawed at my spine.

1

Her voice oozed about me like a malignant force. 'Liffey Gate,' she went on, 'is the latest example in a long line of Celtic Tiger apartment blocks to suffer problems as a result of being constructed with scant regard for rules and regulations. Major defects have now been identified in many of these ...'

I wasn't interested in other apartment blocks. Only the one we'd lived in.

'... Liffey Gate residents have had their tenancies terminated,' she continued, 'and legal proceedings are proving complex due to the apartment block being owned by a group of several investors, the original developer now declared bankrupt.'

She spoke about Liffey Gate's enviable dockland location, the camera panning across the river, the choppy surface glinting with sunshine. It skimmed over the Convention Centre and onto the grey, harp-like cables of the Samuel Beckett Bridge, before it panned back to the south side of the quays, fastening on the apartment block where we'd once loved and laughed and lived with no heed for tomorrow.

But all was changed.

Hoarding covered the lower floors, plastered with lurid-looking safety warnings. Above that, the top two storeys of the six-storey block had already been stripped to a skeletal framework of concrete floors, bone-bleached pillars and redundant lift shafts. Steel tangles protruded from the top of the ghostly structure like mocking limbs.

From high-octane celebrations to an inglorious destruction: a perfect metaphor for our lives.

I could just about make out the third-floor apartment where we'd partied until dawn, coming out onto our tiny balcony to see the sunrise streaming up Dublin Bay. Then later, the partying days over, the sleepless nights, and later again, near the end of it all, when Luke had smashed a set of china mugs against the balcony door, cracking them one by one into a million pieces, cracking my heart into smithereens as he sat on the floor afterwards, put his head into his hands and wept.

'Did you know about this?' I asked Luke, my voice hoarse.

'No … no, I'd no idea.'

I didn't know whether to believe him or not. Had he known, he surely would have done his best to keep this disaster from me. Liffey Gate being demolished meant walls, floors and ceilings being taken apart, and if the building was harbouring any secrets, the demolition could uncover them. A ripple of foreboding ran through my veins.

'*You think you're clever, getting rid of the evidence …*' Jay had snarled that snowy, fateful night, '*You won't get away with this, Holly.*'

I tried to prevent my imagination from exploding in a billion directions, to convince myself that there was nothing to worry about, least of all the threatening words Jay Slater had thrown at me. I told myself it had all been over seven years ago. I'd watched the late-night news footage coming from Grand Canal Dock where divers had brought up his remains from the murky depths of the water, the area shadowy and dark save for pools of light picked out by temporary arc lamps. By the following night the media had moved on to other tragedies, Jay's sad time in the spotlight fleeting and temporary. But our lives had never moved on, even though we liked to pretend they had. His ghost still stalked the emotional rubble in my head, blasting out pockets of anxiety, sometimes jolting me into rude wakefulness at three in the morning.

'I'm not watching this shit,' Luke said, channel-hopping again until the screen filled with soccer pundits arguing about whether or not a goal had been offside.

I rose on shaky legs, went into the bedroom and took a pill I kept for emergencies. Outside, there was nothing to see except a blanket of dark Kilkenny countryside staring in at me through the rain-streaked window pane. I pulled down the blind. Even though I was in my mid-thirties, the impenetrable pitch black of the night still scared me. I closed my eyes and willed myself to dive down into that place deep inside me where nothing at all existed except a pool of dark stillness. No past, no pain, no hurt. But most of all, no Jay Slater.

CHAPTER 2

Alice

ON THURSDAY MORNING, WHEN SHE SAW the February date on the calendar and felt the cold shadow of his absence rippling silently across the kitchen, Alice Clarke picked up the glass vase that had sat for years on the windowsill and dropped it into the sink so that it cracked.

Thirty-six years was too long to be filling a vase with early daffodils as a sort of magic spell to draw her father home and make him stay. Her six-year-old self had begun that tradition because she knew he loved their beauty and symbol of new beginnings after a cold, dark winter, but he'd never come home to see them.

Distracted, she left the house without an umbrella, and as she joined the throng of commuters swarming out of the Dart station on Westland Row, dark clouds opened and sheets of rain bucketed across the city centre streets. Juggling her tote bag, which was weighed down with her packed lunch and a hard-backed novel, she freed the hood of her coat from its zipped compartment. Dodging as many umbrella spikes as possible, and veering away from sprays of dirty water churned up by passing traffic, it took her ten minutes to reach the staff entrance of Abbey Lane Library. Thankfully, the steel shutters were already open. She keyed in the code for the door release and stepped into the passageway, dripping a trail of fat raindrops across the tiled floor as she dashed to the bathroom. Her hood was sodden, her shoulders wet through and her fine dark hair stuck flatly to her head. She peeled off her coat, eased off her boots and slid down her leggings, hanging them over the back of a chair.

From the depths of her bag, her mobile chimed. She was tempted to ignore it, but in case it had anything to do with her daughter Chloe, who'd been brought to school that morning by her childminder Maeve, she wiped her damp hand against her jumper and fished it out. Just as well. It was Ronan – he who must not be ignored.

'Yes, Ronan?' she said, glancing at her reflection in the mirror. Besides her saturated hair, mascara slid down her cheeks like matted tyre tracks. Just as well he couldn't see her because her ragged appearance would be further ammunition in his artillery of unfit-motherhood bullets, which he regularly fired off in his attempts to have more access to Chloe. Ronan had already told her he wouldn't be happy until he had main custody of their precious daughter.

'You haven't forgotten this evening?' he said, his voice disjointed as though he was on the move. She pictured him marching across the floor of his office, barking the reminder to her in between commands to his staff.

'No, I haven't,' she said. 'Chloe will be ready.'

'I'd better get parking outside,' he said. 'Your road is mental at rush hour.'

A flat tone in her ear told her he'd terminated the call.

Of course he'd get parking. Ronan was quite capable of bulldozing his way along Victoria Row in his tank of a Merc and commandeering an undesignated spot, or double parking if needs be, with scant regard to cycle lanes or double yellow lines. Chloe was always ready for a quick handover, because the less Alice had to see of Ronan, the better. Most of the time what Ronan said or did was filtered through a huge safety net – Alice had some ammunition tucked away. Compromising to say the least. Still, as he had pointed out, if she tried to use it against him, he had friends in high places. Ronan L. Russell hadn't cemented his reputation as the brainchild behind one of Dublin's most successful corporate law firms without having plenty of contacts in judicial positions, as well as high-powered business contacts across the city. The sooner their divorce was finalised, the better.

But whatever about the disintegration of relations between them, Ronan had never taken any of his annoyance out on Chloe. He adored his daughter. Ronan spoiled her rotten as some kind of compensation for the harrowing fact (his view) that Chloe was being raised by a separated mother and a dad who only saw her on Sundays unless there was a special occasion, such as this evening, when he was bringing her to his young nephew's birthday party.

All Alice's fault, of course. Nothing whatsoever to do with Ronan.

Alice turned towards the wall-mounted hand-dryer to dry her hair. There was nothing but an oblong of lighter-coloured paint indicating where it had once sat. She'd forgotten it had been replaced last week by a new waist-level air-blade model that only pumped hot air when your hands were inserted. It would work for drying off her leggings, so her lower half was sorted, but her hair was the biggest problem. Putting one hand into the innards of the dryer, she bent her head as far as she could, hoping to catch an upwards drift of warm air. No such luck. Today, she would just have to brave the world with the less-than-well-groomed Alice Clarke mask. When she went out onto the library floor, her leggings still slightly damp, she hoped it would work its magic on her rising irritation.

Abbey Lane Library, in an earlier incarnation, had been a small, perfectly proportioned grey-stone church, the only surviving part of an old south-inner-city Dublin abbey. The library incorporated a lot of the church's former glory, and Alice liked to think that reflections of the still, calm ambience lingered in the beautifully arched doorways, the smooth wooden shelves offering books to satisfy every need and the soft glow that flickered through high stained-glass windows, even on dull days.

Finbarr, the senior librarian, was over at a table with Ralph, the library attendant, who was putting reference stickers on that morning's newspapers before slotting them into a holder behind the counter.

'Morning, Alice, quite a bad one out there,' Finbarr said.

'If there was anyone waiting outside, I'd open the public door early,' Ralph said, 'but it's all quiet.'

'Not surprised, with that deluge,' Alice said.

The library was open from 10 a.m. to 5 p.m., Monday to Saturday, with late-night opening until 7 p.m. on Thursdays. Alice worked four days a week.

Gwen arrived in, bundled into a huge plastic raincoat, breathless from having hurried from the Luas stop on Dawson Street, followed by Julia, equally muffled up. There was no sign of Sharon, even though she was rostered for counter duty that morning, so Alice would have to stand in and show her rain-sodden face to the customers, although she'd planned to go through the boxes of new books delivered the previous evening. It was her favourite job, inhaling the new-book scent, feeling the heft of them in her hands, anticipating the mysteries within. Ralph and Finbarr were setting up the computer room – a volunteer from Age Action was coming in that morning to put some pensioners through their internet paces. Gwen was looking after the tiny tots' story-time.

Sharon eventually arrived, forty-five minutes late. The rain had stopped and she swanned in through the main entrance brandishing an unopened golf umbrella, wearing pristine silvery boots, a pair of white jeans and an emerald jumper under her open cream trench coat. Her blonde hair fanned about her shoulders in a cascade of waving perfection. At twenty-one years old, she was half Alice's age and the newest member of staff. Sometimes Sharon was so dazzling and immaculate and beaming with sunshine that she reminded Alice of Holly, her younger sister, and made her feel drab and dull by comparison. This morning was one of those times.

'Sorry I'm late,' Sharon said, giving everyone the benefit of her brilliant smile, 'the weather was so bad that I waited to get a lift from my dad.'

''Tis far from lifts by adoring dads that you or I were reared,' Julia said under her breath as she elbowed Alice.

Adoring dads.

Alice lifted a stack of returned books so hurriedly that most of them slipped from her grasp, slid across the counter and toppled to the floor.

◆

By lunchtime, Alice's hair resembled a crumpled sheet of frizz. She sat in the kitchen with her sandwiches and fruit while Sharon picked daintily at a mixed salad bowl, bought at some expense in the artisan deli down the road.

'I won't be doing this too often,' Sharon said, noticing how Alice's eyes strayed to her bowl. 'I think I'll copy your sensible example and bring in my lunch.'

Sensible. Sharon was right and it stung.

'Anyway, I'm saving hard,' Sharon went on.

'Are you?' Alice felt obliged to ask.

'Yes, I feel I can trust you, Alice, but not a word to the others for now,' Sharon confided. 'I'm going to spend a year trekking around the world, with my best friend Emma. Just us and our backpacks and the stars at night. It's going to be a wonderful adventure.'

Sharon lived for excitement. Her weekends and days off were filled with new experiences. The previous weekend she'd gone zip-lining in Tibradden, in the Dublin Mountains. Everything about her life seemed to be a glittering adventure of sorts.

Echoes of Holly.

Let me breathe, she'd said.

Let me have a life of adventure.

And for God's sake, keep out of it.

Alice's apple tasted sour.

What happened, Holly? Why are you hiding away in the depths of the countryside?

'I'd hate to end up like Finbarr,' Sharon said. 'Don't get me wrong,' she leaned forward, her big blue eyes earnest, 'I love Finbarr to bits – he's an absolute dote – but almost forty years in the exact same job? And he goes to Benidorm on holidays every single year. Jesus – how boring is that?'

A lot of people would feel blessed to hold down a permanent, pensionable job with a guaranteed income for the span of forty years, and have an annual holiday in Benidorm, Alice wanted to say. Apart from a three-year career break during which she'd married and had Chloe, she'd been in the library service since she'd left school, and she fully intended staying there in her role as senior assistant for the next twenty years. She counted herself lucky to have an annual holiday in Majorca with Chloe.

No doubt Sharon would consider her lifestyle to be as boring as Finbarr's.

'You'd think Finbarr would do something more exciting with his life,' Sharon said.

Alice could have told her that excitement often came with a sting in its tail. She'd had her thrill ride into the danger zone when she'd met and married Ronan. Never again. There was a lot to be said for a humdrum, sensible life.

Wasn't there?

After lunch, Alice stayed back, channelling a vague irritation with herself into tidying the kitchen; even so, when she went out onto the library floor, Sharon's remarks were still darting under her skin like pinpricks. The library hummed with activity, students grouped around study desks, others working in the computer room, Ralph looking after printing and photocopying requests. Mr Woods, a pensioner whose wife had dementia and who escaped into the library for an hour every day when their home help came in, was relaxing with the newspapers in his usual armchair in the reading area. Finbarr was going through the range of online resources with a customer. A man was standing at the front desk, looking in Alice's direction, smiling in expectation.

'Here's Alice Clarke now,' she heard Sharon say, with a laugh in her voice. 'She'll sort you out. Alice is the dedicated one with years of experience – I'm still the newbie.'

CHAPTER 3

'HI, ALICE,' THE GUY SAID, 'I'D LIKE TO BOOK A place at this evening's author event.'

He was medium height with a pleasant face. Neat dark hair. Mid-forties-ish. Well educated, with a successful career, Alice guessed, judging by his beautifully cut suit and expensive tie, the intelligent expression in his hazel eyes.

'Please?' he added, with a confident smile.

The library was hosting an event that evening with Ian Donohue, an American bestselling science fiction author. Ian was holidaying in Ireland, exploring his family roots, and he was giving an informal talk in the library because it was close to the inner-city area his great-grandparents had hailed from. It had booked out swiftly.

'It's fully booked,' she said, wondering why she was being unusually abrupt with a customer. She even sensed Sharon glancing at her quizzically.

'Are you sure?' he asked. The guy smiled at her as if she'd be able to conjure up a place especially for him, simply because he'd asked her in the nicest way possible. But charm offensives didn't cut any ice with her, no matter how well presented. Ronan had oozed charm, in the beginning.

'I'm positive,' she said.

'Do you not need to look up the thingamajig?' he said, his gaze flickering expectantly to a computer screen behind the desk.

'No. I do not need to look up the thingamajig.'

'I told you Alice was super-efficient,' Sharon said in a slightly apologetic voice.

'I've been away,' the man went on. 'I only heard about the event at lunchtime. I'm a huge fan.' He smiled again. 'Could you squeeze in an extra chair? Or I could bring a fold-up stool. I could stand. Better again ...' he paused, 'I could bring chocolates.'

He sounded mannerly. His eyes, when they rested on Alice, were kind and considerate. She was conscious of her frizzy hair and hurriedly repaired face. Then she understood why she had been so abrupt with him. In another kind of life, where Ronan and the impending divorce didn't exist, or even before him, in a life where a younger Alice might have felt stronger, more confident on the inside, this was the kind of man she would have been drawn to, the kind of man who might have loved and cherished her and shared a full life with her, but it was too late now and she was quietly angry with herself and her lost opportunities.

'Oh, don't tempt *me* with chocolates.' Sharon laughed. 'I'm minding my figure, but Alice would enjoy them.'

'I'm sorry, but we can only accommodate a certain number of attendees,' Alice said, striving to be polite. 'Health and safety.' He looked like a thoughtful person who'd respect such regulations.

'Ah,' he said.

'And, officially, we're not allowed to take gifts from the public,' Alice went on, realising she sounded ridiculously prim and proper.

'No way,' the guy said, laughing easily.

'Don't mind Alice,' Sharon said. 'She's far too inclined to play by the book. Haha, *library* book.'

'Could you take my name in case there's a cancellation?' he asked.

'We can add you to the waiting list,' Alice said.

'Thank you, Alice,' he said. 'I appreciate that. My office is nearby. I can come at the last minute.' He took out his wallet and extracted a business card, handing it to her. She glanced at the details. Damien Maher. Senior Analyst, KLW Investment Management.

'Well then,' he said, backing away, 'enjoy the rest of your day. It must be lovely to spend it in this environment instead of looking at double computer screens.'

'That all depends on what's on the screen,' Sharon said with an infectious giggle.

He left then, an unsettling energy rippling in his wake.

'I'd have squeezed him in,' Sharon said, staring after him. 'He's gorgeous, for a middle-aged man.'

Middle-aged? Alice had to forcibly remind herself that when she'd been twenty-one anyone over forty was getting on in life.

'So you would have flouted health and safety?' she said sourly.

Sharon laughed. 'Chill, Alice. You're far too serious at times.' She drifted away, examining her nails before she began to sift through the books on the returns trolley, mindful of her shellac.

◆

Ronan didn't come into the house when he dropped Chloe home that night. He waited out by the kerb, the engine of his gleaming Mercedes purring like a sleek black panther, keeping out of Alice's hair because he knew he'd had Chloe out late on a school night. As soon as Chloe was safely through the hall door, he gunned the engine and roared off.

Chloe had the fidgety look in her blue eyes of someone overdosed on sugar, and sticky streaks ran up her flushed cheeks. She was just seven years of age. At times Alice wanted to weep at the way the innocent baby and toddler years had flashed by in the blink of an eye, but she was grateful that Chloe seemed to be growing up happy and healthy, and turning into a well-adjusted person in her own right. She hadn't botched things entirely with her daughter.

'Daddy's in a hurry,' Chloe said, clutching a goodie bag and playing imaginary hopscotch as she skipped down the hall, her auburn hair loosened from her ponytail. 'He has to go back to his friend.'

His friend. 'You mean Amanda?'

'Yeah, Amanda. She's nice.'

Alice had lost count of the women Ronan had taken up with after the break-up of their marriage, details of which she'd gleaned from the weekend supplements, with the commentary that they were helping Ronan come to terms with his heartache and move on in the aftermath of his separation. Chloe had not seemed aware of any of them, until Amanda.

'He asked me again if you have any friends that call here, but I said no,' Chloe said, oblivious to the connotations of the question.

Friends? She'd lost contact with a lot of her schoolmates, drifting apart over the years thanks to the way her life had mainly revolved around Mum, Holly, her job and Victoria Row. Then later, any tenuous friendships she'd held on to had been severed when Ronan had come into her life. She avoided social media whereas Ronan revelled in his Instagram account. According to him, he had thousands of followers who loved being updated with details of his social life, his golf and his favourite eateries. Alice stayed close to home most evenings. Ronan had a habit of calling the land-line two or three times a week, ostensibly to say good night to Chloe, but also checking on Alice, making sure she was there, preferably alone. Any sign of her wavering off the straight and narrow path would be ammunition in his ongoing battle for main custody of Chloe.

As it was, he only saw Chloe on Sundays, preferring to have his Saturday nights free for socialising. He wanted full weekday access, with Alice being relegated to the weekends. She was determined to retain her existing custody rights and see through the next six months as quietly as possible, until their divorce was finalised.

He resented his daughter going to the local school

and being ferried there and back by Alice's cousin Maeve, who looked after Chloe along with her own young children when Alice was at work. He would have preferred Chloe to attend the fee-paying school in his privileged south Dublin enclave and to have had a personal nanny for her. Chloe was his. She even looked like him. He insisted he could give her a far better lifestyle than Alice could. When Alice tackled him about his 'friends', he glibly informed her that it was his way of finding out who was the most suitable in his efforts to set up a stable home base with a mother-figure for his daughter, seeing as Alice hadn't cut the mustard. However, as far as Ronan was concerned, the same rule did not apply when it came to Alice having men friends.

'If there's even a hint of another father-figure sniffing around, thinking he can step into my shoes with my precious Chloe,' he'd said, 'I'll … I'll …'

'You'll do what, exactly?' Alice had asked, raising her chin, giving him the look that reminded him she had something in her back pocket that could be used against him, even though she knew she hadn't really got it in her to stoop that low.

'You don't want to go there,' he'd blustered.

In dark moments, she asked herself how she'd ever become involved with Ronan in the first place.

CHAPTER 4

FRIDAY EVENING BROUGHT MORE HEAVY rain, and when Alice came out of the library the sky was a low, leaden-grey bowl, the city centre gridlocked with traffic, pavements clogged with pedestrians wielding dripping umbrellas. She went to dash across the road close to the pedestrian crossing, before the amber light flickered to red, but was so intent on avoiding the onslaught of people rushing towards her that she misjudged her step and tripped, her bum hitting the kerb as she fell, landing on her back. Pain shot through her lower back and her hips. Dazed, she blinked up at a forest of wet raincoats and jackets and curious faces, sheets of rain beating down on her upturned cheek. Voices drifted down to her.

'Are you okay?'

'What happened?'

'Don't try to move – you could have broken something.'

Some of the circle shifted and separated as onlookers moved on, their curiosity satisfied. Someone had stopped the oncoming traffic and car horns blared, drivers up ahead unaware of what was causing the hold-up. Then a man bent down, blotting out the spitting rain and dark grey sky.

'Alice? It *is* you, isn't it? What happened? It's Damien,' he said. 'I talked to you in the library. Yesterday. Where does it hurt?' he asked, his dark hair and face beaded with raindrops.

'I'm perfectly fine,' she said, unable to pinpoint the exact source of the waves of pain, embarrassed at the undignified sight she must make lying there, legs splayed, her hood askew and hair soaked with the rain.

'I'm calling an ambulance,' he said, taking out a mobile.

'Don't be ridiculous. I'll be grand in a minute,' she said, deciding not to attempt the ungainly job of getting to her feet while he was there to witness it.

'I'm sure you will be,' he said pleasantly, 'but in the meantime you need to get checked out.'

'I can move,' she said feebly, flexing her legs and lifting her head. 'There can't be much wrong. Just bruises. Go home.'

'You could have slight concussion,' he said. 'Hold on a minute …'

He stood up and she heard him talking to another man, an answering reply. Then he bent back down. 'We're going to see if you can stand up, Alice. There's a taxi right here and we'll get you to the nearest hospital. It'll take a while for an ambulance to arrive in this traffic.'

'I'm fine, honestly.'

'Of course you are.'

Gently and slowly, Damien and another man levered Alice to her feet. Alice glared at the remaining onlookers and more of them drifted away, satisfied that the drama was over.

'My bag ...' Alice looked around. Her tote was on the pavement, some of the contents spilling out. Damien scooped up everything, tucking it back into the bag. She felt as though her lower back had caved in as he helped her into the taxi and leaned over to secure her seat belt, so close she saw the green flecks in his hazel eyes and dark eyelashes. He hopped into the back beside her, putting her bag between them.

'What are you doing?' she asked, as the taxi edged out into the traffic.

'I'll see you to the hospital.'

'There's no need.'

'I can't leave you alone. If there's someone you can call on, I'll wait until they arrive. Okay?'

'Oh God— Chloe. Maeve is minding her. I'm supposed to be picking her up soon.'

She found her mobile, safely tucked into the zipped compartment of her bag. She keyed in her PIN code and scrolled to Maeve's number. The pain slicing through her hips was reminiscent of the agony of the labour ward. She did her best to tell Maeve what had happened without alarming her.

Maeve's voice was reassuring; she wasn't to worry one bit, Chloe could have a sleepover with her daughter.

'Hugh is out at a work do right now,' Maeve said, referring to her husband, 'but as soon as he comes home, I'll be over to the hospital. I don't like to think of you in there on your own.'

'I'm not on my own,' Alice said, explaining briefly about Damien. As soon as she finished the call, she turned to him. 'I don't mean for you to stay,' she said, 'of course not. I'm trying to save Maeve the hassle – it's enough that's she minding Chloe.'

'Is Chloe your daughter?' he asked.

'Yes.'

'Is there anyone else you want to call?'

'No,' she said. 'I have a sister, Holly,' she went on, 'but she moved out of Dublin years ago.' The realisation that there was no one else to call filled her with loneliness and a sense of failure. She was glad that Damien stayed silent and didn't ask if Chloe's father was around. Presently the taxi arrived at the hospital entrance and halted outside A&E. Alice reached into her bag for her purse.

There was no purse. She took out her lunchbox and book, the better to check, but there was no sign of it. 'I'm sorry,' she managed to stutter, appalled at this fresh humiliation, 'but I can't pay. I can't pay the hospital charge either,' she went on in a quavery voice. 'My purse is gone. It must have been robbed when I fell.'

'Jesus,' Damien said. 'Was there much in it?'

'About a hundred euro along with my bank cards and store cards.'

'You'll have to cancel those,' he said. 'First things first, let's get you inside.'

He thrust some notes at the taxi driver, who waved half of them away, mentioning something about the circumstances, mortifying Alice further. Damien took her bag and insisted she hold on to him as he eased her out of the taxi. She'd no choice but to do so, as together they stepped gingerly around the yellow criss-crossed no-parking zone, into A&E.

◆

On a normal Friday night, Alice would be at home in Victoria Row with Chloe, making popcorn and hot chocolate, watching an early-evening movie before she tucked Chloe up in bed and herself on the sofa in her PJs, with a book and a glass of wine. Oh, for it to be a normal Friday night instead of sitting here in the triage cubicle, in the middle of the seething cauldron that constituted A&E.

'You might need an X-ray to see if your coccyx is fractured or bruised,' the triage nurse said, keying something into her computer when Alice admitted that most of the pain seemed to be radiating from her tail-bone.

'Like tonight?'

'Either tonight or we'll give you an appointment for early next week. What were you saying about your head?' the nurse asked, peering into her screen.

'I whacked it when I fell.'

'Any dizziness or brain fog? Nausea?' the nurse asked sharply, looking at Alice.

'No.'

Sometimes she got brain fog when Ronan was around, or when she woke up at three in the morning and thought of the years she'd been married to him. Sometimes she felt dizzy when she thought of the way her mum had died, and that she was no longer around. The mother she'd loved, who'd laughed and moved and inhabited the rooms in Victoria Row; gone now. Grief and bereavement were cold and hard and metallic; sometimes they were colourless and flat, but always painful. Sometimes she felt a surge of nausea when she wondered where she'd gone wrong with Holly, or why Holly had chosen to bury herself with Luke in a remote part of the country just as Chloe had been born. Sometimes she felt dizzy when a sudden memory of her dad sliced across the kitchen in the soft-lit morning and sucked her underwater.

The questions continued as the pain in her tail-bone set her teeth on edge.

'You'll need to see the doctor,' said the triage nurse, 'but there's a bit of a wait.'

When she went back out to the waiting area, Damien was still sitting there, like the only steady anchor in a sea of shifting chaos. The electronic board indicated an estimated five-hour wait.

'Why are you still here?' she asked, anxiety rising inside her. It had been embarrassing enough that he'd paid the A&E charge with his credit card, saying that Alice could pay him back before his bill arrived the following month. He knew where she worked, he'd joked, in case she tried to renege on the debt.

'I was keeping your seat for you,' he said pleasantly, indicating the overcoat folded on the seat beside him, which he picked up. 'They're in short supply around here.'

All the plastic chairs were occupied by a cross-section

of humanity. Most people looked resigned to the dubious fate of A&E on a Friday night. Some were grumbling about having to wait when they clearly needed urgent attention. An elderly man in a wheelchair was crying quietly, his son trying to comfort him. A television high up in a corner was turned to a news channel, and the air was muggy with the scent of damp clothes, the windows heavy with condensation.

'I rang the police and told them about your purse,' he said. 'I gave them my contact details in case it turns up, but you'll have to call the bank yourself.'

'You didn't have to do that.'

'I had the number of Store Street station on my phone. It was no trouble.'

'Thanks for your help,' she said, sitting down beside him as gingerly as possible, 'but please go home now.' There was mud on her trousers and a gash on the side of her face. Her hair was a mess. Pain flared out from her hips to her lower back, as though someone had taken a blow-torch to it. She had no money. Even in the crowded A&E, she felt alone in the world, and the last thing she needed was this stranger witnessing her humiliation.

Her mobile rang. Ronan.

Damn.

CHAPTER 5

'HI, RONAN.'

'Where are you?'

'I'm not at home.'

'Obviously not, seeing as you didn't answer the land-line. Who are you with? Where's Chloe? Can I talk to her?'

The thought of admitting to Ronan that she was in A&E having slipped and fallen filled her with fresh annoyance. Pretending she was doing some late-night shopping might account for the noise around her. Then the sequence of events played out swiftly in her head. He would phone Maeve next, to check on Chloe, and there was a chance Maeve would chat about what had happened to Alice, including her good fortune in having a nice man escort her to the hospital.

'Chloe's with Maeve. I'm in A&E, I fell,' she rushed on, 'I need to get checked out.'

'How the fuck did you manage that?'

'I fell on the way home from work.'

'Silly Alice. Now Chloe's routine is all upset.'

'She's fine. She's having a sleepover.'

'I'll call Maeve and satisfy myself about that.'

'In case you're interested, Ronan, I'll be fine too. A

library customer made sure I got here okay.' She knew it was preferable for her to introduce the part Damien had played rather than Ronan hearing it from Maeve.

'Yeah? Who was that now, exactly?'

'A guy who saw what happened and knew I needed help,' she said, cringing internally.

'How did he see what happened? Was he with you?'

'No, Ronan, he was passing by and recognised me from the library.'

'Is he still there?'

'No. I sent him home.'

'I'll check on Chloe and collect her as usual on Sunday,' he said.

When the call ended, Alice was reluctant to meet Damien's eyes. He had surely heard every strident word out of Ronan's mouth as well as her replies. Still, it was safer for Damien to witness her little white lie rather than having Ronan go into meltdown at the thought of her being with another man.

'That was Ronan, my ex-husband,' she began.

'Ronan. I kind of sussed that.'

'He was worried about our daughter.'

But you probably guessed from the call he wasn't worried about me. Feck you, Ronan.

She contacted the bank and cancelled her cards, and then she exchanged numbers with Damien. 'I'll text you next week and arrange to pay you back,' she said. 'I appreciate what you've done. I don't even have the money to get home, once I'm out of here,' she went on thoughtlessly.

'I can see you home,' he said.

She was sorry she'd spoken, hot and cold at the idea of him sitting there throughout the long haul. 'No way. You go on off, I'll sort something out – I've money at home. The taxi driver will wait.'

'I'm not going to abandon you now,' he said. 'Tomorrow's Saturday, so it's not as if I have to be in the office at eight in the morning. Seriously, Alice, it's fine. Tell me about Chloe, your family.'

She was reluctant to go there, to the place she felt she had failed, between her rift with Holly and her marriage. To take the spotlight off herself she turned the conversation around and asked Damien about his favourite books and authors, surprised to find that over three hours slipped by while they chatted about various genres, how some bestsellers never lived up to the hype, how movie adaptations were never the same as the sensory experience of a book. He told her he'd lived in Hong Kong for a few years, had come home over a year ago and had been working in KLW ever since. He went to the vending machine, Alice refusing anything but a bottle of water while he got crisps and chocolate.

'You're probably starving,' she said.

'Nah, I was out for dinner earlier today, a celebration for a retiring colleague, so no worries there.'

'Good, I owe you enough as it is without having you pass out from hunger.'

She was glad he was there when some of the crowd got restless and unruly, the ambulance sirens kept shrieking up to the door of A&E and, later that night, a fight broke out between two drunks in the back seats. Eventually she was called through to the other side: more bedlam and a logjam of trolleys and scurrying staff. Her injury was more than likely severe bruising, she was told. She was given strong painkillers to see her through the night and a prescription for more, then an appointment for an X-ray the following week, just to be sure there was no hairline fracture, plus a note for work – she'd have to rest up for a few days.

'Sit on a pillow or two,' the nurse said. 'Better still, get a swimming ring.' She didn't look much older than Chloe, and Alice wondered how she was going to deal with the burly and disorderly drunks outside.

'I'll live,' she told Damien, deciding that the less she mentioned pillows and swimming rings, the better. They went out into the night. It was almost two o'clock in the morning and the rain had stopped, the damp air cool and soft. She could have been in a dream of sorts – she had that insubstantial feeling that she was seeing everything through a haze. She wasn't sure if it was the effects of the medication, the aftermath of the shock or the man beside her, helping her gently into a taxi.

'Where to?' he asked.

She gave her address and watched as the late-night city centre streets glided by the window, revellers tumbling out of clubs, queues jostling at taxi ranks. Presently they arrived at Victoria Row. Damien helped her out of the taxi. When she was standing on the pavement, Damien looked around him, absorbing every angle of the scene in front of him. She saw a smile breaking out across his face as he looked at her in the lamplight.

'Is this where you live?' he asked.

'Yes.'

'Wow.' He stood looking, in no hurry to move.

Alice had had many reactions to where she lived before, but none as satisfying as this. Victoria Row was a terrace of eight cosy red-bricked Victorian houses, fronted by small railing-enclosed gardens, tucked between handsome period properties and grander Edwardian residences. 'Bijou', they'd been labelled when a couple of them had been put on the market in recent years. 'Two up, two down', they were more commonly referred to in the vernacular.

But the most desirable feature of all was the location: Victoria Row was situated along the seafront in Sandymount, where the Poolbeg peninsula sat at one end and the southern flank of Dublin Bay at the other, the coastal villages of Killiney and Dalkey floating on the near horizon like a grey, curving arm. Now, at half past two in the morning, the sea was a dark, murmuring expanse beyond the green on the far side of the road. The cool air carried a briny scent as it rippled over Alice's face. Up high and down to her left, lights on the Poolbeg chimneys twinkled into the night, silent signals that had landmarked home to Alice and winked at her all through her life.

Damien scanned her face in the shadowy light. 'Well,

Alice Clarke, you work in a library and live by the sea. It's perfect. I'm jealous.'

He was right. Her world was perfect in lots of ways. Chloe, her job, her small, cosy home. She mightn't see all that much of Holly, but her sister insisted she was happy – which was all that mattered. The spectre of Ronan was something Alice only had to endure for a few minutes each Sunday.

'Sorry,' Damien said, 'I'm standing here like a gobshite and you're in pain. Let me see you safely inside.'

And then, partly because of the strange night that was in it, and partly because Damien seemed so charmed by where she lived and worked, and it warmed a part of her she hadn't realised was cold, she heard herself say – half-expecting him to refuse: God knows what she looked like after her ordeal, between her usual mask in shreds and her self-esteem on the floor – 'Why don't you come in for coffee? A drink?'

'Thank you,' he said. 'But only if you feel up to it.'

She could have backed out then and cut the intangible connection she felt thanks to the time she had spent in his company, but even this moment was surreal, this man called Damien Maher smiling kindly at her, having said her job and the place where she lived was perfect, and in doing so giving her something she didn't understand yet.

'I am up to it,' she said, mentally sticking her finger up at Ronan.

CHAPTER 6

ALICE'S FRONT DOOR OPENED ONTO A SMALL square hall. To her right, a door led into the living room. A staircase straight ahead led up to two bedrooms and a bathroom. She disconnected the alarm, hung her coat on a peg and went into the living room, trying to ignore the ache in her bum as she switched on lamps and closed curtains.

'This is lovely and cosy,' Damien said, looking around.

'Thanks,' she said. Lamplight glowed on a grey sofa softened with blue and green cushions and a cream throw; an alcove by the fireplace was shelved from top to bottom, arranged with books and CDs and scattered with photographs and mementoes; there was a coffee table, a television unit, a mirror over the fireplace reflecting sparkly candle-holders on the mantelpiece, more photos on the walls, and an armchair drawn up to the front window – which had a fabulous daytime view.

'The kitchen is through here,' she said, indicating a door at the back of the living room. 'Would you like tea or coffee?'

'I'll look after that,' Damien said. 'You relax. I can find my way around a kitchen.'

She was too woozy from the additional painkillers to do anything but sit down, easing a cushion under her bum – she couldn't think about the tidiness or otherwise of her kitchen. She wanted to laugh at the total weirdness of having this guy making himself at home, when she rarely invited people in. It was another mad moment to add to the whole craziness of the evening, when it seemed her life up to now had skidded off the rails and lurched onto a different track.

'I could make you a sandwich if you're hungry,' Damien said.

'No, I'm fine, but help yourself to whatever's out there.'

He disappeared and presently a comforting aroma filtered into the room. 'What's that smell?' she asked, when he came through to ask if she took sugar or milk.

'I'm making toast for you.'

'That sounds lovely.' A wave of emotion washed over her. A simple gesture, but she couldn't remember the last time anyone had made tea *and* toast for her. Damien pulled the coffee table up beside her, before going back out to the kitchen and returning with tea and perfectly buttered toast.

'This is great, thanks,' Alice said.

'By the way, your vase on the windowsill is cracked. I shoved it into a corner of your counter – can't have you picking it up and injuring yourself further.'

'Thank you. I was great at putting a few daffodils into that vase every spring.'

'New beginnings?'

'Yeah, that kind of thing. Fresh starts ...' she swallowed, 'after a long dark winter.'

Damien brought out tea for himself and a chocolate bar. 'I can resist everything except chocolate,' he said.

'Chloe loves those bars too,' she told him.

Damien was looking at the photographs on the wall and she suddenly realised that she had invited an almost-stranger into her home in the small hours of the morning. But something was happening to her. The painkillers had kicked in big time, and her limbs softened and sank into the sofa. With that, her critical faculties seemed to be dissolving. Any notion of alarm blurred at the edges as calmness swept through her.

'Is that Chloe?' he asked, nodding towards a framed photograph.

'That's her all right – she was seven in January.'

'She must have been born around the time I went to Hong Kong,' Damien said, sitting down in the armchair. 'She's gorgeous. She looks happy.'

'She is, most of the time.'

'Who are these two?' he asked, indicating another photograph.

'My mother and my sister, Holly.'

Damien looked closer. 'I can see you resemble your mother,' he said.

'Yes.' She knew she was the image of petite, dark-haired Hannah Clarke.

'But you wouldn't think you were related to your sister,' he went on.

'She's the image of our dad,' Alice said.

34

'Where is she now?'

Alice blinked. 'Where's who now?'

'Your sister. Did you say she wasn't around?'

'She moved to Kilkenny with her husband, Luke. And Chloe's the image of her father,' Alice said, focusing on her daughter rather than the memory of Holly leaving Dublin so abruptly. 'I'm so grateful to have her in my life. She was the one wonderful thing to come out of my crap marriage.'

'If your marriage gave you Chloe, then it wasn't crap.'

'That's a—' she paused, swallowed, 'another way of looking at it. Ronan and I should never have married,' she said.

'I don't suppose you've any photographs of him hanging up?'

'No.' Alice shook her head. 'I don't want any reminders of my failure.'

The failure was always there, a black cloud hovering over her head. She was surprised to find herself admitting it to this man. Instead of being Ronan's beautifully groomed wife, enjoying a glittering, work-free lifestyle, mixing in the best social circles, living in a fabulous house in south County Dublin where she'd be looking after Chloe full-time, she had reverted to being Alice Clarke, separated mum, going back to work in the same job she'd had since she'd left school, even back living in her old childhood home.

'I'm partly at fault,' Alice said, 'because I was dishonest with Ronan from the start.'

How on earth was she talking like this? Telling

Damien things she'd never admitted to anyone? 'Irreconcilable differences' was what she usually said on the few occasions she explained why she was separated and awaiting a divorce.

'You, Alice, dishonest?' Damien said, smiling.

'You ask a lot of questions,' she said.

'Sorry. I'll leave you in peace – I'm sure you need to rest.'

To her surprise, she was in no rush for him to go home, leaving her alone with her thoughts. She gripped her mug as images dizzy-danced through her head: Ronan, his gaze flickering distastefully from her head to her toe, twirling someone else around the dance floor, a blonde woman, whispering in his ear. The coffin lid being screwed down over her mum's body. Holly telling her she was far too over-protective and co-dependent. Her dad ... Alice wiped away the image of Gus Clarke in her head. It was always the same one – her dad admiring the first flowering of the daffodils in their front garden, the last ever morning he'd walked her to school.

Don't go there ...

She felt as though her usual armour had been ripped off and her life lay in shreds before her. Sometimes this happened when she awoke in the dark reaches of the night. She knew by now to ride it out, and she was usually okay by the time she put on her face in the morning. Tonight it was caused by the shock of falling, being without any money in a vulnerable situation, the frenetic A&E, this strange man in her house, calmly making tea and toast, looking at her with interest despite her bedraggled appearance. Right now, he was the only thing that sat between her and the prospect of being sucked under a dark tide.

'Don't go,' she said. 'Actually, Damien, it's weird – I've never felt more wide awake and woozy at the same time. Would you like more tea? There's wine out there as well. I don't have beer but there's some –' she tried to think, '– gin, I think it is.' Gin that Maeve had brought over one evening when they were having a girls' night in, bingeing on Netflix.

'I might have a glass of wine. If you're sure.'

'There's white in the fridge and red somewhere in the wall press, beside the glasses.'

'White is fine.'

'Will you pour me one as well? I know I'm on painkillers, but what the hell.'

When he came in from the kitchen and handed her her drink, she took a long slug.

'Do you see much of your sister?' he asked.

'We were close once,' she found herself saying. 'But we've drifted apart. Holly and Luke used to live in a posh dockland apartment by the Liffey, and then almost overnight they gave up their high-flying lifestyles. I rarely see her now and I miss that closeness.'

'That's a shame. Is she gone long?'

'She moved away around the time Chloe was born.'

There was a silence.

'And my mum died suddenly,' Alice went on, feeling the urge to talk. 'Twelve years ago now. She was forty-eight.'

'Sorry to hear that,' Damien said. 'She was young.'

'Heart attack. No warning. Looking after Holly kept me sane. She was distraught.'

'I'm sure you were equally distraught,' Damien said. He put his glass down on the table beside her and leaned forward, his forearms resting on his legs.

'I was the eldest by six years,' Alice said. 'I was a bit more mature than Holly was.'

She used to envy Holly her easy tears when she felt freezing cold and numb inside. She'd kept her grief hidden, not wanting to inflict herself on Holly and upset her further. Somehow that became a habit. She knew now that it wasn't good to hide things or let grief fester for too long.

'You must miss your mother,' he said, his eyes empathetic.

Alice took another slug of wine. She nodded when Damien went to refill her glass.

'I do, still,' she said. 'By now, people generally assume you've moved on …'

'I know from my family that there's no such thing as moving on from grief. You eventually learn to live with it, but it alters everything.'

'Ah, feck it, Damien, when it hit me, about three years later, I felt ambushed. I didn't know what it was, at first. I didn't like the person I was changing into, but all I could think about was that I'd never see her coming home from her line dancing again, all happy and excited; I'd never hear her singing along to the Bee Gees, out of tune as usual. The physical pain was indescribable. How come I'm telling you this?' Alice paused. Another gulp of wine. 'I don't like this time of night,' she went on, her brain unable to stop her words. 'I don't like the dark and the way things can come crowding in, things you don't want taking up space in your head.'

'I've had late-night moments myself,' he said.

'Sometimes when I wake in the night, I look out the window and watch the lights from the Poolbeg chimneys,' she told him. 'They've been there all my life, and night after night, they're still there, like good friends. No matter how dark it is, they're always winking at me, reminding me that with every wink the seconds and the minutes are ticking by, and in time the night will pass and morning will come.'

'That's a good way of looking at it,' he said.

She took another long slug. 'I need to fix myself,' she said. 'Big time.'

'I don't think you have anything that needs to be fixed, Alice.'

Oh, but she had. Everything seemed worse tonight, as though she was in shreds. How had this happened? She didn't want a man in her life. She'd sworn off all things love and romance, they only brought grief and pain. Besides, Ronan would have a field day, and the last thing she wanted to give him was any ammunition to fire back at her – yet this almost-stranger was sitting here in the sanctuary of her home in the dark, loneliest hours. She blinked slowly and swallowed hard. Her tongue felt thick, her mouth loose and wobbly. She shouldn't have had wine on top of her painkillers. She shouldn't have invited Damien in. She shouldn't have tripped up against the kerb in the first place. She saw Damien getting to his feet, coming over to her, his image hazy, felt her rigid fingers being peeled away from her glass before it was lifted gently out of her hands.

It only seemed a minute later when she became conscious that she was lying down, a cushion behind her head, the cream throw placed over her. Her bum was sore, the pain radiating out in waves. Her eyes flickered open. She realised she was lying on the sofa in the living room. Light pressed against the curtains. She heard traffic rumbling slowly along the main road outside. It was morning.

Then she remembered. Last night. The hospital. Damien. Her words running away from her, talking about light and darkness. Her chest tightened in panic. How could she have been so silly and stupid as to invite a stranger into her home, then fall apart and fall asleep in front of him? He'd obviously been considerate enough to cover her with the throw before he'd left, but he could have been anyone, anyone at all.

CHAPTER 7

Holly

HOW LONG DOES IT TAKE TO FORGET someone? Seven years is clearly not long enough.

After the shock of seeing Liffey Gate on TV, Luke and I moved around like puppets on autopilot for the rest of the week, being incredibly polite to each other, avoiding any talk of Wednesday night. I had a deadline approaching, and a freelancer can't afford to ignore those, so I was busy proofreading a script. Even so, my whole body was held in a vice grip of dread. It squeezed my chest and filled my sleep with nightmares: visions of the hulk of Liffey Gate rearing up against grey skies, supporting pillars silhouetted like bleached skeletons rising demonically out of a grave.

Visions of Jay and his cheeky gait.

Waking up early in Rose Cottage on Saturday morning after another disturbed sleep, my stomach churned with a sickening anxiety. Luke's side of the bed was empty. He was in the kitchen, sitting on a stool by the counter, clad in a T-shirt and jocks, despite the cold February morning. He'd raised the blind and was staring out the window onto the pale early sky, so lost in thought that he didn't hear me until he sensed me behind him and he jumped. Nuzzling into his back, I put my arms around him and buried my head into the curve of his spine. He turned his face sideways and I kissed his cheek.

'You're up early,' I said.

'I can't sleep.'

'Can't you?' I was afraid to ask – *Are you remembering it all? Do you see the ghost of Jay? I've never forgotten him.*

Luke rubbed his face.

'The other night …' I ventured, 'it seemed strange to think of the building being demolished.' I couldn't even mention its name. The words clawed at my throat.

'Relax, Holly, it was all over long ago,' he said.

'You don't think they'll find anything?'

'Absolutely not.'

'So we've nothing to worry about?'

Luke smiled. It didn't quite reach his eyes. 'You have nothing at all to worry about, Holly darling,' he said. 'You know I'll always look after you.'

I let the silence fall between us. Outside the rain that had persisted all week had finally stopped and a watery yellow sun was breaking through, slanting white-gold light across the valley. Down by the back fence, a line of daffodils was dancing in the breeze. I remembered the way Alice had always put a vase of new daffodils on the windowsill in Victoria Row each spring – to cheer us up after the long, grey winter, she'd say. A wave of homesickness swept through me.

I thought of Alice, innocently going about her life in

Dublin, perhaps seeing something about the demolition in the papers and remembering the few short years I'd lived there. The way she'd viewed our lives with slightly mocking eyes had irritated me in those days. I know now she'd only been concerned for me – rightly so, as it happened. Since we'd moved to Rose Cottage, I kept as much distance from her as I politely could. We spoke on the phone regularly enough, but we only met three or four times a year, including lunch to celebrate our respective birthdays, in some neutral place, a garden centre café or a shopping-outlet restaurant close to the motorway between Dublin and Kilkenny. I knew it disappointed Alice that she rarely saw me, and that Luke always came with me for support, which gave no opportunity for a sisterly tête-à-tête. But I had to avoid being interrogated by her as much as possible – Alice needed to reassure herself at every opportunity that her younger sister was alive and well and, most important of all, happy. I don't think she ever suspected the way our lives had imploded and the sadness that underlined everything I did after that. Otherwise, she would have made it her personal crusade to try and rescue what was beyond fixing.

We spent that Saturday quietly, as we often did in Rose Cottage, having a lunch of soup and sandwiches, lounging on the sofa in front of the telly, letting easy afternoon programmes wash over us. I couldn't even concentrate on reading. No matter where we went, or how much Luke tried to protect me, I knew I'd never forget, and the memory of all the times our lives had collided with Jay's was lodged inside my chest like a second beating heart, only this heart was constantly pumping rancid images through dark capillaries that reached deeply into every part of my body.

How young we'd both been at the start of it all in Ocean City, how innocent, the future stretching brightly ahead of us like a shimmering mirage. Sometimes I wondered at what stage I could have changed the course of our lives. Usually I came to the conclusion that we had all been complicit in setting up our downfalls, and that it was a long time since our lives had ever been bright and innocent.

CHAPTER 8

Holly, 2005

THE SUMMER IN OCEAN CITY, MARYLAND, USA; a golden, carefree hiatus that bubbled effervescently in the three months before my final college year. In my early twenties, I rejoiced in being young and alive. I, along with my mates, knew that after college we were going into a world that was waiting to welcome us and our talents. Both Mum and Alice had told me often enough that with a college degree under my belt, and the thriving economy, I could get a wonderful job and have a fabulous career. I grew up on a diet of their constant reminders that I could be anything I wanted in this life and have everything I wanted to have.

Except a father.

I didn't believe my mother when she said that neither she nor my father had had any idea that she was pregnant with me when he'd jumped on a ferry to England on a grey morning in February, deserting his wife and daughter. It was the first leg in his escape to Australia and he'd taken nothing but a backpack and my barely formed heart. I arrived into the world six months later, on a hot afternoon in August, so of course he had to have known. Therefore, it was the news of my impending arrival that had sent him running to the far corner of the world. When confronted afterwards, Mum had denied this, telling me that I'd been born a month prematurely, and she'd had no symptoms of pregnancy until after he'd left. Mum said it was Gus who'd missed out on the joy of me, and all the love I had to give, not the other way around.

I decided then, at eight years of age, that Mum was telling me a big white lie to spare me the awful, ugly truth, and that both Mum and Alice were overcompensating for Dad's absence to stop me from coming to the terrible conclusion that I wasn't worthy of love. Because they more than made up for his desertion. I spent my childhood wrapped up in thick layers of the love and care they lavished around me. And although she was only six years my elder, Alice could have been my second mother such was the way she cherished me. We shared a bedroom in Victoria Row, and whenever I was afraid of the dark or cried over birthday or Christmas cards that never arrived from Australia, Alice was always there to comfort me.

Both of them had cheered me on the day I'd started my business studies degree. Alice had never gone to college, settling for a job in the council library when she'd left school, but she'd been happy to champion me through every exam, every assignment, bringing me home suitable reference books. My summer in Ocean City would be the first time I'd been apart from them. Mum and Alice were going to occupy themselves with redecorating the house, now that I wasn't around trying to study, when the smell of drying paint might have given me a headache or distracted me from my books.

'You look too young to be going so far away,' Mum said as I began to pack my case as soon as the exams were over at the end of May.

'Do I?' I knew that I'd need to have my ID card handy if I wanted to buy booze in the States. Even though I was coming up to my twenty-second birthday, my blonde hair had retained its baby-fine texture, and my eyes were misleadingly innocent looking. I'd gotten away with half fare on the bus for years. If it was a disadvantage at times, I blamed Mum and Alice for my childlike, unsophisticated face, thanks to the way they'd always spoiled me and protected me from the realities of life.

Both of them failed miserably to hide their tears when they said goodbye to me in Dublin airport. I was upset too, a wall of tears pressing at the back of my eyes in that emotional moment of farewell. I wondered, dramatically, if I would ever see them again; they seemed so precious and familiar that I clung to them until the last possible moment and decided I was mad to be leaving them. But all that dissolved the instant I caught up with my college friends in the departure lounge. The drinks were flying and the sense of freedom was intoxicating. When the plane lifted into the sky, I felt the past dropping down and away from me. It was a metamorphosis of sorts, and I was transformed into someone brand new, ready to take on the world.

There were twelve of us students heading out to

Ocean City for the summer, some of whom I only knew slightly. The group included my friends Tara, Niamh and Megan. Tara's boyfriend, Conor, was with us, along with a mate of his, Jay Slater, from the accounting and finance stream at college.

'It'll be handy to have the guys along,' Tara had said. 'Conor has his uses. We might need a stray spider killed or a sink unblocked or defending from a big American baseball player – who knows?'

'I mightn't want defending from one of those,' Niamh had sighed.

I'd seen Jay now and again on campus. He hung around on the edge of the group by virtue of living around the corner from Conor, and their parents were friends. He made no secret of the fact that, as soon as he graduated, he had a job lined up in his uncle's financial firm and his main aim in college was to sleep his way through the female population. His fuckit list, he called it. His attitude occasionally pissed off some of the group but he could also be funny at times and good for a laugh.

◆

Ocean City glittered and sparkled: long sandy stretches by the rolling Atlantic, buzzy waterfront cafés, side streets and quaint narrow parts of the town. Even our basic apartment glimmered under the rays of a high, bright sun, which held everything in some kind of benevolent smile. Coming from a life where I'd never had the chance to venture abroad, it shimmered with magic. I knew I was viewing it all through the lens of where my life was right then, poised on the edge of a dazzling, charged-with-endless-possibilities future.

Outside of our jobs in cafés, hotels or restaurants, where the pay was lousy but the tips were great, life in Ocean City was one long party. We shared adjoining apartments and our sleeping arrangements were haphazard. A lot of the nights, we hauled our mattresses out onto the balcony to sleep under the stars. When our gang settled in, we met up with other Irish young people. Most of the block seemed to be rented out to students, and sessions went on every night.

We were about a month in when Jay got drunk on beer and shots and cornered me at a party in an apartment on the second floor. He'd been eyeing me up since we'd met in the airport, and if I'm honest, his blatant approval turned me on a little and made me strut my stuff as sexily as I could under the glare of his laser-beam attention. Out here, mixed with the dazzle of the summer and the untrammelled freedom of being away from Victoria Row, it gave me the charged feeling of being on a constant high.

'You're the last on my fuckit list,' he said, his voice slightly slurred as he weaved over to me, dangling a bottle of beer in his hand. In a pair of shorts and a sleeveless T-shirt, he looked bulky and strong. 'The beautiful Holly,' he said. 'I'm doing it in reverse order and was keeping the best until last. So you're really my number one. I've been waiting all year to have the pleasure.'

'You might have to wait a bit longer,' I said, teasing him.

'No rush, I'm enjoying the anticipation.' He wriggled his hips. 'I'm looking forward to losing my virginity with you.'

I must have looked startled because he grinned widely. 'Cos that's what it will feel like,' he said, moving closer. 'You're so special, it'll be like the first time all over again.'

'Yeah right.' I laughed, my ego boosted a little more.

He looked at me with unfocused eyes. He clutched his crotch, thrusting it forward. 'Seriously, Hol, I've something here that can't wait to get inside you.'

'I'm worth the wait,' I said, backing away, realising he was far more drunk than I'd first thought.

'Bloody sure you are,' he said, staggering forward, spilling some beer on my top.

'Hey, watch it.' I pushed him back. He swayed again, falling against me. In the crowded throng, with The Killers' 'Mr Brightside' belting out, no one noticed what was going on. Jay was in front of me, concealing me from everyone else.

'Do that again, but lower down,' Jay said, angling his hips so that they pressed against mine.

I stayed completely still, trying to decide the best way out of this without making a scene. We were all enjoying the Ocean City experience, and I didn't want to be the one to mess it up. Though why was I trying to be nice? The answer wasn't something I wanted to acknowledge but I knew it went back to my father, to the way I'd always felt the need to behave as nicely as possible to keep everyone onside and not give them a reason to abandon me. Still, Jay was being a real nuisance now. He slumped against me, almost pinning me to the wall. I pushed at his shoulders with as much strength as I had. 'Jay, you feckin' eejit, you're totally pissed. Get off me.'

Then a voice said in an Irish accent, 'You heard her, get off her.'

CHAPTER 9

Holly, 2005

THE GUY WAS TALLER THAN JAY, BUT MUCH thinner. His voice was calm and steady and behind the stern look he gave Jay, I sensed a gentle demeanour about him. His most striking feature was thickly lashed grey eyes. He asked me if I was all right, and when I nodded, he gave me such a lovely smile that it melted something inside me. Jay teetered backwards, into the side of the wall.

'What's it to you?' Jay said to the new arrival.

'Didn't you hear?' he replied. 'The lady wants you to leave her alone.'

Jay looked as though he was about to lunge.

'I wouldn't,' the other lad said. 'Unless you want to grapple with a Munster hurler.'

'Yeah, Jay, run off and save your pretty face.' I saw him recoil at my words, delivered in a mocking tone of voice.

'Prick tease,' Jay said, leering at me.

'You're hammered,' I said.

Jay scowled at me and then at the guy. 'Cork dick,' he muttered.

'Dublin wanker,' the other guy said, quite clearly and pleasantly, as though he was paying him a compliment. There was a pause in the music and his words were heard around the room. People turned to stare at Jay, and there were a couple of stifled giggles.

'No one calls me that,' Jay said, before he staggered off.

'Thanks,' I said to the grey-eyed newcomer. 'He was drunk and it got messy.'

'No worries.'

'I haven't seen you around, have I?'

'No, I think I'm at the wrong party.'

'That's a shame. Are you really a Munster hurler?'

A smile played around his lips. He had a lovely mouth. 'What do you think?'

'I dunno what to think,' I said. Looking at his pale indoors face and the leanness of his body, I doubted it very much.

'I'll stay for a bit and make sure he doesn't come back. Or I can walk you home in case he starts bothering you again. I'm Luke, by the way, and you are …?'

'Holly. Thanks for the offer, but it's okay,' I said, explaining that we all lived on the next floor. 'Jay's as drunk as a skunk. He'll conk out once his head hits the pillow and we'll be complaining of his snores. He'll sleep in tomorrow and have forgotten all about it by the time he wakes up, late for work as usual.'

'Good.'

We looked at each other for the longest moment. His grey eyes held mine, a gleam in the depths of his giving me the weird sensation of something passing between us, as light as air but as strong as tensile steel. Then both of us laughed at the same time. He looked away before his eyes slid back to my face, studying it intently.

'What party are you off to?' I asked, mentally kicking myself for reminding him he had somewhere else to go when I really wanted to ask, *Who are you? What are you doing here, in Ocean City? Are you here for long? In other words, is there the remotest chance that I might see you again? Because there's something about you that's sparking happy feelings all around me. Something about you I'm drawn to, as though I'm slotting into my personal energy bank.*

The Holly I'd left behind in Dublin had never been attracted like this to a guy before. This was Ocean City Holly, the girl who felt freer and lighter and unencumbered, away from the ever-watchful eyes of Mum and Alice.

'It's a party for another Cork guy,' Luke said. 'My mate Steve should be there already, probably wondering where I've got to.'

'There's a bunch of Cork guys staying in a house on the corner of the next block,' I said, deflated at the thoughts of him leaving.

'That must be it.'

'I'll show you,' I said, wanting to prolong my time with him, wildly imagining he might ask me to join his friends. I was filled with a breathless excitement as we pushed our way through the throng and went down to the ground floor. Outside, the evening air was balmy and fresh. As we went down the path, the shrieks and loud laughter flooding out from the party faded a little.

'Hey, wow, look at that sky,' Luke said, staring up.

I followed his gaze. The sun had set, and the sky in the west was still splashed with lingering colour, crimson and purple splashed across the perimeter of the sky in variegated strands, streaking the heavens and setting the underside of puffy clouds aflame.

'It's beautiful,' I said. I'd had a couple of beers, and Jay had unsettled me, but as we stood there, all sorts of feelings rushed through me, including the sheer certainty that it was wonderful to be alive in the world at this moment, a world where Luke looked at my face as though it interested him.

'Seems a shame to go back into a sweaty hot party,' I ventured.

He grinned. 'I can hold off joining my mates for a few minutes.'

'Great,' I said, wondering furiously what on earth I could talk about that might sound remotely interesting. We sat on a low wall further down the road but I needn't have worried about chat-up lines. Luke looked at me keenly and got straight to the point. 'So who are you, Holly? Tell me about yourself, your life, your dreams.'

'Just like that?' I laughed, a bubble of excitement rising inside me.

In the space of fifteen minutes I gave him the short history of my life: Victoria Row, school, college, my family. He looked at me with empathy when I spoke of the father I'd never known. I found myself admitting that

I blamed myself for his departure, that sometimes I felt it was a huge wedge between me and Mum and Alice.

Luke shook his head. 'Remember one thing,' he said. 'Your dad's actions had nothing to do with you. Nobody really does anything because of someone else. They do things because they've made that choice all by themselves. His decision to leave came from where he was right then in his own life.'

I didn't bother to say that right then, in his own life, his wife would just have found out she was expecting baby number two.

Luke was from Fermoy in County Cork, where his father owned a pub. 'Dad wasn't happy that I wasn't interested in joining him in the business. But he accepted it. I didn't want to be stuck in Fermoy for the rest of my life. My brother Pierce is quite happy to settle down there but I always wanted to spread my wings. I've finished a computer science course. It'll be a passport to everything.'

'It sure will,' I said, falling a little bit more in love with him and the way he spoke of spreading his wings.

'My plan is to get a great job in Dublin for nine months of the year,' Luke said, 'save up as much as I can, then take off the other three months to go travelling the world.'

'Sounds amazing,' I said.

'Yeah, and no reason why it can't be done.'

We talked hopes and dreams as we sat on the wall that evening, my head sparking with the idea that life could be as exciting as you made it, my heart aching and expanding in turn as he spoke. I understood that our worlds had intersected for this short while, in Ocean City under a scarlet sky. Luke was off on his travels and I'd be going back into my final year in college, our lives diverging so much that there was no point even attempting to keep in touch. Before he joined his mates, he walked me back to my apartment.

He kissed me, and I kissed him back, wanting to brand myself and my kiss on his heart, like he was branding mine.

'Make sure you have a good life, Holly,' he said. 'Follow your dreams.'

'How will I know what I really want?'

'You'll feel it, in your heart. If I wasn't heading off …' He hesitated and scanned my face.

'Enjoy your adventures,' I said, unable to comprehend how my heart was wrenching given that I'd only met Luke a couple of hours ago. Then I turned and walked away.

The next morning, as I called out orders and balanced huge piles of food in the restaurant, I kept seeing a pair of grey eyes and how they'd made me feel. I didn't see Jay until late that night. He seemed subdued, thanks to his hangover. He hardly spoke to me in the days after that and I wondered how much he remembered. Then a few days before we came home, he cornered me out on the balcony.

'We have unfinished business,' he said.

'As I said, I'm worth the wait,' I replied, keeping it light, determined to avoid any aggro. And still, desperate as it was, feeling a little empowered that he still had the hots for me.

'You certainly are, Holly.' He grinned. 'Our time will come. Jay Slater always gets what he wants.'

'So does Holly Clarke.' I laughed, swanning off and leaving him standing there.

CHAPTER 10

Holly, 2005–2006

ARRIVING BACK IN DUBLIN ON A DRIZZLY early morning in September, everything seemed grey and drab under swollen dark skies, the buildings squashed together, the landscape small and insignificant compared to the wide-open spaces in Ocean City. Coming through the door of the house was like being enveloped in a constricting hug, Mum and Alice waiting to greet me, the familiar rooms closing around me, even if they had been treated to a fresh coat of wall-to-wall magnolia.

Mum and Alice looked as though they'd stood perfectly still while I'd been away, whereas I, oh, wow – I felt more alive, brighter, sparkly from the inside out, as though the sunshine I'd soaked up all summer was still dazzling around me. Especially compared to same-old same-old Alice. My adventure had opened a gap between us that hadn't been there before.

'You should go travelling yourself, Alice,' I said to her that evening. 'You could get leave of absence from the library, head off around the world for three months, and you'd come back a brand new person.'

'Why? What's wrong with me now?' Alice asked.

'You're not exactly following any dreams, are you?' I didn't wait for her to answer. 'You should think about doing something adventurous next year,' I went on, 'after Maeve is married.'

I shouldn't have reminded Alice that Maeve, up to now Alice's holiday companion, was to be married next April, and it would mean that their annual two weeks in Spain would be a thing of the past. Especially when Alice seemed to be having no luck whatsoever with men. Of course, her job in the library with a handful of staff, mostly married, didn't help. She went out on occasional dates, but nothing much came of them. No one seemed to last longer than a month, and she never brought them home.

'When I've graduated,' I said, 'I'm going to travel to the far corners of the globe. There's a lot more to life than Victoria Row. Who wants to be stuck here, or in a dead-end job, when New York, Washington or Peru are all waiting? I can't wait to be gone.'

'Gone where, darling?' Mum asked, coming in from the kitchen.

'I was telling Alice of my plans to travel the world,' I said airily. 'Three months in Ocean City was the start. As soon as I've saved enough, I'll be off.'

Mum's face dropped.

'It won't be for a while yet,' I conceded. 'I need to have some dosh behind me.'

All the same, I found myself galvanised with a new sense of purpose during that final college year. Occasionally, as I sat in lecture halls, I wondered where

Luke was then. Coming up to Christmas, I figured he must have arrived back in Ireland, probably to work so he could save for his next backpacking adventure. After Christmas, I was busy with the push towards the final exams, hoping to start my career in a go-ahead firm. Up to now, I might have thought I didn't deserve certain things, like three months in America or feeling as happy as I did, but being away from the cosy cloisters of Victoria Row and meeting Luke had changed me. That confidence helped in my job application process, and by the time graduation day came around, over a year after I'd come home from Ocean City, I was already working in the graduate programme in Clery Consulting, a development and training firm with offices beside the IFSC, in the training resources section.

I didn't see much of Jay Slater in the year after Ocean City. It was my final year in college so I had my head down, studying hard. According to Tara, he had a new girlfriend who was playing hard to get, and so I wasn't alone with him until graduation day.

After the conferring ceremony in St Patrick's Cathedral, we returned to the college for refreshments. Both Mum and Alice had taken time off work to be with me, but we were separated in the crowd when Jay caught up with me. Right enough, he'd just about passed his exams and had started work in his uncle's financial firm.

'Here you are, Holly,' he said, his eyes scanning the gap in my robe, beneath which I wore a V-neck red dress. 'Nice one, but I wish you wouldn't tease me like this.'

'Hello, Jay,' I said coolly. 'How's the new girlfriend?'

'Am I hearing a note of jealousy?' he asked. 'Don't worry, you know I'm still waiting patiently for you.'

I felt annoyed that his comment gave me a small kick of satisfaction. Was I that desperate for male validation?

'I thought we left all that behind in Ocean City,' I said.

'No way,' he said. 'I'm counting the days.'

'I hope you've lots of patience – you'll be waiting a *looong* time.'

'How's life in Clery Consulting?' he asked.

'It's fantastic,' I said.

'Sounds like the way we'll be together. I'm already on the road to hell, with all the sexy thoughts I have about you.'

I saw Mum and Alice coming towards me. I did not want them to meet. I didn't want Mum to see the blatant look Jay was now giving me, although I knew not to take him seriously.

'Goodbye, Jay,' I said, moving away from him.

Mum had booked a table in a hotel on Golden Lane for a celebration meal for the three of us. Her eyes shining with happiness, she said how thankful she was to have such beautiful daughters, she was blessed, she was the luckiest woman in the world. She'd never thought she deserved to have her life turn out this brilliantly.

Afterwards, whenever I looked back, my heart squeezed painfully when I remembered her happiness, her proud, smiling face. Hannah Clarke's life didn't end up so brilliantly after all. Four months later she was dead.

CHAPTER 11

Holly, 2007–2008

YOU'RE NOT SUPPOSED TO HAVE SUDDEN heart attacks in Arnotts department store bargain basement. You can't be there one minute, breathing, alive, comparing the price of stripy tea towels, and then be gone in the moments it takes to lurch sideways, scrabble in vain for a grip on the counter, pulling towels with you as you slither to the polished linoleum floor, and by the time a shop assistant comes running and customers reach your side, it's too late.

That's not how it's supposed to go.

But that's exactly what happened.

Summoned from a meeting for an urgent call at my desk on an early March morning, I heard Alice's strained voice. Something had happened to Mum, she said, sounding as though she was measuring out the words carefully. I was to jump into a taxi, go straight to the Mater hospital. When I saw my sister waiting for me, pale-faced and looking as though she was being held upright by a man I didn't know, my head began to freeze. Mum was in a side room, lying on a narrow bed. Her eyes were closed. She looked fast asleep. I wanted to shake her and wake her up and tell her to stop pretending to be dead. Mum's sister, Aunt Kate, and Maeve were on the way. They'd help get Mum out of bed. She might listen to them. She wasn't listening to me.

She didn't listen to them either, and later, when they said it was time to go, I refused.

'We can't leave Mum like this,' I said, staring from Alice to Maeve to Aunt Kate. 'We'll have to wait until she wakes up, tell her we'll see her in the morning.' I gripped the rail at the end of the bed. 'I'm not going anywhere until Mum opens her eyes. I need her to open her eyes.'

Eventually Alice peeled my fingers, one by one, off the rail. I could have been sleepwalking when they shunted me away from the bed. My eyes never left Mum's still, white face, until they propelled me out of that room.

Alice saved me. Alice soothed and comforted me. Alice said a few words at the funeral, her pale face giving nothing away. After Mum was lowered into a hole in the ground on a cold, blustery morning – how barbaric *was* that – Alice held me tightly, as though she was safeguarding me from a physical assault, and listened to my hysterical and incoherent words.

From the blurry circle of mourners, faces detached and moved towards me: relatives, friends from college – I felt stiff and strange in their arms, as though I'd been cut out of my own life and pasted onto a strange cardboard world, while they were still living in the warm world of happy times and bright ambitions. Then I saw Jay standing at the back of the circle, watching me crying as Tara held me. I hadn't expected him to be there, but he still kept in contact with Conor. In my defenceless state, I was glad he didn't come near me. From the look in his eyes, he was still as hung up on me as ever, even though it was over eighteen months since Ocean City, and now I found it unsettling.

◆

The first year without Mum, I see-sawed between huge troughs of grief and loss, interspersed with normal enough days when I joined in the camaraderie going on about me in Clery Consulting. There were days when I felt numb and empty, days when I forgot Mum was dead, and then painful reality would crash in over my head, taking my breath away.

Alice looked after everything, including me. We still shared the same bedroom and Alice was nearby in case I cried in the night. Alice said it was good she had me to look after as well as all the red tape. It gave her no time to think. When I claimed responsibility for Mum's sudden death – after all, hadn't she been upset when I went off to Ocean City, never mind my plans to go travelling the world – Alice shook me sternly.

'Mum died of a heart attack because her muscles were damaged over the years,' Alice said. 'I have the death certificate. You can read the medical terminology if you like.'

'Oh, no,' I said. 'I couldn't bear to look at it. I couldn't bear to see her date of death written down.'

'It had nothing whatsoever to do with you.'

◆

We went on holidays together that September.

'Mum would have loved this,' I said, as we sat on a terrace overlooking the sea in Salou, spooning cold ice cream from frilly-edged glass dishes. I looked across the promenade at the shimmering blue of the sea and my heart ached. Always close to tears that year, the need to have a good cry swelled up inside me at the thought of Mum not being here in this beautiful place.

'Of course she would,' Alice said in a pragmatic tone of voice. 'But she'd be happy to think we're here, having a good time, together.'

I stared out at the moving carnival of brightly dressed holidaymakers. Everyone looked happy and relaxed. But surely in that cavalcade there were people like me? People who were grieving, missing loved ones; people whose lives had fallen apart for one reason or another. People who were dealing with problems and illnesses. Yet they were all going around looking normal enough on the outside, as though they had false faces on, like masks. I wondered if Alice was the same, if she was pretending to be okay with everything, but deep down she wanted to cry like I did. Nah, not my big sister. She was made of sterner stuff. She was great at getting over it and getting on with things.

Then I saw him in the middle of the moving crowd, walking along with that mocking smile on his face – Jay. I didn't realise I'd dropped my spoon until I heard it clattering against the glass dish. Had he somehow found out about my holiday and followed me here? When I looked again, I realised it wasn't Jay at all, but a dark-haired man who had the same cocky walk.

'Holly? Are you okay?' Alice's eyes searched my face.

'I'm fine,' I said.

'You had me worried for a moment.'

Sometimes I wished Alice wasn't always monitoring me so carefully. I knew she meant well, but there were times when I found her attention too vigilant. Even now she was over-reacting. I had no intention of trying to explain Jay. Alice would make far more of his irritating carry-on than I did.

'I'm okay,' I said. A family arrived at the table beside ours, busy with small children and buggies, and I distracted myself by smiling at the babies and moving my chair to accommodate them. But as the days went by, I found myself scanning crowds, searching for his eyes – the eyes that had stared insolently at me across the graveyard on the day of Mum's funeral. He must have spooked me more than I'd realised.

CHAPTER 12

Alice

'WHAT'S THE STORY WITH THE GUY?' MAEVE asked on Saturday afternoon.

In the kitchen in Victoria Row, Alice watched her cousin pretending to be engrossed in unloading the shopping: prescription painkillers she'd picked up for Alice in the chemist, along with fresh milk, bread and eggs, a pizza and a lasagne. From upstairs came the drift of high voices; Chloe and Lucy, Maeve's daughter, were playing up in Chloe's bedroom.

'What guy?'

Maeve gave her a magnificent smile. 'Your knight in shining armour. I want to know all about him. Who is he? Where did you meet him? This is breaking news, Alice.'

'There's nothing to know.' The less she remembered of the previous night, the better. Alice felt a tide of embarrassment consume her. How could she have fallen apart in such a stupid way in front of an almost-stranger? And to think that he'd stood there while she was unconscious, long enough to decide he'd best cover her with a throw and put a cushion behind her head. What had she looked like in her semi-drugged sleep?

Had she been snoring? Had some dribble leaked from around her mouth?

She'd ignored the texts he'd sent her that morning –

'I hope you're feeling better, I made you as comfortable as I could. Damien.'

Then later –

'Let me know you're all right or if you need anything. D.'

He was being polite, because that seemed to be in his nature. God knows what he privately thought of her after all her crazy talk about falling to shreds and hating the dark. She'd even mentioned the Poolbeg lights winking at her, hadn't she?

'Pull the other one, Alice,' Maeve said. 'From what you told me, he sees you on the street, he recognises you from the library, he not only brings you in a taxi to A&E but he pays the fee, and then he pays for your visit, and then –' Maeve paused for dramatic effect '– he waits the *whole time*. In A&E. On a Friday night. *And* brings you home. Don't tell me there's nothing going on – which, by the way, I hope there is.'

Alice swallowed hard. Putting it like that, the chain of events only served to compound her embarrassment. 'Sorry to disappoint you but I hardly know him. I was lucky he came along when he did.'

'You *do* disappoint me. I'd love to give you a good shake. You're still young and sexy – you shouldn't be wasting your life away on account of that prick Ronan.'

'I'm not wasting away. I'm busy, I'm happy.'

'Don't tell me you're living your life to the full. You've been looking out for your family for so long that you've forgotten how to look out for yourself. You were more devoted to your mum than any other woman I know, and as for Holly? You've picked up after her since she was a baby, always putting her first. You need to start doing things for yourself. It was no problem for Holly to go off and make a new life for herself. She didn't stay still.'

'I married Ronan, didn't I?'

'I'm sorry things didn't work out with him – no, I'm not, he doesn't deserve you – but it's not too late to make another new life. You should be out there having fun and lots of sex.'

'I'm forty-two. I'm not young and sexy.'

'Of course you are. That's only a number. It's all about how you feel, how much you love. And stop glaring at me.'

Alice sighed. 'Yes, you're right.'

'See?'

'I'm glaring at you.'

'And I know you're not going to take a blind bit of notice of me.' Maeve sighed. 'Come to me for dinner tomorrow, instead of shoving a frozen something into the oven.'

'Thanks, Maeve, but you do more than enough. I'd rather flake out here and not have to talk to anyone. Ronan will have Chloe for the day.'

'Give him my fondest regards,' Maeve said, making a face as though she had a particularly bitter piece of fruit in her mouth.

◆

'So who's the bollocks you were with the other night?' Ronan asked on Sunday morning, when Chloe went back upstairs to get her Minnie Mouse teddy. He didn't ask Alice if she was okay. He didn't even mention the word hospital. Ronan hated hospitals. He told her before Chloe had been born that he never wanted to step inside one, but he would make an exception in their baby's case. Not that he'd be witnessing the birth or anything messy like that – he was far too sensitive for all that gory stuff – but as soon as the baby was out and cleaned up, he'd be there. He couldn't help it if anything to do with sickness or infirmity repulsed him.

Alice thought of Damien's calm kindness and something inside her rebelled.

'He's my latest toy boy,' she said, 'and you've no right to speak of him like that.'

'Toy boy!' Ronan laughed and shook his head.

'You're the one who's a bollocks,' she said, 'not even asking how I am.'

'You look okay to me.'

'That doesn't mean I feel okay, but I know you don't give a shite.'

Chloe came back downstairs, full of excited chatter, oblivious to her parents' cutting words. The one thing they'd agreed on was to have no arguments or cross words in front of her. To Alice's gratitude, Ronan stuck to this, making sure his daughter didn't witness any acrimony between them. Alice wasn't fooling herself, though. She knew it had nothing to do with her wishes or her daughter's happiness. It was purely for Ronan's benefit alone that he ensured his daughter only saw his charming side.

No one except her and Ronan knew the true circumstances of the break-up. No one commented when she mentioned 'irreconcilable differences'. It must have been glaringly obvious to everyone that Ronan Russell had been way out of her league.

'I hope you feel sick every time you see me, when you remember what I have in my back pocket,' Alice had said to him the day she moved out of his apartment.

'I'll return that favour as soon as the opportunity comes along. One mistake, that's all you need to make,' he'd said, giving her a sour grin. 'I have my spies. I'll find out and I'll get you back.'

He'd phoned Maeve on Friday night to check on Chloe, but it had also been a way of checking Alice's story. He was arrogant enough to believe his continuous checking up kept Alice under his thumb. Well, to hell with that, she decided, waving goodbye to Chloe as she skipped down the path to her father's car.

CHAPTER 13

ON TUESDAY MORNING, A BOUQUET OF flowers and a get-well card arrived from the library crew and Alice was touched by their thoughtfulness.

Sharon phoned that afternoon.

'Sharon? What's up?'

'Chill, Alice, we're managing fine. Stay out as long as you like. I'm calling you about the guy.'

'What guy?'

'Damien. The Ride. He was in here asking for you at lunch hour. He seemed to know you were sick.' Sharon's voice rose on a questioning inflection. 'He said he hoped you were on the mend. How come he knew you weren't out on annual leave …?' Sharon's voice was dripping with curiosity.

'I haven't a clue,' Alice said. She hadn't supplied any details other than she'd fallen and hurt her back when she'd phoned in sick on Saturday morning. She was relieved Damien didn't appear to have expanded on that, although surprised he'd bothered to call into the library.

'So there's nothing going on?'

'No way,' Alice retorted.

'Awww, that's a pity,' Sharon said. 'He seems nice. I'd encourage him if I were you.'

Damien had followed up his texts with a phone call on Monday evening, which she didn't answer. Later, she'd finally texted him back, telling him she was resting up and thanking him for looking after her, and that she'd arrange to repay him as soon as she was on the mend. She hoped that would be the end of it. No doubt he felt sorry for the forty-plus woman who'd all but admitted her life was in tatters, who couldn't even fall down in a street without having a major drama attached to it. And it had to be something mortifying, like an actual pain in the actual ass.

The doorbell rang at lunchtime on Wednesday: Damien, carrying a large bouquet of flowers.

'What are you doing here?' she asked.

'I'm dropping these off,' he said.

'You shouldn't have,' she said, folding her arms, half-flattered but hugely disconcerted by his arrival at her door.

'If you don't take them off me, I'll have no choice but to sit on the bench with them.'

'What bench?'

'The one over by the seafront. The one I'm going to sit on while I admire the view.'

She shook her head. 'There was no need for this.'

'Why not? They're just flowers, Alice. It's good to have something beautiful to look at if you're feeling sick. Although,' he grinned, 'you have the fabulous sea to look at every time you open your hall door.'

She was glad he only saw the beautiful sea. Ronan had always dissed it, preferring to complain about the incinerator further down on the Poolbeg peninsula, denouncing it as a blot of pollution on the landscape and another reason why he hated Chloe living in Victoria Row. Alice felt it was enough distance away not to interfere with the air quality or detract from the endless vista of the sea and sky.

A wave of embarrassment swept through her. 'I owe you money.'

'I'm not here to collect my debts,' he said, a smile crinkling his eyes. 'I have a sheriff who looks after that for me.'

She laughed and surrendered to the moment. 'Come in. This time I'll make the tea.'

◆

She brought him through to the living room.

'How are you feeling?' he asked.

'Much better.' She didn't elaborate. *My sore bum has eased a lot. I'm not a big pain in the arse any more.* 'I can't thank you enough for Friday night.'

'No problem,' he said.

It was strange, seeing him here on her territory in the daytime. He was quite good to look at, with those green-flecked hazel eyes. His dark hair faded slightly to silver above his temples. He had a nice voice, calm and measured. She recalled how patient he'd been with her in A&E – she found it hard to believe they'd shared the frenzy of those few hours. Even so, he was a stranger, and she was aware that once more she was alone in her house with him. Maeve was collecting Chloe from school, and even though Alice was off work, Maeve was bringing Chloe home to her house to give Alice time to rest up.

'I'll put the kettle on,' she said, going out to the kitchen, bringing the flowers.

When she came back into the living room with mugs of tea, he was standing in front of her shelves, scanning the contents.

'I was in the library yesterday,' he said, turning to her. 'I could have picked up some new books for you.'

'I've plenty to read,' she said, putting down the mugs on the low table.

'How long have you worked there?' he asked, sitting in the armchair by the window.

'I'm almost four years in Abbey Lane but twenty years working in the service altogether.'

'Wonderful.'

Ronan had thought it was 'cute' that she worked in a library.

'Don't you find it boring?' he'd said, 'surrounded by nothing but shelves of books all day?'

'At least books don't talk back to you,' she'd said, not attempting to explain what had drawn her to the library in the first place. She'd sensed Ronan would never appreciate or be interested in the Alice who really wanted a quiet life, who felt safe in a library. There would be no nasty surprises lurking on the bookshelves, and although the books themselves offered worlds that were exciting, sometimes dangerous, so different to her own life, if they got too much, she just had to close the book, easy-peasy. And in addition to the books, libraries provided such a brilliant range of free community services that Alice found it a thoroughly satisfying job. Ronan would never have understood that version of her.

'Books don't give me any trouble,' she'd said to him, searching for an answer that would fit into his world. 'If I worked – for instance – in the beauty industry or event management or PR, I'd be spending most of the day rushed off my feet, trying to solve problems.'

Ronan had laughed. 'I love it! No hassles, a free and easy number. You're a clever lady behind that lovely face.'

She sensed Damien understood as she chatted about the library.

'I've always enjoyed reading,' she said. 'It seemed like the perfect job when I left school. I didn't bother with college.' Not when her library job meant that Hannah Clarke was able to drop one of her cleaning shifts and take life a little easier.

'Not every graduate can say they're in a career they love. I see your sister went to college.'

'Holly?' Alice was surprised at this comment. 'How did you know?'

Damien smiled easily. 'I saw her graduation photo on your shelf and I was wondering where she'd studied. Thought I recognised the sash.'

'She did a business degree,' Alice said, for some reason unwilling to satisfy his curiosity.

'And are you living here long? You are Dublin-born and -reared, aren't you?' he asked.

'What's this? Twenty questions?' She was unused to such interest in herself, which made her feel nervous.

'Oops,' he said, leaning forward and giving her an apologetic smile. 'I can't help imagining what it must have been like to grow up with the sea across the road.'

'It was great, Holly and I loved it,' she said, relenting a little to answer some of his queries, but not enough to tell him that the house had been her mother's childhood home, and when Hannah Clarke had married, her dad had moved in. Apart from the three years she'd lived with Ronan, it was the only home Alice had known.

'And yet the city is so accessible to here,' Damien said. 'Jobs, colleges and so much culture, right on your doorstep.'

'I've the best of both worlds,' she said.

'You certainly have. Anyhow,' he stood up, 'I'd best get back to the office.'

'I've taken up your lunch hour.'

'No bother. I usually get out for a walk in the park, but this was a nice change.'

'So do I,' she said. 'It was kind of you to call in considering the state I was in the last time you saw me.'

Damien smiled. 'One minute you were talking and the next you were out for the count. I guess it was the tablets.'

'Those and the wine,' she said wryly.

'Well,' he said, at the hall door, 'might see you around some time. The library's not that far from my office.'

'Sure,' she said.

When she went back into the living room it seemed emptier than usual. For a short while, Damien had given her a tantalising glimpse of a life that she considered closed to her now; a life that included an attractive man, who had seen her at her worst yet it hadn't turned him off, who'd bring flowers and be happy to sit by her window and talk about libraries; a man who was interested enough in her to ask a lot of questions.

That was why, surely, she felt thrown into confusion for the rest of the day.

CHAPTER 14

AFTER A WEEK OF ENFORCED REST, ALICE was glad to get back to work. On Wednesday, she took a lunchtime stroll in Merrion Square Park, which was close to the library. It was bright but chilly; everywhere she looked there were signs of spring, tiny buds visible on tree branches etched against a piercing blue sky, yellow drifts of daffodils blazing in the silvery sunshine. Then she saw him rounding a bend and coming towards her.

'Well, hello, Alice Clarke,' Damien said.

'Hello, Damien,' she said. For a moment she stood there uncertainly. She thought of his recent texts that she'd mostly ignored, asking how she was keeping.

'Lunchtime stroll?' he said.

'Yes,' she said. 'Funny to bump into you like this.'

He smiled easily. 'I often come here at lunchtime – who knows, we've probably passed each other by hundreds of times.'

They probably had, for all she knew, both of them part of the procession of anonymous strollers. They fell into step, taking a path that led up along the side of the park, where a bed of daffodils glowed vibrantly.

'Lots of new beginnings for you, Alice,' he said, indicating the flowers.

'They're beautiful,' she said.

'What are you up to in the library today?' he asked.

'I'm working on a spring reading programme for the juniors,' she said. 'It's good fun.'

'And rewarding. Great to be able to nurture the habit of reading in the little ones.'

'Absolutely,' she said, knowing how much she enjoyed the faces that beamed at her in the library. If things had been different with Ronan, she'd have loved more children. 'Do you have children, Damien?' She shook her head. 'Sorry, I'm not usually so personal.'

'I don't have any children, contrary to my expectations.'

'Oh.'

He surprised her by elaborating. 'I was in a relationship when I lived in Hong Kong. Eve and I … I thought it was for keeps.'

'But it wasn't?'

'We were talking about marriage and babies, and then I came home from work one Friday evening and she was ready and waiting with a bottle of wine and her bombshell. She'd met someone else. She said she'd been perfectly happy with me – until she met Rick through a work thing.'

'Oh dear.'

'She moved out that evening, and a month later I moved back to Ireland. I'm home a year now.'

'Do you miss Hong Kong?'

'No. Not a bit.'

They had reached a far corner of the park, and they

turned back along a path that cut through the centre, bordered by a riot of primroses.

'Thing is, Alice,' he said gently, 'I know what it's like to lie awake in the dark.'

So that was why he'd confided in her about Eve. He was being kind, smoothing over the way she'd spilled her guts to him that Friday night. She was beginning to think that Damien Maher was on the high end of the more-decent spectrum of human beings.

'Sorry to hear you had a bad time,' she said. 'Has it got any easier?'

'Now it has.'

'Have you family here?'

'Yeah, in Maynooth, where I grew up.'

'Good to have family.'

'We've had our share of crap, though,' he said. 'I guess every family has something hurled at them and this was big shit, but people are trying to get on with things.'

'Life doesn't always turn out the way you'd expect,' she said, wondering what happened.

'I presume you mean your marriage to Ronan.'

Ronan. He was interested enough to have remembered the name.

'It was great in the beginning,' she said. 'But there came a time when I knew staying with him would destroy me, and it wouldn't be good for Chloe either. I didn't want her to grow up with the example of a woman who put up with shite for the sake of a luxury lifestyle.'

'Absolutely,' Damien said. 'Far better to set the example of someone who had the courage to take responsibility for her own life and walk away from a bad situation.'

'That's me,' she said. 'I'll never find myself in a situation like that again.'

It was the first time she'd walked out on someone. Usually they left her: her father, her mother dying too soon and Holly, twice.

'I'm sure Holly was a support when your marriage broke up.' There was a question in his voice.

They'd reached the gates of the park and she was glad there was no time to answer. *Anything but*, she'd been tempted to say.

'It's a shame to go back to the office on such a nice day,' Damien said. 'You can see the Poolbeg chimneys from the sixth-floor canteen,' he went on conversationally.

She cringed when she remembered how she had waxed lyrical about them that Friday night, sounding like a hopeless case.

'And I still remember seeing them winking through the grey morning when I flew into Dublin from Hong Kong,' he continued. 'I knew I'd come home.' He began to walk backwards so he was still facing Alice, his hands in his coat pockets. 'They make me feel good too … just sayin'.' Then he grinned, turned around and headed back to his office.

Courage, he'd said, the word resonating with her as she walked back to the library – far from the pig-headedness Ronan had described.

Ronan had been at pains, many times, to list the ways in which Chloe was being short-changed thanks to Alice's pig-headedness. She knew them off by heart: Chloe would have her father a lot more than just every Sunday; she'd be living a life of luxury; she'd be privately educated. Alice would be a stay-at-home mum, instead of farming her out to relatives.

They'd never have married, she knew, but for her pregnancy. Ronan had insisted on it. He was thrilled he was about to become a father. He'd admitted to her that he'd thought he might never have children. He was forty-three and most of his girlfriends were afraid to get pregnant, not wanting to spend a few months in baggy clothes, much less give birth. This wonderful baby would be the start of the Russell dynasty, so *of course* Alice had to be his lawful wedded wife. He wanted to portray a squeaky-clean image and have everything tied up legally from the get-go, including Alice, as the mother of his child. Marrying him would ensure that Alice would have every comfort, everything she possibly needed.

Until as time went on, and things changed, she realised she hadn't.

Courage, not pig-headedness, Alice whispered to herself as she went into the library, focusing on that alone and blocking the image of Damien's parting smile, because it was bringing her into dangerous territory.

CHAPTER 15

Holly, 2008–2009

MUM'S BEDROOM, A YEAR AFTER SHE DIED; my heart in my mouth, something buzzing in my ears as Alice and I stepped across the threshold, and the threshold of finally realising that Mum was never coming home. I'd slipped in to her room often during that year – a shrine of sorts where I could cry in peace. This morning I freeze-framed the image of the room in my head, so that I'd remember exactly what it had looked like as she'd walked out of it a year ago. It seemed that the room was holding its breath, waiting for her to return; there was a scarf she'd allowed to drift over a chair, perfume she'd sprayed and left with the lid uncapped, the pink slippers she'd aligned by her bed, books arranged on her bedside locker, one half-read; the final fingerprints of her life, all overlaid with a gossamer veil of dust and heartache.

Then Alice opened the wardrobe door and heaved an armful of clothes onto the bed; the air was disturbed and the waiting came to an end. I swallowed back a formless panic and steeled myself as a cascade of memories along with her clothes unspooled around the room.

'Right. Here goes,' Alice said. We kept a few special

mementoes for ourselves, packing up most of Mum's modest wardrobe for a charity shop. Alice let me have Mum's old jewellery box, even though Alice had bought it for her. Then I nearly cracked completely when we found the letters, stuck together in a brown envelope in the bottom drawer of Mum's dressing table. The letters had been written by Mum and sent to the address in Australia that Gus Clarke must have given her. They'd been returned, 'not known at this address' scrawled across the front. The postmarks were faint, but we could make out that they'd been posted the year I'd been born.

'Will we have a look?' I asked.

'Yes, and then we'll burn them,' Alice said.

'Alice!'

'Believe me, Holly, it'll be more cathartic that way.'

But after the first letter was opened, my chest bloomed with pain and I couldn't read any more. It was clear from the way Mum wrote about my arrival into the world that Gus Clarke had gone off to Australia blissfully ignorant of the fact that he'd fathered me.

'Mum was telling the truth,' I said, sitting back on the bed, my head reeling. 'He didn't know about me.'

'She told you that all along.'

'I didn't believe her,' I said, feeling as though I was speaking through a frozen mouth. The letters changed everything, pulling the rug out from whatever I'd known about myself up until then. I was too shocked to cry. 'I thought she was only saying that to make me feel better. I thought he'd gone running when he heard she was pregnant with me, that I was to blame.'

'Even if you didn't believe Mum, how could you have been to blame if you hadn't even been born? The people he left were me and Mum,' Alice said. She had a pale, strained look on her face.

'But something had to make him leave. I thought it was the idea of me being born. It made me think there was something wrong with me. Even though you and Mum always loved me to bits, I felt deep down Dad had rejected me, like faulty goods, and you were both making up for it by spoiling me. That was why –' I hesitated, the beliefs that had driven me and prompted my behaviour up to then torn to shreds.

'Why what?'

'I always tried to be as happy and cheery and nice as possible. And to love people, especially you and Mum, as much as I could, to help make up for Dad going off.'

'Dad going off was never about you, Holly,' Alice said. To my surprise, there was a hard look in her eyes I hadn't seen there before.

'Sorry, I've annoyed you.'

'You haven't,' she said. She turned away and began tying up the bags for the charity shop before lugging them downstairs.

Later, when we were having a takeaway pizza and watching a rom-com that Alice insisted would be best for taking our minds off things, I said, 'Maybe he'd have stayed if he'd known.'

'What are you talking about?'

'If he'd known about me and had been around when

I was born, Dad might have stayed. Whatever about walking out on one child, he might never have walked out if he'd got to know me and love me.'

Alice made a funny noise like a strangled cough. She stood up, cleared away the pizza box and brought in another bottle of wine from the kitchen.

◆

Alice arranged for a decorator to come in and paint Mum's bedroom in a pale pink colour, and I moved into it, accenting the candyfloss shade with purple cushions and throws. The second year, the pangs of grief came less often, yet when they did, they squeezed me with an intensity I'd never expected. I began to work harder and go out more, and then I bumped into Jay at a concert in Iveagh Gardens when I was on my way to queue for some beer. I'd seen him in the past year on the rare occasions the college gang had met up, and his continued but very casual jibes about us getting together were beginning to annoy me. I was relieved to see him with a dark-haired woman I didn't recognise because I wasn't in the humour for his banter.

Not that that stopped him.

'Holly!' he said, greeting me as though I was a long-lost friend. 'I didn't expect to see *you* here. Otherwise I'd have …' He didn't finish his sentence. He glanced down at the young woman and made a face. Standing beside him, the woman couldn't see his expression, but she must have guessed he was up to something because she twisted out of his embrace.

'Is this another one of your good friends?' she asked coolly.

'Holly, meet Sonia,' he said. 'Holly's not a good friend – at least not yet,' he said, grinning at me. I'm not sure if the inference was lost on her but his meaning was clear to me.

'Lovely to meet you, Sonia,' I said, deliberately excluding Jay from my smile. I walked away, my whole back prickling, raging that I hadn't seen him coming. I joined a queue at the far end of the drinks station, where I ordered vodka in addition to the beer – a quick shot to take the taste of him away. When I was walking back across the field to join my mates, trying to carry the tray of beer without spilling any, he appeared in front of me, smiling brazenly.

'What do you want?'

'You, Holly. The sooner the better.'

'Go back to your girlfriend.'

'She's not my girlfriend. Ah, Holly, if I'd known *you* were going to be here today …'

He moved in closer to me and snaked out his hand. I lifted the tray of beer and tipped it all over him. It didn't matter that I had to queue all over again. The sight of Jay Slater with beer-drenched hair and a saturated T-shirt made it worthwhile.

◆

Then Alice began asking me what was wrong.

'I'm fine,' I said. 'Why do you keep asking me?'

Alice put her head to one side. 'You never really got

over that flu. You look tired and wrung out to me. You're coughing a lot.'

I'd had a bad dose of the real, actual flu in the late spring. I'd gone back to work and socialising too soon, not wanting to be sick. 'I'm working and partying too hard,' I said.

Two weeks later my cough had become much worse. I was short of breath and suddenly fatigued in a way I'd never been before. I came home early one Saturday night because I was shaking with chills and almost collapsing with chest pain. I'd never wanted to darken the door of the hospital where Mum had been pronounced dead, yet thanks to Alice's insistence, I found myself sitting in A&E later that night. And thanks to Alice I was in the right place. I was terrified when they diagnosed pleurisy, and absolutely devastated when I found myself in a hospital bed being hooked up to intravenous antibiotics.

'I can't stay here,' I said to Alice on Sunday evening. 'It's where they brought Mum when she died. It's bringing it all back to me. Take me home, please.'

'Forget what happened to Mum,' Alice said. 'Nothing will go wrong with you while I'm around.'

In the end I was so upset that they let me home to Victoria Row on the Tuesday morning on the understanding that Alice would look after me.

She organised her life around me with the verve and purpose of someone who'd been injected with a high dose of energy and adrenaline. She changed her shifts in the library. She bought new cushions and cuddly-soft throws and made a day-bed of the sofa in the living room so that I'd be as comfortable as possible. She prepared my favourite foods, tempting me with treats; she pampered me with scented candles and hot-water bottles; and she brought home audiobooks for me to listen to when she had to go to work. Some evenings she even read to me. She arranged flowers and get-well cards on a low table close to where I lay on the sofa.

'You shouldn't be doing all this,' I said halfway through the second week, when Alice brought through yet another mug of hot chocolate. 'I feel I'm taking over your life.'

Alice plumped up the cushions propped behind my back. 'What else would I be doing? I couldn't save Mum, but I'm sure as hell going to save you.'

'Save Mum? How could you have saved Mum?'

Alice sighed. 'I dunno … she must have been feeling tired beforehand, or sensed that something was wrong. If only I'd noticed …'

'Mum seemed fine to me. There were no warning signs.'

'We'll never know. But in the meantime, you're going to be fine.'

'You should be out there enjoying yourself, meeting men, finding love …' My words trailed away. There was a funny moment when I seemed to step outside myself, and I looked, really looked, at my sister. By rights, Alice should have been in a steady relationship by now, maybe married with children. There had been occasional dates with men, but nothing serious. Alice most resembled

Mum. She had straight, shoulder-length dark hair that she sometimes caught in a loose knot at the back of her head. No matter how tidily she fixed it, a few tendrils always escaped, framing her pale oval face. Her eyes were a shade of light brown, almost cinnamon. She wasn't pretty, but she could be striking, and she looked lovely when she smiled. Her face had smiled at me all through my life. I used to think she was overcompensating in case I felt bad for sending Gus Clarke away. Now I knew I hadn't sent him running and I was still coming to terms with the way that dark cloud had been lifted off me. Which was another reason why I hated being sick. I wanted to get out there and have lots of fun and make the most of my social life.

'I'll have plenty of time for the hordes of men panting after my body when you're well,' Alice said. 'No harm in keeping them waiting.'

'Is there someone waiting?' I asked.

'Not right this minute.'

'I'll get well soon, won't I?'

'You certainly will, if I have anything to do with it.'

I came through it all right, due in no small part to Alice's love and dedication. Six weeks after I'd almost collapsed, I was deemed fit to return to work. I couldn't wait to pick up the pieces of my life again. But there was a price to pay.

◆

'You're not going out *again*, are you? Don't be late home,' Alice said, frowning, standing between me and the door as though she'd prevent me from leaving if it were physically possible.

'There's no need to wait up,' I said.

'I can't really sleep until you're home safe.'

'That's ridiculous. I'm well able to take care of myself.'

'Hello? You do realise you've had a major illness?'

'I wish you wouldn't fuss so much.'

'I'm not fussing. You've been seriously ill, Holly.'

'I don't want to be reminded, thank you. I'm not sick little Holly any more. I wish you'd let go of the idea of me being some kind of invalid, needing your care and attention. I don't know why you're so hung up on it.'

I thought of the new red top I was wearing, the new mascara that gave me ultra-long eyelashes, the iridescent smoky eyeshadow that brought out the blue in my eyes and the cool bar on Dawson Street in which my workmates were gathering at this moment, the club we might go to afterwards. I itched to join them.

'Coming home at four in the morning every weekend night is not a great idea,' Alice said, pursing her lips, 'not after what you've been through. You could have a relapse.'

'For God's sake, let me breathe, let me have a life of adventure, and keep out of it. I'm cured. It's over now, right? Being sick has made me want to live life to the full and party as much as I can. Have you any idea how trapped I felt, being stuck at home for six weeks?'

'I do have some idea. I thought I made it as easy for you as possible.'

'You did,' I said, 'and you were brilliant. I'll never forget that. But I want some fun. Fun, remember that word? There hasn't been much of it around here in the last few years. You could do with some fun yourself. Maybe then you wouldn't object to me going out and enjoying myself. Yeah, actually, maybe that's what's really biting you. You need to get out there and make the most of life just as I'm doing.'

Alice went into the living room and turned on the TV, the sound of the evening news bulletin droning into the hallway. Some of my excitement fell flat. I bit back an expletive and went out the door.

CHAPTER 16

Holly, 2009

FRIDAY EVENING A COUPLE OF WEEKS LATER, I was leaving the pub after post-work drinks with Shauna and Rachel and some of the office gang. I felt a tip on my shoulder and a voice close by said, 'Hey, it *is* you, isn't it? Holly?'

I turned around, and when I saw his face, everything about my life flipped into the most beautiful place imaginable.

Oh, my God. 'Ocean City?' I said.

He grinned. 'I didn't think you'd remember.'

I'd never forgotten. 'Luke.'

'Yeah, Luke Summers.'

'Summers,' I said, feeling a smile break out across my face. 'Cheerful and bright.'

Someone pushed past me, jostling me slightly.

'Holly?' Shauna asked, looking with interest at Luke. 'Are you coming?'

I glanced at Luke again before saying, 'No, it's okay, you go on ahead.'

'Does that mean you have time for a drink?' Luke asked.

'Yeah, but not here.' The pub was heaving with Friday-evening roars of exaggerated laughter and ultra-loud jollity. We walked up the quays until we came to a hotel where the bar was quieter and we had a chance to hear ourselves think. I watched him going up to the counter, taking in the neat suit and white shirt that told me he'd also come from the office. His dark hair was shorter than it had been in Ocean City, but his grey eyes warmer. I felt a solid contentment, as though a missing piece within me had been filled. He seemed like someone I'd always known, floating around in a corner of my heart, the lovely guy who'd rescued me from Jay that evening in Ocean City.

'You've probably been around the world twice since I saw you,' I said, when he came back with drinks.

'North America, South America, Vietnam, Cambodia, Thailand ... it's been amazing watching sunrises and sunsets, going from blistering sunshine to torrential rains, and,' he smiled at me, 'wondering how a girl I met one night in Ocean City, with hair like a sunbeam and eyes the colour of a sapphire sky, was getting on with her life and hoping she was happy.'

My stomach fluttered. 'Yeah, right.' I laughed shakily, secretly thrilled with his description of me.

'I've never forgotten you, Holly,' he said earnestly. 'I'm working in Dublin now, an IT firm. I knew I'd find you sooner or later.'

'Did you now?' I grinned happily.

'Yeah, even if I had to search half of Dublin for you.'

'You didn't, did you?'

'Maybe I did, but never mind that now – how are you?'

'I haven't exactly been around the world since Ocean City, but I've been to places I never expected to be.'

It all poured out of me, like I'd been saving it up for him: the awfulness of Mum's sudden death, the horribleness of grieving for her, and then being ill. 'Sorry,' I gulped, 'it's not as exciting as a sunrise off Machu Picchu.'

'*I'm* sorry to hear all that. It's so sad about your mother. She must be a huge loss.'

'I can't believe how desperate I still feel when I stop for a moment and think of her gone. It's like that part of me is stuck and can't move on.'

'Your feelings are perfectly normal. Grief is so difficult to get your head around.' His arm slid around my shoulder and a warmth spread through my body. 'I kind of know how you feel,' he said. 'I've been there too. Sort of. I was in a car crash at sixteen: one of my friends died; another one walked away without a scratch. I was in hospital for months afterwards, staring at the ceiling. It was horrendous and life-changing, I couldn't process it for ages, but when I was stuck in that hospital bed, thinking of my friend who'd died, I couldn't wait to get back on my feet again and start living, really living.'

'My sister has been great, but she's almost too protective,' I said. 'She doesn't like to see me upset about Mum, and after being sick I can't even blow my nose without her worrying. She's hovering so much that it's beginning to feel like a millstone around my neck. And as for going out … that's almost forbidden territory.' I couldn't help rolling my eyes.

'Yeah, I got that from my parents after the accident. They meant well, but still … You only get one chance at life – you have to make it amazing.' He looked at me as though I was amazing. 'I'm sorry I wasn't around for you,' he said.

'You're here now.'

Luke gave me a hug. 'Hey, you'll be okay,' he said in a gentle voice.

I felt an even deeper connection to him. He understood. I felt tears gathering at the back of my eyes and was unable to stop one or two from trickling down my face. It was the beer, wasn't it? I was on my fourth by now. Still, it was a relief to hear him reassuring me, telling me my feelings were normal, that I'd be okay. Better than Alice telling me not to get upset or insisting that nothing would go wrong as long as she was around to look after me – to the point of trying to keep me far too safe.

'No one knows what might happen tomorrow,' he said. 'You have to make the most of every day. Make it amazing.'

After that I was finished. The thoughts that I could go on to have an amazing life, that Luke Summers was telling me this, filled me with happiness.

'You're so lovely,' I said.

'So are you.' He held my face in his hands. 'My sweet Holly.'

We met every night the following week, Alice getting tetchier and tetchier with me for going out so much as the week went on. We had another row in the hall the following Friday evening, when she caught me coming down the stairs with my overnight bag and I told her I wouldn't be home. I knew it was too soon to tell her about Luke or that we planned to spend the night together in his bedsit in Rathmines. I didn't want a major escalation of hostilities, when already the fizzing anticipation that had heightened inside me as I'd counted down the hours until the evening approached began to fall a little flat in the face of her annoyance.

Funny, the best thing that was happening to me and I was half-afraid to tell my sister. I sidled past her, closing the hall door quietly as I escaped, feeling like a ten-year-old child who'd been chastised by the teacher for talking in class. But joy bubbled up once more inside me when I saw Luke waiting for me in a pub. I wasn't poor, sick Holly any more, whom Alice wanted to safeguard with military force; I was someone whole, someone beautiful, someone desirable.

When I woke up late the following morning, his body curving around mine, I don't think there was anything at all about me that he didn't know. I felt fragile, as if I'd been cracked right open to my deepest insecurities. At the same time, I felt wonderfully strong and euphoric. I lay in a cocoon of heat and remembered how brilliant it had been between us the night before, how beautifully he had looked at me as though he could see right into my soul, how slowly we had made love, Luke drawing it out for hours, with a sweetness and gentle sensuality I'd never expected. I knew that the tight, constricted world I'd been caught in for so long had opened out, like a beautiful butterfly emerging from a chrysalis.

CHAPTER 17

Holly, 2009

A MONTH AFTER I MET LUKE AGAIN, I FINALLY told Alice I had a boyfriend.

She'd guessed, she said.

'How?' I asked, detecting a sour note in her voice.

'All those late nights *and* the times you don't come home? It doesn't take a genius to work that out.'

She was still bickering with me over my hectic social life, still annoyed that I wasn't – according to her – taking good enough care of myself.

'Aren't you pleased for me?' I asked.

'I hope he's treating you properly.'

'Oh, he certainly is.'

Then a month later, on a Monday morning when we were having breakfast, I told her I was moving out of Victoria Row and moving in with Luke the following weekend.

'I've a whole new adventure in front of me,' I said. 'I want to forget all about the bad things that happened here – Dad, then Mum, then being sick. I can't wait to put this house behind me.'

She rose awkwardly, jostling the table. 'Whose idea

was this?' she asked. 'Luke's? It seems very sudden. I hope he's not pressuring you into anything.'

'Pressuring? I hoped you'd be happy for me.' I didn't want her to be dismissive of the amazing turn my life had taken.

'I'd no idea you were that serious about Luke, and now, hey presto, you'll be gone by next weekend.'

'Maybe I was afraid to tell you how serious it was getting.'

'*Afraid* of me?'

'I told Luke how hard it was going to be to tell you I was moving out – as it is, I get the third degree whenever I stay over with him.'

'The third degree?'

'You mean well, Alice, but it's like I'm your comfort blanket … as if you're dependent on looking after me to make you feel validated, and Luke agrees with me.'

It was actually Luke who had suggested Alice was being overly dependent, using me as a way of propping up her own self-esteem. All I knew was that I didn't want Alice to put a dent in my fragile, newfound happiness.

'*What?*'

'Look, I know I'm not explaining this well,' I said. 'I'll never forget the way you cared for me over the years, you've been brilliant, but you can't seem to let me go. You want everything under your control including me, safe and tidy and tucked up tightly. Sometimes I feel I can't breathe. I need to get away from here … from your co-dependency. I've had more than enough of your fussing.'

She stared at me.

My conscience was pricked at the hurt look in her eyes. I softened my voice. 'You never let me forget,' I said. 'The pleurisy. Like something you want to hold on to for your own sake.'

'I thought I was taking care of you.'

'You do too much, that's the problem. You hover around me as though I'm going to break into smithereens any minute. If I'm off my food for some reason or have a runny nose, I sense you watching me. You should be making a life of your own instead of being obsessed with mine. Believe it or not, this is tough love.'

'Says who?'

'Says me.'

'Is Luke prompting you?'

'He understands how I feel. About how Mum dying and me being sick brought home to me that we only have one shot at this life. He helps me to realise I'm a beautiful, vibrant person.'

'And I've never treated you like that?'

'Look, I want you guys to be friends. You're both on the same side. Team Holly, remember? Only now it's going to be Team Holly and Luke.'

Team Holly. The rally cry Alice had come up with when I'd been recovering.

'Go to him if he means all that much to you.'

'I *am* going. It'll be an exciting, brand new start. You should try it sometime, Alice – you're still young enough to reinvent yourself.'

I knew I'd said the wrong thing when she looked at

me with a hard gleam in her eyes. 'Why? What's wrong with me the way I am?'

'You're stuck in a rut. You should go out there and make a life for yourself. Find love. It's wonderful. I want to be with Luke all the time,' I said. 'I want to sleep with him every night and wake up beside him every morning. What's between us – it's like, God, totes amazing. Perfection.'

'Too much information.' She clattered dishes into the sink, her back ramrod straight. 'There's no such thing as perfect in this life, Holly. Everything, no matter how good it seems, has a downside.'

'Why can't you be more positive?'

'Right then, what's the plan? When am I going to meet this wonderful Luke? Where will you be living?'

'Luke found an apartment to rent in a complex down along the quays – Liffey Gate. It's ultra-modern and has a tiny balcony overlooking the river.'

I'd fallen in love with Liffey Gate the minute Luke had shown me around, almost as quickly as I'd fallen in love with Luke. It was compact, with one bedroom and a neat living-space-cum-galley-kitchen, both rooms with glass doors leading out to a small balcony. What's not to love about an apartment overlooking the river?

'Luke loves being near flowing water,' I told Alice. 'It calms him.'

'You'd want to keep the windows closed at low tide,' Alice said. 'He must be well heeled, this Luke guy, if you can afford the rent on that.'

'It's been empty for a while and the landlord has reduced the rent.'

I didn't tell Alice that the previous tenant had lost his job. I was determined to ignore the financial crisis Ireland was sliding into. It was like a gloomy fog on the horizon of our sunshiny lives.

'Still. That can't come cheap.'

'We'll manage with both of our salaries. And you'll meet Luke tomorrow evening, if that suits you.'

'I can't wait.'

◆

We didn't get off to a great start. Luke was waiting for us in a bar off Grafton Street and he stood up and kissed Alice on the cheek as soon as we arrived.

'Luke, meet Alice. Alice, this is Luke,' I said.

'It's good to finally meet you, Luke,' Alice said, sitting down directly opposite him. I sat beside Luke, conscious that we were on one side of the table and Alice was alone on the other. Like an interview.

'I'm delighted to meet you, Alice,' Luke said warmly. 'Holly has talked about you a lot.'

'I believe you two are setting up home together very soon? That was quite a surprise.'

'Yes, isn't it great?' Luke said, his arm curving around me. 'Next weekend.'

'I hope you'll take excellent care of Holly,' Alice said.

'Alice,' I said, 'don't start.'

'I'm not starting anything,' Alice said, smiling

innocently. 'I want to make sure Luke knows how lucky he is, having someone as wonderful as you sharing his life.'

'I do know, Alice,' Luke said smoothly. 'And Holly knows how much I appreciate her. I can't do enough for her.' He squeezed my shoulder. 'I intend to take excellent care of her, just as you have.'

'Hey,' I said, 'I'm well able to take good care of myself. I'm not a parcel to be passed around.'

'I wouldn't call all those recent late nights good care,' Alice said.

'Alice, please,' I said, 'there's no need to come on with the big sister act.'

'It's not an act,' Alice said.

'It's fine, Holly,' Luke said in a calm voice. 'I see where Alice is coming from. The late nights were my fault. It was hard saying goodbye to Holly at the end of an evening. It will be different when we're living together, in our own little world. I can't wait to look after Holly, and I promise you I will, Alice.'

'See, Alice?' I said. 'Happy now? And can we move on, now that the introductions are done?'

Luke ordered drinks, Alice refusing a celebratory cocktail, settling for a white wine spritzer. I turned the conversation around to our new apartment, how lovely it was, how convenient it was going to be. Luke spoke a little about growing up in Cork and his travels around the world.

I tried to see him through Alice's eyes, watching him objectively. I'm sure Alice was wondering how come a tallish, rather lean guy, with a soft, sensitive face had turned my life around. But I knew Alice wouldn't see what I found wonderful about him. It was the light in his eyes and the intense way they looked at me that made me feel beautiful; and the way he talked to me, making me want to grab life with both hands and soar with it. The way he made love for hours, as though I was infinitely precious and made of delicate glass.

We didn't stay out too long and whatever Alice thought of Luke, she kept her opinion to herself, but I knew she wasn't happy with me moving in with him, especially on Wednesday evening when I said I was going to clear my bedroom.

'You don't have to do that,' she said, following me upstairs.

'I won't be coming back,' I said, snapping open a roll of black bin bags.

'There's no need to make such a clean sweep, in case it doesn't last.'

'Of course it will last,' I said. 'I'm done with my old life. Luke and I have plans to work for, oh, maybe nine months, then take time off to travel.'

'That's some plan all right,' she said, her eyes faintly mocking.

'I might store a few things in the attic. You'll have more space for whatever you want to do.'

'Thanks,' she said grudgingly.

'You really can't stand it, that I'm moving on while you're being left behind, can you?' I said, in exasperation.

'I don't understand why you feel the need to reject

your old life so thoroughly for the sake of someone you met two months ago.'

'Jesus, Alice, why should I want to bring reminders of my crappy life in Victoria Row into my new one? Why can't you just be happy for me?' I asked, conscious of her watching me as I chucked a load of old, well-thumbed diaries, full of the ramblings of my teenage angst, along with old soft toys and patchwork dolls into a plastic sack destined for the dump. They'd been sitting on a shelf in my bedroom for far too long. I had vague memories of Alice busting her gut to put up that shelf for me, but, hey, I was moving on to better things.

'That's mine,' she said, when I was about to lob a worn and faded Holly Hobbie rag doll into the sack.

I looked at it for a moment; it had been languishing at the back of my shelf, long forgotten, and I didn't associate practical Alice with soft toys of any description.

'It was the last thing Dad bought for me,' she said, her voice neutral. 'Stupid me, I was attached to it so much that when you were born Mum called you Holly. You always had your eye on it, and you asked me for a loan of it when you were sick with chicken pox. Then you didn't want to give it back.'

I couldn't recall this, although I knew I'd had the chicken pox when I was nine or ten. 'I'll leave it here so,' I said, popping it back on the now empty shelf, something guarded in her face preventing me from going over and handing it to her. She said little to me after that, watching quietly as I finished sorting my belongings before selecting the clothes and whatever necessities I was bringing to Liffey Gate. In the fever of anticipating living with Luke, I didn't let Alice's air of negativity dampen my spirits.

Luke called to collect me in his new jeep on Saturday afternoon.

'Impressive wheels,' Alice said in a deadpan voice when she saw him pulling up outside the house. I half-expected her to say something caustic about the need for such a monster vehicle when Liffey Gate was so central. I was glad she didn't. The jeep was Luke's pride and joy. It was silvery and shiny, a perfect symbol for our new lives.

Then when Luke put my belongings into the jeep, I turned to Alice to say goodbye. She was standing by the garden gate, hugging herself with her arms, her dark hair tossed by the brisk on-shore breeze rolling in off the sea. The tide was out, but huge swathes of wet strand glimmered in the sunlight.

A sweep of nostalgia took my breath away. All those growing-up years with Mum and Alice in Victoria Row had come to an end. It seemed only yesterday that I had been five, six, ten, fifteen. All the times that Alice had been on hand to comfort me, love me, care for me, were over now. I felt disjointed for a moment, torn in two between both worlds, so much so that I stood on the pavement, frozen, unable to speak. I wondered if Alice was feeling the same. Maybe this was how she'd been feeling ever since I'd told her I was moving, that something special between us was coming to an end. Scarcely though – Alice was more resentful of me for turning my back on my old life. Still, I forgot that when she drew me into a hug. She patted my back. She held me for a long moment, and then she gave me a little push.

'Go,' she said, her voice gruff. 'Luke's waiting.'

I turned back to the jeep and saw Luke waving at Alice from the driver's seat. On autopilot, I climbed up into the seat beside him. Then I, too, was waving Alice goodbye as we drew away from the kerb, thinking that this was it, she was being left behind, and how solitary she looked, how empty the house must seem now, empty of the people she'd loved so much. I waved until she was out of sight.

CHAPTER 18

Alice

'WHAT ARE YOU DOING HERE?' IT WAS A WEEK since Alice had seen Damien in Merrion Square Park; now he appeared beside her in the library while she was gathering up picture books in the junior section.

'Is that how you talk to your customers?' he asked, laughter in his voice.

'Of course not, but this is where we keep the children's books,' she said, managing to sound as if she was surprised to see him in that section, as opposed to being disconcerted at his sudden appearance. He was impeccably dressed, wearing a navy overcoat over a navy suit. His blue and silver tie was set against an ice-white shirt.

'Sometimes junior sections have the best books with the most amazing adventures,' he said. 'If I had a child, I'd look forward to a feast of bedtime reading. Where are all the Roald Dahls? I used to love those.' His gaze swept around the low shelving. The area was welcoming to little ones with primary-coloured seating and bean bags sized for small bodies, as well as picture books arranged in blue and red low-level containers.

'So did I,' she said.

'Which was your favourite?'

'*Matilda*.'

'I haven't seen you in the park lately.'

'No.'

Had he been watching out for her? Did something about her interest him?

'A daily walk would be good for you,' he said. 'Fresh air, endorphins ... the list of positives is endless.'

Was he inviting her?

'I called in to let you know your purse has been found,' he said.

'Oh.' Even to her ears, her voice sounded flat, as images of walking in the park with him dissolved in an instant.

'I had a phone call from Pearse Street station this morning,' he said. 'Unfortunately your cash and bank cards are gone.'

'How did the police know the purse was mine?'

'There are store loyalty cards in it and a gift card with your name. And a hall-door key. Luckily, that wasn't taken – otherwise you would have had to change the locks. If you don't mind me saying, it's best to keep your key separate from anything holding your name, in case your address could be identified.'

'You won't find me on social media, and there could be hundreds of Alice Clarkes in Dublin. Anyhow, no one could have opened the door with that key.' Whatever about the number of Alice Clarkes in Dublin, she bet none were going around with an old key in their purse.

A key that had been discarded on a kitchen table thirty-six years ago.

'No worries, then,' he said.

'Thanks,' she replied, belatedly remembering her manners, acutely aware of the trouble he'd gone to – yet again – for her. 'You're probably on your break, so I appreciate you taking the time to call in.'

'I was passing by,' he said. 'I'm on my way to a meeting.'

Duh to her. She was getting this so wrong.

'Have fun,' she said.

'Oh, it'll be great fun all right. As far from a walk in the park as you could get.'

He turned to leave. Was that it? What else did she expect? Alice Clarke didn't want anything to interfere with the safe running of her life until her divorce was finalised, not even a casual lunchtime stroll with a nice guy. Seemed like her courage didn't extend that far, after all.

'Damien?' she said, on impulse.

He paused.

'I might see you there some lunchtime.'

He smiled. 'Like tomorrow? I won't make it today.'

'Yeah, maybe.' She tried to sound careless, mildly panicked by the spark of pleasure she felt at the warmth of that smile. Then, in case it showed in her eyes, 'It beats sitting in the kitchen.'

Well done, Alice.

◆

The park was lit by a pale disc of sunshine that flitted behind the banks of grey clouds. It illuminated the soft drizzle, turning it into tiny jewels that danced in the air and glittered on the tips of the grass. Alice took a few deep breaths, inhaling the cool rainy scent of it as she saw him coming towards her, carrying an industrial-sized navy umbrella emblazoned with the KLW logo.

'Hello, Alice, yours or mine?' He lifted his umbrella, smiling at her.

She folded up her barely adequate chain-store version, moving under his. 'No contest.'

Soon, however, the clouds darkened and the drizzle turned to a downpour. They ran to the nearest gate, taking refuge in a pub around the corner. Damien ordered caffe lattes and, with the busy lunchtime crowd, the only available seat was in a corner snug, which was a tight squeeze for them both.

'I hope I won't run the risk of getting thumped by your ex-husband,' Damien said. 'Ronan, isn't it?'

'You might,' she said. 'He's the one and only Ronan L. Russell.'

Damien's eyes sparked with interest. 'The solicitor guy? I've heard of him.'

'I'm sure you have. Solicitor extraordinaire, respected businessman, influential investor. My ex. The father of Chloe. I'll be glad when the divorce is signed and sealed,' Alice admitted, 'and when Chloe's custody arrangements are a little more secure.'

'Where did you two meet?'

'The library sent me to a literary event in Dublin Castle and there he was.'

'Love at first sight?'

'He said I intrigued him. That I was unlike anyone he'd ever met before. Thing is, at the time, I was pretending to be someone else. The Ronan Russells of this world don't normally give the Alice Clarkes a second glance. I was flattered that he paid me attention. It was a careless fling of sorts until I found out I was pregnant.'

'Ah.'

'Yes. Ronan has conservative values and being married to the mother of his child was a matter of pride for him. He wanted us to stay married for Chloe's sake. He doesn't like not getting his way and can't stand being a loser.'

'So, no pressure.'

'Absolutely none,' she said wryly.

'I'd better watch my back so,' Damien said with a grin.

She wondered what Ronan would make of her sitting there with Damien. She told herself there was nothing to make of it, changing the subject and asking Damien about his family, realising she knew little about them. But he didn't go into any details, telling her that his parents had both retired and were on a two-month trip to Australia and New Zealand and that he'd one sister now living in Kerry, who was married with young children. His expression was shuttered, and whatever terrible thing life had thrown at them that he'd alluded to previously, he kept to himself.

The heavy shower was over by the time they left the pub and Damien gave her a quick hug before they parted.

'Might see you here again?' he said. 'I'll text you.'

'Sure,' she said, feeling the imprint of that hug all the way back to the library. She wondered what Ronan might think of that and realised she didn't give a toss.

CHAPTER 19

'WELL, YOU'RE CERTAINLY A DARK HORSE,' Sharon announced loudly a couple of weeks later as she walked into the library, late as usual. She winked at Alice.

'Am I?'

'You might have told us, instead of keeping it a secret,' Sharon said.

'Keeping what a secret?' Julia asked.

'He's gorgeous,' Sharon said. 'I'm glad I nudged you in the right direction.'

'Ooh, Alice,' Julia said, putting on a fake squeal, 'what have you been up to? This sounds exciting.'

Alice braced herself.

'Abbey Lane Library – where love stories begin,' Sharon announced, clearly enjoying every word.

Finbarr looked up from where he was checking a spreadsheet. He glanced from Sharon to Alice but remained silent.

'Who knew the passions that were smouldering behind the quiet shelves?' Sharon continued, grinning broadly.

'Tell me more,' Julia said.

'Romance in real life,' Sharon went on, 'not just between the covers of a steamy book.'

'Sounds like you should be writing those steamy books,' Julia said.

'Not me,' said Sharon, 'I wouldn't have the sexual experience. But a certain member of staff might have.' She grinned at Alice. 'I thought I was the adventurous one. We were up at the Giant's Causeway at the weekend and I even did the rope-bridge thingy – it was scary, but that was nothing compared to Alice's adventure.'

Julia squealed. 'Come on, I'm bursting to know …'

'Merrion Square Park – lunchtime rendezvous. It looked like he was waiting for you, as though it was prearranged. You can't keep it a secret any longer. Aren't you glad I brought you two together?' Sharon said.

'The suspense is killing me,' Julia said. 'Who is it?'

'It's none other than Damien, one of the library customers, a regular, especially in recent weeks. Now we know who's drawing him in. Our own Alice.'

'Damien who?' asked Julia.

'You know – he looks like Jake Gyllenhaal without the beard and 'tache – regular guy-next-door but dripping with testosterone. A bit old for me,' Sharon went on, 'so I shoved him in Alice's direction. Didn't I, Alice?'

'Excuse me, I'm needed elsewhere,' Alice said, flustered at the word testosterone in practically the same breath as Damien and the rush of heat it brought to her face. She was relieved to see a customer needing her assistance with the automatic kiosk, giving her an excuse to leave the counter.

◆

'Sharon means well,' Finbarr said.

'I'm sure she does.' It was lunch hour. Alice wasn't seeing Damien today because he was at a day-long meeting. She looked up from the book she was pretending to read. Even the latest Tana French couldn't distract her from thinking about Sharon's comments and Damien. There was a pause. Alice got the impression that Finbarr was readying himself to say something. She saw a variety of expressions chase across his face until he glanced at the closed door, put down his newspaper and took off his reading glasses.

'If you don't mind me saying, Alice, I think it's lovely for you to find someone to share things with. It can't be easy raising a young daughter on your own. Time runs on quickly,' he said. 'You need to make the most of any opportunities that come along. You don't want to reach my age and have regrets.'

She wondered what regrets, if any, Finbarr might have. He always seemed so calm and contented with his lot. He knew how cut up Alice had been when she'd returned to the library service after her separation from Ronan and had been assigned to Abbey Lane. Finbarr had kept her busy, as she'd asked, treating her with nothing but kindness and compassion while she found her feet during those first fraught weeks.

'I know you have Chloe,' he went on, 'but it's good to have friends, someone to do nice things with, happy things ... You're a lovely young woman and you deserve happiness.'

'Thank you, Finbarr,' she said, touched by his words

and the effort it had taken him to say them. 'I wish my ex-husband felt the same.'

'In that case, isn't it just as well he's your ex,' Finbarr said.

'Yes, actually, it is,' Alice said, his words somehow finding a space inside her, nestling like a little seed, taking root.

◆

'I'm bringing Chloe to Euro Disney,' Ronan said when he called to collect her on Sunday morning.

Chloe had gone back upstairs to fetch another soft toy, leaving her parents in the hall. Alice had noticed her doing this several Sundays in a row and she hoped Chloe wasn't deliberately giving her parents time alone, thinking it might bring them back together.

> It will never happen, my darling. I'm going to raise you
> to be so strong and resilient that no man will catch you
> off guard. I'll show you how to live a life full of courage
> and guts.

'You're not bringing her to Euro Disney,' Alice said flatly. There had been no discussion, no advance agreement. She could imagine Ronan's apoplectic fit if she was to casually announce she was taking Chloe off to another country.

'Oh yes, I am,' he said, smiling easily. 'It's all booked. A belated birthday treat, seeing that I was up to my tonsils in January. We're going with my sister Myra and her boys next Friday. For a week.'

'What about school?'

'They won't give me any hassle. A nice donation to the sports fund will go down well.'

Alice shook her head. 'And will there be anyone else tagging along? Who goes by the name of Amanda? Chloe has told me about her.'

'Mind your own business.'

'It *is* my business. I'm supposed to be squeaky clean, but you're well able to do whatever you like.'

'What's got into you?'

'How come there's one rule for you and a different one for me?'

'Let me remind you, you're the one who wants this divorce, not me. Can't have you being a bad example to Chloe. That wouldn't go down well with the judge.'

'How dare you,' Alice said. 'You'd want to watch your step. I might want to add another piece of blackmail to my collection.'

'No chance.' He grinned. 'You might think you have one over on me, but it's in your best interests not to use it. I doubt if your little blackmail would impress any judge in the land.'

Chloe came down the stairs clutching her teddy.

'Would you like a big surprise?' Ronan asked her.

'What surprise, Daddy?'

'I'm taking you away for a week – would you like that, poppet?'

Chloe looked anxiously from Alice to Ronan. 'Where?'

'We're going to Euro Disney in Paris,' Ronan said. 'Next Friday. With Aunt Myra and your cousins.'

Chloe's upturned face reddened. 'Really?' she squealed, staring at her father and twisting her teddy around and around in her hands before glancing back at Alice. 'Is that okay, Mum?'

Ronan's teeth smiled at Alice. 'You're hardly going to deprive Chloe, are you?'

Alice hugged her daughter, willing away the anxiety in her young face. The depth of her love for Chloe burned through the marrow of her bones. She wished she could protect her forever, wrap her up so securely that nothing would ever trouble her, but she knew that was impossible.

'Of course it's okay,' she said smoothly. 'You'll have a wonderful time.' She avoided Ronan's gaze completely, not wanting to give him the satisfaction of witnessing the fury in her eyes at the way he had manipulated her.

◆

'Ronan and Chloe in Euro Disney for a whole week? Woo-hoo – the perfect opportunity,' Maeve said when Alice called to collect Chloe after work on Monday evening.

'What for?'

'For you and lover boy.'

'What makes you think I'm seeing him?'

'You look different. Happy. Warmer in your eyes. You're moving around with a lighter step. A sexier step. Maybe Ronan sensed it and that's why he's pulled a fast one on you with Chloe.'

'No way.'

'Have you looked in the mirror lately? Really looked?'

Alice didn't need to look. She knew something was happening, something she'd never expected. She'd met Damien in the park several times. The previous Friday they'd gone for coffee again because it had been raining. For those moments in time, it had been good to leave everything to one side and be just a woman chatting to a man who was kind and attentive. And attractive as hell. Only that morning, on her way to work, words that Holly had spoken to her about Luke had somehow jarred themselves loose from her memory bank, words to the effect that Luke was helping to bring out the best version of herself, because she was beginning to feel like that about Damien. He was bringing out an energy in her, a version of herself who was fed up playing it safe and living by Ronan's rules, and fed up arguing with him in her head. When it came to Chloe's security and happiness, she would fight Ronan all the way. And if she wanted to raise Chloe to be strong and resilient, and to live a life full of courage and guts, well then, she had to lead by example.

But she felt more alive, as if a protective binding she'd wrapped around herself over the years had started to unravel. Yet she was also playing with fire. Damien was too easy to talk to, and she was becoming aware that she had so much bottled up inside her, words and feelings she'd never expressed, sadness and disappointment with Ronan and Holly, and emotions she'd put into cold storage, right back to the time she'd been young. Sometimes, now, under Damien's kind gaze and warm attention, she felt them bubbling to the surface. She was afraid that one of these days she might become completely undone, and they'd come pouring out of her at the wrong time.

What would she be like, she wondered, if all that baggage was unloaded? If everything was sliced back cleanly, to the very heart of her? Damien might have seen her vulnerable side one Friday night, but he hadn't seen the real Alice Clarke yet.

Neither, she sensed, had she.

CHAPTER 20

Holly, 2009–2011

IN ONE SENSE, MY SISTER WAS RIGHT. THERE is no such thing as the perfect life – everything is subject to light and dark. The higher you fly, the harder you fall. In the beginning, our life in Liffey Gate was magical, as though fairy dust was sprinkled all over it. We were living in a dream world, no worries, no cares, just happy-ever-afters like all the good fairy tales.

We had less than three years before it turned into a nightmare.

The first year, I felt I was a modern-day Sleeping Beauty, waking up after years of being smothered by Alice and Mum thanks to Luke's love. The apartment already contained the basics, but I spent my lunch hours shopping for all the little touches that added a cute cachet to our lives – china mugs and pretty cake plates, crystal glasses and scented candles, designer photo frames that I filled with happy pictures of us, sequinned cushions and warm white fairy lights that I trailed around the balcony doors and bed rail. Most mornings, Luke was up first, showering and dressing quietly so as not to disturb me, then he'd bring me coffee, kissing me awake softly.

'What's it like out today?' I'd ask.

'It's beautiful,' he'd say. 'It will be a brilliant day, the best day so far.'

He'd open the curtains and gently plump up the pillows behind me. I couldn't see the river from our bed, but I could see the sky, the gulls drifting about and the sun reflecting off windows of buildings across the quays. Every morning, Luke said it was the best day so far. Even if it was dull and rainy. Because each day with me, he said, was making his life richer and happier. Before he left for his office, he made sure I was organised with my shower and clothes, and after he was gone I often took my coffee out on to our tiny balcony. I loved watching the way the Liffey rippled and glided between the ancient walls in its run to the open sea. Luke was right: there was something calming about the movement of the water. I didn't even mind if it was a bit stinky at low tide – we could close the doors and be in our own perfect little glass bubble suspended above. Sometimes we took a bottle of wine outside in the evening, pulling on fleeces if it was chilly, watching the wavy reflections of lights across the river dance on the surface.

Even though we were perfectly content to spend as much time as we could on our own, I invited Alice over for a glass of wine a few times in the early months, but I still felt she resented Luke for what she regarded as him taking me away from her.

'He's great, Alice,' I said, trying to get her onside one evening when Luke had gone around to the off-licence. 'He sorts out all the financials, does the grocery shopping – he even collects the dry cleaning. Otherwise,' I giggled, 'they might get overlooked. I'm hopeless when it comes to the everyday stuff.'

'You're not that hopeless,' she said.

'He likes to look after me,' I went on. 'Sometimes he even picks out my clothes for the day, and I love that he's so caring.'

'Do you not find that a bit much?' she asked.

'Not at all,' I said. 'I feel so cherished. And he's great with the cooking. Just like you were. You know me,' I giggled, 'having different pots on the go *and* something under the grill freaks me out totally.'

'It's just practice, Holly,' she said. I could see by her face she was still unimpressed. 'Have you seen much of your friends lately?' she asked.

'Yeah, not so much the college gang – Luke is shy in big groups – but we're going out Saturday night to a new club with a few mates.'

Luke loved to have me all to himself, but we went out at least once a week, treating ourselves to dinner in one of Dublin's best restaurants, and we kept up with a small circle that included Tara and Niamh, who insisted on dragging us out clubbing some Saturday nights, occasionally coming back to ours for wine or cocktails when we'd party until dawn light glowed up along the river, less frequently meeting up with the wider college gang. There was rarely a night when we didn't make love. Luke never rushed it, making it a slow, sensual experience for both of us, buying me expensive lingerie, setting the atmosphere with candles and low music, sometimes arranging my limbs and my hair carefully across the bed before he got naked, other times using my chiffon scarves to blindfold me or tie my hands – but always gently – he wanted nothing to distract me from his touch. He always took the lead and made me come first, and he loved watching my face as I climaxed. Occasionally, when he stared into my eyes with that fiercely intense, almost unblinking gaze of his, and I felt it was taking me too long, I faked orgasm. But mostly I drank in the perfection of it all, the sublime beauty of the way he loved me. Weekend mornings in bed were an extra treat, followed by brunch somewhere along the quays or Grand Canal Dock. Sometimes when we sat at an outdoor café, I fancied that the intense pleasure I'd felt from the fantastic sex we'd just had was oozing from every pore in my body.

And on one such morning, we encountered Jay. He still hung out sometimes with the wider college gang, but I'd always managed to avoid him on those occasions and I hadn't come face to face with him since I'd moved in with Luke. His eyes flicked across my body, and I knew he was mentally undressing me – same-old same-old Jay – but being on the receiving end of Luke's love seemed to have surrounded me with some kind of magical armour against him.

'I heard you'd moved in with your Cork dick,' he said, eyeing us with a mocking grin as he came up to our table. 'What's it like playing house and pretending to be grown-ups?'

'What's it like being a loser?' Luke asked with uncharacteristic snappiness, recognising him immediately.

'Oooh. Tetchy.'

'Get lost.' Luke's jaw was set.

Luke would have been better off ignoring him. Anything Jay said was bound to be mega-irritating to the gentle Luke.

'Cheer up,' Jay teased. 'Things not going so well in Liffey Gate?'

I hadn't realised he knew where we lived, and it surprised me. Jay put the palms of his hands flat on the table, leaned towards me and said in a jocular tone of voice. 'I've heard all about your place on the third floor. Can't wait for you to realise you need a real man in your bed.'

Luke's hand shot out and grabbed Jay's wrist. His face taut, he looked like he wanted to punch him. It was the first time I'd seen Luke so angry and it appalled me. Besides, Luke would have been no match for the brawnier Jay. I reached over and stroked Luke's arm. 'Leave it,' I said. 'Just ignore him.'

'I'd never ignore *you*, Holly.' Jay laughed as though it was all very funny, straightening up as Luke released him. 'You're still top of my list, remember? By the way,' he winked, moving away from the table, 'we're practically neighbours.'

I wasn't happy about that, any more than I still wanted to be on his list. I was living the dream with

Luke and certainly didn't want Jay popping up from time to time with his sleazy comments, even if they were delivered in a teasing manner. And, God forgive me, even if they still delivered a tiny lift to my ego. He strode off with his usual cocky gait and even had the gall to salute as though he knew I was watching.

Luke said, 'I'm sorry you had to listen to that asshole – you should have let me shut him up for good.'

'How? By giving him a black eye?' I smiled at Luke. He was the gentlest man I knew. 'He's only a stupid pest and not worth your energy.'

For a while, Jay rarely crossed our paths. Sometimes when we went to parties or clubs I found myself scanning the room to make sure he wasn't around because I didn't want to run the risk of Luke and him trading insults. I heard from Tara that he was sharing an apartment on the far side of the river with some other guys. He'd become involved with a girl who lived in Galway and he spent a lot of his weekends there.

But as one year slid into the next, the recession was biting deeper. We heard of friends who were made redundant, some emigrating, others moving back in with their parents. It was a rude awakening. We'd only ever been used to having plenty of dosh, swigging cocktails and flashing cards in high-end restaurants and boutiques. It was all changing for the bright young things who had graduated with high hopes and the world at our glitz-encrusted stilettos. Keep-you-awake-at-night change. Then Luke had to take a pay cut at the same time our taxes went up. It was a double whammy, so we put our travel-the-world plans on hold, not wanting to jeopardise our jobs by looking for career breaks. I made up for that by booking a couple of city breaks.

'Imagine being so broke that we couldn't pay our rent or the loan on the jeep,' I said, tucking my head into the nook of his neck the night we heard another of his mates was moving back home.

'We'll be fine,' Luke said, holding me close. 'We'll always find somewhere cheaper to live, but no one's going to take my pride and joy off me.'

I smiled at him in the dim lighting. 'I thought I was your pride and joy.'

He pulled me back into his warm embrace. 'You're far more than that,' he said, stroking my hair. 'You're my one and only soulmate.'

I loved being called Luke's soulmate, the idea that our hearts were two halves of the one whole, bound together at some deep level. When he asked me to marry him, it seemed so right, as if all the edges of my life had finally slotted smoothly into place.

'We could plan the most marvellous wedding and honeymoon,' I said. 'It would take our minds off this horrible recession.'

'I didn't mean splashing out on a big wedding. I just want you to belong to me in every way.'

'Oh, Luke. Well, I want a big wedding to show our love off to the world, and what Holly wants,' I teased, 'she gets.'

◆

I hadn't seen much of Alice in recent months. She and Luke had never really hit it off and I found it annoying that she still didn't seem to appreciate how much he cared for me, although Luke assured me that her attitude didn't bother him too much – I was the one he was living with. As I guessed, she wasn't completely happy with my wedding news, partly because in the same breath I asked for my share of the Victoria Row inheritance. Mum hadn't made a will, but by default, the house belonged to both of us. I hoped Alice wouldn't have a problem with buying out my share.

'The money would be useful for our wedding and honeymoon,' I said, thinking of other things it would be useful for: the mad credit card bill I'd somehow racked up; the loan I'd taken out to cover recent weekends away in Amsterdam and Prague.

'What happened to saving up?'

'Please don't begrudge me, Alice,' I said. 'We want to be married early next spring. We won't fritter it all on the wedding. We'll have plenty left for a wonderful honeymoon, some travel and to tide us over the worst of the recession.'

'Would it not be best to use the money towards a house of your own, now that prices are dropping? Even Victoria Row is not worth anything like it was in the boom. It's not a great time for you to look for your share. You know that, don't you?'

I resented her practical advice. And even though there

was a nugget of truth in it, I saw it as another obstacle raised by Alice, now that I was cutting the final apron string. 'We don't want to take out a mortgage yet,' I said. I didn't tell her about Luke's pay cut or our rent going up, or that we hadn't even looked at trimming our budget. We hated the thoughts of having anything gloomy sour our lovely lifestyle.

'It's your money,' Alice said. 'If you feel this is what you want, I'll make arrangements to buy out your share. But go easy, Holly.'

'What do you mean?'

'I think Mum and I wrapped you up in too much cotton wool and fed you a diet of wishful thinking. We shouldn't have kept telling you that you could be anything or have anything you wanted in life; unfortunately it doesn't work like that.'

◆

On a cold, sunny day in February, we were married in the local church, a stone's throw from where I'd grown up. I would have loved an Italian wedding, but I knew a lot of our friends couldn't afford it, so I had to curb my extravagance a little. I stayed in Victoria Row with Alice the night before the wedding.

'You really are in love with him,' she said to me on my wedding day, as she helped me into a soft cream ballet-length dress – so beautiful, I decided, it had been worth the few trips to London to source it.

'Of course I am,' I said, smiling at her reflection in the mirror. 'It's amazing between us.' Alice stared back at me as if seeing me with different eyes. I knew I looked beautiful that day. I felt it radiating around me like a tangible glow. It had little to do with my dress or the flowers in my hair or my silk-covered sandals. It was something that shone out of me, a happiness that lit my face and sparkled my eyes, thanks to the knowledge that Luke and I were making the ultimate commitment. In spite of my sadness that Mum and Dad weren't around for this special day, I felt happy, and I realised that happiness and sadness could quite easily coexist inside you: it was your choice which emotion you wanted to respond to the most. I also realised that Alice was alone in the house, in a life that was empty of love and commitment compared to mine.

'Will you be okay?' I asked her, my conscience suddenly squeezing.

'Me?' she scoffed, raising an eyebrow in the dismissive way that only Alice could. ''Course I will. Why shouldn't I be?'

I wanted to tell her I loved her, to say that I hoped she would be as happy as I was. I wanted to thank her for being the big sister who'd climbed on a chair to reach the breakfast cereal for me, and cleared the empty wine bottle off the table the weekend mornings Mum had a lie-in – one of my earliest memories, when Alice must have been about nine; to tell her that I'd appreciated the way she'd had my back during all those growing-up years, minding me when Mum died, taking care of me when I was sick. But the words stuck in my throat. *Don't you dare get soft*, her eyes said. *Don't you dare show me or my singleton status any concern.*

She walked me up the aisle to the sound of Tom Baxter's 'Better' – Luke's choice – her hand warm where it rested on my forearm, and when we reached the top and she took it away, I felt a cold spot on my arm and I shivered. I looked into her eyes – there was nothing there but love. 'Be happy,' she mouthed silently as she stepped back into the first pew. There was something about her – a single, solitary figure, her sometimes spiky demeanour cloaked today by a quiet dignity in deference to the occasion – that caught at my throat.

Then I turned around and there was Luke.

◆

At our wedding reception in a four-star hotel in Ballsbridge, we sipped champagne and laid on a free bar for most of the night. With a lot of the legacy of Victoria Row sitting in our bank account, I could afford it. There was an odd moment during the speeches when Pierce, Luke's brother, read out greeting cards and messages.

'To Luke and Holly,' he read out, 'sorry I'm not there, but I'm with you in spirit. Happy wedding night from Jay.' Pierce's voice faltered and he made a droll face as though he didn't know what to make of it. There was a ripple of faint laughter. Luke had been holding my hand and now he squeezed it so hard that he hurt me a little. I smiled reassuringly at him and rubbed his arm in a comforting gesture. I was married now and out of Jay's reach.

We spent our wedding night in the luxury presidential suite. I made love with more abandon than usual and Luke thought I was amazing.

'If this is what getting married means, bring it on,' he said hoarsely, barely able to talk.

Two days later, we flew to Paris for a week-long honeymoon in a five-star hotel, followed by a week in a luxury hotel in Èze, on the Riviera. No expense spared. You only ever have one honeymoon. Holly and Luke deserved only the best to celebrate the start of their wonderful married life, didn't we?

CHAPTER 21

Alice

'I HAVE JUST THE TICKET FOR YOU, ALICE,' Finbarr said on Friday. 'Are you free tonight?'

'Why, what's up?' It was after break time and she was processing the inter-library loans in the office off the reception desk.

'Ian Donohue rang – you know, the American writer.'

'Yes.' Alice nodded, wondering where this was leading.

Ian Donohue was coming to the end of his five-week holiday in Ireland. His night-with-Ian-Donohue event in the Convention Centre, as a precursor to the Dublin International Literature Festival, was scheduled for tonight. He was being interviewed by Lorna Molloy, one of Ireland's leading literary critics. Damien had told her he'd tried to get a ticket but they'd sold out early on.

'Ian said there'll be two tickets at the desk tonight for a member of the library staff. I think you should go, if you're free. Bring a friend. It's last minute – two of his family members can't make it and he thought of us.'

'Is that fair? Shouldn't they be raffled or something?'

'I think you should have them,' he said. 'You're the most senior after me in terms of length of service. Provided you're free, of course. And if you can get someone to accompany you.'

For all his quiet calm, Finbarr didn't miss a trick.

She *was* free. Chloe had left for Euro Disney in a whirlwind of excitement that morning. Whatever reservations Alice had felt had melted into the background at the sight of her daughter's ecstatic face. Ronan, to give him his due, had made a big occasion out of calling for her in his car, arriving at Victoria Row brandishing a new Minnie Mouse wheelie case and matching accessories.

'You have five minutes to repack everything,' he'd said. 'I'll help. I'm sure Mum will help too, won't you?'

It would have been churlish not to. Then Chloe had had to fix her passport into the shiny Minnie Mouse holder that Ronan had also bought. Alice watched Ronan waiting patiently as Chloe insisted on fitting it in herself, her fingers fumbling with excitement until she eventually gave up and thrust it at him.

'You do it, Dad.'

'Sure, honey.'

He'd barely looked at Alice as they went off; she'd sensed his relief as he went through the door in Victoria Row. She'd wondered if the lovely Amanda was accompanying them and, when she'd looked out at his car to see someone blonde sitting in the passenger seat, something inside her had hardened.

'As it happens, I am free,' she said to Finbarr.

◆

Alice texted Damien and he replied straight away, arranging to meet her for drinks in the foyer beforehand. It took Alice four changes of clothes before she was happy with her appearance. Nothing overtly sexy, she said to herself, holding back silent tears of mirth as she riffled through her clothes – there was nothing remotely sexy in her wardrobe, not since her separation. But she wasn't going to wear anything that screamed Alice-Clarke-is-so-out-of-touch-she-looks-like-she-hasn't-been-on-a-date-in-a-million-years either. Not that this was a date – it was a library event. No need for a babysitter, therefore no one to explain her absence to. And no need to feel nerves trapped in her stomach, she told herself futilely as she checked the mirror one more time before she left – black jeans and a thin blue sweater, topped by her ancient but comfy black leather jacket: perfect.

When she reached the Convention Centre, she collected the tickets from the desk. She nipped into the bathroom, her jangling nerves making it difficult for her to breathe. She swallowed hard, smiled at herself in the mirror and strode back out into the busy foyer. Damien was standing by a pillar near the entrance, scanning the crowds.

This was nothing at all, she reminded herself.

Nothing. At. All.

Until he turned and saw her.

Then it was everything.

She walked over to meet him and felt his light kiss on

her cheek, and for the night that was in it, Alice took all her baggage, every last scrap of it, and mentally tied it up with a big white ribbon. Then she imagined herself flinging the bundle into the depths of the River Liffey outside.

◆

They brought their drinks to the second floor, where there was plenty of space to stand at the rail and look out through the huge plate-glass windows that faced the river.

'So the library sent you?' Damien asked. He was wearing dark jeans and a casual jacket over a dark grey jumper.

'There were complimentary tickets going. Finbarr insisted I use them.'

'Good for Finbarr. Who's looking after Chloe?'

'She's away,' Alice said. 'With her father, in Euro Disney. For a week. Eight nights to be exact. They went this morning.'

'You're not happy about that?'

'Right now, it doesn't matter. Right now I'm a woman at a literary event, no past, no future. Out on the town and going to have a blast.'

'*And* you've a free gaff,' he said to her with such a mischievous glint in his eyes that she burst out laughing.

When she realised he was staring at her thoughtfully, her laughter died in her throat.

'You should laugh more often, Alice Clarke. It suits you.'

She tried to hide her discomposure by taking a large sip of her wine. She didn't quite carry it off because her hand shook and wine slopped onto her chin. She took out a tissue and dabbed it away, his eyes following her movement so that they rested on her mouth.

She stared out into the dark evening. 'Great view from here, isn't there?' Lights from the buildings on the far side of the Liffey were quivering on the surface of the inky water. To her right, the Samuel Beckett Bridge, with its iconic structure, raised graceful, harp-like cables into the night.

'The view is beautiful,' he said softly.

She gave him a sidelong glance. He wasn't looking out the window. He was looking at her. How was all this happening? How come Damien was still sticking around?

'My sister and her husband used to live over the far side, down a bit further,' she said hurriedly. 'She worked near the IFSC and lived in a luxury apartment with a balcony overlooking the river. Liffey Gate.'

'Holly lived in Liffey Gate? Until when?' Damien gazed intently at the buildings along the other side of the river. For a funny moment she thought he'd forgotten she was there.

'She and Luke moved out seven years ago and went to live in the depths of Kilkenny,' she said.

'Yes, I remember you saying something about that. How come they uprooted themselves so drastically?'

'They wanted to get away from the bustle of Dublin and get back to nature,' she said. 'A new adventure, so Holly said.'

'You weren't happy with that?' he said, picking up on the hint of sadness in her voice.

'I was disappointed,' she admitted, 'selfishly so. I'd just had Chloe, I was wiped out and I'd hoped to have her around for support. I thought that being an aunt would be a new adventure for her.'

'I don't think that was being selfish, Alice – naturally you'd want your sister close by at such a special time.'

'You're too kind,' she said.

'You know it's being demolished,' he said, 'Liffey Gate.'

'It's not!'

'Yeah, something to do with fire-safety standards. It'll take a few weeks to strip it before they raze it to the ground.'

'I didn't know that.' Alice searched the far quays but found it difficult to identify the apartment block. Then she saw hoarding shrouding the lower floors of a building where there had once been a beautiful plant-filled foyer. 'That's giving me a shiver,' she said. 'When Holly lived there it was fab.'

'A Celtic Tiger casualty,' Damien said. 'Like so many buildings thrown up in a hurry. Although the worst casualties of that time were the ordinary people who lost their futures.'

'Absolutely. I heard some sad stories but thankfully none of my immediate family or friends were badly affected.'

'You were lucky, so.'

Then the five-minute call went out and they finished

their drinks and went into the auditorium. 'We'll talk later,' he said, smiling at her and gently squeezing her arm. All the way through the event, she had half a mind on the entertaining discussion and the other half wondering what exactly 'later' would mean.

◆

'Later' meant Damien holding her hand as they joined the crush of people surging out of the auditorium. It meant a stroll further down the quays to a rooftop bar in a hotel near the 3Arena. Two armchairs close together by a window overlooking the river. Twinkly lights scattered throughout the bar behind them were reflected in the glass in front and superimposed on the nightscape outside. A table drawn up with a white wine for Alice and a beer for Damien. His eyes looking at her warmly as they spoke. Crinkling at the corners when he laughed. His mouth curving in a smile. Alice was amazed at how relaxed she felt as they chatted about the evening and discussed Ian Donohue's humorous answers to some of the more outrageous questions.

'Later' was a short taxi journey home, Damien dropping her off, walking her up to the hall door, turning to look at the sea, dark silvery ink in the night, and turning back to kiss her.

And Alice – leaning in to kiss him back. Knowing she had wanted to do this all night. It felt so good that she did it again.

Eventually they drew apart. 'Thank you,' he said. 'Tomorrow night?'

'Text me,' she said, opening the door and watching from the hallway as he loped down the path and waved at her before he jumped into the taxi.

She felt too wound up to go to bed immediately, so she made chamomile tea and sat for a while, replaying the evening in her head. When she got into bed and switched off the light, the darkness filled with the unsettling image of Liffey Gate as she'd seen it that evening; torn asunder it would leave an ugly, gap-toothed blot in the smooth, polished lines of the south city's regenerated docklands.

She wondered if Holly knew. She hadn't spoken to her in a couple of weeks. She wondered if she could talk to her without mentioning Damien or what it would be like if both of them ever met.

It wouldn't, she knew, be a repeat of when Ronan met Holly.

CHAPTER 22

Alice, 2011

ALICE FELT LOST AFTER HOLLY MOVED OUT. Holly's words about Alice needing to get a life had stung deep. Alone in Victoria Row, she was surrounded by memories and ghosts, and a wall of unresolved grief at the loss of her mother rose up inside her – grief turned rancid and bitter. She didn't like herself in those days: the way she resented Holly, with her fun and adventures and amazing sex; the way she envied Holly getting married; the way she felt dull and stuck in a rut compared to Holly's vivacious personality. Alice was thirty-four now and after Holly's wedding she found it harder than ever to put on her nice face in work.

One Friday evening, a month after Holly's wedding, everything erupted inside her. In Victoria Row, in a fit of rebellion directed against herself, she marched upstairs. She went through her wardrobe, casting aside most of her dull clothes, trembling as she secured the top on the fourth recycling sack, and wondered how soon she could get rid of them.

She spent Saturday in the city centre on a buying spree, realising when she came home that she'd spent a small fortune and that most of her new clothes mirrored Holly's bright and sparkly style. She decided that this wasn't going to put her off wearing them. She practised a bright, sparkly smile in the mirror and a laugh that sounded as carefree as Holly's. She even tried raising her voice a notch, so that it sounded more girlish. On Sunday afternoon she went to a city centre hairdresser's and had her dark hair restyled and highlighted with blonde streaks. Then she went into Brown Thomas and bought a new and expensive range of make-up. She went into the Central Library on Monday morning, where she'd worked at the time, her brand-new image sitting on her awkwardly like an ill-fitting coat, getting a few surprised glances from her colleagues at her transformation. Then, the following week, when they were looking for someone to represent their branch at a literary event, they chose Alice by a unanimous verdict.

Her reinvention was working.

She glided into Dublin Castle acting as if she were Holly – her bubbly, effervescent sister. Her hair was freshly styled, her eyelashes long and feathery, like Holly's; she was wearing a cobalt blue dress with a neckline skimming her cleavage that Holly would have rocked to perfection. Alice knew she had never rocked anything in her life. Until now. And while ordinary people like Alice Clarke usually fell far beneath the radars of powerful men like Ronan L. Russell, tonight, she caught his attention.

'I don't think I've ever met anyone quite like you,' he said, his head tipped to one side.

'You probably haven't,' she replied, taking in his

146

bright blue eyes, shock of auburn hair, beautifully tailored suit and aura of power and entitlement that only comfortable affluence could bestow.

'You're a mixture of fun and loveliness but behind your sparkly smile I sense a soft heart.' He smiled at her. 'And in these days when everyone is out for themselves,' he went on, 'and Dublin is crammed with women climbing all over each other to get into a man's trousers en route to his pockets, that's sweet.'

Sweet? She wasn't sure if she liked that label but he seemed to find it attractive. Ronan told her he had to work the room, but he gravitated back to her every so often, and it made her chat more animatedly and laugh louder and more often. He had to rush off to another reception before the night was over, but he took her mobile number and said he'd call. Which he did, saying that there was something inscrutable about her that intrigued him. She didn't dare admit that the mixture of fun and sparkle she was putting out there was really a carefully contrived effort to reinvent herself.

Then one sunny Sunday in early April, Ronan met Holly.

Alice was sitting with him outside a pub off Grafton Street, trying to act as if afternoon drinks with a hot-shot solicitor while she wore a revealing top and far too much make-up was a regular occurrence, when she saw Holly coming up the middle of the street, laden with glossy carrier bags. Her eyes shaded by oversized sunglasses, she was wearing skintight white jeans and a shirt under a denim jacket.

It was two weeks since Alice had met Ronan. She'd seen him three times since, but surely if Ronan laid eyes on Holly, with her shimmering blonde hair and huge, sparkling blue eyes, her unique air of warmth and effervescence, he'd realise that Alice was trying to be a carbon copy of her sister? And only managing a faint one at that. The street was busy with shoppers, and she hoped that Holly would walk on by without seeing her because she wasn't ready for them to meet yet. No such luck. Holly stopped, dropped her bags right there in the street, took off her sunglasses and stared at Alice, her eyes widening in surprise. Then her gaze slid to the man beside her and widened further.

'Alice? It *is* you. I thought I was seeing things.'

'Holly! Hi. What are you doing here?'

'I was about to ask *you* that question.' She looked at Ronan, gracing him with a big, beaming smile. Alice had no choice but to introduce them. Ronan stood up and kissed Holly on the cheek, a chair was brought, Ronan picked up her shopping, and Holly arranged herself with a flourish.

'What can I get you to drink?' Ronan asked, summoning a bar assistant.

'A gin and tonic would be lovely, thank you,' Holly said.

'Tanqueray or Hendricks?'

'Hendricks please,' Holly said, without batting an eyelid. Alice didn't know what she meant until she realised it was the label on the bottle. All of a sudden her wine tasted acrid.

'This is great,' Ronan said. 'I'm delighted to meet the lovely Holly.'

'Lovely? I wonder what Alice has really been saying about me.' Holly laughed, her blue eyes full of merriment.

That was the thing about Holly. She was so natural with everyone, even here now with Ronan. She came to the table infusing the atmosphere like a breath of warm, fragrant air. Still, Alice could do that too, couldn't she? She didn't have to sit by quietly while Ronan and Holly became acquainted.

She sat up a little straighter. 'Not much, yet,' she said. 'Then again, Ronan and I are just getting to know each other,' she went on, smiling privately at him, pleased with the familiar way 'Ronan and I' slid so easily off her tongue.

'You've had your hair done,' Holly said, her eyes round with interest. 'It's amazing – I love the glamour. Well done, sis, it's about time. I hardly recognised you,' she finished, her eyes dropping to Alice's revealing top.

'And you've been shopping,' Alice said, nodding in the direction of her glossy bags, delighted Holly seemed impressed with her transformation.

'Yes,' Holly said. 'Mind you, I'll have to run these outfits by Luke first. He likes to manage my wardrobe.' She gave a soft laugh. 'So what have you guys been up to?'

'This and that,' Alice said, as nonchalantly as possible, a little buoyed that, for once, she had one up on Holly.

'You'll have to come to ours for drinks some evening,' Holly said.

'For sure,' Alice replied, waving her hand carelessly.

'But come to mine first,' Ronan said. 'Next weekend.'

'And where is yours?' Holly asked, her eyes sparkling with interest.

'Leopardstown. I have a place near the race course.'

'Oh, wow, nice one. Have you been there, Alice?'

'I have, it's *soo* amazing.'

It wasn't just a 'place'. Ronan had a huge open-plan penthouse suite, four times the size of Victoria Row, with modern cutting-edge furnishings the kind of which Alice had only seen in a *Better Homes* magazine. The previous weekend he'd had friends in for drinks and had invited Alice. She'd worn a turquoise dress cinched with a slim gold belt, and had glided around pretending she owned the apartment. It was all part of replicating some of her sister's effervescence, but in the enormous bathroom with the mirrored wall, she'd wondered what she was doing there. Then she reminded herself that she was getting a new life for herself and it was turning out to be a rather exciting life. Ronan was charm personified, including her in conversations with his friends, introducing her as his lovely and enigmatic new friend. Alice knew she wasn't contributing very much, feeling a little out of her depth, but Ronan seemed to be happy with her once she smiled at his friends and laughed at his jokes. Even though she knew he was aroused, she didn't sleep with him that night, half-afraid she wouldn't live up to his expectations. She finally slept with him the night Holly and Luke came to Leopardstown, fired up in the wake of the younger couple's sexual vibes, needing to prove to herself that she and Ronan could be equally passionate.

Holly floated around Ronan's apartment in a white chiffon dress and glittery sandals, looking like she'd stepped off a yacht in the French Riviera. Her enthusiasm for the apartment was contagious. The sound system pumped out sultry Alicia Keys, and out beyond the huge balcony the sun slid down into a mauve sky. Alice soaked up the sensuality of it all. She knew Ronan wanted sex by the heavy look in his eyes, by the silent messages they were sending her, the invisible flares of electricity that sparked about him as he moved around in a crisp white shirt and pair of dark jeans. Then Holly and Luke dashed off in a whirl of laughter and an air of expectation, looking like two over-excited children who couldn't wait to be alone. The apartment was still ringing with Holly's silvery laughter when Ronan met Alice in the middle of the floor, kissed her hard on the mouth and wrenched her dress apart.

Ronan knew what he wanted. Alice knew what she wanted. Afterwards, she lay in the queen-sized bed under tossed white sheets, listening to his snores, and asked herself how Alice Clarke had inspired such passion. He'd been wild for her. And if she felt a little deflated because it hadn't fulfilled her as she'd hoped, she knew that was her fault. Even in bed, she'd been acting a part, enjoying the physicality of it all but hiding the true Alice Clarke, avoiding any real and heartfelt connection.

There were more dates, Alice gliding through those early weeks with Ronan, making it look as though she belonged in his affluent, cosmopolitan world. She was flattered by Ronan's attentions, knowing they were poles apart but determined to get a life and break out of her shell. She knew she had no exciting social circles to boast about, no amazing travel anecdotes to contribute, and that Ronan was way out of her league. To keep up with his sophisticated world, she bought glossy magazines and devoured the contents, noting must-have perfumes, must-have drinks, must-have techniques to drive a man wild in bed. She bought sexy underwear. She scoured newspaper gossip pages for suitable soundbites to drop into conversation. In trying to reinvent herself, she deliberately – and mistakenly – cut herself loose from what she regarded as outdated friendships. She didn't kid herself that she was the only woman in Ronan's life; still, she sensed he expected to be the only man in hers, calling her the evenings he didn't see her to ask what she was up to. There was no question of inviting Ronan to Victoria Row – it would have been like inviting a wild, golden lion into a sheep's pen.

They were asked over to Liffey Gate at the end of April. Holly looked fresh from the shower, her pale blonde hair rippling softly down her shoulders. She was wearing white jeans that showed the outline of her thong – something Alice found too uncomfortable – and a white shirt, top buttons undone to show a tantalising sliver of her lacy bra.

'This is the start of Luke's birthday celebrations,' Holly said, opening a bottle of champagne. 'The week after next, we're off to Marbella.' She wound her free arm around Luke's shoulders and kissed the top of his head.

'Sounds very romantic,' Ronan said.

'It will be,' Holly said. 'Megabucks, but for Luke, worth it.'

She served a three-course meal, giggling that Luke had prepared it all, moving around the table in a waft of flowery perfume. Afterwards, Alice helped Luke tidy up, but she couldn't help watching Ronan and Holly out on the balcony, chatting and laughing as if they were old friends: Holly moving in to tip Ronan affectionately on the arm, her cheeks flushed; Ronan throwing back his head and laughing; Ronan bending towards her to say something that caused her to giggle helplessly. Something about the cosy way they stood together prevented Alice from going out and joining in, as if she was going to interrupt something.

Holly was her *sister*, she censured herself; there was no need to feel excluded. Surely what seemed like deliberate flirting to stick-in-the-mud Alice was just the two of them becoming acquainted? She saw Luke gazing in the same direction before he went out and joined them, placing himself between Holly and Ronan. Did it bother him that Holly seemed to be enjoying Ronan's attention?

Afterwards, they got a taxi back to Leopardstown, and it was Alice who threw herself into lovemaking with a renewed passion, determined to banish all thoughts of her sensual sister from both their heads. Ronan responded to her with vigour. When a condom burst, she assured him that it was okay – she was at the safe end of her cycle. But she wasn't, and afterwards she realised that that was the night she became pregnant.

CHAPTER 23

Holly

IN THE DAYS AND WEEKS AFTER THE TV show about the demolition of Liffey Gate had aired, the vice-like grip of dread and sickening anxiety that had clamped around me on the night of the programme became stronger and darker. My sleep was more disturbed than ever, my nightmares deeper and more frightening. I was having rows with Luke, arguments we'd never had before.

'What the hell is wrong with you?' he asked eventually.

'I can't help thinking of Liffey Gate. With every day that passes, I don't know if it's good because another day has gone by and the axe hasn't fallen yet, or bad because surely we're getting closer to the time when it will.'

'For God's sake, Holly, forget about it. You're safe here. No axe is going to fall. You know I'll take care of you.'

I wanted to say it was too late, that my fragile peace of mind had already been shattered, that there was only a thin veil between the compartments in my head, one of which was permanently marked with the ghost of Jay. It was ready at all times to be wrenched open, like a curtain going up in a theatre, Jay strutting across the stage as he'd strutted in real life, his jaunty, full-of-bravado self. What deepened my unease was that, for all his reassuring words, Luke seemed distant and preoccupied. As though his thoughts were somewhere else, focused, for instance, on a building being demolished in Dublin.

Then Luke began to get annoyed when I started saying I couldn't live like this any more; the uncertainty of it all, wondering and waiting, my heart in my mouth, it was slowly killing me.

'Stop imagining the worst,' was his usual response. 'We've talked this through already. I told you, you'll be fine.'

'How do I know for sure? Can you promise me that?'

'I promise, Holly.'

Words were easy to say, though, weren't they?

I began to talk about going back. 'Some days I think … that I'm about to go mad. That maybe it would be best to go back. Back to Dublin.'

That made him very unhappy. '*What?* Are you for real?'

'Maybe it's the only way … go back and face things. I can't sleep, I can't eat, my insides are in ribbons. I can't live like this any more, honestly, Luke – I'm finding it impossible …'

'Let me remind you,' he said, a steely note in his voice, 'if you do go back, whatever you're feeling now will become a hundred times worse. That I can promise you.'

Then the phone call I'd been half-expecting and half-

155

dreading arrived: Alice. It was Saturday morning, six weeks and three days after the programme had aired – I'd counted every one. I was making coffee in the kitchen. Luke arrived in the doorway, having heard the ring of my mobile.

'Hi, Alice,' I said brightly, conscious of him watching me and listening in. 'How are things? How's Chloe?'

'Chloe's great,' Alice said. 'She's in Euro Disney this week with Ronan.'

'Ah, lovely. I'm sure she'll enjoy it.'

'I won't delay – I'm sure you're busy. Did you hear about Liffey Gate?'

'What about it?' I asked, as nonchalantly as possible, my gaze fastening on Luke.

'Did you know it's being demolished?'

'Yes, I heard something about that,' I said, forcing my voice to sound casual for Luke's benefit as much as mine. 'Just as well we're long gone – it sounds like a right mess.'

'I only found out last night, when I was –' Alice paused '– down that direction. Which made it all the more funny – funny peculiar.'

'How?' My voice was sharp. Something told me to brace myself.

'I was in the Spar this morning, and one of the neighbours up the road was chatting at the counter. Her husband is involved in that demolition, but, like, overnight it's been halted.'

'*What?*' I stared at Luke. He was listening intently.

'They're still at the stripping-out stage, she said, but

the work has been stopped and she thinks it's something serious. So God knows what was going on with your neighbours, Holly. Who knows,' she laughed lightly, 'there could be bodies in the basement.'

Somehow, despite the icy chill creeping up around my head, I made the supreme effort to find my voice and form coherent words. 'It's so long since we were there, Alice, I doubt if we know any of the present occupants.'

I knew by Luke's face I'd said the right thing, although nothing about this was right at all, and I shivered, feeling the blade of an axe bite into my neck.

CHAPTER 24

Holly, 2011

AT THE END OF MAY, ALICE ASKED TO SEE ME, insisting I call to Victoria Row, so I made a rare visit to my childhood home.

I wondered if by some telepathy she'd found out I was frittering away a lot of my inheritance. The economic crisis was biting deeper. More of our friends had less disposable income, and some were losing their jobs. Even the older generation wasn't immune. Two of Luke's friends saw their parents' businesses crashing to the wall. What was even sadder was that one of his friends' fathers thought his family was better off without him and he jumped in front of a goods train one dark night. I'd cried torrents at this news, imagining how utterly devastated he must have felt to have deliberately ended his life.

In my attempts to cheer myself up and make everything bright, shiny and happy, I kept on spending without thinking about the future: designer bags and clothes, hotel breaks, spa trips, a designer watch for Luke. Although Luke looked after our joint finances, I knew I was dipping into my inheritance quite a bit, and when he began to comment on my extravagances, I justified them by reminding him life was short and you had to live in the moment. As well as that, Tara and Conor planned to marry in late August and were buzzing with an excitement that I envied. The college gang would be there, maybe Jay as well. If so, I'd have to keep him away from my gentle, sensitive Luke. Then I decided we'd go to Paris to celebrate my birthday. It would help recapture the glow of our wedding and honeymoon and surround us with another layer of loved-up togetherness in front of the mocking Jay. As I pointed out to Luke, if the economic climate was preventing us from taking career breaks to go travelling, a five-star week in Paris would help to make up for that.

'I know it would,' he said, 'but things would be better if my salary cuts were reversed, never mind the tax increases. They've started to trim back staff as it is.'

I didn't want to know.

◆

When I stepped over the threshold of Victoria Row, I knew I was a different person to the Holly Clarke who'd grown up there. I didn't fit into this small, confined space any more. I had moved on to better things.

But what Alice wanted to say had nothing to do with my spending.

I squealed with joy when she told me she was pregnant.

'Oh gosh, oh Alice, this is so *exciting*.'

The appropriate words came out of my mouth. I hugged her tight and kissed her. But I didn't exactly feel joy. I felt Alice had stolen a march on me. After all, *I* was the one who was married, *I* was the one in love with my husband – I *had* a husband. It came to me then, in an uneasy niggle, that being part of the loved-up team of Holly and Luke who lived in sexy Liffey Gate and had everything had made me feel I had one up on Alice.

'I'm barely pregnant,' she said, 'and already I'm as sick as a dog. Ronan's asked me to marry him.'

I subsided into the nearest chair.

When I'd met first Ronan, I'd been surprised that a man with so much power and wealth was interested in my sister, even if she was finally getting some style and he was bringing out a bubbly, light-hearted side to her. I hadn't seen him as the settling-down type, never mind with Alice. Now she'd be the one with everything and jealousy surged through me.

'I thought he was kidding at first,' Alice said. 'But he's over the moon that he's going to be a father. He sees it as the start of his Russell dynasty. Family is important to him. So are outward appearances when it comes to the heir to his throne. The baby is due in January, and he wants us to be married in the autumn. I haven't decided yet.'

'Why not, you mad thing!' I said, making a superhuman effort to curb my sickening envy. 'Jesus, Alice, you'd be set up for life. Think how thrilled Mum would be, her daughter married to a wealthy man like Ronan Russell *and* her grandchild born into a life of privilege.'

'That's the other thing,' Alice said. 'Even though I'm amazed that I'm carrying brand new, wonderful life within me, and I'm going to be a mother, I'm having sleepless nights wondering how I'd manage financially with a baby on my modest salary. I can't help thinking how hard Mum had to work and how much she struggled after Gus Clarke swanned off. She held down three jobs when you and I were going through the expensive teenage years. If I married Ronan, the baby would want for nothing.'

'Well, there you are, then – problem solved.'

Alice gave a half-smile. 'Whatever I decide, you'll be the first to know.' She put her hand hurriedly to her mouth. 'I need the bathroom.'

◆

I wasn't surprised when she rang and told me that she and Ronan were planning a September wedding, the reception to be held in Beverly Court, a luxury hotel in Wicklow. As the summer drifted by, I found myself obsessing about the fact that Alice was the one who suddenly had it all while life in Liffey Gate had become bland and boring, thanks to Luke beginning to talk more seriously about curbing expenses. I hated the dark clouds of recession that were engulfing us and our friends. I wanted something new to look forward to, something exciting.

Like having a baby.

Alice's news had been quietly eating away at me, and I felt the only way I could cope with my sudden jealousy was by having a baby of my own. Once I had made that decision, I was consumed by it. In the back of my head, as soon as I had a positive pregnancy test, I'd plan a romantic meal for Luke and me, I'd put a pair of tiny baby bootees on a plate and serve it to him at the same time as the dessert as a way of breaking the exciting news.

But it wasn't so easy to make a baby. When the second month came along and my period arrived once more, Luke found me crying in the bathroom. I hadn't told him I'd come off the pill. I couldn't understand myself why I'd decided this, but I knew it was more than wanting to give him a wonderful surprise.

'What's up, darling?' he asked.

'It's my period – it means I'm not pregnant.' If sheer wishful thinking had been enough to make me pregnant, I would by now have been expecting quadruplets.

Luke's jaw dropped. '*Pregnant?* When did we talk about this?'

'Well, we didn't,' I conceded. 'I thought I'd surprise you with the wonderful news.'

'Holly – Jesus – surprise is right. This isn't a good time.'

'Why not? We can't go travelling so we should use this time to start our family. Then when the economy is okay again, the baby will be old enough to come travelling with us. I would absolutely love, love, *love* to have our baby.'

'Yes, in time. But bundles of joy don't come cheap. We can't afford it right now. I didn't want to alarm you but things in Mahoney Solutions are very unsettled.'

'Couldn't you look for another job?'

'They're not exactly growing on trees right now. Anyway, I want to have you all to myself for a while longer.'

'You mean you don't want to share me with a baby?' There was a dull thud of disappointment in my chest. I knew in a corner of my mind I was being unreasonable, but I couldn't help it. I badly wanted some distraction from all the greyness around me, some diversion from envying the life my sister was now enjoying, and I didn't like being told I couldn't have what I desired. What had happened to being able to do anything I wanted?

'It's not that,' Luke said. 'Apart from the expense, having a baby would change everything. You can't imagine how much time a baby takes up, how much extra work. I know from Andrew in the office, he hasn't had a full night's kip in a year.'

'That's really what this is about – you're afraid a small baby would come between us?'

'That's not it at all. And now is not a good time to have this conversation.'

'*Conversation?* About one of the most magical things that could ever happen? This isn't a work meeting, Luke, this is about our love together and sharing it with our own little bundle of joy.'

'Dear God,' I heard him mutter, along with something about me needing to get real. Then he walked out of the room. Luke had never walked out of the room like that before or told me to get real, and my heart dropped down to my feet. After that, he rarely made love to me, and when he did, he wore a condom. For the first time ever, Alice was the one whose life was on the rise and I couldn't get over my resentment.

◆

'Are you sorry Dad won't be around to walk you up the aisle on your special day?' I asked Alice one evening when I called over to Leopardstown to talk wedding plans.

'Nope,' she said. 'I'm quite capable of walking up the aisle all by myself.'

I was even jealous of her careless attitude towards our father, remembering how emotional I'd been that he didn't know I was getting married, let alone of my existence.

Ronan walked into the room in time to hear us. 'Just as well,' he said. 'It would be impossible to bring him back from the dead.'

I shot a look at Alice – she gave me a warning glance that urged me to stay quiet. I guessed then she'd told Ronan that Gus Clarke was dead, rather than admit he'd done a runner. I filed that nugget of information away. I'm not sure why I found it comforting to think Alice hadn't been totally honest with Ronan. My sister might appear to have it all, but she didn't trust her husband-to-be with the truth about a major incident in her childhood.

'We'll all be family now,' Ronan said to me. 'You mightn't have a father but at least you'll have me for a brother.' He put his hand on my shoulder, squeezing it with what I considered to be more than brotherly affection, leaving it there a little longer than was necessary. I looked at Alice to see if she'd noticed anything amiss, but she was already heading out to the kitchen, saying something about coffee.

Ronan smiled at me. 'Do you want coffee, Holly, or can I get you anything else?' He raised an eyebrow and I had the strangest feeling that he was looking at me with a hint of suggestion in his eyes – something else I filed away in a corner of my mind. But by the time I arrived home, I had convinced myself I had been imagining it all. Ronan loved my sister enough to insist on marrying her when a baby was on the way – not a course of action many men took nowadays. Besides, I loved Luke, even if things had become a little stale between us. I wished we could reverse time and go back to those halcyon days with the economy booming again.

Not that any crumb of austerity was affecting Alice's life. I met her for lunch in a gastro pub in Duke Street just before the wedding, envy slicing through my heart when I noticed the soft swell of her belly. Ronan was spending a fortune on the wedding, she said. There would be over one hundred guests, the majority of whom were family and friends on Ronan's side. He was picking up the tab for the wedding-party rooms, and I wouldn't have to put my hand in my pocket.

Which was just as well. My careless spending was catching up with me. I was surprised to realise at the beginning of September that I owed a lot more than I thought on my credit card, and to my annoyance, I didn't have enough funds in my current account to cover it and would have to dip into the last of my dwindling inheritance from Victoria Row. Which made it more difficult, two weeks later, to hold back the gut-wrenching tide of jealousy that swept over me on Alice's wedding day.

Maeve had helped her to pick out an empire-line dress in embroidered satin and lace. Thanks to Alice's almost constant nausea and despite careful application of make-up, her face was pale. Nonetheless, she looked beautiful.

It didn't help that I was there without Luke.

CHAPTER 25

Holly, 2011

I COULDN'T BELIEVE IT WHEN LUKE TOLD ME he'd be unable to make Alice's wedding.

'I've been offered overtime for that Saturday,' he'd said, 'an urgent go-live job, all hands on deck. It'll be a late night – we might have to work through it – but if I don't show willing, I could be next for the chop.'

'You're not serious.'

'I am. Mahoney's is … struggling to say the least. I can't afford to turn this job down. I'll get brownie points and double rate, money we could do with.'

I argued, but Luke stood firm. Maybe that was why I responded to Ronan with a little more interest than I should have. I bumped into him on the corridor outside my room when I nipped back to put my mobile on charge. The champagne reception was in full flow and we were both carrying champagne flutes.

'Aren't you going to congratulate me?' he asked, tipping his glass to mine before knocking back his drink.

'I already have,' I said, thinking of the chaste peck on the cheek and the few words I'd said to him after the ceremony.

'I mean properly,' he said, a smile of amusement curving his mouth as if it was a pleasant joke. 'My brand new sister,' he said. 'Welcome to my world.' Dropping his glass to the floor, he put his hands on my shoulders and drew me close. Somehow, whatever way I turned my head, his lips managed to graze my mouth. I felt a moment of shock, then surprise, especially when they stayed there instead of moving to my cheek. Slightly alarmed but hugely flattered, I couldn't help opening my mouth, and he deepened the kiss in a most un-brotherly way before I sprang back.

'Hey – hang on,' I said, confused.

'Relax, no harm done,' he said in a slightly bored voice, as though I was a child who didn't understand the adult way of doing things. 'A man's entitled to a nice kiss on his wedding day. Especially if it's family.'

'I wouldn't exactly have called that brotherly.'

'Would you prefer a different kind of kiss?' he said.

'You've just married my sister – this is your wedding day,' I pointed out, hardly able to believe I was having this conversation.

'So? Alice will always be my wife and I'll never replace her. But I know she'll probably believe in her marriage vows with more dedication than I will – I can't help enjoying a bit of fun with a beautiful woman.'

'You know you're a misogynistic bastard?' I said. Still – *beautiful woman.*

'Alice will want for nothing, I promise you that. I'll make sure she's happy at home looking after my child. She'll be living in luxury and what she doesn't know won't harm her. We have to take care of each other, Holly dear, now that we're family. The best families stick together, don't they?'

'Less of the Don Corleone, thank you,' I said. 'Anyhow, Ronan dear,' I continued ultra-carelessly, 'you'll have to join the queue.' I delivered those words with a sweet smile.

He smiled, equally as sweet. 'I don't do queues, darling – did nobody tell you that? I'm an impatient kind of guy.'

To my shame, I couldn't help feeling a boost to my ego that my sister's big, powerful husband was coming on to me on their wedding day. I knew he was playing cat and mouse with me but, hey, streaks of envy that had weighed down my heart eased a little. I met his gaze and widened my eyes, a vision of Jay Slater in my head. 'You're not the first person to try and come between me and Luke, so you'll have some stiff competition.'

'I like a challenge. Who is he?'

'That's classified.'

'Interesting,' he said, sizing me up as though I'd become a more exciting proposition. 'Luke is a fool to let you loose on your own. Anything could happen, Holly dear ...' He raised a suggestive eyebrow and touched me lightly on the buttock. 'If I want something, I take it, queue or no queue. I have ways of getting rid of competition. Stiff or otherwise.' He chuckled with laughter as he marched away.

I enjoyed the rest of the wedding after that, thanks in part to the free-flowing champagne and the thoughts that the impressive Ronan Russell had taken time out of his wedding day to tell me I was beautiful and tease me about bed, and I floated on such a high that I rose way above the sobering knowledge that I was flirting with my sister's new husband. Flirting – that's all it was. A little fun to oil the dull wheels of what my life had become, I told myself, finishing yet another glass of the bubbly Ronan had had imported from France. Champagne that Alice was unable to drink on her wedding day.

'Can you not even have one?' I asked, when we were talking later and she said I seemed to be knocking it back.

'I'm not going to chance it. Ronan would have a fit.'

'Pity, it's gorgeous. Not even half a glass? And what's Ronan got to do with it? It's your body.'

'Not quite. My body is carrying his child. To Ronan, it's the most precious thing in the world.'

I wished she hadn't reminded me that she was pregnant. It was like a shower of cold water all over my Ronan-and-champagne-induced glow. He was going to be a father. He'd been playing with me, probably trying to prove to himself he could still do it. And like a fool, I had lapped it up. My guilty conscience made me reach for more of the crystal flutes that were flying around on silver trays. And when the night was over and Alice and Ronan disappeared to their suite in a fanfare of ceremony, I gravitated into the residents' bar and sat with wedding stragglers, not sure what I was doing there with people I didn't know or how the happy-ever-after dream of me and Luke had begun to fray around the edges. In the early hours of the morning I tottered out of the bar, so unsteady on my feet that I stopped to wrench off my strappy sandals before crossing over to the corridor that led to my room. As I bent forward, my mobile fell out of my bag and slid right across the marbled floor. That's when I saw Ronan again.

Far from enjoying his first night of marital sex with my sister, he was back downstairs, sitting in a tall armchair, deep in conversation with a man sitting beside him, who was leaning forward deferentially. Ronan looked like he was holding court. They were screened from the general foyer area by a bank of tall indoor plants and we wouldn't have spotted each other only I went chasing my mobile. He looked up, his eyes narrowing slightly. Then he got to his feet, buttoning his jacket and murmuring something to the other man. He strode across the foyer and, in that moment, perhaps as a result of the conversation he'd been having, he seemed to carry a deeper aura of power around him.

'Holly, are you okay?' he asked in an even voice.

'Yeah, great,' I said, not sure how to react. I'd had far too much to drink and was liable to say something wrong, never mind go flying across the polished foyer. 'Lovely day,' I said inanely, conscious that my teeth were suddenly chattering. I told myself it had everything to do with the way it was chillier in the foyer compared to the snug surrounds of the residents' bar, and nothing to do with the flicker of displeasure in Ronan's eyes. I shivered in my dress, the hem clutched in my fingers so that I wouldn't trip up on it as I padded across the floor in my bare feet.

'I'll see you to your room,' he said. 'Can't have my sister-in-law wandering the corridors half-cut. It doesn't look good.'

He seemed a lot cooler than the Ronan who'd kissed me earlier. We walked in silence, me suddenly conscious of how much he towered over me in my bare feet. We stopped outside my door and he looked me up and down. 'Key card?'

It seemed to take ages but eventually I fished it out of my bag and passed it to him, knowing I would have made a mess of opening the door in my hammered state. He pushed me into my room with his free hand.

'There you go, safe and sound,' he said. I turned to look at him. He stood there watching me, his eyes flinty, and then he spoke, arching an eyebrow. 'Kiss goodnight?'

'I don't –' I began. Suddenly he stepped into the room and held my upper arms. Then he kissed me hard on the mouth.

'Until the next time, Holly dear,' he said. 'And don't drink so much in future,' he censured. 'It doesn't suit you.'

There wasn't going to be a next time, I told myself as I lay sleepless in bed, unable to get him out of my head. I'd seen a side to Ronan I hadn't before and I sensed he took no prisoners. Yet how dare he caution me on my drinking, considering the way he'd behaved with me. I eventually fell asleep wondering how my sister would cope with this man.

Luke called for me the next day. He'd been working in Mahoney's until four in the morning and he was white-faced with exhaustion. We met Alice in the foyer and wished her all the best. I was sorry to leave the sumptuousness of the hotel and go back to the dull routine that life in Liffey Gate had become. For twenty-four hours I'd been wrapped in a bubble of affluent luxury. Now Alice was married into a life of it but at what cost? I was thankful there was no sign of Ronan. I thought of the way he had laughed yesterday afternoon when I spoke of competition – there were no prizes for guessing who'd come out on top if he and Jay Slater ever came face to face.

CHAPTER 26

Holly, 2011–2012

IN DECEMBER, THE BEGINNING OF THE END arrived out of the blue. We were spending yet another quiet weekend in Liffey Gate. Luke made a shepherd's pie to stretch to both days, and he produced a cheap bottle of wine for Saturday night.

'Come on, we're not that badly off,' I said, when I spotted the label.

'Wanna bet? The last few credit card bills were huge. Sorry, Holly, but the spending-spree days are over.'

I knew he was right, but it was such a contrast to Alice's life that I wanted to cry. She and Ronan had honeymooned in the Seychelles, travelling first class. When she'd arrived home, she'd let out Victoria Row and moved permanently into the luxury of Leopardstown. She'd taken an indefinite career break from the library. Sometimes I remembered the pressure of Ronan's mouth on mine on his wedding day and I told myself I was a rotten sister for having sexy thoughts about Alice's husband.

'Are we poor now?' I said to Luke.

He turned around from the sink and, in an unusual

display of pique, threw a tea towel onto the counter. 'Don't start.'

We were prevented from having a row that evening by yet another one of Luke's friends arriving with the news that he was next to emigrate. Cian was off to Melbourne straight after Christmas. His sister, her husband and two small children were also emigrating. They were so far behind on their mortgage that they'd no option but to walk out the door and hand the keys back to the building society. Their parents were inconsolable. Luke was quiet for the rest of the night. So quiet and withdrawn that I was afraid to ask why he was so upset – hadn't he got me? We had our jobs. We could also have a baby. A baby would distract me from the feelings of impending doom that were slithering around my stomach, shore up the slight rift I felt between us, and ease my jealousy of Alice. On Sunday evening I mentioned it tentatively to Luke. He looked as though I'd suggested a trip to the moon.

'Holly,' he said, 'you'll have to stop this obsession.'

'Obsession? Is that what you think it is?'

'Can't you understand? Money is tight, there's talk of my job being on the line, the time could come when we can no longer afford this apartment.'

'Or *your* baby,' I said.

'*My* baby?'

'The jeep,' I pointed out.

'I'd give it up if I had to. It would be the last straw in a poxy life –'

An old childhood fear of not being good enough rose

up in a tsunami that left me trembling. 'Poxy? Is that what you call being married to me?'

'I didn't mean it like that. This recession is poxy. I hate the way this country is going down the tubes, ruining all our dreams.'

'It hasn't ruined my dreams,' I pointed out. 'I'm married to you and one day soon we'll have a baby.' I knew deep down we couldn't afford a child, but I couldn't help pushing it.

He turned away from me. 'Oh, for fuck's sake, grow up.'

I couldn't believe my gentle, loving Luke had spoken to me like that. It upset me so much that I was edgy and nauseous when I went into work on Monday morning. In a moment of tetchiness, I pulled down the inspirational message about following your dreams that I'd pinned up over my workstation, and I tore it to shreds.

Naturally, that didn't go unnoticed.

'Oh dear, someone's not her usual cheery self this morning,' Shauna said in a silky voice.

'Yeah, I wonder what happened over the weekend,' Amy said, eyeing me speculatively.

They spoke lightly, as though it was only a joke, and although I pretended to ignore them, they got to me, adding to the slow-burning anger I felt over Luke's comments and the dread that our lovely lifestyle was falling apart. As the morning went on, Shauna and Amy continued to be overly polite, pretending to walk on eggshells around me. I found it irritating, on top of my heightened state of anxiety. The flashpoint came in the canteen at coffee break, when Rachel joined our table.

'Don't tell Holly your news,' Shauna said. 'She's feeling a bit emotional this morning.' Her tone of voice was like fingernails on a blackboard to me.

'What news?' I said, knowing intuitively by the glow on Rachel's face.

'Dylan and I are expecting a baby,' Rachel squealed. 'I'm *so* excited, I can't believe it. Dylan thinks I'm wonderful. I *am* wonderful, aren't I?' She looked down at her minuscule tummy. 'I can't believe there's an actual baby growing in there. Coming from our wonderful love. It's a beautiful miracle. *Our* miracle.'

It was exactly how I'd imagined myself breaking the news as soon as I'd become pregnant, with that warm glow on my face and a sparkle in my eyes, only it wasn't happening for me. I stared at Rachel as the waves of jealousy I'd felt rocking the pit of my stomach since Alice had announced her news rose up and swelled, almost blinding me. I picked up my half-eaten muffin and lobbed it at Rachel's beautiful, miraculous belly and told her to fuck off.

I was lucky that Rachel decided not to take any action against me – she was satisfied that I'd been fired on the spot.

I couldn't believe what I'd done and I was sick with anxiety as I went home from work, terrified of what Luke might say, wondering how we'd get by, given that I was now out of a job in the middle of a recession. But I didn't tell him the truth. At a time when so many people were losing their jobs, I found it easy to pretend I was one of those statistics. Two weeks' pay in lieu of notice was better than some of our friends had received when firms crashed to the wall overnight, Luke said. He was sympathetic, and although I knew I didn't deserve his sympathy, I didn't care. I liked him being extra kind to me, asking me if I wanted him to come with me to the local social welfare office so I could sign on for unemployment benefit. It was the last place I wanted to be seen in.

'Give me a week or two,' I said. 'I need to get my head together. After Christmas.'

I still hadn't done anything when, at the beginning of January, Luke lost his job. Mahoney's collapsed overnight and the receivers arrived in that morning, sending all the staff home, with no indication of when their final salary would be paid, never mind any redundancy entitlement. It didn't even register in the media, given that larger firms were collapsing on a daily basis with bigger consequences.

'We're fucked,' he said.

'We'll survive,' I said. 'We have to.'

'With what? We won't have rent money next month. Unless a miracle happens we won't be able to pay the jeep loan. And I owe a fortune on my credit card.'

That was news to me. I thought of Alice and of the luxury lifestyle she was now enjoying. Ronan had whisked her away to the Canaries for Christmas and she was now settling comfortably into married life, although she was still plagued by nausea and raised blood pressure.

She had taxis to bring her to her antenatal visits, to save her the stress of driving, and she had a cleaner coming in on a twice-weekly basis – she let it slip one day when we were talking and I could hear a vacuum cleaner in the background. I could have asked Alice for a loan to tide us over, but there was no way I was going to go begging. I didn't want any lectures or 'I told you so's; I didn't want to be the sister who needed looking after. My skin crawled with humiliation at the idea of Ronan finding out about our dire financial straits.

I didn't know how much longer we would last in Liffey Gate. There was little of my inheritance fund left. Luke sold his music system and the watch I'd bought him to help pay January's rent. The television would be next. I popped out for milk and bread one morning and, to my utter humiliation, my card was declined. When Luke said he'd have to hand back the jeep, I couldn't help thinking of the day he'd collected me from Victoria Row in it – it had symbolised the start of what I'd thought would be a glorious life.

I was conscious of something thick and black opening up in front of me, like a long, dark tunnel waiting to swallow me.

Which it did.

CHAPTER 27

Alice

'I THOUGHT OASIS WERE THE BEST THING ever,' Damien said, in the wait between the starter and main course. 'Better than The Beatles, although my dad wasn't impressed. Especially after I'd been reared on a diet of Paul and John.'

'Oh dear,' Alice said, smiling. She could tell by the warmth in his voice that he was fond of his father. She knew by now that his mother had been a nurse, his father a teacher and their current trip to Australia and New Zealand was including a visit to his mother's brother, who lived in Auckland. His sister Ellie, who lived in Kerry, was married with young children and ran a B&B with her husband. They sounded like a normal enough family. He had never given Alice even a hint of whatever calamity had befallen them.

'Dad and I agreed to differ and respect each other's opinions,' Damien said. 'I'll never forget going to Cork to see them live. Ten of us college mates together. We had a crazy time. But my musical tastes have moved on,' he said. 'So if you ever do make it over to my wonderful abode, I promise not to bore you with floor-to-ceiling 'Champagne Supernova' or 'Wonderwall'.'

'What would you play?' she asked, enjoying this glimpse into his life.

'I'm starting a new vinyl collection – Dad thinks it's hilarious that I've gone out and bought some Beatles stuff – so I'd play some of that, as well as David Bowie, The Killers, maybe Bruce Springsteen …'

'Good choices,' Alice said, finding it hard to imagine a situation where she'd be in his flat, listening to music. Yet she'd never imagined this either – being out with him in a restaurant, on a Saturday night, twenty-four hours after she'd met him at the author event in the Convention Centre. She'd dithered over her clothes so much that she'd left a taxi running outside her house for ten minutes while she finished getting ready. When she saw Damien waiting for her in the cosy restaurant off South William Street, at a table for two set by an original reclaimed wall, she marvelled that he'd walked into the library just over six weeks ago, looking for a ticket to an event, and now she was out on a date with him. A quick glance around the restaurant assured her that she'd got it right in her black skirt and grey chiffon top. She saw her reflection in a mirrored wall; who was this version of Alice Clarke? Whoever she was, she liked her. Best of all, she wasn't pretending to be anyone she wasn't.

'Bros were my first big crush,' she said, picking up their conversation after their mains were served. 'Sort of. I think I only liked them to fit in with my peers.'

'I can't imagine you ever trying to fit in, Alice.

You seem way too independent to me. And that's a compliment, by the way.'

'Not everyone would agree with you.'

He looked at her keenly. 'On what? Your independence or the compliment part?'

'Both. Either. Depending on whether you're my sister or my ex.'

'Why, what does your sister think of you?'

'She wouldn't regard my independence as a positive thing.' Alice sighed and sipped her wine. 'From what I can see, Holly is so coupled-up with Luke that she relies on him for everything and thinks that's wonderful. That *he's* wonderful. That married life together is brilliant. And by definition, Alice is in a much poorer place with her broken marriage.'

'Has she actually said that to you?'

'Not in so many words, but it comes off her in waves. She and Luke seem to be joined at the hip, they're so seldom apart. I only see her a few times a year and he's always with her. She seems to lap it up, as though she can't bear to be apart from him. Whenever I manage to get her alone for a few minutes, she insists she's very happy.'

'That's the main thing, isn't it?'

'Yes, so long as she's not putting on a big act.'

'What makes you think that?'

She fidgeted with the stem of her glass. 'Nothing, really,' she said, shrugging slightly. 'Just a thought I had once or twice.' She smiled at him. 'But if anything was majorly wrong with my sister, I think I'd know by now.'

Wanting to change the subject, and a little unsettled at the turn the conversation had taken, Alice chatted about the latest box set she had on loan from the library.

'So you get first dibs and preferential treatment, do you now?' Damien teased.

'It all depends,' she said. 'But you have to agree I deserve some fringe benefits.'

'I'm sure you do,' he said, smiling at her in a way that warmed her heart.

Later, Alice passed on dessert, and they left the restaurant, taking the long route to the taxi rank as if by silent consent, in no hurry to end the night. People spilled out of restaurants and pubs and the cool air was redolent with various spicy scents and drifts of perfume, and lively with laughter and snatches of conversation. A large and raucous hen party jostled up the street, and Alice moved closer to Damien to allow them room to pass. On Grafton Street the flower sellers were long gone home, remnants of bruised flower petals skittering across the pavement in the slight breeze, and a lone busker stooped over his guitar and sang plaintively about searching for a heart of gold. Alice felt a sudden longing to spend the night with Damien. He hailed a taxi and insisted on seeing her safely home to her door. This time, as he said goodbye his kiss was longer and deeper, and she found herself responding in a way she thought had been dead to her.

Afterwards, she lay sleepless in bed thinking of the way he smiled at her, the sound of his voice and soft laughter, the pressure of his mouth on hers, knowing she wanted more, although it would be difficult to open herself up to possible hurt again, especially after Ronan.

She thought of Holly, surprised she'd voiced her occasional worry that her sister was putting on an act. She'd had too many glasses of wine. But the concern had been there since Holly had moved out of Dublin, hadn't it? Alice would recognise it, after all: she was the champion when it came to putting on a smiley, carefree, laughing façade.

She'd done that on her wedding day and had suffered the consequences.

CHAPTER 28

Alice, 2011–2015

EVERYONE AROUND HER – MAEVE, THE library staff and most especially Holly – thought her wedding day was the stuff of dreams. Even though on one level, her whole life seemed to sparkle with the wonderful knowledge that she was carrying precious life within her, all Alice could remember of that day was the pain in her face from her fake smiles, hiding the fact that deep down she knew she was marrying Ronan under false pretences, chiefly because, being pregnant, she felt a primeval urge for security and she wanted the best for her child. She loved him in a fashion because he was the father of her child, and it was more a self-survival instinct.

And all she could remember from the blur of the following months was being bogged down with constant nausea along with varicose veins and pendulous breasts, then, as the birth approached, floundering around like a beached whale, coupled with anxieties as to how this melon of a baby was actually going to come out of her body. Ronan was carefully attentive, insisting she put her feet up and relax instead of getting glammed up for one social event after another. It didn't matter that she couldn't keep up her blonde highlights or seemed to have lost her sparkle. Her health and the baby's development were the important things right then.

Then after a long and difficult birth, Chloe finally arrived, screaming into the world on a snowy January morning.

Ronan was ecstatic.

Alice knew, underneath the tsunami of exhaustion, that something amazing had happened.

◆

For the first couple of years, mind-numbingly fatigued, both physically and mentally, her hormones on a see-saw, Alice found it impossible to recapture the frothy, effervescent persona that had attracted Ronan, never mind try to make a go of a marriage that had been built on false ground. They began to drift apart. Terrified of getting the whole motherhood thing wrong, her only reassurance was the fact that she knew she loved Chloe with every fibre of her being; she'd kill for her if needs be. Living in Leopardstown, she felt like a flower that had been plucked out of familiar soil. It might be a luxury apartment but the big echoing rooms, cleaned regularly and efficiently by people she didn't know, didn't feel like home to her.

Looking back, she suspected Ronan had begun to play away less than a year into their marriage. He'd gradually become impatient with her lack of enthusiasm for his glittering social life, her withdrawal into a shell of sorts, her inability to put on a sparkling front; there were late nights at the office and occasionally he brought home bouquets of flowers or an expensive piece of jewellery that spoke of a guilty conscience; there were hushed mobile phone calls, and he didn't look for sex half as often. Depleted of energy, she'd ignored the signs because he was such a good father to Chloe.

Then he started not coming home. The first time she asked him where he'd been, he said it was none of her shagging business.

'So it's definitely shagging,' she said, feeling nauseous now that it was out in the open.

'Hey, I've rescued you from a dog-box house. I've saved you from a dead-end job. I'm giving you a life of luxury. That doesn't happen without hard work on my part. Your only job is to look after my child. You should be grateful and not annoying me with stupid questions. Besides, the girls are discreet – there won't be a whiff of scandal to touch either of us.'

Alice was too hurt and too shocked to respond.

He threw a lavish birthday party for himself the summer after Chloe's second birthday. He invited his family and friends, and in amongst the guests in the hotel venue was a blonde woman whose eyes constantly followed Alice around. She knew instinctively that she was Ronan's latest girlfriend, the reason he'd been missing for a night the previous week.

'How dare you flaunt your woman in front of Chloe,' she said, shaking with anger. 'I'm not having it.'

'And what do you propose to do about it?'

'I want a divorce,' Alice heard herself say.

Ronan laughed. 'Me bollocks.' His laughter died away as he stared at her. 'Are you for real? Over my dead body. You're my wife. This is Chloe's home. I want you here, under this roof, as Chloe's mother.'

'You have no respect for me, either as your wife or Chloe's mother, with your behaviour. I know you're seeing other women. How could this be a stable, loving home for her, let alone me?'

'Chloe wants for nothing. She has the best clothes, the best toys, and she'll have the best schooling. Get those divorce ideas out of your head. If you start anything stupid, I have friends who'll make sure Chloe stays with me.'

'You wouldn't.'

'Look at the life of luxury I'm giving you – you should be feeling indebted to me, you thick bitch.'

You thick bitch.

'So now I know what you think of me.'

'You hardly think I was after your beautiful body? You don't exactly make the cut between the sheets either.'

Nothing changed in the following months, and after Chloe's third birthday Alice knew for sure that her marriage was over, and she had to find a way out of it before it destroyed her. She had no idea that Holly and Luke, with their fiercely guarded privacy, their perfect close-knit coupledom, were going to inadvertently help her obtain her get-out-of-jail-free card.

◆

Ronan didn't object to her visiting her sister, not that it earned him much in the way of brownie points. He knew Alice had seen little of Holly since she'd moved to Kilkenny. 'Good luck with that,' he said. 'Make sure you bring my daughter home.'

'Aren't you going to wish me well?' she said.

'Hah!' He laughed.

She followed the unspoken rules and regulations when it came to visiting Holly and Luke and gave them two weeks' notice. Holly was happy for her to pop down on a Friday afternoon and stay for a couple of nights. Talking to Holly and enlisting her support might help, Alice thought. Even if they didn't see each other that often, the sisterly bond was still there, and it would be good for Holly to get to know Chloe a little more.

But down in Rose Cottage, Alice never got the chance to talk to Holly alone. Holly and Luke were glued to each other like industrial-force sticking plaster. They cooked together, cleared up together, sat together on the sofa when they watched a television programme. At no point during the visit did Holly peel herself away from Luke's side long enough for Alice to confide in her. At no point did Luke disappear with the words, 'I'll leave you both to have a natter – I'm sure you've lots to catch up on.' All of Alice and Holly's conversations took place within his earshot. It was as if he was determined, Alice sensed, not to let Holly out of his sight. Then again, Holly didn't make any effort to have a sister-to-sister chat.

She seized the moment the next morning when Luke

brought the kitchen waste outside to say to Holly, 'Is everything okay?'

'Why shouldn't it be?' Holly said, smiling brightly. 'We love it here. We're happy.'

'Good,' Alice said. 'You'd let me know if anything was up, wouldn't you?'

Holly laughed. 'You worry too much, Alice.'

Then Luke asked her what time she was going home at that afternoon.

'You mean today?' Alice was nonplussed. 'But I thought –' Hadn't Holly said to come down for a couple of nights? Alice had intended staying until Sunday.

Both Holly and Luke smiled at her expectantly. 'We're going out this evening,' Luke said, and she knew by the look on Holly's face that they weren't doing any such thing.

She wasn't wanted. By her own sister. Humiliation rose up inside her. Swallowing hard, she said, 'Right. I'll leave straight after lunch.' Holly's look of relief was palpable and Alice's lunch stuck in her throat. As if picking up on the atmosphere, Chloe became cranky and unsettled, screaming and making her whole body go rigid when Alice tried to strap her into her car seat. Alice felt scalded, conscious of Luke and Holly waiting to wave her off, succeeding eventually in strapping in her daughter by promising her a treat. Chloe cried for most of the journey, falling asleep when Alice was almost home.

She lifted a sleeping Chloe out of the car and put her in the buggy, taking the lift up to the apartment. Ronan would laugh at her curtailed visit, saying she couldn't stay away from him. She expected the apartment to be empty – he usually went to the golf club for drinks on Saturday afternoon. Instead she was hit by sultry music coming through the sound system.

It was still engraved on her memory: the cloying scent of perfume and, through the open door into the living area, the sight of a bottle of champagne in a cooler. A pair of red stilettos abandoned on the floor. Likewise a skirt. The door to the master bedroom slightly ajar. Her skin prickling at the realisation someone was in there. With Ronan.

Up to now, Ronan had been discreet. But bringing someone home to the marital bed was a new level of deceit. Instinct took over. She pushed a sleeping Chloe in her buggy into her nursery and closed the door. She slid her phone out of her bag, keyed in her pin code and selected the video setting. They didn't hear her. At first. Making sure the marital bedroom was included in the frame, she got Ronan's pale buttocks as he pounded into her. The woman's answering screams. His snort as he came relatively swiftly. Then footage of both of them springing apart when she coughed gently, Ronan getting off the bed in one bound, giving her a perfect post-coital full-frontal shot.

Alice fled, running into the bathroom, locking the door. Ronan thumped on it, but she forced herself to take deep breaths and concentrate, forced her trembling fingers to obey, as she emailed the video to herself, not once but twice. Afterwards she threw up all over the bathroom. By the time she opened the door, the woman was gone and Ronan was dressed and red with fury.

'How dare you,' he said, grabbing for her phone. 'No one pulls a stunt like that on me.'

'Stay away from me,' Alice said, pushing past him. 'Even if you get your hands on this phone, I've already sent the video off beyond your reach.'

'You fucking bitch.'

'Let's discuss our divorce plans,' she said, her legs weak in the aftermath. 'Otherwise this could go viral.'

'You can't threaten me like this.'

'Can't I?'

She knew she'd never have it in her to do that, much less get away with it, but she also knew that Ronan didn't want anything to soil his polished, sophisticated image, especially a full-frontal, post-sex shot.

'You put one foot wrong,' he said, 'and I promise I'll find out. You'll be forever looking over your shoulder.'

And he kept tabs on her. All the time.

CHAPTER 29

'I THINK YOU SHOULD CATCH SOME OF THE endorphins over this side of the city,' Alice said, when she called Damien on Sunday.

'I think that's a very good idea,' he said.

By the time he arrived at Victoria Row on Sunday afternoon, the sun had broken clear of early-morning cloud and the sea behind him dazzled with glittering light. They went for a long walk, Alice knowing by the lift in her heart that this was something special.

On their way back down the strand, their shadows were thrown in front of them by the westerly sun, silhouettes lengthening across the path, and Alice followed them with her eye, an old childhood memory dislodging itself from a dark corner of her mind, sending a dart of unease through her: a sharp memory of two shadows, both elongated, one long and skinny, the other smaller. She took slow breaths of the tangy air and centred herself in the moment with Damien, relieved that the memory dissolved.

They went to the movies on Monday night, and on Wednesday afternoon, on a glorious, sun-drenched spring day, Damien took leave to coincide with Alice's day off and he brought her to Wicklow, to the waterfall in Powerscourt. Driving up a narrow incline that twisted and turned between pine forests, she forgot about Ronan and Chloe and the complications of it all as she soaked up the presence of the man beside her. They chatted in low voices, filling in gaps in their lives, while sunlight flashed through the trees, throwing lacy patterns on the windscreen, and they caught glimpses of blue-grey mountain slopes plunging down to valleys fuzzed with gorse and heather. Later, after they'd strolled around by the waterfall and down woodland tracks where white-tipped water gurgled and bubbled over centuries-old stones, they went for food.

'Why don't we pop in on your sister?' Damien said. 'It would be nice to meet her.'

'Holly and Luke are not the "pop in" sort,' Alice said. 'They both work from home and would need advance notice. She's way off the beaten track, anyway – a decent journey from here.'

Besides, she hadn't mentioned Damien to Chloe yet. How could she suddenly introduce him to Holly?

'A big change from Dublin,' he said.

'By the way, did you hear about Liffey Gate?' she said.

'What about it?'

'The demolition has been halted,' she said, 'for some reason or other. Funny, we were only talking about it last Friday night.'

'When did you hear about this?'

'In the local shop last weekend. I rang Holly to tell her about it, but she said she's gone from Liffey Gate so long now that she wouldn't know any of the residents.'

'Has it something to do with the occupants?' he asked.

'Who knows. It must be serious enough.'

Silence fell between them and then Damien ordered coffees.

'How's Ronan getting on?' he said. 'I mean, with Chloe this week.'

'They're having a great time,' she said. 'He makes sure she calls me every morning before I go to work. For all his faults, he's very good with Chloe.'

'What kind of guy is he?'

'Exactly the guy you see and read about in the papers: big, brash, clever, successful and quite wealthy.'

'And yet you walked away.'

'I had to. Even on my wedding day, I knew I was doing something wrong. Ronan didn't know the real me, so I guess that makes me guilty of false pretences,' she admitted. 'After the birth, I'd no energy to put into our marriage, and we were so mismatched it was doomed to fail.'

'Don't feel you failed, Alice,' he said. 'Sometimes in fraught situations the survival instinct drowns out everything else and seems to be the only solution.'

His words softened something inside her.

'For Chloe's sake, the last thing I wanted was a broken marriage,' Alice said.

She wanted to say that when you grew up without a father, when you wondered what you'd done wrong to make him flee the country, when he wasn't there for concerts and sports days, when you saw other children being swept into fatherly arms, you grew a hard skin from pretending you were happy without him, but you knew deep inside it had eaten a piece of you away – and the last thing you wanted was for your child to grow up in a broken marriage, a marriage that had fallen apart because after all those years, Alice had been unable to piece herself together again, or give her heart fully away. The words were on the tip of her tongue, ready and waiting, but she couldn't go to that painful spot and free them.

'Shit happens, even in the best of families,' Damien said. 'Things go wrong, circumstances alter people. We've had upsets in my family that have changed the whole shape of it.' He stared at her for a few moments, and she had the feeling he was about to tell her something, but then the moment passed. Sensing his hurt, she put her hand on his, hoping the universal language of touch might help, and eventually he smiled at her.

Afterwards, she brought him into Victoria Row, poured wine and put on some music. And, with Florence and the Machine in the background, she put her arms around him and pulled his head close, enjoying his kisses, opening her mouth to his, straining to be close to him, lost in the heat of him and the blood rush to her head.

Eventually he said, 'I'd best be off.'

'Yes, I think so.'

'I'd love to stay, but –'

'I know, but –'

Not yet – but soon, the thought rose like a bubble of certainty inside her.

She didn't know where this was leading. There was Chloe to consider. There was Ronan and the impending divorce. But most of all, there was the Alice who'd locked her heart away many years ago, before even Ronan, and wanted it kept there safely, free from harm.

CHAPTER 30

ON THURSDAY MORNING WHEN ALICE WENT into the kitchen, the usual shadow was waiting for her: wraith-like, cold. How, she wondered, could emptiness feel so comprehensively solid? Sometimes she sensed it as a formless shape hanging by the window; other times it was around the cooker or the sink. The more she strained to see it, the more ephemeral it seemed.

Until this morning.

'*You've a great imagination, Alice, you get that from me.*'

His voice in her head was as unexpected as it was clear. As she stood there, transfixed, confronting that inchoate shadow, the years contracted and rolled back, and a flood of memories, normally locked away, sprang free and opened up, images as crystal sharp as if they had happened yesterday.

Dad, downstairs in the kitchen, in the early-winter mornings when it was still dusky outside, pale light edging across the bay. The scent of milk heating on the stove. Alice swinging her feet at the kitchen table, able to see the top of Dad's dark blond head as he hunkered over the grate, coaxing the yellow flame to spiral up through the coals. Their special time, just her and Dad, Mum already left for her first cleaning job of the day. Dad pulling stories out of his head, like a magician pulling a rabbit out of a hat, as he poured warm milk onto her cereal, buttered bread for her lunch, and Alice sitting in the comforting glow of a fire warming her toes, milk warming her tummy, Dad warming her heart with his stories.

He'd been a dreamer. He talked of adventuring on the high seas, of stargazing nights, of magical stories. Sometimes he'd have her late for class because he'd pause by the front window, looking out to sea, gazing at the ships crawling across the flat bay, bound for distant shores. Far better shores than here, according to Dad.

'There they go,' he'd say, hoisting her up onto his shoulders in time to see the big, bulky tanker reduce in size until it became a dot on the hazy horizon. 'Getting out of this rotten grey hell-hole of a country, off to more exciting places. Places where there are jobs and money, not like this arsehole of nowhere. But don't tell your mum I said that,' he'd continue, winking at her. She didn't understand the full meaning of his words, but she knew they made her feel uneasy, like the loose tooth in her gum.

He'd grin, his bright blue eyes sparkling. 'Don't worry, sweetheart, some day my ship will come in. One day I'll strike it lucky. Then we'll be rich and I'll be famous.'

She dimly remembered a time when her dad used to go to work in the mornings and come home in the evenings grumbling about the man in charge, but since she'd started school, he'd been at home all day. That should have made him happy.

She came down one morning to a cold, dark kitchen, last night's ashes still in the grate, a hall-door key abandoned on the table. When she went back upstairs to her parents' bedroom, her dad's side of the bed was empty and, instead of being up and at her cleaning job in fresh overalls with her hair pinned back, Hannah Clarke was sprawled across the pillow, sound asleep, her hair knotted and untidy, a stale smell and trickle of moisture coming from her open mouth. Alice pulled at her arm and eventually her mum woke up and looked at her through half-closed, bloodshot eyes. She lifted Alice into bed beside her. She held onto her so tightly that Alice could hardly breathe.

'It's just you and me, lovey,' she said in a husky voice. 'You and me against this whole shitty world.'

The days began to blur together, and as a cold, wet spring turned into a damp summer, Alice looked out the window and watched the ships coming in across the bay, growing from tiny specks on the horizon to full-bellied hulks, hoping her dad would be on one of them.

Mum told her they were going to have a new baby.

'Are we getting a new baby so that Dad will come home?'

'No, lovey, Dad won't be coming home. He has an important job in a place called Australia – it's on the other side of the world and it's too far away for him to come home.'

'Not even on a big ship?'

'Especially not on a big ship.'

Still, for a long time afterwards, Alice watched the

ships and waited to hear his knock at the door. What would she have done differently if she'd known, that fateful day, that it had been the last breakfast in the kitchen, the last walk to school, the last time Dad had marvelled at the row of dancing daffodils opening up in the tiny front garden, the last cosy bedtime story …?

She went back over everything, wondering what she'd done wrong to make him go away in the middle of the night without even saying goodbye. Had it been the time at Christmas when Dad had brought her to Santa Claus in the local community centre? When Santa had asked her what she wanted, she'd asked for a Cabbage Patch doll, because half the girls in her class were asking for them. Dad's face had looked sad and he'd been cross with Mum. Later on, she'd heard him crying and his big sobs had frightened her.

Had Alice asked for too much?

When the new baby was born, Alice marvelled that she was so tiny and beautiful. Holly had perfect fingernails, and miniature eyebrows, and delicate, curving eyelashes. Her skin was incredibly soft to the touch.

'We'll have to look after her together,' Mum said. Alice stared down at her perfect sleeping sister and knew she'd have to love her with all her heart to make up for Dad's absence.

A dad who wasn't around because silly, stupid Alice had asked for too much and sent him away.

An absence that was forever cold and empty.

◆

Time rolled forward again. The images dissolved. Alice's scalp prickled and she felt dizzy. She poured a glass of water and drank it while she waited for the kettle to boil. Then she made coffee and sat by the front window, cradling a mug in her hands as she gazed at the iridescent sea outside, the gulls drifting on invisible wind thermals. Old knots that had festered in the depths of her stomach for far too long began to unravel as she realised that that six-year-old child had never been silly or stupid. And a six-year-old child, even if silly or stupid, couldn't possibly be held accountable for the irresponsible behaviour of a grown man.

She didn't know if Gus Clarke was alive or dead, if he'd ever missed his wife and child, if he'd ever regretted his decision to walk away. She didn't know if he would ever come home, and she realised she didn't care and it didn't matter. What mattered was now, today, her life at this moment and from now on.

When she left the house, instead of going to the Dart station, she went over to the strand. Far out across the glimmering bay, the hulk of a ship was disappearing into the pearly grey horizon. She took an old key out of her pocket, took aim and, running forward, threw it with all her might into the swirl of waves. She stood for a while, inhaling deep breaths of fresh sea air, listening to the shush of waves on the strand, knowing she'd be late for work. No matter. She was meeting a new side to herself for the first time, and this was too important to be rushed.

CHAPTER 31

ON THURSDAY EVENING, IN THE GASTRO PUB in Drury Street, Alice abandoned the last of her baked salmon, rested her elbows on the table and looked at Damien.

'I wouldn't mind going back to your place and listening to some of your vinyl, even if it is The Beatles or The Boss,' she said.

She'd been on edge in the library all day, deciding one minute that she was going to be brave and meet this new version of Alice head on, the version of herself who wanted to sleep with this man; then deciding in the next breath that she had foolish notions – she'd forgotten what to do, she'd ruin a beautiful friendship, and how did she know if he was interested? Yet she'd gone home, showered and changed as if in a daze, putting on good underwear and a blue and white Zara midi dress. She'd taken a cream leather jacket out of her wardrobe and then a taxi into the city centre, still not knowing what she was going to do or say.

Then the words had been said, and there was no taking them back.

'You wouldn't mind … listening to my vinyl …?' Damien said.

'If it's okay with you,' she said.

'Okay? Do you mean what I think you mean?' Something glowed in his eyes.

'I'm not sure if you're, ah – interested?' Was this really her, talking like this?

'Are you kidding?' A huge smile broke out across his face.

'Although –' She paused for a moment.

'Although?'

'It's a long time since I listened to vinyl.' She had to be honest.

'That makes two of us,' he said, his gaze resting fondly on her.

'Well, then, what are we waiting for?' she said, slightly alarmed with this new, emboldened Alice. She seemed to be possessed by a heedlessness that didn't care what tomorrow might bring. She could no more halt the sea tide than she could her rush of excitement and the conviction that she was doing exactly what was right for her. She didn't care that her legs seemed to be made of jelly as she got to her feet, but she was glad Damien took her arm as they left the restaurant and didn't let go of it until they got into a taxi.

They said little on the journey to his apartment. Alice looked out at night-time streets swishing by the window, people she'd never met and would probably never see again strolling or scurrying about, illuminated by lights shining out from bars and restaurants and fast-food cafés; anonymous people who had no way of knowing that the pale-faced woman in the taxi was on her way to a momentous event. Then over the bridge at Portobello where sodium street lights reflected on the canal water like a looping necklace chain. She had a sudden memory of standing on the balcony of Holly's apartment, watching the night-time river reflecting the city lights as it glided by, and Holly saying it was a sight she would never tire of because they looked like beautiful jewels. She would tell her soon, about Damien. She wanted to share her good news, and letting Holly know what was happening to her would be a good way to soften the rift between them.

What was happening to her … She looked at Damien's profile in the shadowy taxi, and her throat went dry.

Damien asked the driver to pull over to the kerb, and her breath caught in her chest at the way he looked at her. Her body hummed with tension as he opened a hall door and led the way up a flight of stairs; he turned and grinned at her as they neared a doorway and he said something about ignoring the mess – he hadn't known he was going to have a special visitor that night. She didn't see any mess. They went into a small hallway, and she saw a door to a bedroom left slightly ajar. Taking off his jacket, he led her into a room beyond that, a living space with a kitchen at one end. He closed curtains and switched on a lamp.

'Some wine?' he asked, moving over to a press.

She stood in the middle of the floor, suddenly frozen, staring at him in the lamplight, her eyes travelling over his tousled hair, grey jumper and black jeans. She marvelled at the ordinary look of him, when he was anything but ordinary. *This* was anything but ordinary. She opened her mouth to speak but no words came out beyond a quivery, 'I – thanks, but –'

He walked back across to her and smoothed her hair. 'Alice, it's fine if you want a drink and we can chat, nothing else.'

She shook her head. 'No, that's not what I was going to say. I don't want any wine, thank you,' she said. She stepped away from him. She took off her jacket and let it drop to the floor. She stepped out of her shoes.

Damien pulled off his jumper, revealing a black T-shirt underneath. He toed off his shoes and yanked off his socks. Then his T-shirt was gone. He stood there in his jeans, gazing at her. Alice couldn't breathe with the thick tension in the air and the speed of the blood pumping through her veins. He moved in closer and kissed the side of her neck so softly she barely felt it, and she caught his musky scent and felt the heat coming off his body. She lifted her hair so he could reach the zip at the back of her dress and he slid it down, painfully slowly, until her dress pooled at her feet and she stood there in her underwear. He opened his belt and zipper and shrugged out of his jeans, laughing and hopping around as one leg got stuck.

Then, her heart galloping, she reached behind her and unclasped her bra, letting it drift to the floor. He gazed at her, and he wasn't laughing any more. They met in the middle of the floor, kissing greedily. Her hot skin pressed against his; his hands in her hair locked her against him as the kiss deepened.

Eventually he lifted his head, tilted it back, looked at her face. 'Hello, Alice.'

'Hello, you,' she said, dizzy with need, her nerve endings on fire.

'Just realised I never got to put on that vinyl,' he said.

'Oh dear,' she said weakly, 'you know that's all I came for.'

'Give me a minute,' he said. He went across to a turntable. She looked at the gentle slope of his shoulders, the vulnerable curve of his neck, the long, perfect indent of his backbone. His thighs. A minute later, music tumbled around the living space. Damien took her hand and began dancing her to the sound of Bruce Springsteen's 'Secret Garden', twirling her slowly, looping her around under his arms, spinning her gently across the floor, kissing her face, her neck, whenever he spun her back towards him, his gaze fastened on her at all times. When the track was over and 'Paradise' came on, he danced her across to the sofa. His fingertips trailed over her skin, followed by his mouth. Alice's throat was tight with longing, her heartbeat racing, her insides quickening.

The music stopped. There was the sound of cushions being thrust aside and slipping to the floor. Then there was just the two of them.

CHAPTER 32

Damien

ON SATURDAY MORNING, DAMIEN SHOVED bed linen into the washing machine, added detergent and fabric softener, and switched it on. He turned to the pile of dishes. He hadn't bothered to clear up on Friday evening, staying in bed as long as he could with Alice. She'd come to him straight from work, leaving early that morning because Chloe was arriving home from Euro Disney later that day.

He had all morning to put the flat to rights, but with every item he picked up, images of Alice and the night before came back to him in a pleasant wave of recollection. Her eyes, teasing him over the balloon glass of gin – he'd pulled out all the stops: crushed ice and pink grapefruit …

'You're trying to seduce me,' she'd said.

'How did you guess?' he'd replied.

The food they'd eaten – a straightforward pasta dish that she'd enjoyed, breaking off crusty bread to mop up the last of the sauce – her slim fingers curved around a glass of wine; strawberries and ice cream for dessert; more wine, low music, soft voices chatting about their respective days, the air around them crackling with expectation.

Alice's brown eyes soft and calm as they met his. 'You've changed me,' she'd said. 'I was never like this before.'

'Neither was I,' he'd said. 'It's different with you.'

◆

Damien Maher hadn't expected all this to happen with Alice, especially the way it began, with something as innocuous as a library visit, followed by a fall in the street, when he couldn't very well have abandoned her. A few things she'd said that evening had snagged his interest and made him stick around and see more of her, waiting to hear what else she might say about her life and her family, if maybe she'd supply some missing answers, answers she wouldn't even be aware that she had. He'd been on the brink, a couple of times, of telling her what had happened to wrench his family apart, the tragedy that had sent some of his loved ones abroad to try to make a new life – in a vain attempt to wipe out the past.

But then as the weeks went on, he'd begun to enjoy her company – the way her eyes lit up, the way she laughed, the vulnerability he sensed behind her sometimes spiky self: it all found an answering resonance inside him. Gradually, he became aware that his life was opening up in a new way and giving him another chance – at happiness? Love? It was still early days. He found it difficult, then, to take out the dark, unexplained history of his family in front of her, in case it broke the tentative, warm connection that was growing between them.

He filled the dishwasher with plates and cutlery; he plunged pots and pans into soapy water. When his mobile rang and his uncle William's number flashed up, he ignored it. He wanted to stay caught up in the warm memory of Alice for a little longer and not have to make small talk with someone who invariably reminded him of the downsides of life, the times when things could – and did – go horribly wrong. Instead he focused on recapturing the essence of Alice last night, her breath on his chest, her fingers in his hair, her hands on his body causing his breath to stall, her smile. Sleeping with her had been wonderful and never had anyone, even Eve, made him feel so replete.

When the pots were draining and he had cleaned the kitchen countertop, he went into the bedroom and smoothed clean sheets on his bed, ignoring the ringing of his phone. His uncle, again. He would call him later, when he felt more up to talking to him without having his good mood evaporate. He called Alice instead, her voice warm and low, her laughter light. She was up already, showered and ready for Chloe.

'It won't stop me – us, I mean,' she said.

'Good. This week has been wonderful.'

'Yes, it has. I'm going to tell Chloe that I have a new friend, very soon. I'll deal with Ronan after that.'

He was having his first coffee of the day when his mobile rang again and he decided he'd better answer this time.

'Damien Maher?' It wasn't his uncle. The voice was clipped and authoritative.

'Who is this?'

'You are Damien Maher?'

'That's me.' *Feck.* Why had he bothered to answer? He hated cold calls. They were training them differently these days. And they had his name. He was about to hang up and say he wasn't interested when the man said, 'I'm Detective Inspector Kelly. I need to talk to you about a sensitive matter.'

'What matter?'

'We'll discuss that when we see you.'

His mind raced over possible reasons why the cops would need to see him. Parking offence? Traffic violation? Nothing came to mind. It could be a wind-up, one of his mates taking the piss.

'At least give me some idea of what this is about,' Damien said.

'We're outside your apartment building,' the detective said. 'You're floor 2, apartment 3 – is that right?'

'Yes.' *Holy shit.*

He buzzed them into the building, answering the peremptory knock on his door a minute later. There were two of them, the other being Detective Fitzpatrick. They were dressed in casual clothes – they could have been heading up Temple Bar for a pint on a Friday night. Somehow he found that more sinister. He checked their ID cards and realised he was still in his bare feet.

'Tea, coffee?'

'No, thanks.'

Detective Inspector Kelly came straight to the point. 'We were talking to your uncle William last night. He's out of the country and he advised us that you might be able to help.'

'With what?' Damien said, even though if his uncle was involved he'd already guessed.

'It concerns your cousin Jarlath.'

'I was away when he – when it happened,' Damien said.

'You might recall that the coroner's verdict was one of accidental death. We've informed your uncle that we're reopening the investigation. At the moment it's all at a highly sensitive stage.'

'How can I help?'

'We want you to look at a photograph and see if you recognise the woman.'

Detective Inspector Kelly showed a document to Damien. It was a copy of a photograph of a woman's face, whose eyes appeared to be half-closed.

'We're showing you this in strict confidence,' he said. 'You're the closest next of kin in Dublin at the moment and your uncle said you were to be trusted.'

Damien stared at the image.

'Have you any idea who this woman is?' Detective Inspector Kelly asked.

'What's the connection to my cousin?' Damien asked, avoiding the question.

'We want to talk to this woman in connection with Jarlath's case,' Detective Inspector Kelly said. 'We know she's not Sandra, his girlfriend at the time.'

'So? What's the problem?'

'In our initial investigations,' Detective Inspector Kelly said, 'both our request and the family's appeal for information were well publicised. However, this particular woman never came forward, although it appears from new evidence found in Liffey Gate, an apartment block that's being demolished, that she was with Jarlath around that time and there could be a link between this woman and Jarlath's death. We need to establish whatever connection they had, or if we can rule this woman out of our enquiries. We're also cognisant that the family were never convinced it was an accident, and the new evidence has raised fresh concerns regarding that.'

'*What?*'

'Your uncle wasn't aware of any woman Jarlath was involved with apart from Sandra,' Detective Fitzpatrick went on. 'He asked us to talk to you and show you this photograph in case Jarlath might have mentioned another woman to you, or maybe you saw him with this woman at some stage, and this would help jog your memory?'

Damien shook his head. 'Jarlath and I weren't that close.'

'We've enhanced and rechecked the original CCTV footage of the dock area close to the scene of the accident,' Detective Fitzpatrick continued. 'That has also raised new questions, enough to warrant a reopening of the investigation. If you think of anything at all that might help us, please contact us immediately.'

They gave him a card with contact details and he saw them out to the door, his head beginning to explode. He looked at his mug, half-full of cooling coffee, and wished he could go back to the innocent moment he'd been drinking it and thinking of Alice.

Alice.

How could he tell her about this? He'd have to, no question of it, along with the sad tragedy that had devastated his family. He'd wondered if there could have been a connection, and now he knew there was – and it could be darker than he'd thought. He knew the woman in the photograph; he'd recognised her immediately. He'd seen that face smiling out at him from more than one photo frame in Alice's house – her sister, Holly.

He'd been right.

CHAPTER 33

Alice

THERE WAS SOMETHING WRONG. ALICE sensed it when Damien phoned and asked if he could call over that evening – a guardedness about his voice, completely at odds with the warmth she'd begun to hear and allow to find a home inside her.

No. This couldn't be over. It had barely begun.

'Can you wait until Chloe's in bed?' she asked, knowing intuitively that this was not the occasion to be introducing Damien to Chloe as Mum's new friend. Chloe had arrived home at midday, chattering non-stop about the wonderful time she'd had, too wound up to hear Alice properly when she'd casually mentioned that she had a new friend.

'That might be best,' Damien said soberly, deepening Alice's anxieties.

She hoped that when she saw him later he'd be back to the kind, warm Damien she'd begun to let into her heart. Maybe a problem at work had distracted him. But when he arrived he gave her a look of such bleakness she felt dizzy. It had started to rain and she closed the hall door on the dark clouds rolling in across the bay, pressing down on the sea, sheets of grey rain sweeping across the surface of the water. In the living room, rain pockmarked the front window. In a savage way, she was glad it wasn't bright and sunny.

'We have to talk,' he said.

'About what?' she said, her heart knocking against her chest. She should have guessed something would go wrong. She should never have risked getting close to him. Surely she knew by now that love always ended sourly for her?

'Can we sit down?' he said. 'You might need to.'

'Do I look as though I'm going to faint?'

'I don't know where to start,' he said.

A flare of anger inside her. 'Start anywhere. Just get this over with.'

'It's about Holly.'

'*Holly?*' A moment of disconcertion. She subsided into a chair.

'I had a visit from the police,' Damien said.

'The *police?*' What's that got to do with Holly?' Alice's head filled with white noise.

'That's what I'm trying to find out. The police have reopened the investigation into my cousin's death, Jarlath Slater.'

The name meant nothing to Alice. She sat there, bewildered.

'Seven years ago he fell into the dock at the Grand Canal basin and drowned,' Damien said. 'It was classified as an accidental death. An unfortunate tragedy. There was never any proper explanation. He was supposed to have been in a pub that night but no one came forward to verify that, although someone must have seen something, spoken to him, whatever. The family were left devastated. Now the police have reopened their file on his death following a new lead, and they want to talk to Holly about it.'

She couldn't grasp the magnitude of what he was saying. She asked him to repeat himself, which he did. 'I'm so sorry to hear about your cousin,' she said, 'but I don't see what that has to do with my sister.'

'The police found something … evidence … that links Holly to Jarlath around the time of his death.'

'None of this makes sense to me. How do you know it was Holly with your cousin?'

'The police showed me a photo of the woman they want to speak to. It was Holly. I recognised her from the ones on your mantelpiece.'

'But what has Holly got to do with your cousin?' Alice said, fighting back unease.

'That's what the police are trying to establish.'

Alice stayed silent; hairs rose on the back of her neck.

Damien looked at her, an unreadable expression on his face. 'It seems Holly was involved with Jarlath in some way around the time of his death, but what I don't get is she didn't come forward when the police and the family were appealing for help in trying to establish his movements.'

'If Holly ignored something, she must have had good reason for it.'

'What reasons are there to ignore a cry for help?'

A thread of fear tightened inside Alice.

Damien continued, his face pale. 'Have you any idea what Jarlath's accident did to our family? It broke us. It smashed us up. Jarlath's father and my mother are brother and sister. They were close. It affected all of us. His parents and sister were so devastated that they sold up in Dublin and went to live in New Zealand. They couldn't continue to live in the same city where he'd died.'

'As I said, I'm really sorry, but I don't like the way you're talking about Holly as if she's done something wrong. No way. Not my sister.'

'The family don't know what happened,' Damien said. 'They agonised over that, the not knowing. Not knowing what frame of mind he'd been in those days leading up to his death, not knowing who he'd been with that night, maybe earlier that evening. Maybe even the night before. What had he been talking about? How did he end up in Grand Canal Dock? They were desperate for information, and they appealed for help on national television. Had your sister come forward, she might have been able to answer some questions and put them out of a little of their misery.'

'Holly obviously knew nothing,' Alice said, the words feeling like glass in her mouth.

'I didn't tell the police I recognised her. They're making their own enquiries, and they'll find her eventually. I'm probably not supposed to be telling you any of this.'

Alice stood up, her whole body vibrating with fear and anxiety. 'Get out.'

'What?'

'Leave me alone,' she said, hugging herself to control her shaking body. 'How dare you come into my home and insult my sister, and by association, me.'

'Alice, this is not easy for me. The police found something questionable in Liffey Gate, isn't that where she used to live? And it's not a million miles from the docks. Didn't you tell me she moved away when Chloe was born? Which, incidentally, was around the time my cousin died.'

'I'll make it easy for you,' she said. 'Leave. Now. If that isn't clear enough, go fuck off.'

After Damien left, the house was filled with waves of thick silence that almost hummed aloud in their intensity. Alice put her hands up to her ears but it only deepened the noise. She realised after a while that the anxiety was reverberating from her own body, every single cell quivering in outrage and fear. Could Holly have deliberately ignored a family's pleas for help, in case she got sucked into something unpleasant? Or was she involved in some way? Her mind cascaded with images of Holly over the years, a Holly who'd moved away from her sister emotionally, as well as physically, in her quest for a carefree life of fun and adventure. And, Alice realised, she had no way of knowing how far her sister was capable of going to safeguard that happy-go-lucky life.

CHAPTER 34

'WILL HOLLY BE ALL EXCITED WHEN SHE SEES me?' Chloe asked. 'I haven't seen her in *ages*.'

Neither have I. Alice tried to relax her grip on the wheel as she chatted to Chloe. It was Sunday morning. She had taken the wrong exit off the motorway and found herself travelling through a series of roundabouts and a plethora of signage exhorting her to 'Keep Kilkenny Tidy'. Ronan, for once, had not insisted on his Sunday access, having been away with Chloe for over a week. Yesterday, when he'd brought Chloe home, he'd even stayed for a while, almost as enthusiastic as Chloe as he showed Alice some of the photographs he'd taken. It was certainly a change from his usual swift drop-off.

Sideswiped by Damien's later bombshell, that innocent interlude seemed a million years away.

Alice had called Holly's mobile the previous night and again this morning, getting no reply. Then Holly had eventually texted to say she was up to her tonsils with a rushed deadline and had no time to talk. To hell with that, Alice had decided. She needed to see Holly face to face. Though, on a day as perfect as this, nothing could be all that wrong, could it? It seemed spring had arrived overnight, trees covered with brilliant, bright green fuzz, carpets of fields blazing with yellow rapeseed. She took an alternative route to Thomastown and onto Inistioge. She crossed over the stone bridge, almost missing the turn for the long, curving side road that led to Rose Cottage.

'I can't wait to tell her about Euro Disney,' Chloe said, in a voice brimming with excitement, as Alice turned into another narrow laneway bounded by clusters of buttercups and straggling whitethorn hedging, where there was barely room for one car. Two miles on, she arrived at the white-washed cottage. Pulling into the driveway, she felt a renewed jolt of anxiety. There was no sign of Luke's car. The blinds were pulled down. The grass was overgrown and hadn't yet got its first cut. Primroses in planters showed signs of neglect, the soil dry, faded blooms not yet deadheaded.

This was unlike Holly, who had impressed Alice in recent years with her new-found dedication to all growing things. There was post stuck in the letter box that hadn't been pulled through. She plucked it out and saw that it was three days old. She rang the bell, hearing it echo through the hall. No answer. She pressed it again. She walked around to the back of the house, peering in through windows, unable to see anything. The back garden was similarly neglected. She stood for several moments, her scalp pricking with tension, while Chloe chatted away. Then she took out her phone and called Holly.

Her call went straight to voicemail. She fired off a text, asking Holly to call her immediately. She didn't say she was outside Rose Cottage because, quite suddenly, she felt like an intruder of sorts. When there was no reply she knew she had to do something she'd never done before. She plucked her key ring out of her bag and selected the shiny, never-used key that Holly had given her on Chloe's christening day, insisting she hold it 'in case of a dire emergency'.

'What kind of dire emergency are you expecting?' Alice had asked her, surprised.

'Nothing at all.' Holly had smiled brightly. 'But no harm for you to have it put away, in case we lock ourselves out.' Alice could have said she wasn't exactly in the neighbourhood for that kind of call-out, but caught up in the day itself, never mind the exhausted aftermath of giving birth, she'd let it go.

She held her breath as she went around to the front door, opened it and stepped into the hall. She stood there while Chloe dashed down to the kitchen. She didn't need to hear Chloe's cry of disappointment to know that Holly wasn't there. Neither was Luke.

'Holly?' she called out, moving through rooms where everything was still and silent.

The bedroom was tidy and, feeling as though she was snooping where she shouldn't, Alice opened wardrobe doors and scanned the contents. Clothes were hanging neatly on the rails or folded into cubbyholes, bags and shoes lined up across the bottom shelf. She couldn't say if anything was missing because she wasn't familiar with the contents of Holly's wardrobe, but there didn't seem to be any gaps. She checked the spare bedroom that

Holly used for her work – it held a bed and free-standing wardrobe, a desk by the window, shelves overhead and a press alongside.

Holly's laptop sat on the desk.

She checked the bathroom: neat and tidy, toothbrushes and toothpaste still sitting on the shelf, no traces of water residue in the sink or shower. Towels were folded neatly over the rail, as dry as a bone. Likewise, the big natural sponge in the bath had dried out. In the kitchen, the drainer was clear of mugs and plates, and a dish cloth, hardened with disuse, curled over the mixer tap. She peeked into the fridge: vegetables and fruit, low-fat spread, yogurts, cheese and milk. She steeled herself to check the best-before dates, her heart crashing down when she saw that the yogurts and milk had reached those; given the life span of processed foods, they could have been bought over a week ago.

How long had Holly and Luke been gone?

She looked out the kitchen window. The rear garden was bounded by a low beech hedgerow, beyond which the terrain sloped down to a valley and a further vista of pine forests and mountains. Alice had always thought it was incredibly beautiful. Now, in the cool silence of the kitchen, it seemed nothing but incredibly lonely and remote.

What had really brought Holly and Luke to this isolated place? Had they been running away from something? At the time, Alice had been too caught up in the exhaustion and exhilaration of new motherhood to read any clues in Holly's face. A fragment of memory came back to her: Alice, blanketed in a fog of fatigue after Chloe's birth; Holly, leaning against the black granite island in the kitchen in Leopardstown. 'You know me,' she was saying with a smile, 'I'm always up for adventure. This will be something completely different. An alternative life. Getting back to nature.'

Not only had Holly's move coincided with Chloe's birth, it had also come tight on the heels of Jarlath Slater's accidental death. Everything Damien had said hit her again, the fresh shock punching her in the chest. She struggled to fill her lungs with air. Something else clawed at her brain – hadn't she phoned Holly last Saturday and told her about the demolition of Liffey Gate being halted? Could there be some connection? She thought of the big, bright smile Holly had always presented along with assurances that she was perfectly happy; the way some inchoate concern had occasionally whispered to Alice that all might not be as it seemed; and the way she'd disregarded that, caught up in the break-up of her marriage and the struggle to form a new life with Chloe. A painful headache pulsed through her temples; once so close, what did she really know of her sister's life?

'They're not here.' Chloe pouted, her arms folded around her middle. 'I was dying to tell Holly all about Euro Disney.'

''Course you were,' Alice said soothingly. 'I'm sure we'll see Holly soon.'

She went into the spare bedroom to Holly's laptop, lifting the lid in case it yielded anything, thinking hysterically that she'd hardly be able to get into her sister's emails. As she expected, the log-on was password protected. But then she noticed a page torn out of a notebook. Alice picked it up and turned it over: a short message, scrawled, as if in a hurry – *'I'm fine, I'm with Luke, please don't worry about me, see you soon x'.*

CHAPTER 35

ON MONDAY MORNING, IN ABBEY LANE
Library, Alice took the returns trolley and lost herself
amongst the polished shelves. She inhaled the scent of
the books, felt the texture of them in her hands, heard
the murmur of voices coming from the reception desk,
students chatting to Ralph by the photocopier, Mr
Woods over in the reading area with the newspapers.
Light filtered down from the stained-glass window,
bathing the shelves in hues of yellow, red and blue.

If only she could stand there forever, in a kind of
limbo, and not have to go forward into the next moment,
or the one after that, or the next day, or the next week.
If only she could cut off all her feelings so that her nerve
endings weren't jerking around like the frayed ends of
exposed electrical wires. But once again her thoughts
went around in an endless spiral.

Holly had gone somewhere, but was pretending she
was at home.

She'd left a funny kind of note that made little sense.

The police were looking for her, having reopened a
file on an accidental death.

Somehow, it seemed Holly had been with Damien's
cousin, Jarlath, shortly before his death.

Jarlath's family had been devastated by his death,

urging members of the public to come forward if they had any information about his final movements.

Holly had never come forward. Instead she'd moved to a remote part of the country.

Where was Luke in all of this?

More importantly, where was Holly?

Damien's face … his *face*. Her heart, so tight it almost suffocated her, pain spreading out to all her limbs, even her fingers and toes.

Voices floated by.

'Did you have a good weekend, Alice?'

'I can't believe it's Monday already.' This was Sharon. 'Another week closer to my freedom. Yay!'

'What freedom?'

'I'm heading off to travel the world and have some fun and adventures.'

'Did you hear that, Finbarr? Sharon's deserting us.'

'I heard.'

'Not yet, I need to save up loads. But guess where I went this weekend!'

'I can't keep up with you …'

'I went on a helicopter ride.'

Alice went through the motions. She answered her colleagues and smiled at customers, had some banter with Steve when he brought in the boxes of new books. But as the week went by, she felt her edges beginning to crumble. Thursday was her day off and it seemed an impossible place to reach. At lunch hour on Wednesday, as they sat together in the kitchen, Finbarr asked her if she was feeing all right.

'I'm fine, why?' Considering she'd had little or no proper sleep since Sunday, lying rigidly in bed as the hours passed, it was remarkable that she wasn't the least bit tired. Rather, she felt wide awake, on an emotional high of fear blended with heartache.

'You seem a bit pale,' he said. 'If you don't mind me saying, Alice, you haven't been your usual self this week.' He looked at her gently.

His kind expression almost broke her.

She was too raw to pretend. 'How did you know? I thought I did an excellent job.'

'I recognised the signs,' Finbarr said. 'I know what it's like when things get on top of you. You keep going for so long, then suddenly – wham, it's like you get sucked under a tsunami.'

'How do you know?'

'I don't mind telling you, Bridie and me – well, we've had our problems. We lost a beautiful baby boy years ago, before his second birthday. Now and again it jumps up to bite us.'

Alice was freshly stunned. 'Oh, Finbarr, I'm so sorry. I had absolutely no idea.'

'I'm not looking for sympathy, or to compare our respective lives, but just so you know, I understand what it's like when life gets on top of you. Mostly Bridie and I keep on keeping on, not rocking any boats. It's safer that way.'

She knew then, far from boring old Benidorm and forty years coming in and out of the same job, same building, it was a question of keeping the show on the road. Words floated into her head, something about everyone fighting a battle you might not be aware of.

Did that include Holly?

'We can talk again,' Finbarr said. 'Why don't you take the rest of the afternoon off, go home, have a good rest, and I'll see you on Friday? I'll make excuses to the others – a tummy bug or whatever.'

'That might be an idea,' Alice said. Home, her refuge, her place of safety. The library was also a place of safety, but it wasn't home, and she had no energy left to keep up a front.

◆

Victoria Row felt different when she was home unexpectedly in the mid-week, early afternoon. The street seemed quieter, more relaxed, as though it was snoozing in the pale April sunshine, taking a hiatus before the bustle of the evening commute. Even the sea was calm and benign. Alice unlocked the hall door, stepping into the hall, reaching to key in the alarm code on the pad. But there was no warning beep. Stupid Alice. She'd forgotten to set it that morning. No surprises there, given her distraction. She was about to shut the hall door behind her when she heard a noise upstairs. Her scalp prickled. Instead of closing the door, she left it open. She rummaged in her bag for her mobile, having it ready before she called up the stairs.

'Who's up there? I can hear you. Come out before I call the police.'

Upstairs, a floorboard squeaked, the loose one in

front of the wardrobe in what used to be Holly's room, now used by Chloe. Holly! It had to be Holly. A flood of relief crashed through her. There was no need to be concerned for her sister – she wasn't hiding somewhere, she was here, safe and sound in Victoria Row. All would be explained.

'Holly?' She closed the hall door. She started up the stairs and heard someone moving across the landing. Then a face appeared over the banisters and looked down at her.

'Ronan! What the hell are you doing here?'

'Where the fuck is Holly?'

CHAPTER 36

Holly

THE MOBILE HOME PARK WAS TUCKED INTO a sheltered spot behind undulating sand dunes. Luke was keeping me safe there. He said I wasn't to worry about anything at all, but I didn't know if it was a good idea to leave Rose Cottage. We were here ten days now but running away solved nothing – it was like putting sticking plaster on a festering wound, where the poison within would grow and become fetid and eventually burst out. I was tired of running away and hiding. But I knew I had to go along with him for now – he had my best interests at heart.

He still loved me in spite of everything.

Most days we went out for a walk along the cliff, the swelling Atlantic rollers down below making a dull crumping sound as they broke across the long, curving strand. Up above, the eggshell-blue sky spun away to limitless infinity. My life had been like that once, the life where Alice and Mum had told me I could have anything and everything I wanted. The life that Luke had said I could make amazing.

The life I'd messed up big time.

◆

After Alice's phone call, talking about the demolition of Liffey Gate, the fault line I'd been living on for years cracked open, tossing me into the abyss.

We'd had a quiet Saturday – Luke putting the finishing touches to a project, and me completing work on a script and returning it to the publishers. He decided we deserved a little celebration. That evening he went down to the convenience store in the nearest village to pick up a bottle of wine and a pizza. As soon as he left, I googled Liffey Gate, something he'd told me never to do. A succession of links to various articles appeared, all concerning the faults in the building. I almost logged out before I saw it, an article flashed with a breaking-news banner – the very thing I'd been dreading. I clicked on the link and read the short piece – as Alice had said, demolition work had been suspended. However, what made my head burst, as though fireworks had imploded in my brain, was the fresh news that, following the discovery of items in the building, the file on an accidental death was being reopened. No further details were being released to the media at that moment.

I looked around at our cosy little cottage and the now familiar walls layered up with the years we'd spent there, where Luke had looked after me and taken such good care of me. It was over.

He arrived home from the village, organised the pizza and wine, and then I fell apart.

'It's all over,' I said, my hand shaking when I lifted my glass.

'What do you mean?'

Tears poured down my cheeks. 'They've found something, in Liffey Gate. That's why the demolition has been stopped.'

'Fuck's sake. How do you know?'

'I know I shouldn't have, but I googled Liffey Gate when you were down in the village. The police have reopened a file on an accidental death. It has to be Jay. They didn't mention his name, but it has to be him.'

Luke sat immobile, a slice of pizza halfway to his mouth. He looked like he was carved out of stone, his face was so fixed. I shivered at what I saw in his eyes. It was fear. He didn't even get cross with me for googling the building and upsetting myself.

He was sleepless most of the night, as I was. Both of us afraid to speak, to break the complicit silence we'd maintained since the events that had haunted our final days in Liffey Gate. Then at four in the morning, we talked. He suggested we leave Rose Cottage, quietly, telling no one. He needed an hour or two to sign off on his current project, and then he could put everything else on hold.

'Where are we going to go?' I asked.

'To my parents' mobile home in west Cork. The park isn't opening officially until the end of April and most of the mobiles will be unoccupied.'

'What good would that do?'

'There's no broadband, no Wi-Fi. We'd have no

internet access. Therefore you wouldn't see any updates on Liffey Gate. Therefore you wouldn't get all nervy and agitated. Therefore you'd be less likely to do something silly, or say something silly. I think it's best for your peace of mind. This thing … it probably has nothing to do with Jay. Hundreds of people have lived in that apartment block over the years. And we checked, didn't we? I want to keep you safe from harm.'

Luke. Always thinking of me.

I agreed to pack as few items as possible, so it wouldn't look like we were running away – just in case. I didn't ask him what he meant. I knew. In case the police happened to come calling, we wouldn't look like we were in hiding. And, Luke said, I wasn't to talk to Alice under any circumstances. After all, I was so nervy I was liable to say something foolish. I was satisfied she hadn't a clue about my connection to Jay and his death, apart from him having being a fellow student. If Ronan had let anything slip at the time, she'd have mentioned it to me, but he'd remained silent, just as we had. However, Luke didn't know I'd given her a spare key to the cottage. I knew that if anything blew up about my connection to Jay, or if the police were looking for me and I wasn't answering her calls, Alice would be down to Rose Cottage to assure herself everything was all right. So I left a little note for her tucked into my laptop because I didn't want her worrying. Funny, now that my world had caved in, I was finally beginning to realise that my sister had always put me first, and her fussing was a reflection of her big-hearted love.

We left Rose Cottage that Sunday morning. I bit back a sob as we turned out of the driveway and headed down the lane. Luke reached for my hand. He didn't want anything to happen to upset me, he said. He didn't want anything to happen that might separate us.

After all, we were soulmates.

CHAPTER 37

Alice

'WHAT DO YOU WANT WITH HOLLY?' ALICE asked, anxiety freezing her on the spot.

'Where is she?' Ronan bounded down the stairs.

'You haven't answered my question.'

'Any more than you've answered mine.'

'I expect she's in Rose Cottage.'

'You know full well she's not down there.'

Chloe. Of course Chloe had told her dad about their failed expedition to Holly's last Sunday when he'd called her later that evening to say goodnight.

'What are you doing here anyway, sneaking in like a thief?' she said, playing for time as she recovered from the shock of finding him there, looking for Holly. 'You'd no right. That wasn't part of the agreement.' She'd given him a door key purely for emergencies. If she hadn't come home early from the library, she might never have known he'd been there.

'Or is this an emergency?' she asked.

Her anxiety swelled when he stayed silent.

'You'd better tell me what's going on,' she said, 'explain this sudden interest in my sister.'

'I've always been interested in Holly,' he said. 'She's family. Family is important to me – you should know that.'

'You always had a soft spot for her, hadn't you?' Alice said, taking a stab in the dark, recalling how cosy they'd looked together in Holly's apartment, how easily they'd chatted, telling herself at the time that it meant nothing.

'What makes you say that?'

'I saw the way you looked at her from time to time.'

'For God's sake, Alice, she was your sister – of course I was fond of her in a brotherly way. Anyhow, you should be relieved I'm prepared to overlook the fact that you've been seeing someone while I was away.'

'*What?*' Her head spun.

'Oh, come on, you were spotted in town. For all I know you brought him back here, to your free gaff, but that's not my priority at the moment. I need to find Holly.'

Her blood ran cold. Whatever was going on with Holly, it was significant if Ronan prioritised it over a new man in Alice's life. Although that was over now. 'It's none of your business where she is,' she said.

'It might be, actually.' For the first time since she'd met him, Ronan Russell looked uncomfortable.

'What's going on?' Alice asked, swallowing her anxiety.

'The police are looking for her,' Ronan said.

'How do you know?' *The police already had Holly's name? Had Damien identified her?*

'I have friends. I went down to Rose Cottage myself to talk to her.'

'You went down to *talk* to her?'

'Yes, but the house was empty.'

'How do you know she just wasn't answering the door to you?'

'Believe me, Holly would have answered the door to me had she been there. She's not answering her mobile either.'

'I'm sure your friends must be able to tell you where it's located.'

'I don't want to bring unnecessary attention to her or the fact that she's uncontactable.'

'Or unnecessary attention to you,' Alice said, hazarding a guess, knowing by the cagey look in his eyes that she was right. 'I don't understand. Why do you need to talk to her?'

'She's your sister. Any muddy scandal with her will stick to you, and you're still my lawful wife. Therefore it will stick to me. However,' he paused, 'that's not important now. The most important thing is finding Holly.'

'Why should there be any scandal with Holly?' Nausea rose inside her. She couldn't believe she was having this conversation.

'You really don't know, do you?' Ronan said, a funny glint in his eye.

She shook her head, unwilling to admit what Damien had told her.

'I've heard through my friends that the police have reopened a file on an accidental death, a guy called Jay Slater.'

Jay Slater. That name rang a bell. Jay for Jarlath.

'He was a college mate of Holly's,' Ronan said, 'but he wanted to be more than a friend. Your sister didn't mention his name, did she?'

'I don't remember.' She'd heard his name before but she couldn't remember when.

'The police want to talk to Holly about Jay.'

Alice gripped the counter and tried to breathe slowly. First Damien, now Ronan. Damien had every reason to be involved – Jay was his cousin. But Ronan? She wondered how much he knew and why he was so agitated. Surely Ronan was only interested in whatever affected himself?

'I don't believe a word you're saying,' Alice fibbed. 'And I don't know why you're so concerned. Surely it would suit you to have my family's name dragged down? I'm sure the great Ronan Russell would be well able to deflect any unwanted attention from himself, or use it to his benefit. It's only more ammunition in your quest to rescue Chloe from my clutches. Well, that's never going to happen.'

'You don't realise how urgent this is. Your sister is missing. The police want to talk to her about Jay's death. I think he was stalking her.'

'*Stalking* her?'

'I'd say Luke was glad to see the back of him, probably Holly too,' Ronan said, compounding her worry with the intent look he gave her. 'Do you know what that could mean?'

'It means nothing,' Alice said, with far more bravery than she felt.

Ronan looked around the hallway. 'I really thought Holly might have been hiding out here.'

'*Hiding?* My sister has no need to hide from anyone.' She had to turn away from him to shield her distressed face.

'How come you called out her name when you walked in the door? Either you're concealing her somewhere, or you're expecting her to turn up here. Which she will. Begging for your help, most likely, knowing you, Alice, but even you won't be able to help her out of this shit.'

'Get out.'

'Hold onto your knickers, I'm going,' he said, heading for the hall door. 'Look,' he paused, 'I know you won't believe it, but I'm genuinely concerned for Holly. This isn't the last of this, this is only the beginning.'

His final remarks turned the blood in her veins to stone. Ronan L. Russell didn't concern himself with anything that was the slightest bit unsavoury unless it was truly serious.

Oh God, Holly, what on earth were you covering up with your big, bright smile? Did I know you at all?

CHAPTER 38

'I'M HERE TO TALK ABOUT HOLLY,' ALICE SAID.

'What about Holly?' said Maeve.

On Thursday morning, Maeve's kitchen seemed such a haven of domestic reassurance, that Alice almost convinced herself there couldn't be much amiss in the world. The radio was on low in the background, the washing machine thrummed through its cycle and the air was infused with lemon-scented washing-up liquid. She had tossed and turned the previous night before falling into a deep sleep an hour before the alarm went off. Thankfully, it was her day off, and when she'd met Maeve coming out of the school yard, having dropped Chloe off, she'd asked if she could pop in to see her.

'There's something going on,' Alice said. 'I'm not sure yet, but I'm determined to get to the bottom of it.'

'Like what?'

'For starters, did Holly ever talk to you about other guys being interested in her? Or did she ever talk about anyone annoying her?'

Standing by the sink, Maeve picked up a tea towel and, lifting a glass from the drainer, she began to wipe it. 'No, not that I can remember. I've hardly seen Holly since she moved to Rose Cottage,' she said, looking slightly relieved that she had this fact to latch on to.

'I know. I'm talking about before that.'

'Before Rose Cottage,' Maeve said slowly.

From the careful way Maeve was wiping the glass, taking great pains with it as though it was spun crystal, Alice sensed Maeve knew something but was using distraction to prevent herself blurting it out.

'It's really important, Maeve,' she said. 'There's a ... problem, with Holly. I need to get it sorted quickly. It concerns a man who could have been annoying her. Something happened around the time Chloe was born, and I guess I was too wrecked to pay her much attention. Then again, she mightn't have wanted to bother me if she had any problems.' Alice's voice cracked. That was surely the understatement of the century. Even before she'd met Luke, Holly had begun to drift away from her.

'Do you know his name?' Maeve asked.

'No,' Alice said, her denial too forceful for her own liking. 'Look, if there's anything Holly said to you ... in the past, I mean, not now.'

Maeve sat down.

'If you knew anything at all, you'd tell me, wouldn't you?'

'That all depends,' Maeve said.

'On what?'

'On what you mean by annoying her. Or being interested in her.'

Something in her tone of voice, her choice of words and the empathetic look Maeve was giving her alerted Alice. She thought of Ronan in Victoria Row, saying he was interested in Holly ... the two of them, cosying up in Liffey Gate ... laughing over Sunday afternoon drinks ... Ronan's sudden need to see her.

'Ronan,' she said.

Maeve's face cleared. 'Did you know?'

'Know about Ronan?' Her heartbeat tripped, thoughts slamming into her head.

'I don't think it meant much, Alice – that's why I never bothered to tell you – and then Holly moved, and we saw little of her after that.'

Light-headed, Alice sat there, her hands gripped together in her lap. 'You had better tell me everything,' she said to Maeve. 'I'm not quite sure what you're talking about.'

'Aren't you?' Maeve's face was stricken. 'I'm sorry I didn't bring it up sooner, but you were gone on honeymoon by the time I found out, and after that you were so sick with Chloe, I couldn't bear to upset you, and anyway Ronan seemed to be looking after you well, and Holly moved away –'

'What happened?'

'Hugh saw them, at your wedding. Ronan and Holly. Together.'

'*Together?* In what way?' There was a sudden heaviness in her limbs.

Maeve looked embarrassed. 'He was going back to our room when he saw them in a side corridor during the champagne reception. They were kissing, and it wasn't just a congratulatory kiss. Then later—' Maeve paused.

'Later?'

'Hugh went into the residents' bar after the reception.

243

I had to go straight to bed – I was wrecked. The feckin' eejit stayed drinking until four in the morning. Holly was there too, quite drunk, so Hugh kept an eye on her and followed her when she left to make sure she'd get to her room okay. But she met Ronan in the foyer and they both went back to her room.'

'I don't believe you.'

Her wedding night. They'd left the reception together in a whirlwind of ceremonious well-wishing, and Alice's only thought, at the end of that long, extravagant day, was falling into bed and getting a good night's sleep. Ronan had even said that he, too, was exhausted but he'd obviously got dressed again as soon as she'd fallen asleep and headed back to the party.

But Ronan and Holly … *Holly*!

Her *sister*! Whom she'd loved to bits all her life. Yet whom she'd always instilled with the idealistic but totally unrealistic belief that she could have anything she wanted in life. That hardly included Alice's husband. Or had Holly really been that spoiled? Anger surged through her body.

'Hugh was plastered but not plastered enough to be seeing things. Ronan didn't stay long, though,' Maeve went on. 'Our room was right at the end of the corridor, and when Hugh was messing around with his key card and trying to open the door, he saw Ronan heading back up towards the foyer.'

'And that makes it all right,' Alice said, her voice rising. 'It must have been a quick bonk, a Ronan Russell special.'

'From what Hugh said, it couldn't have been long enough for sex. But still … oh, Alice, I hoped this would never come out. I never wanted you to be hurt.'

'And you've known this all along,' she said bitterly.

'Hugh told me the evening after your wedding. He spent most of that day in hangover hell. By then you were heading off on your honeymoon.' Maeve's face was creased with worry. 'I didn't know what to do, Alice, talk to you or talk to Holly, then if Holly was angry with me word might have got back to you, and I didn't want your marriage to be over before it had a chance. I certainly didn't want to do or say anything while you were pregnant with Chloe. You weren't a bit well. Then things seemed to sort themselves out for the best: Ronan seemed to be taking good care of you and Holly moved away. I really hoped you and Ronan would make a go of it.'

'From the sound of his carry-on, Ronan had never any intention of making a go of it, and wait till I get my hands on Holly.' Alice fumed.

Maeve looked puzzled. 'They're not at it again, are they? Is that the problem?'

'I don't know, Maeve.' More confused than ever, she felt a wave of exhaustion wash over her.

'If I were you I'd forget about Holly and Ronan,' Maeve said. 'You should be putting that energy into your own life. How's Damien?'

The mention of his name caught her unawares. Her head spun. 'Not good,' she blurted out.

'I'm sorry to hear that. From what you were telling

me of last week, you seemed happy with him. I really thought …' Maeve's eyes were full of questions.

'Don't think,' Alice said. 'Don't ask. I know by now I'm better off alone.'

'That's not true.'

'Yes it is.'

'At the risk of being chewed out of it for daring to give you advice, I think you should leave Holly to sort out her life and look after your own. Holly's an adult. You can't take her problems on board, and you can't fix things for her as if she's Chloe.'

'You're right,' Alice said, anxiety nibbling at her exhaustion.

She imagined the look on Maeve's face were she to tell her the truth.

Damien thinks my sister knew something about the death of his cousin and ignored his family's pleas for help. How could he think that of Holly? Whatever there was between me and Damien is over.

Yet questions plagued her as she walked home from Maeve's. Supposing, by some cruel twist of fate, that Jay had been stalking Holly – what might Ronan have thought of this, given his affection for Holly? What was the real reason he was so anxious to talk to her? Now that the police were asking questions about Jay Slater's death, it was all too convenient that Luke and Holly had disappeared. It appeared she was in some kind of trouble all right, but was Alice prepared to help her?

CHAPTER 39

THEY CALLED TO VICTORIA ROW ON Thursday evening, showing their identity cards, Detective Inspector Kelly and Detective Fitzpatrick.

'May we come in?'

Alice nodded. She'd been half-expecting them. They were casually dressed, both younger than she was, Detective Fitzpatrick looking as though he was barely old enough to shave, let alone have graduated from Templemore. Thankfully Chloe was up in her bedroom, having a play date with two of her school friends, and they were making too much noise to have heard the doorbell.

The detectives stood around awkwardly, the living room suddenly suffocating to Alice. They refused to sit down, saying this wouldn't take too long.

'Have you any idea why we're here?' Detective Inspector Kelly asked.

'No,' Alice said. Her first lie.

'It's in connection with your sister, Holly Clarke,' Detective Inspector Kelly said. 'She is your sister, isn't she?'

'Has anything happened to Holly?' Alice asked.

'That's not why we're here.'

'Then what's this all about?'

'We'll come to that presently. Could you confirm, please, that Holly is in this photograph?'

Detective Fitzpatrick withdrew an envelope from his folder and slid out a group photo of the students in Holly's college year, taken at the time of their graduation. Alice stared at the rows of faces, spotting Holly immediately in the middle row, her bright smile as she stood in her cap and gown, blonde hair caught to one side and flowing down the front of her gown in a soft wave. She spotted her friends, Niamh and Tara. She knew Jay had to be there somewhere but the rest of the faces swam in front of her eyes.

'She's there,' Alice confirmed, feeling wretched, wondering oddly if it was how Judas had felt, 'middle row, third from the left.'

'Fine, thank you. And she lived at this address when she was in college?'

'Yes, she did.'

'Then she moved to Liffey Gate?'

'Yes, that's right.'

'Can you confirm her current address?'

There was no way she could refuse. She gave the address, the words sticking in her throat. Detective Fitzpatrick seemed satisfied that it matched the address in his notebook.

'She's still with her husband? Luke Summers?'

'Yes.'

'When was the last time you saw her?' Detective Inspector Kelly asked.

'I haven't seen Holly in a couple of months,' Alice answered.

'Is that normal?'

'We're both busy people. We don't exactly live around the corner from each other. I might only see Holly four, maybe five times a year. That's normal for us.'

'When did you speak to her last?'

'Oh gosh, let me think. It was about two weeks ago,' she said, 'Saturday morning. We sometimes spoke then, because we were both busy during the week.'

'How did she sound?'

'Fine, much as usual.'

'Did she give you any indication that she might be going away? On holidays, perhaps?'

Alice hesitated. For a wild moment she realised she could take the spotlight off Holly by telling them she'd gone away, couldn't she? That Holly was off travelling abroad for a few months – she could work from anywhere in the world. Then they might discover she was lying, and it would only make matters worse.

'No,' she said. 'From a text she sent me recently, I understood she was busy with a work deadline,' she explained, deciding it was best to stick to as much truth as possible, in case they investigated Holly's phone records.

'Ms Clarke, does the name Jarlath Slater mean anything to you?'

'Jarlath Slater,' Alice echoed, the name on her tongue making her feel nauseous. 'Slater – I think Holly knew someone in college by that name.'

'They were in the Institute of Technology at the same time,' Detective Inspector Kelly said. 'However, we're interested in the years after college. Jarlath Slater died seven years ago, a death that was ruled accidental at the time. Due to new material coming into our hands, the investigation into Mr Slater's death has been reopened and we need to talk to Holly in connection with this.'

'You hardly think my sister had anything to do with that terrible tragedy?' Had she said the right thing?

'So you remember it?' Detective Fitzpatrick was tense. 'What did Holly have to say about it?'

'I don't remember much,' Alice said, a pulse of fear sliding around her chest. 'I knew Holly was upset about a friend who'd died, but I'd just given birth to a baby and I had other things on my mind. I really don't see how she can help you with this.'

'That's for us to talk to Holly about,' Detective Inspector Kelly said. 'Just so you're aware, we'll be putting out a renewed call for information on the news bulletins over the next couple of days, along with some fresh CCTV footage.'

'CCTV?'

'Yes. We're hoping it might help to jog people's memories. If you're talking to Holly, tell her to get in touch with us or to drop into any police station as soon as possible. In the meantime, we'll be continuing our efforts to locate her ourselves.'

As they were going out the door, Detective Inspector Kelly said, 'You're married to the solicitor Ronan Russell?'

'I was. We're separated. What's that got to do with Holly?'

'Nothing that I'm aware of,' the detective inspector said. 'We heard he – ah, had an interest in the case and, in the matter of Mr Slater's death, we're following every line of inquiry, no matter how insignificant it might seem. Our investigation is fully open at the moment, Ms Clarke, and it would be in your sister's best interests to come forward as soon as possible.'

It certainly would, Alice decided grimly, closing the door after them.

She was annoyed that she only had a fuzzy memory of the time Jay had died. She recalled the afternoon after Chloe had come into the world, Holly and Luke landing into her private room with a big gift bag full of baby clothes and teddies. Even though she'd been torn between total exhaustion and giddy elation, she'd noticed and commented on Holly's wretched face. She hadn't wanted to mention it, Holly said, but one of her college mates had just died tragically and she'd rather not talk about it, it was far too upsetting. Luke had curved his arm around her in support.

Upsetting in what way, though?

And why had the police brought up Ronan?

CHAPTER 40

ON FRIDAY, FOR THE FIRST TIME IN HER career, Alice called in sick when she was perfectly well. That afternoon, she marched into the Georgian townhouse in Upper Mount Street where Ronan L. Russell Solicitor occupied two floors. It spoke volumes that, having phoned him that morning, Ronan allowed her to breach the citadel of his office on a busy Friday afternoon.

She was treated to a blatantly inquisitive stare from the assistant ordered by Ronan to get some coffee, who was clearly wondering how this rather ordinary-looking woman had managed to wangle a wedding ring out of Ronan L. Russell.

'I'd rather have tea,' Alice said to the assistant. 'And after that my husband and I are not to be disturbed.'

'That's usually my line,' Ronan said, as soon as the assistant left the office. 'And what's this with the "my husband" business? I'd laugh, only I guess that what you want to talk about is not remotely funny.'

'You're still technically my husband,' Alice said. 'Whatever you get up to, any muddy scandal you're involved in, can still affect me.'

'You're certainly stealing my script today,' Ronan said.

He was uneasy. She knew by the way he was arranging

and rearranging the mobiles on his plush leather-topped desk. He had three. He never did things by halves. In every walk of life. Sometimes she could hardly believe she'd been intimate with this man.

He chatted about Chloe but waited until a tray was brought in and he was sure they wouldn't be disturbed before he asked, 'Have you talked to Holly?'

'No,' she said, 'but try this for size.' She leaned across the table. 'What the hell were you doing with Holly on our wedding day?'

'What do you mean?' he asked, his eyes unblinking.

'Don't pretend you don't know.' Her voice shook. 'You were seen. How long was it going on?'

'Nothing happened, for Jaysus' sake.'

'You were seen kissing her. On our *wedding* day.'

'A kiss for my new sister-in-law. That's all.' He leaned back in his chair and laced his fingers behind his head. He was wearing a red tie and a crisp white shirt.

'You bastard. You were even seen going into her room. Much later. *After* we'd gone to bed.'

Ronan sighed. He threw up his hands in capitulation. 'Right. I couldn't sleep. I went down to the foyer to talk to John Macken. We were having a chat when Holly came along in tatters. I saw her back to her room, and there was a quick kiss.'

'Fuck you anyway,' Alice spat. 'How long was this crap going on?'

'There was nothing going on. I had to see her back to her room because she was sloshed. Yeah, and I kissed her goodnight. End of story.'

'How dare you, with my sister, and on our wedding night.' Alice picked up one of his mobiles and threw it at him.

'Jesus, woman, calm down, you're making a mountain out of a molehill. It was years ago. Why should you care? We've split now.' His eyes narrowed. 'You've been talking to her. Where is she?'

'I don't call badgering my sister a molehill and I don't get your sudden need to see her when you haven't mentioned her in years. What did you do to make her run out of Dublin?'

'*What?* I had nothing to do with that. Hand on heart.'

He looked so genuine that Alice was tempted to believe him. 'I was wondering why Holly was avoiding me,' she said, her voice shaking. 'I couldn't understand why she moved so far away when I'd just had Chloe. Was that to get away from you?'

'You have it all wrong.'

He got up from his chair and went over to the window, staring out at the rooftops of buildings as though they were suddenly of great interest. Something in his rigid stance alarmed her. Then, 'Holly moved out of Dublin because of money problems,' he said evenly.

'Money problems?' Alice froze in the act of picking up her tea cup. 'I don't believe you.'

'A golf buddy of mine was a landlord in Liffey Gate. I heard about it after she'd moved to Rose Cottage. They'd no choice. They were broke, her and Luke.' He was still standing, facing out the window, the breadth of his back set in silhouette against the grey-skied Dublin afternoon.

Holly *broke*? 'How come I didn't know?' Alice clattered her cup on the saucer.

'I guess she didn't want to worry you.'

'This is insane,' Alice said. 'You've managed to change the subject and give me another problem to think about on top of everything else. You're not going to deflect me that easily. Why are you looking for Holly?'

'I'm concerned for her welfare.' Ronan turned away from the window.

'Yeah. Right. The only welfare you've ever been concerned with is your own.'

'For Christ's sake, Alice, haven't we more important things to discuss?'

'I'm furious with you,' Alice said. 'It's not every day you tackle your ex-husband about getting up close and personal with your sister. But I'm parking that for now.' She sighed. 'I haven't heard a word from Holly. I'm worried sick. I'm trying to work out what kind of involvement there was between Holly and Jay. You seem to think he was stalking her?'

'I'm sorry I let that slip. I didn't want to add to your worries.' He sat down heavily, raking his hands through his hair. 'I saw them, together, Holly and Jay.'

'Where? When?'

'In Arabella's. One evening. About three weeks before Jay died.'

'Arabella's?'

'A bit of a kip, down near the docks. It was once the coolest gastro bar, but it's long closed. There's a new vegan place there now. Holly and Luke were there with some mates. I was with my accountant, sussing it out for investment. I saw Holly heading out to the ladies and a few minutes later Jay followed her.'

'How did you know that he was Jay Slater and that he was following Holly?'

'I didn't know who he was at the time.'

'But you found out later? How?'

'Jaysus, what's this? The inquisition?'

'How later? What made you remember him?' Alice pressed.

'I saw his photo in the news around the time he died, and I recognised him.'

'How come I've a gut feeling you're not telling me the truth? There has to be more to this.'

'You're suspicious of everything, Alice. Everything to do with me. It's always been a battle between us. You're always far too ready to believe the worst of me – you never give me credit for anything. Don't you realise how disheartening that is?'

'Poor Ronan. And once again, you've neatly slithered away from my questions.'

'Take it or leave it,' Ronan said, picking up a paper clip, bending it out of shape and flicking it across the room. He rested his elbows on the desk and leaned forward, looking as though he was talking to a prospective client. 'Is there anything else I can help you with?'

'You're lying.'

'Thanks a bunch. I didn't spare valuable time to listen to this bullshit.'

Alice eyeballed him. 'How did you know Jay Slater was following Holly out to the bathroom that night? That's the bullshit bit I don't understand.'

'I don't get you.'

'Picture it,' Alice said, forcing herself to breathe slowly. 'You were busy in conversation. You saw Holly going by. Okay, no surprises you spotted your sister-in-law. Then you saw Jay going by. What made you connect them? How did you know he was following her?'

'Did I say that?' Ronan plastered an innocent look on his face. 'I went out to the jacks myself, soon after Holly. That's when I saw him.'

'Oh, go to hell,' Alice said, 'you're hiding something. I need to find Holly before the police do. You want to find her too, but you're not helping me. The police might come looking for you next.'

'They won't find anything on me,' Ronan said.

'You hope. They mentioned your name to me.'

He sat up straight, suddenly alert. 'When?'

'When they called to me, last night.'

'Why didn't you tell me?'

'I'm telling you now. They were confirming we'd been married.'

'See? I told you. Mud sticks.'

'You looked worried there for a moment. You'll hear all about it on national television soon. They're reissuing an appeal for fresh information.'

'What did they say to you?'

'They're looking for Holly. They hope she'll come

forward as soon as possible so that they can eliminate her from their enquiries. They heard you had an interest in the case.'

'Well of course I do, Holly is family.'

'Soon it'll be all over the media. They'll have her photo plastered across it next. I feel for the family – it's heartbreaking for them – but I'm also climbing the walls wondering what this all means for Holly.'

Even saying the words made Alice feel ill. She slumped in her seat, feeling deflated. Ronan gave her a look of such genuine solicitude that she heard herself admitting, 'Oh, Ronan, I don't know where she is or what's going on.'

It was the second time in as many moments she found herself confiding in him, speaking from the heart. What kind of relationship might they have had if she'd been willing to speak honestly to him from the start?

'The minute you talk to her, tell her to contact me.'

'Why?'

'I could help, couldn't I? If she's in any kind of trouble, I might be able to sort it out for her. I'll do the best I can.'

'Sort it out for your own selfish ends, you mean,' Alice said, rallying a little, putting his declarations of concern to the test. 'Make sure that whatever's going on, you emerge squeaky clean.'

Ronan smiled at her ruefully. 'I guess I deserve that. I know I don't have a particularly good track record with you, and believe it or not, I regret that. Did you ever stop to think for a moment that I might, somewhere, have a decent bone in my body? That maybe, although it seems inconceivable to you, I want to help? I care about my reputation, but I'll do whatever I can to protect family. Have you talked to any of Holly's friends from college?'

'I saw them occasionally in Liffey Gate, Tara and Conor and Niamh, but I think they drifted apart in recent years.'

She hadn't seen or heard much of them since Holly had left Dublin, Alice realised. Why hadn't she spotted that? Had she really been so wrapped up in her own marital problems that she'd neglected to see that her sister had withdrawn in lots of ways from her circle of family and friends?

'Why aren't you having a big splash for your thirtieth?' Alice had asked, a year after she'd moved to the cottage.

'I am,' Holly had said, 'with Luke. We're off to a spa hotel for a luxury weekend – I call that splashing out.'

Still, no party, no friends, no get-together, no birthday cake. And no way of knowing if Holly and Luke had actually gone away, because she hadn't heard anything about it afterwards.

'I'm not going outside the family on this,' Alice said. 'I haven't seen any of Holly's friends in years. I can't very well start asking about Jay all of a sudden, especially in the circumstances. Apart from them, you're the only one I know who saw them together.'

'The only one, eh? That's why you're talking to me? For a moment there, it was nice to feel I was included in your definition of family.'

'For heaven's sake, Ronan, don't change the subject

again. Just tell me what you know about this guy and why he was following Holly.'

He gave her a thoughtful glance. 'I was hoping to spare you, Alice, really. You won't like what I have to say but Holly wasn't the perfect angel you think she was.'

'Explain that.'

'Look, I'm not proud of coming on to her at our wedding. I know it was out of order.'

'Wow, that's a change. Ronan Russell admitting he made a mistake.'

'I've made lots of mistakes,' he said to her, his gaze subdued. 'As for Holly, there was something soft and vulnerable about her that I couldn't help being drawn to.' He put his hands up, as if to forestall Alice's objections. 'I know, I know, I was out of line and I sincerely apologise. Thing is, the part you're not going to like is that Holly flirted right back at me and more or less told me I'd have to join the queue.'

'What queue?'

'Exactly. According to Holly, there was a queue. Of men, I guess. And from the look of him in Arabella's, Jay Slater was on it, probably first in line.'

'I don't believe you.'

'When I followed them out that night, Jay had Holly cornered outside the jacks.'

'He had her *cornered*?'

'Sort of. Holly passed a comment about him stalking her, before turning it into a joke. I gave him the evil eye and he slunk off. I wanted to clock him one.'

'*You* wanted to clock him one?' Alice said. 'Was that because you wanted to take his place?'

'Alice, please.' He sighed. 'Right then, I felt more protective towards Holly than anything else. I never thought much of the lily-livered Luke, but I didn't like this guy.'

'What was it about Jay that made you feel like you had to protect Holly from him?'

'A gut feeling I had, more of an instinctive thing – he seemed a pushy kind of guy. I can't say for sure he was intimidating her, but I didn't like the look in his eyes.'

Alice suppressed a shiver. Intimidating? Things were a lot darker for Holly than she'd first thought.

When she left, more anxious than ever, Ronan insisted she call him the minute she heard from Holly, and while she was relieved to have the support of influential solicitor Ronan L. Russell at her back, she could hardly bear to think that his insistence on helping could be due to some unwholesome knowledge he was keeping to himself.

CHAPTER 41

Holly, 2012

ARABELLA'S: A BIG, BRASH GASTRO PUB OFF
Grand Canal Quay, it had been one of Dublin's ultimate
destination venues during the Celtic Tiger, and it was
still a popular hangout, boasting several huge television
screens designed to draw in the crowd on sporting
occasions, but there were rumours that it was now in
financial difficulties. In spite of the circumstances of
losing their jobs, Luke's colleagues decided to go out
all guns blazing by having goodbye drinks there, and
although money was tight, we went, mainly to prove to
ourselves that we could still do these things.

It was Friday night in early January and the place was
jammed. There were about a dozen of us taking up a
corner area, and I was so distracted by the reason for us
being there that I forgot to do my usual sweep around
when we entered. To my annoyance, it turned out Jay
Slater was over in another corner with a large group of
mates, none of whom I recognised. I avoided making eye
contact with him, and didn't even mention his presence
to Luke. Later in the evening, I thought I was seeing
things when Ronan arrived with another man in tow, the

guy he'd been chatting to on his wedding night. They sat on stools further up along the bar and ordered a bottle of wine. With Ronan's body angled towards the other man rather than in my direction, I was satisfied he'd have no reason to turn around and spot me. But Jay must have seen me and been watching for an opportunity. Later in the night I had to go to the bathroom, and when I came out of the ladies into the small corridor, he was waiting for me.

'Well, Holly,' he drawled, his eyes slightly unfocused. He put his arms out either side of me, effectively pinning me against the wall. 'Don't I get a birthday kiss?'

'Sorry, not tonight,' I said, shrinking back a little, the smell of alcohol on his breath making me nauseous.

'Ah, come on, I deserve a kiss and a cuddle. I'm the big three-oh today and I'm celebrating.' He put on a sad face. 'I bet you're not, though. Celebrating, I mean. I heard things went south with Luke's job. You should have known he was a loser.'

'Piss off,' I said.

'That's no way to talk to me,' he said, his words slurred. 'I'd have looked after you.'

'Get out of my way.'

He leaned in closer. 'I could still look after you,' he said. 'It's not too late. You're so beautiful, Holly.' His mouth was inches from mine. His hands dropped to my shoulders. He was telling me I was still number one on his fuckit list, when the door to the bar area opened.

As fate would have it, Ronan had chosen that moment to come to the gents. He looked from me to Jay, sizing up the situation immediately. 'For Jaysus' sake, what's going on here? Who the hell are you?'

'He was leaving – weren't you, Jay?' I stared at him.

'I hope this fucker's not bothering you, Holly.'

'Not at all, Ronan. Jay's harmless. Just your average, everyday stalker, isn't that right, Jay?' Anxious to defuse Ronan's concerns, I spoke lightly, as if it was all a big joke.

'Why don't you stalk off?' Ronan growled at him.

Jay eyed the taller and more stockily built Ronan. 'Well if it isn't Ronan Russell, Mr Celeb Solicitor. You're keeping posh company, Holly,' he went on, turning back to me. 'Give me a shout, anytime. I'd be happy to help you out. And fuck you, Ronan,' he said, giving him the finger as he went out the door.

'"Happy to help you out"?' Ronan said, mimicking Jay so comically that it made me laugh and released some of the tension. 'Happy to reef the clothes off you, more like,' Ronan went on, his eyes sweeping over me speculatively. 'Christ, Holly, don't tell me he was some of the "stiff competition"? What's going on?'

He'd remembered. It was a tiny sop to my crumbling ego.

'Mind your own business,' I said.

'That's no way to talk to your brother-in-law,' he said. 'You're family. You *are* my business. I wouldn't like to see you hurt. Jay. Huh. I'll remember that prick. If I thought for one moment he was annoying you …'

'You'd what?'

'I'd do a Don Corleone on him, of course.' Ronan

laughed at his own joke. I must admit I was relieved that he'd chased Jay away, and I envied Alice for being married to a big, strong protective man who'd keep the world at bay – until his next words.

'In the meantime,' he said, 'I'm jumping the queue. What about you and me?'

'Why aren't you at home looking after my sister?'

'Your sister is being well looked after, she wants for nothing.'

'Except a good husband. Who's out on the prowl without her.'

'I am being a good husband. I'm here on business. I've been offered an investment opportunity in this kip to save it from going under, and I'm checking it out.'

He cupped my cheek. I was surprised at how gentle his touch was, given the coiled-up strength I sensed about him. 'Dear Holly, no wonder Jay's in lust. You're so hot when you're angry. But I shouldn't be teasing you, there can never be a "you and me", although if things had been different ...'

If things had been different, I know I'd have jumped into bed with Ronan, no sweat. I sensed he'd be a passionate, exciting lover and I bit my lip, shocked at my thoughts.

He backed away and straightened up. 'Let me know if that fecker comes sniffing around you again, I don't like anyone upsetting the family.' He escorted me back to my seat to make sure I was okay, saying hello to Luke, and I held my breath in case anyone in the group let slip they were drowning their sorrows. I couldn't bear for Ronan to know we were down on our luck, no doubt passing that juicy gossip onto a judgemental Alice. Thankfully they didn't, and we left soon after.

I didn't sleep a wink that night. It was torturous to have tasted the highs of the good days in Liffey Gate, the magic of that first year, the promise of a golden future, only to have it wrenched away, replaced by worries and bills, upsets and tensions. Then the next day, when Luke was offered a job in Liverpool, fate came rolling inexorably towards me – like a car-crash ad on the television you see happening in slow motion: you know it's all going to end badly but there's nothing you can do to prevent the propulsion of the car, the crump of the collision or the cutting down of innocent life.

'Dave called me,' he said, referring to one of his Mahoney Solutions mates. 'His brother Brendan lives in Liverpool, and they're looking for two guys urgently. Casual work, a week or so, starting Monday, cataloguing and clearing out the contents of a warehouse. The company has gone into liquidation. It would be cash in hand. Too good to refuse. We need every penny we can get our hands on.' For the first time in weeks, there was a hint of enthusiasm in his eyes. 'Dave and I can get the boat across. It'll be cheaper. Brendan will put us up. It'll be another month's rent, Holly – it'll give us time to sort ourselves out.'

Yes, sure, we'll wave a magic wand and it will all be sorted.

◆

'Don't worry about our money situation when I'm gone,' Luke said, when I said goodbye to him on a Sunday afternoon. He and Dave were starting work in Liverpool at eight o'clock the following morning. 'And please don't answer any calls unless you know the number, or open the post, especially if it looks like it's from the bank. I'll sort everything out when I get back.'

'I hope to get some work myself,' I said. I'd been trained in document proofreading as part of my job in Clery Consulting, when we'd proofed training guides and business manuals. I had planned to pick up some freelance work in that area once I made a few contacts, but so far my efforts had been fruitless.

There were plenty of other items on my to-do list:

Fret over our dwindling bank account.

Look for somewhere else to live.

See if there is anything else I can sell.

But I didn't know then that I was about to put a gigantic wrecking ball through the rest of our lives …

CHAPTER 42

Holly, 2012

IF ONLY I COULD HAVE TURNED BACK TIME to the Sunday Luke left for Liverpool. It was a beautiful January afternoon, sunlight bouncing off the surface of the river outside reflecting on the apartment walls like silvered watercolours. Walls that were starting to close around me.

On Monday it lashed rain, which suited my mood. Alice phoned, inviting me out to Leopardstown. The last weeks of her pregnancy weren't going too well: her blood pressure was elevated, she needed bed rest and it would be lovely to have a chat with me. I hadn't seen her wedding photos yet, she said, we could have a cosy evening in – there was champagne she'd open for me.

I made an excuse not to go. I'd been avoiding her as much as possible. I still hadn't told her that both Luke and I were unemployed. I had some pride left. I didn't want to let anything slip about our financial affairs and give her the opportunity to be critical about the way I'd frittered my inheritance. Neither did I want to run into Ronan, given how easily we had flirted. Besides, Luke and I had got to the stage where we had to be draconian in eking out whatever cash we had left. Our bank cards were off limits, and I had ten euro to get through the week or so until Luke came home, so even the bus fare to Leopardstown was out. Then I let it slip that Luke was in England.

'What's he doing over there?' she asked.

'A training course in Liverpool,' I said, thinking it was laughable that I was sticking to a small part of the truth while leaving out the biggest truth of all.

'He must have some hold on you,' Alice said, 'if you won't leave Liffey Gate even in his absence.'

'I've a lot on this week,' I said, lying through my teeth. 'When Luke comes home, we'll go out to Leopardstown together.' I had no intentions of doing any such thing.

On Tuesday afternoon, I forced myself to do some basic sums. Luke planned to sign on for benefits with Social Welfare as soon as he was back from Liverpool. I had been holding out for a job, thinking I'd get one after Christmas, but I'd soon have to swallow my pride and sign on also. Even so, what we'd both be entitled to would come nowhere near to covering our rent, never mind the car loan. Without the loan repayments and with moving out of Liffey Gate into basic accommodation, we might manage to live a meagre existence. As it was, the freezer was empty and the fridge contained nothing but a packet of cheese, a few eggs and half a pint of milk. My mouth watered with longing at the thoughts of a warm croissant fresh from the oven, a juicy steak and skinny fries, a bar of milk chocolate, a glass of chilled bubbly – even a budget wine; luxuries I couldn't afford.

269

My stomach clenched and I realised I was still hungry. I'd had tea and stale toast for lunch, needing to keep the eggs and cheese for my evening meal, so in desperation I threw on one of Luke's sports jackets and went out for fresh air.

I marched down the quays, facing the chilling breeze, trying to get some air into my lungs, and Jay Slater strolled out of a coffee shop close to Liffey Gate, almost as if he'd been watching and waiting for me. Right then, I didn't care one way or the other. I think I was so overwhelmed by the sorry state of my life that everything else paled in comparison.

'Holly, the very person,' he said.

'I could swear you were sitting in there waiting for me,' I said, too wrapped up in my own misery to be unsettled.

'Maybe I was.' He had a grin on his face that went back to our carefree Ocean City days. I so did not want to be reminded. 'See, Holly, we need to talk.'

'No, we don't.'

'We do, and it's important. I've a thick file on my desk with Luke's name on it.'

'What file?' Alarm bells shrieked in my head. The arctic breeze snatched at my hair and I held it back from my face. I was freezing cold. A gull screamed, wheeling in close, unnerving me further.

Jay was talking. 'Your big, fancy jeep is in the balance thanks to defaulted payments.'

I should have walked away. Had I done so, everything would be different now. Instead, I said, 'What do you mean?' And that was my first mistake.

'I was moved to the debt-recovery unit of my uncle's finance company last year,' he said, speaking hurriedly, as if he was trying to get the words out before I stalked off. 'It's extremely busy – you've no idea. I prepare the paperwork before the cases are handed to our solicitors. They pursue the legal side of the recovery of the monies. I have one such file on my desk. Concerning a certain jeep. There's also paperwork to be put through for a repossession order.'

I felt chilled to the bone. Right now, Luke was ignoring a lot of post marked urgent that had been piling up, some of which was surely from the car finance company. He must know we'd defaulted on the payments.

'Luke is the person you should be talking to,' I said.

'Luke's away,' he said. 'This won't wait.'

'What makes you think he's away?' A sliver of unease broke through my fog of gloom.

'I still have some friends who talk to me. But I might be able to suggest a way out of your troubles. Why don't we talk about it over coffee?'

I shoved my hands into the pockets of Luke's jacket and clenched them tightly. 'I've nothing to say to you.'

'Look, Holly,' Jay said, his voice softer. 'I know we've had our moments, but for old times' sake, I'd like to help out a mate of mine.'

'You don't fool me, Jay Slater.'

'I'm serious, hand on heart.'

He looked at me steadily. I wavered, biting my lip. I badly needed to know what was going on with the jeep, Luke's pride and joy. I couldn't wait until he arrived home.

And the thought of a warm, delicious cappuccino sliding down into my cold, empty stomach was comforting, no matter the circumstances.

If anyone had told me that I'd agree to coffee with Jay while Luke was away, I would have said they needed their head examined. But that's exactly what I did. It's frightening what you'll do when your back is to the wall. The café close to Liffey Gate was quiet in the early afternoon. The lunchtime crowd had returned to their offices; the staff were in that relaxed zone between a busy lunch period and the onset of the evening crowd. And, oh, how I envied all of them their jobs. My coffee arrived just as I liked it: large and creamy, accompanied by a chocolate treat. I tried not to dive hungrily into it. I even envied Jay the careless ease with which he shoved the ten-euro-note change back into his pocket.

He sipped some coffee and then he looked me in the eye. 'What do you think of me, Holly? Come on, you might as well tell me.'

'I thought we were talking about Luke's jeep?'

'We'll get to that. What's your opinion of me?' He waited, looking at me with a faintly mocking smile.

This was a crazy conversation to be having in the middle of my debris-strewn life. I didn't know how to answer him, groping for words, knowing my poor opinion would annoy him just as much as false flattery. 'You're self-assured, you know what you want out of life, but can be a bit of a pest at times. You breezed through college and came out sweetly at the other end.'

'I'm disappointed, Holly. You're like everyone else, seeing what's on the surface.'

I shrugged. 'What's there to know?'

'That swagger was mostly a front. I was never that big guy with the frenzied sex life. See, Holly?' – he rested his arms on the table and drummed it lightly with the fingers of one hand – 'I didn't have the brains for college. I don't know how I scraped in. I could never keep up with my clever scientist dad and genius sister. I knew I was a disappointment to him, so I played the fool. It was the only way I could cope with the displeasure I saw on his face year after year when my results didn't come up to scratch. Have you any idea what it's like to be judged and found wanting? By your own parent? To have to face him time and time again, knowing that no matter how hard you tried it would never be enough? Only for my mum putting in a word with her brother, so that at least I'd have a job after college – have you any idea how much that can eat away at you?'

'I'd no idea,' I said, fidgeting with a lock of my hair. I was tempted to tell him I'd never known my own father, an ache that had never been resolved.

Jay stared at my hands. 'I'd hoped you would have seen me differently, the woman at the top of my list. How did that make you feel? Knowing you were my number one?'

'Why should I feel flattered that you wanted to have sex with me?'

But you did, Holly, even a tiny bit.

'Did you ever think about getting it on with me?'

I hesitated. Had I? Nah, not Jay. 'I don't know how we got started on this,' I said, uncomfortable with the look in his eyes. 'We've other business to be getting on with.'

'Ah, yes,' he said, 'the business of separating you and Luke from your jeep. Sorry to be the one with the bad news, but I have a copy of the paperwork on my phone.' He scrolled through his mobile, eventually looking up at me. 'Including all interest and penalties, there's a total of twelve thousand euro owed after the repossession.'

I didn't move a muscle. Jay might as well have said one hundred and twelve thousand euro. It didn't make any difference because we couldn't pay it.

'Some of that figure is to pay for the repairs necessary to bring the jeep up to a resale condition,' he said.

'What? How do you know?'

'I've checked it out already and reported back the damage.'

'How did you check it out?'

'I was having a nosy around Liffey Gate basement, and hey presto – there was no mistaking Luke's pseudo-symbol of his virility.'

'You'd no right to be down in our basement.'

'Nothing to stop me,' he grinned, sensing my discomfort, 'and it's part of the job. I estimate about four grand's worth of damage.'

I saw Luke deliberately scraping the jeep off a pillar in the basement, only last week. 'If they think they're getting this back in one piece, they can think again.' He'd turned to me and said, 'This is the last straw, Hol. After this, it's over and out.' He'd thumped the dashboard so hard he'd almost dislocated his wrist. Then he'd rubbed his face and slumped in his seat, resting his head on the steering wheel.

'You mean you're not only taking back the jeep,' I found my voice, 'but we still have to pay for it. Through the nose.'

'Thing is, the money you borrowed is still owed,' Jay said evenly. 'And on top of that there are administration and towing charges.'

'You mean we've to pay for having it taken away?'

'It's standard.'

'I never heard such crap in my whole life.'

'And there's a penalty clause for –'

'Don't tell me.' I couldn't listen to any more. I imagined myself turning into a tiny dot and floating up into the air and out through the window of the café to the cold, clear afternoon outside.

'However, there is a get-out clause,' Jay said softly.

I stopped in the act of floating down along the Liffey, past the docks to the wide expanse of Dublin Bay and beyond.

'What are you talking about?'

'Like I was saying … I might be able to … arrange something.'

'Arrange what?'

'I can do all sorts, Holly. Shred documents, write the debt down … delete some spreadsheets … It's happening all the time in some of our exalted financial institutions. Luke would love to hang onto his jeep, wouldn't he? You could tell him whatever story you like to explain it.'

'And what's the price of this favour?' I was playing the game. Suddenly I knew exactly what he wanted, what he'd been looking for since Ocean City, but I needed him to spell it out so that the words might shock me into rejecting outright the crazy thoughts that had begun to creep around my head.

'One night with you, and Luke gets to hang on to his jeep.'

'No, this is off the wall. Anyway, you can't fix this.'

'I can. I've pulled off a few little favours for friends already. And we're so inundated with work that I've gotten away with it.'

'That's out of order.'

'I call it adjusting the figures. It's only chickenfeed compared to some of the financial crimes that have been perpetrated against the innocent victims of this recession, the likes of yourself and Luke. Rich bastards out there are getting away with millions – it's happening all the time. There are files being shredded, spreadsheets being deleted and millions being adjusted, but the people who owe relatively small amounts, the innocent people who never caused this recession in the first place, are the ones who are being squeezed to death. Doesn't that make you angry?'

'It does.' Angry, furious, frustrated. I'd had this fruitless conversation many a time with Luke. 'But ...'

But sleep with Jay.

Sleep with *Jay*. 'Does it have to be a whole night? How about we just have sex?'

Just have sex. Was I for real?

'One night,' he repeated. 'That's the deal. Imagine if the loan on the jeep was cleared completely.'

I stayed silent, his startling suggestion falling down

into my consciousness like dangerous shards of glass. One cut and I'd be scarred for life.

One night out of thousands of nights. In my mind's eye I could become a tiny dot, almost invisible, and float away from my body as I opened my legs. It meant Luke could save some of his pride. And it would help to make up for the way I'd stupidly lost my job, which could have been avoided.

Luke could never know. I'd slept with guys before we got together but I'd never told him, not wanting to spoil our perfect lovemaking. And I knew I daren't ruffle his jealous streak by putting images of me with other men into his head. Would this be much different? And how could I explain the debt being paid off? A further redundancy payment that Clery Consulting realised I was entitled to? Surely there would be some kind of correspondence from the car finance company? Unless Jay was able to fix that as well. I was shocked at how easily I was finding a way around obstacles.

'How do I know you'd keep your side of the bargain?' I asked Jay. 'That you can actually do this? How can I trust you?'

'You have my solemn promise, Holly. I'm not the bollocks you think I am. Give me a chance to prove that. This is my way of helping old mates, of making up for the times I pissed you off. I've told you things about me I've admitted to very few people. And I have to trust you as well. If I don't carry out my side of the bargain, you could get me into serious trouble.' He smiled. 'You were always the one that got away. The one I wanted more than anyone else. Think how happy I'd be for one night with you.'

Taking these words out of context and standing them alone, in a life where dreams had turned into ashes and hopes to dust, who couldn't help being moved by such devotion, even a little? I went along with him for a moment to see how it felt. I was already as low as I could go. I had tumbled to rock bottom and I was fed up watching every single cent and feeling battered and squeezed under the onslaught of crippling debt. With Jay's help, I could make sure Luke held onto the jeep, take some of the desperation off his face and a massive financial burden off our shoulders. I felt something I hadn't felt in a long time – a sense of purpose, no matter how foolishly misdirected it was.

'How do I know you wouldn't tell Luke?' I said.

Jay spluttered. 'Do you think I'd want Luke to know I'd slept with his wife?' he said.

I stared at him steadily. 'I think that's exactly what you'd want.'

'Christ, Holly, Luke would be so mad with me I'd be looking over my shoulder for the rest of time. You have my word. With Luke away, it's the perfect opportunity.'

'You've thought all this through already.'

'I have. From the moment I saw your file in the office.'

Jay's words kept me awake all night. One night with him and the humiliation of a repossession order on Luke's pride and joy, never mind a nightmare debt, would be wiped out. The night would be over before I realised it.

Or was I out of my mind?

CHAPTER 43

Holly, 2012

THERE WERE MORE ENVELOPES WITH RED warnings stamped on them in our post-box the following morning and my stomach reached up to claw at my throat. Jay phoned twice, but I ignored him. Then Luke phoned that evening.

'This is just a quick call,' he said. 'Don't answer the phone unless you know who it is, right, Holly?'

'You rang just to tell me that?'

'That's how important it is.' Luke's voice was tinny and far away, but I heard the note of agitation in it.

'Has someone been calling you? Someone you don't want to talk to?'

'Never mind, I'll sort it. Don't go near the post and don't talk to any strangers. I'll be home soon.'

Later, I took a deep breath and opened some post. I knew Luke would be annoyed. Even during normal times, I was never allowed to open his post, although he had sometimes opened mine – all the better to look after me, he'd say. But this wasn't normal times and he'd no right to keep me in the dark or treat me like an incapable adult with his over-protectiveness.

Then I saw why he'd been so adamant. Figures danced in front of my eyes, jumbling and twisting together as I grappled with the extent of the debt we were in. It was clear Luke had been borrowing without my knowledge to cover the rent and jeep repayments; now those loans were also outstanding. The money due on his credit card was another shock, even more than the debt owed on mine. I spent a sleepless night tossing and turning, working out that if the jeep debt was cleared, selling it would give us funds to keep some creditors off our back, hardly able to believe I was thinking this. But just a few hours of sex would lift Luke and me out of this nightmare. All I had to do was close my eyes and pretend I wasn't there. The following morning I ignored my hammering heartbeat and I called Jay – he'd given me the number of his new state-of-the-art mobile that he was using exclusively for us – and agreed to have sex with him.

'I need to know in advance that you'll keep your side of the bargain,' I said.

'I'll give you the original file. You can tear it into pieces yourself. I'll have a letter from the company addressed to Luke to say the loan is cleared and nothing else is due.'

'I want to see that letter first,' I said.

'Of course.'

'Luke must never know, Jay, seriously, and if you start any rumours I'll deny it. Or else I'll pay you back in a way you'd never expect.' I hadn't a clue how I might do that, but it sounded good. Then again, if he thought Jay was messing me about in any way, a word in Ronan's ear might sort him out.

'That won't happen.'

'Jay –'

'I love the way you say my name, I want you to keep saying it to me when we … when we … can't you imagine it, Holly? I'm already feeling hot thinking about it. Sooner rather than later. Tomorrow night. Time to anticipate it, but not too long to wait.'

I spent the rest of that night and most of the next day at a cold, calm remove. For the first time in my life, I realised that people were capable of doing anything at all, depending on the circumstances they were in. I couldn't believe what I was about to do. Not that I was going into this in my senses. I walked up town, going into a shop on Parnell Street to sell a white-gold bracelet Luke had bought me to celebrate moving into Liffey Gate for far less than what it was worth, buying a couple of bottles of wine and paracetamol with some of the proceeds, figuring they'd help to deaden any pain or emotion. At five o'clock I had a shower and dressed in clean underwear, a pair of jeans and a white shirt that belonged to Luke over a sleeveless T-shirt. Did I really think that wearing something of Luke's was going to help me feel connected to him while I broke our marriage vows? I drank a full bottle of wine and took some paracetamol to help numb my feelings.

Then at seven o'clock, Jay knocked on the apartment door, and my third mistake was letting him in, because the moment he stepped into our hallway, he was like a dark presence invading the home that Luke and I had set up, just as threatening as the envelopes with red warnings, and I knew with a sickening lurch that I had made a terrible mistake in agreeing to this. 'I've changed my mind,' I said, the effects of the alcohol and tablets making me unsteady on my feet. 'I can't go through with this. You can take the jeep, I don't care.'

'You'd give up your jeep rather than spend one night with me?'

'Yes.'

'Am I that repugnant?'

'It's not that —'

'It's too late now,' he said, propelling me down to the bedroom. 'You had me all excited.'

'I can change my mind whenever I want,' I said, conscious that my head was spinning.

Why, Holly? Why the hell did you drink so much in such a short space of time?

'If you don't leave immediately,' I said, grappling with words, 'I'll report you to the company.'

'And what will you tell them?' He let go of me, dropping his backpack on the bed and sliding off his jacket. He was wearing a black jumper and jeans.

'Exactly what happened. That you —' I gulped, hugging myself with my arms to hold myself together '— you came here and offered to squash the paperwork if I spent the night with you.'

'And supposing I tell them you offered to have sex with me in return for squashing the paperwork. That you begged me, you were desperate. Who do you think they're more likely to believe? Who do you think Luke is more likely to believe when the company investigates your allegations against me? I'll go when I get what I've come for.' His laser eyes burned through my clothes. 'You've been teasing me for years, Holly. It's payback time.'

'Where is the file,' I asked, 'and the letter saying the debt is cleared?'

'It's all here,' he said, aiming a punch at his backpack, exposing a yellow folder. 'But you don't get your hands on it until you deliver the goods.'

'That wasn't the original agreement.'

'It's the agreement now.'

As if through a fog, I was conscious of an innocent Luke hundreds of miles away, working all hours to scrabble some cash to shore up the remnants of our shattered lives. I was conscious of all the debt we had accumulated, and how ashamed I felt not to have enough money for food, that I was afraid to tell my sister how far I'd fallen on account of my pride, that maybe if I'd hung on to my job we wouldn't be in quite the perilous situation we were in today. Jay Slater was right on one count: I was desperate, even if he was looking at me with eyes that were making me nervous, his face blurring a little as the effects of the alcohol and tablets deepened.

'Think, Holly,' he said, coming closer, pulling a strand of my hair and twirling it around his fingers. 'How would it feel to be free of twelve thousand euro?'

I could do this, couldn't I? It would only last a few hours, and at least I was *doing* something, anything, to stave off the worst of the nightmare for Luke and me. Even if it was sex. Just meaningless sex. Only it wasn't so easy to become a tiny dot, almost invisible, and float away from my body as Jay tore open my jeans, shoving them down along with my pants, kicking them off and away from me, pushing me on my stomach across the bed.

'We have all night,' he said, bending right over me and whispering in my ear. 'And I'm going to fuck you to high heaven. See what I have. Fun and games.' Within my line of sight he rummaged in his backpack, pulling out crimson underwear, a blindfold and sex toys.

'No,' I croaked, my limbs like jelly, unable to move very much thanks to the concoction I'd downed.

'Oh yes, Holly,' he said in a sing-song voice, pulling off my shirt. 'I know you'll do as you're told, otherwise Luke will find out. And we can't have that now, can we? Luke would be all upset. If I had to tell him about this, he'd fly into a rage and, well, I'm stronger than him and anything might happen.'

That wasn't what he'd led me to believe when we'd talked over coffee, making out then that Luke could intimidate him. What else had he led me to believe? I couldn't think this through, not now, in the middle of this horror. It wasn't easy at all to become an invisible dot, and then eventually I did, and I was flying away from this room, this bed, this man, like a screeching gull flailing in the chilly air blowing down along the Liffey.

CHAPTER 44

Holly, 2012

PAIN, THE FOLLOWING MORNING. IT embedded itself in every single one of my cells like thousands of nails, pulsing all over, as far as the tips of my fingers and toes. Pain of regret. Of shame. Of disgust. Of degradation. Of hating myself. Of hating my body. Of hating Liffey Gate. Of hating Jay. I was too shocked to cry. Too paralysed to get dressed. Too petrified to leave the apartment. Too nauseous to be able to force anything but sips of water past my lips.

Dear God, what had I done? Needless to say, there had been no paperwork in the file. I had a vague memory of Jay taunting me before he left – *I enjoyed the sex, pity about the jeep … what a shame … my manager has that file – I saw it on his desk … it was easy to take photos of the paperwork …*

Three days later, Luke arrived home from Liverpool, exhausted and pale-faced but slightly victorious as he brandished an envelope stuffed with sterling. I was relieved that he was too drained to talk. The first evening he was home, he fell into bed early and slept for twelve hours straight. The following morning he had a long shower and made some scrambled eggs on toast, and he went off to the currency exchange office in Westmoreland Street to change the sterling into euro, coming home with some much-needed groceries.

I was terrified he'd sense the dark deed that had taken place in our bedroom. Everything about me was different, was strained, was edgy, down to the sound of my voice. Surely he'd notice? For me, the hours with Jay still hung in the apartment like an oily black cloud, filling every corner as well as every piece of my heart and soul with dark fumes. How could Luke not notice the way it leapt between us like an invisible wall? I was terrified he'd find some trace of Jay, some lingering odour. It was the first time I was hiding something from Luke and I found it horrendous. I'd done something wrong, and whereas before I might have turned to him for a hug and some comfort, now I had to keep it all to myself.

And I had a gut feeling it wasn't over yet.

The following morning, Luke tackled the post. If he noticed I'd opened some of it, he didn't comment, and I had the sense that, far from being down and despairing, there was a new and quiet resolution about him.

Then he said we needed to talk.

I jumped guiltily. Could he see it somewhere in my face, the night I'd spent with Jay?

'Talk about what?' I asked.

'Us. Our situation. We've been ignoring it for too long.' There was a determination about him that hadn't been there before. 'I must have been nuts to ignore the bills – I've started to get aggressive phone calls now.'

'Tell me exactly how bad it is,' I said.

'It's bad,' he said, reeling off amounts. All the pretending was over. No more we'd be fine, we'd get other jobs, we'd weather this, things like this didn't happen to bright, shiny Holly and Luke.

'I've been to see my father.'

'When? How?' We'd hardly seen Luke's parents since we'd married.

'I got back to Dublin two days ago and I took the bus down to Fermoy.'

'And?'

'I didn't realise how lovely it is down home, how beautiful.'

'Didn't you?'

'Nah, I was always too busy planning my escape to the exciting big city. I never really appreciated it all. The house might be small but it's cosy and home, my father's business … always there, the cornerstone of my life. I saw it differently this time. How hard he has worked all these years and never complained, the long hours he put in and sacrifices he and my mother made so we'd have a happy childhood. I really snubbed it all. I can't believe I told him I didn't want anything to do with the pub – his precious livelihood. I took it all for granted.'

'Do you want to go back?' I had a vision of us starting over again, away from Dublin, in a place where Luke had felt secure.

'Nah. Dad's lost trade, he's had to let staff go, Pierce is taking over. There's no room for me there now, but,'

Luke held my gaze, 'Dad has some savings and has offered to help.'

I knew how much that must have cost him, Luke swallowing his pride. 'I have to be totally honest with him. He wants to see the statements for himself; he'll sit me down with his accountant to work out a plan, he'll do whatever he can to help. I told him I'll pay him back every penny, eventually. He said ...'

'What?'

'He said to spread the repayments out as long as I wanted, within reason, of course. He'd rather the money was doing something useful than sitting in a bank getting zilch interest. He said I should have gone to him sooner. He also said if we wanted to move out of Dublin, there's an option of a free roof over our heads, once we pay the utility bills. We won't do this unless you're perfectly happy, Holly. I told him we'd need to think about it because it's such a huge change.'

'Go on.'

'My father's aunt – Great Aunt Nora – her cottage has been lying empty since she died last year. It was left to my father and his sister, but they don't want to put it on the market yet, it's so flattened. However, they'd be happy for it to be occupied. We can have it rent-free for a couple of years, negotiable after that depending on the market.'

'A free roof is a free roof,' I said.

'It's in the wilds of Kilkenny, Holly, off the beaten track. It's fully furnished, although a little dated. We don't have to decide just yet – there's no rush, Rose Cottage is not going anywhere.'

Luke smiled, a thin smile. He looked older, and there was a hard light in his eyes, a wounded, world-weary expression. I knew he'd never go back to the carefree person he'd been when we'd first met. Then again, neither would I. And at that moment, I knew there was no way on earth I could tell him about the night with Jay.

And then I was forced to.

CHAPTER 45

Holly, 2012

I MIGHT HAVE KNOWN THAT IT HADN'T been enough for Jay to humiliate me completely – he wanted to humiliate Luke and shred him of the last vestiges of his pride.

'Jay Slater wants to see me,' Luke said, a few days after he was home from Liverpool.

'What about?' My heart plummeted.

'The jeep. I didn't know he works in the company that organised the car finance.'

'Don't see him.'

'I might have ignored him a month ago, Holly, and the idea of talking to him is sickening, but I have to face up to things.'

'Does it have to be Jay? Can't you talk to someone else in the company?'

'He told me my file was sitting on his desk in the debt-recovery unit. He's up to his tonsils with work, so he's willing to put the file to the bottom of his in-tray until we talk.'

'How do you know he's telling the truth?'

'I've no reason not to believe him.' Luke rubbed his

face with his hands. 'He mentioned a few details he'd only know if he had the file in front of him.'

I thought of how innocent Luke looked – innocent of the total ugliness of what had transpired between me and Jay. I couldn't bear him to find out – it would kill him altogether. It would ruin us and destroy Luke for good. That was why I arranged to see Jay myself, before he spoke to Luke, meeting him in the café, picking the afternoon that Luke went to the social welfare office to sign on.

'This is a pleasant surprise, Holly, you looking for me,' Jay sneered.

'We need to talk.' Every cell in my body trembled with revulsion.

'Talk?' His eyes lacerated me with the sharpness of a knife point. 'I can think of other things I'd rather be doing.'

'You got what you were looking for,' I said, the pain in my chest almost unbearable. There was music on in the background, Adele singing throatily that we almost had it all, and I found it gut-wrenching.

'I want more.'

'No way.'

'Aww. Here was I thinking you'd called me because you wanted a repeat.'

'Go fuck yourself.'

'Not even if it stopped Luke from finding out?'

Icy fingers ran down my spine. 'What do you mean?'

'Another night with you and I might be persuaded not to tell Luke about us.'

I tried to brave it out. 'No way. That's not going to happen. Luke won't believe you. I'll deny it all.'

'You can deny it all you like, Holly. But I have proof. On my lovely new mobile.'

He took out his phone and swiped the screen. Then he held it in front of me as he scrolled through a dozen or so images that wouldn't have been out of place in a brothel. A selection of me, half naked, with crimson knickers around my thighs, a bra around my neck, a couple with sex toys. In most of them my eyes were half-closed, as if in ecstasy or, perhaps, a little drugged. Then there were a couple of selfies of us in the act, slightly out of focus, but unmistakeable. 'How did … you …?' I could barely speak.

'You were so out of it you hardly even noticed me setting up my phone.' His insolent eyes studied my face. 'They're quite explosive, aren't they? Don't worry, they're not on my work mobile. This is just between you and me. But God help me if I pressed the wrong button when I'm feeling a bit mischievous. I might even print out a few.'

'You wouldn't dare.'

'I might. It all depends on you.'

A crippling pain crashed through me as my life fell apart. I couldn't recall Jay taking photographs. Then again there had been times during the night when I'd slipped into a twilight zone, thanks to booze-fuelled drowsiness and blanking everything out.

'How dare you, you absolute bastard!' I lost it, my voice loud enough to attract the attention of people around us, including the staff, who paused to stare at us. I didn't care.

'I wonder what Luke would think of these?' he said. 'Maybe he'd like them, maybe I'll need to print some … unless …' He raised his eyebrows suggestively.

I rose to my feet. I leaned over the table and threw the last of my coffee into his face. I grabbed my bag, sending a small vase crashing to the ground. 'You fucking prick,' I said, heedless of my audience and a manager making his way across. My vision swam and my legs were about to buckle, but somehow I walked away.

◆

There was no hope for Holly and Luke. We could never come back from this. We could never make a life together again, because not even the best of our love could help us climb out of the deep, dark pit into which it had fallen. I was the one who had taken the sledgehammer and pulverised our lives. I had ruined us. I was somewhere outside of myself, an onlooker watching our marriage and the rest of our dreams crumble to ashes. I think the shock of it all numbed me enough to say to Luke that we needed to talk.

'When you were in Liverpool,' I said, after our meal that evening, my mouth bone dry with anxiety, 'something happened.'

'I told you not to answer any calls.' Luke frowned, a chink beginning to show in his fragile new-found positivity.

'It wasn't a call,' I said, my teeth beginning to chatter. 'It was the jeep.'

'What about the jeep?'

There was a silence while I swallowed the huge lump in my throat. 'I thought I had the chance to clear the money we owe on it—'

'You *what*?'

'You see, I found out how much was due,' I gulped, 'and I thought I could ... arrange to have it wiped out.'

'What are you trying to say?' Luke's face was whiter than I'd ever seen it.

I shook uncontrollably. I hugged myself as if I was trying to stop my insides from falling out. Which was ridiculous because I was hollowed out, cracked apart, eviscerated from within. 'I thought it could be written off ... the money we owed ...'

'How, though?' Fear sparked in his eyes, as though he sensed I was about to detonate the equivalent of an atomic bomb in our already shattered lives.

'I was talking to Jay.'

'Jay?' He looked puzzled, as if failing to make any connection. More than anything else at that moment, I wished he could looked puzzled forever, that what I was about to say would remain unsaid, that I wasn't about to destroy his love for me and take that away from him also.

'He has the file ... in his job ...' I said, struggling for breath.

'I know that,' he said, sitting up straighter, suddenly on full alert.

I thought of the photos Jay had on his phone and his

threat to tell Luke. I thought of how this had all started on a party-filled night in Ocean City and the interlinking filaments of all the times we'd met since leading to this. I knew my next words were going to kill something inside Luke. I never loved him more than I did right then.

My heart was fluttering painfully in my mouth. Somehow I managed to form words. 'He said … he could take care of the debt … write it down … shred the file …'

'And why would he do that?' Luke asked, his voice a whisper.

'If I … slept with him.'

Luke stared at me, while a formless panic surged through me. Apprehension flashed across his face. He sprang to his feet as if jolted. He put his hands up to his ears and shook his head from side to side. He said, his voice hoarse, 'You didn't. Jesus Christ, Holly, you didn't, tell me you didn't. Please.'

I hung my head, my silence enough of an answer.

Luke sank down to the floor as though his body had caved in. He sat with his back to the wall, his legs stretched out, his arms wrapped around himself as if he could shield himself in some way against my terrible words. I stared at his trainers, instead of his face, but even that was a mistake. Once upon a time, Luke would have splashed out on the latest in footwear, discarding them as soon as they showed wear and tear. Now his Nikes were fraying at the seams; they were scuffed and dirty and threadbare where his big toe pressed against the material. To see him reduced to this tore my heart apart.

'When? Where?' he said in a broken voice.

'Here. Last week.'

I tried to put myself in Luke's place, and I wondered if there were any words I could use to ease the pain. 'It meant nothing,' I went on. 'It was just meaningless sex. I didn't want to do it, I hated it, but I thought I was doing something to save us from total destitution. One night with me, he said, and he'd adjust the figures and shred the file, but he told me afterwards he was lying. He even took photos of us on his new mobile ... they're ... he wanted to blackmail me ... oh God, Luke, I'm so sorry.'

He looked at me incredulously. '*Sorry?* You're *sorry?*'

'Luke, please!' I knelt down beside him and reached out to him, but he pushed me away and slammed out of the apartment, not returning for hours. Over the next couple of days Luke withdrew from me in frozen misery. I couldn't reach him. He moved around the apartment like a robot. He never once looked at me or spoke to me. His face was shuttered and blank. Whatever private hell he was in – and I knew by the hard light in his eyes that it *was* a hell – he wasn't about to share it with me.

I tried to talk, to reason with him on some level. 'In the fullness of me and you,' I said, 'it was insignificant ... Remember we said nothing would ever come between us? Well, this won't. It's meaningless, compared to the strength of our love ... You and me, we can get through this, we're more than what happened.'

Silence.

Then later, I tried again. 'Look on it as a few hours blanked out of the whole of our marriage,' I said. 'Think of all the hours, all the days and weeks, all the years we've been together. All the time we have in front of us. This was a blip that just took a tiny fraction of those hours.'

In desperation, I said, pain blooming in my chest, 'Think of it this way. Our lives together are a big colourful canvas – like a beautiful Monet painting – and this is just a small dark weed in the corner of the meadow. It doesn't take away from anything. The whole picture is still beautiful.'

One of the worst moments of my life was watching Luke sit on the floor of the kitchen while, one by one, he smashed a set of china mugs against the balcony door, cracking them into a million pieces, cracking my heart into smithereens as he put his head into his hands and wept. Apart from that, there was no response from him. Then the following day, he disappeared. He walked out of the apartment in the morning and didn't come back all day. I drifted around from room to room, thinking of the way our lives had been laid waste, catching sight of myself in a mirror – how thin I'd become since the start of the year, my face full of hollows that hadn't been there before, my stomach a hard ball of steel inside me. I drank coffee and forced myself to sip water. I hated myself in a way I never had before. Late in the evening I took a scourer and washing-up liquid from the kitchen, took off my clothes and stepped into the shower. The water was tepid because we were rationing the electricity. I stood there under the flow, pouring washing-up liquid onto the scourer and using it to scrape my body until my skin was raw.

I didn't notice when I began to cry, helpless tears that poured out through my nose and eyes. I kept scrubbing and scouring, scraping away skin cells, scourging my soul at the same time. The first I knew of Luke returning was when the shower door opened. I stared at him through wet strands of hair. He said nothing as he stepped in beside me, fully clothed. Some of the hardness left his eyes as they scanned my body and he began to weep silently. Then he took the scourer out of my hands and threw it aside. He looked at the marks on my skin, the red rash I had inflicted on myself in all my tender places. He began to stroke my body, getting wetter and wetter by degrees as the cold water spilled down on us. He stroked over and over, until his hands had massaged every sore piece of skin. Then he stepped out and, heedless to his saturated clothes and squelching sports shoes, he reached back and led me out by the hand. He wrapped a towel around me with the tenderness you would grant a new born baby. He pulled me close to him and held me there until my heart felt like it was beating up in my mouth.

He pushed wet strands of hair away from my face. 'I hate what happened to my sweet Holly, but I still love you.'

CHAPTER 46

Alice

'YOU'RE SURE YOU'RE OKAY?' FINBARR ASKED when Alice returned to work on Monday morning.

'I'm fine,' she said, knowing her pale face told a different story.

'Well, don't overdo it today,' he said. 'Ease your way back in.'

'Thanks. I'll take a look at the newspapers.'

She saw it immediately:

'*Who was with Jarlath Slater the night he plunged into the dock?*' screamed the headline on a front-page article. And below that, '*Police have launched a fresh appeal for information in relation to the unexplained death of …*' She didn't need to read any more. There was a small photograph of Jay alongside the article. He looked young and carefree, a guy with most of his life still ahead of him.

Alice moved through the day in a daze. The police wouldn't waste time on an investigation without good reason. And there was so much that Holly had been keeping from her. Why was she missing and not answering Alice's calls? How come she'd left a scrawled message in her laptop? She only had Ronan's word that Jay had been stalking Holly. But supposing Holly had been flirting with Jay, maybe welcomed his attention, like she had with Ronan? According to Damien, she'd been with Jay around the time he died. What good reason could she have had not to respond to the appeals for help?

By the time she was home that evening, Chloe doing her homework at the kitchen table, Alice was weary to her bones.

There was a report on the reopened investigation on the six o'clock news bulletin. She forced herself to watch, unable to comprehend that there was even the remotest possibility that Holly had been involved with this tragedy. The same photograph of Jay that Alice had seen in the newspaper flashed up on the screen. The newscaster was joined in the studio by a uniformed inspector who announced that the original CCTV footage taken of the dockland area around the time of Mr Slater's death had been digitally enhanced, thanks to improved technology, and it was now possible to make out the shadowy outline of another person standing close to a wall. The television screen showed a still image, where the dark outline of a person was visible.

'It's impossible to say if it was a man or a woman,' the inspector said. 'We're satisfied it's not Mr Slater – we have him on camera moments earlier. This person, so far unidentified, was in the vicinity when Mr Slater entered the water. It was a cold night, temperatures below normal, visibility poor due to snow showers, and the quality of the CCTV is not as good as we'd like.'

'It was also the night of a big Manchester Utd match ...' the newscaster prompted.

'That's correct. Mr Slater had told one of his friends he was meeting someone in Arabella's that night. We haven't been able to confirm if he did.'

'Arabella's has since closed?'

'Yes, a few weeks later it went into receivership. I'd like to make a direct appeal to anyone who has information that might help to establish Mr Slater's last movements. Someone must know something. The family are too upset to appeal to the public themselves, but we're keeping them fully informed of all developments.'

Alice couldn't bear to listen any further. She jabbed the remote control and brought up cartoons, much to Chloe's delight. The family. Jay Slater's family. No doubt going through a dark nightmare, revisiting his unexplained death.

◆

The news bulletin was the topic of conversation in the library the following morning.

'I can't imagine what that poor family are going through,' Gwen said.

'It was all over Twitter,' Sharon said. 'There were some vile comments about him taking his own life or being pushed into the water. I hope his family don't see them.'

'He was quite good-looking too. And well educated,' Gwen said, as if this compounded the tragedy. 'His father was a *scientist*.'

'You'd think that if someone had any information they'd have the decency to come forward,' Ralph said.

'Maybe there's a reason why they're not coming forward,' Sharon said.

'They're obviously guilty of something. The police must suspect foul play if they're reopening the investigation.'

Alice moved down to the reference shelves, pretending to be busy even though her vision was blurred. *Foul play*. It had been there all along, lurking in her heart like a poison bud waiting to burst. Now it cracked open, pouring through her veins. If Holly was innocent of any wrongdoing, why was she missing? It was only a matter of time before the police issued a photograph of her and named her as someone they wanted to speak to in connection with the investigation.

And this wasn't a twisty crime novel she was reading: this was her life.

◆

The following evening, when she came out of the library, she ran straight into Damien. She should have expected it; she'd been ignoring his phone calls and texts.

'We need to talk,' he said. He was wearing his navy coat, and he had shadows under his eyes as though he, too, had lost sleep.

'I've nothing to say,' she said, stalking off in the direction of the Dart station.

'Alice, please,' he said, following her.

'Just leave me alone,' she said, stopping for a moment

to push ineffectually at his coat. Her words were saying one thing, but her heart was screaming something else.

It could have been so good. It could have been wonderful and brilliant and oh-so fantastic, but Holly was there between them. Holly with her scary disappearing trick, Holly with her cryptic note under a laptop, her wide-eyed pretences, her lies and more lies, her flirting with Ronan and her photograph taken with a young man who'd died soon after, whose family were devastated. Now when questions needed to be answered, Holly was most conveniently missing. She must have known something was going to break in relation to Jay Slater's case and that Alice would come looking for her – why else had she left a note?

Had she not loved her sister enough? Cared for her, cherished her, even given her her name? Where had she fallen short? How come Holly had been disloyal enough to flirt with Ronan? Why the hell couldn't she have confided in her about her finances, told her what was going on? And why now, when Alice had been on the brink of something wonderful, did Holly have to go and ruin it all? Although, Holly had no way of knowing that Alice had met Damien, who happened to be related to Jay. Or how she felt about him. Or how he'd turned her world around.

Holly was okay, *Holly* was fine, according to her note, but Alice was far from okay.

Damien was still following her, keeping up the pace as she marched as quickly as she could through the evening crowds.

'Go away,' she said.

'Have you spoken to your sister?'

'No.'

'Why not?'

She rounded on him suddenly. 'Don't you get it? I don't want to see you again. How come when the police called to my house they had Holly's name?'

'I didn't give it to them,' Damien said. 'They checked college records and photos, and when they came back to me with her name, I said I'd never met her. Neither did I tell them I knew you.'

'Thanks.'

'They know I was out of the country for a few years, so they didn't expect me to be up to date on Jarlath's social life.' He looked at her closely. 'They don't know that you and I —'

'You and I? There is nothing to know — we're so over.'

They were being buffeted by crowds of commuters heading for the Dart station. Damien took her arm and gently steered her into the porch of an estate agent's office that was closed for the evening. 'Let's talk about this.'

'I've nothing to say. And you shouldn't be talking to me — you could be compromising the investigation. Isn't that what they say?'

He stepped back. 'I thought — oh, Alice.' He turned away for a moment and then he looked at her with concern. 'Surely what's between us is bigger than this? And more important to us than what's going on or what might have gone on with our relatives?'

'Are you for real?' she said, furious and sad all at

once. 'You come into my house. You break the all-time-shitty news that the police believe Holly could have some involvement in the death of your cousin. And I'm supposed to think we're *bigger* than that?'

'Well, yes, I would hope we are.'

'No way, Damien. We're finished. What happened to your cousin is heartbreaking, but I can't believe you'd think, even for a moment, that my sister might have had something to do with this tragedy.' Even as she said the words, a chill ran through her. She knew she was trying hard to convince herself, never mind Damien.

'But you haven't even talked to her yet. She was certainly involved with Jarlath according to the police.'

'I don't believe you. Holly adored her husband. She'd never get involved with another man.'

'Then if she's all that innocent, why hasn't she contacted the police?'

'Either she has no idea what's going on because she's off on holidays somewhere. Or else,' Alice said, ignoring the wobble in her voice, hoping by some miracle this might be true, 'she hasn't come forward because the accident had nothing at all to do with her.'

'Do you really believe that?'

'I love my sister. I trust her implicitly,' Alice said, despite the misgivings crawling around her chest.

'My cousin was loved by his family,' Damien said. 'They're devastated all over again, not that they ever got over it. If there are any answers out there – anyone who spoke to him, any grain of information – they really need to know.'

Alice found it difficult to meet his eyes. They were full of soft entreaty. She remembered how they'd looked at her, full of warm light. She thought she was going to get sick.

'Did you ever meet my cousin as part of Holly's group?' Damien pressed. 'Did you ever come across him at any college activities or any celebrations you might have gone to with Holly?'

'No. Did you?' She tossed the question out, unthinking.

'Yes, I did.'

'*You* did? When?' All her senses prickled.

'It was before the accident, about three weeks. Jarlath was having drinks to celebrate his thirtieth birthday. I hadn't seen him in a while and I was due to start work in Hong Kong so I went along to be sociable and cousinly –'

'Went where?'

'Arabella's. Thing is, Alice, Jarlath mentioned Holly and Ronan to me that night.'

Alice stepped back and stared at him; a fresh stab of anxiety. 'What are you saying?'

'Jarlath got a little agitated when he saw a couple coming up from the corridor to the bathrooms. I happened to be sitting beside him, and I joked about him needing to lighten up.'

'And what made you think he was agitated with Holly and Ronan? If it *was* them.'

It could have been them if it was the night Ronan had mentioned.

The night Jay had followed Holly out to the bathroom.

The night Holly had joked about him stalking her.

Before turning around to flirt with Ronan.

Alice's head tightened with fear.

Damien looked unhappy. 'Jarlath was drunk.'

'What did he *say*?'

'It wasn't very nice. He said something to me about prick-tease Holly going to get what she was asking for, and Ronan could go to hell.'

'And you remembered?'

'It was the last time I saw him, and it stayed at the back of my mind. I left for Hong Kong soon after. I wasn't even home for the funeral – I had just started an intensive training programme in my new job and my family insisted I stay put.'

'And you've known all this time?'

'I didn't think it meant much. Jarlath was pissed, and I never thought to mention it to family the few times I was home, but then you ...'

Something about the sad way he looked at her chilled her to the bone. 'But then,' she said, figuring it out as she went along, 'you met me and I was talking about Holly ... and Ronan ... and the names rang a bell ...'

There was a moment of perfect stillness. Something slammed into her, a fresh pain. Every line of Damien's body screamed regret. She remembered how easily it had curved towards her in bed.

'And you stuck around ... just in case,' she said. 'Please, please, tell me I'm wrong.'

'Alice – look, it kind of caught my attention in the

beginning,' he said in a strained voice. 'I was wondering if there was any link, but then as time went on and I got to know you, it didn't matter. Nothing mattered, except us.'

'Well, fuck you, Damien Maher, fuck you to hell.'

Trembling, she had to forcibly prevent herself from lashing out. She marched off, leaving him standing there, wondering how her feet were moving in formation when her heart was wrenched apart. Wondering how she found the entrance to the Dart station when she was crying; big, heaving sobs; ugly sobs; snotty, noisy sobs that blurred her eyes. She rummaged in her pocket for tissues, letting her commuter ticket fall to the ground in her clumsiness.

She thought she'd been angry with Holly, but it paled in comparison to the incandescent rage she felt for Damien.

CHAPTER 47

THERE WAS SOMETHING ABOUT HAVING every molecule of your life ground into dust, Alice decided. When everything had fallen apart, so that even your skin was stripped back to clean bone, and you'd shed every tear you possibly could, something emerged from the solid core of you. Something raw, and honest and real.

On Thursday morning, her day off, Alice drove to Rose Cottage as soon as Chloe was ensconced in school, just about keeping within the speed limit as she hurtled down the motorway and up the country lanes.

There was still no sign of life in the cottage.

'Holly, where are you?' she called out as she let herself in. 'Come out, wherever you are. What kind of game do you think you're playing? I need to see you, to talk to you.' But her words fell into a still, silent space.

In the living room, she went through the sideboard and bookshelves, looking to see if there was anything at all that would tie Holly to Jay – photographs, documents, college memorabilia. She did the same with the presses in the kitchen, checking them from top to bottom. She went into the bedroom, searching carefully through Holly's bedside locker, her dressing table, the shared wardrobe, Holly's clothes hanging on the left, Luke's taking up the right-hand side.

She checked the locker and wardrobe in the guest bedroom, feeling a clutch in her chest when she recognised her mother's old jewellery box tucked away behind spare blankets. She drew it out, a wave of loss engulfing her. It had been an inexpensive Christmas gift that Alice had bought for Hannah Clarke with one of her first pay packets, and it had housed Hannah's modest items of jewellery, which the sisters had split between them, Holly claiming the box as hers.

She went outside to the tiny shed: garden paraphernalia, paint tins and a stepladder. She brought the ladder inside, placed it beneath the entrance to the attic and took a torch she'd noticed in the kitchen press. Then she lifted the trapdoor and shone the beam around. The attic was small and bare, the eaves of the cottage aligned so it was impossible for a grown person to stand upright.

Then she went back into the living room, mystified.

Apart from Hannah's jewellery box, their wedding album, the same photo of Mum and Holly that sat in Victoria Row and a folder tucked into a kitchen press containing their passports, birth and marriage certificates, plus Holly's university degree, there was nothing at all in Rose Cottage to indicate that Holly and Luke had had a life before they'd moved here. No trace of the ordinary footprints of living. No photographs, documents, bills, receipts, bank statements, tax returns or any kind of paperwork that showed they'd ever lived in Liffey Gate.

Why hadn't she noticed this before now? Then again, her visits to Rose Cottage had been sporadic and she hadn't exactly had cause to notice their lack of evidence of an earlier existence. Holly and Luke must have felt it necessary to eradicate all traces of the life they'd shared in Liffey Gate, just as Holly had done when she'd left Victoria Row, because, Alice's thoughts ran on, she hadn't wanted any reminders of her then crappy life. She clearly didn't want any reminders of Liffey Gate.

She tried to recall what mood Holly had been in around then. After she'd announced she was moving to Rose Cottage, Alice hadn't seen her until Chloe's christening day. It was a day Alice had almost sleep-walked through, still in a fog of exhaustion. Ronan had insisted on a big, lavish christening ceremony, but still feeling weak, Alice had objected.

'Don't you want to have Chloe christened?' he'd said.

'Well, yes, but later on when I feel more up to it. She's only four weeks old. And you don't even go to mass.'

'I'll pay off the priest if it comes to that. I can't wait to show my daughter off to the world. I'll look after everything – you just have to turn up on the day and look beautiful. Get a good massage or facial or something to make you feel better. Get glammed up. Go to one of those personal stylists.'

Ronan had put the day into the hands of exclusive event planners. Alice had been there, yet not there, her expertly made-up face feeling like a mask, her outfit like a strange costume, waves of numbing exhaustion crashing through her. That was the only explanation, she decided, for missing some of the tiny clues Holly might have dropped that all was not perfect in her world. After the private christening ceremony, over a hundred guests celebrated in a five-star Radisson hotel. Then there was the surprising moment when she and Holly had strolled out into the garden, they'd sat on a bench with glasses of wine and Holly had surprised her by giving her a key to Rose Cottage. She was talking about the cottage and her first proofreading commission when Luke came out looking for her, asking her what the hell she was doing, and Alice knew by his tight face that he was barely concealing his anger.

Or could it have been fear?

Holly, she recalled, had been edgy and apologetic. 'We've been chatting about our new home,' she'd said. 'Don't worry, Luke, it's all very innocent.'

Maybe, Alice decided, if she hadn't been so exhausted, she might have taken more heed as to why Holly might have felt the need to assure Luke that her chat with her sister had been innocent.

Innocent? Nothing was innocent about this situation, Alice decided savagely as she took a final look around and left. Not even her sister.

CHAPTER 48

Holly, 2012

'I HAVE A PLAN,' LUKE SAID.

'What kind of plan?'

'A plan to separate Jay from his state-of-the-art-mobile.'

'But I've told you everything that happened, so he can't blackmail me any more.'

'Are you for real, Holly? He could do anything with those photos, anything at all.'

I sank my head down into my hands. I blinked my eyes several times and took a deep breath. It was the evening after Luke had helped me out of the shower. We were having a decent dinner for once, courtesy of Luke's trip to Liverpool, not that I had much of an appetite. We'd even allowed ourselves the luxury of the heating on full blast. The January evening was cold outside, heavy, grey skies turning the river a dark shade of pewter. It reflected my mood.

I stared at Luke. 'And how are we going to get his phone?'

The look Luke gave me turned my insides as cold as the arctic air outside. 'You'll have to do that, Holly,' he said. 'I won't stand a chance with him – he'll be on guard with me, whereas with you ... you have the perfect excuse to talk to him.'

'I don't ever want to lay eyes on Jay Slater again.'

'You'd rather have the threat of what he might do with your sleazy photos hanging over your head, for good?' Luke's face could have been etched in granite.

'I don't want that either.'

'Well then, you'll have to get his phone off him.'

'I'm sure that will be dead easy.'

'I told you, I have a plan ...'

Luke talked me through it, step by step. I was to meet Jay, ostensibly to arrange another night with him to prevent him from running to Luke with the photos. We would meet in Arabella's later that week, the night of a big Premier League match. Arabella's was a mecca for Man United fans and it would be jammed. The match would provide plenty of distraction because Jay was a United supporter. The heaving crowd would work to my advantage, Luke said, going over the finer points.

'He doesn't know I know,' he said. 'Remember that, Holly, otherwise this will all fall apart.'

'I don't think I can do this,' I said. 'It will fall apart anyway.'

'It can't and you have to. After this, the nightmare is over. I'll be seeing my dad, and we can get our lives back.'

Luke went over it again, making sure I knew exactly what to do. It was, he said, the best idea he could come up with to separate Jay – that prick – from his mobile.

'This isn't going to work,' I said. 'I won't be able to stay calm when I see his sneering face.'

'It's the best I can do. I can't sit here and take shit off that pervert. He violated my wife.'

'Don't say it like that.'

'That's exactly what happened, Holly. Now, come on, I won't be too far away. Just do exactly as I say and nothing will go wrong, I promise you.' He stared into my eyes and it reminded me of the times he had told me I was beautiful, the times when we'd be making long, slow love, just the way Luke liked it. I was unable to comprehend how everything, starting from the pink bedroom in Victoria Row, and all the possibilities that life had promised, had run a course leading to this moment. As Luke continued, going over things one more time, I sat frozen in a gut-wrenching fear, telling myself everything would be fine, but not really believing it.

◆

I called Jay and said I needed to see him. Over drinks in Arabella's, I suggested. Thursday night?

'What brought this on?' he said.

'We need to talk about … us,' I said, swallowing my repugnance.

'I hope you're not thinking of trying anything funny.'

'Do you think I'd get away with it if I did?'

'How do I know you haven't told Luke already and that this is some kind of wind-up?'

'Are you joking? Do you want to see me or not?'

'I'll make sure you don't mess me about,' he said. 'I'm taking out some insurance, so no funny tricks, or else.'

'There won't be any funny tricks,' I lied. 'I just want to get this sorted. I'm terrified of Luke finding out,' I continued, staring at Luke as I spoke, who nodded his head.

On Thursday, the weather worsened, temperatures dropping even further. A warning for heavy snow and ice in the west and north of the country was issued and motorists were warned to take extra care on the roads. Snow was also forecast for Dublin. It was weird listening to a weather warning, knowing that it bore little or no relevance to the shattered compass points of our lives. It could rain monkeys for all I cared. All I was worried about was my mission of madness. When it was time to leave the apartment to meet Jay, I begged Luke to forget about it. I didn't care about our ravaged lives. Surely we could make an attempt, however feeble, to patch them up?

He brushed off my arm. 'I'm saving us from more humiliation,' he said. 'If that fucker thinks he can trample us into the ground, he's mistaken.'

We put on our jackets in silence. I was desperate for a drink or two to take the edge off my nerves, but I needed a clear head.

Outside, thick snowflakes slanted sideways in the glow of the street lights, everything distorted in the dirty white gloom. I was filled with foreboding. If I'd known the way things were going to play out that night, I would have given everything I had left in the world to stop us going out the apartment door. I wouldn't have cared about whatever Jay chose to do with the photographs. I would have risen above it and grounded myself in the knowledge that I was alive, I was breathing, the core of me was still there underneath all the crap. I would have told myself that a year, two years from now, it would all have passed, the horrible night with Jay begun to fade, those awful hours with him only a fraction of the whole of my life.

And it might have been fine – everything might have been okay, Jay might still be alive, perhaps married now, with kids, and us not living a half-life of fear and misery – if I hadn't turned the wrong way.

◆

It took us twenty minutes to walk to Arabella's, my head bent against the falling snow, the furry hood of my puffy coat pulled tightly so that as little of my face as possible was exposed to the stinging wet cold. There were just a handful of people scurrying around the pedestrian area by the Grand Canal Dock, huddled into coats and jackets, bent under umbrellas.

Arabella's loomed up out of the murky night like a gaudily lit cruise ship anchored in the middle of a dark, stormy sea.

I said goodbye to Luke. He ran through things, very quickly, one more time. 'You'll be fine, Holly,' he said, 'you know exactly what to do. I'll be watching and waiting.'

I pushed open the door of the pub and was hit with

a cacophony of noise and waves of hot, beer-tinged air, as well as the muggy scent of damp coats and jackets. As Luke had predicted, the venue was packed with football fans cheering on a match that was being relayed from several screens placed at vantage points around the multi-level pub, strategically angled to ensure no one missed any of the action from wherever they were sitting or – most importantly – if they had to go to the bar to order fresh drinks. I shrugged off my hood. As I was squeezing through the throng, someone must have scored a goal because the crowd erupted and I was almost felled by two men in red jerseys who were hugging each other and dancing on the spot. I glanced at a screen to see that Man United were one goal ahead. Then out of the corner of my eye, between the jostling bodies, I saw Jay, sitting on a high stool at a narrow table over at the far side of the pub.

If only, if only ... Afterwards, I marvelled at how easily chance plays a major role in our lives, how a series of seemingly inconsequential actions can come together and trigger the equivalent of an earthquake, destroying the foundations of our lives.

If only I'd turned back then, things might have been okay.

Then again, you could go right back to the start of me and Jay, to the series of insignificant threads that bound our lives together, and unpick it at any point in time. As it was, and as Luke had predicted, no one noticed me when I pushed through the throng, taking a circular route to the bar, where I ordered a double vodka for Jay and a soda water for me, as well as two shots that I poured directly into the vodka, topping it up with some tonic, exactly what Luke had told me to do.

And no one noticed me when I made my way over to Jay, through the knots of bodies and thicket of heaving fans, because everyone's gaze was glued to the screens. As I reached Jay's side, a collective groan thundered around the crowd; grown men thumped their fists and banged glasses off tables, others covered their faces with their hands, in despair at a near miss by their team.

Jay gazed at me with unfocused eyes and a drunken smile. A pint glass half-full of beer and a small glass that I guessed had contained a vodka chaser were lined up on the table in front of him. As was his mobile. That was the first thing Luke had told me to check for. If the mobile had been tucked away in his pocket, I would have had to ask him to show me the photos as a way of getting him to take it out.

'Hey, Holly, nice one,' he said, when I put the drink down in front of him.

I sat up on the stool he had kept for me, so both of us were facing the nearest television screen. I opened the zip of my coat and loosened my scarf, leaving them on despite the warmth of the pub. I wondered where Luke was. He was to come in shortly after me, when I'd have Jay's attention engaged, but keep well away from us.

I forced myself to talk, needing to get close to him to be heard above the escalating noise levels. 'Let me know when you want another one,' I said, conscious that I was on my own with no rehearsed script. It had been impossible to practise the conversation in advance. Be nice, Luke had said, but not too nice.

'Trying to get me to change my mind, are you?' he said. 'This isn't going to work.'

'I didn't think it would,' I said.

'How's Luke anyway?'

'He's okay.'

'Any sign of a job yet?'

'Why?'

'It would mean he'd be out of the way, wouldn't he? How soon can we do this, Holly?'

'You're still going ahead with your threat?' Don't make it too easy either, Luke had said, you don't want to arouse his suspicions.

'What threat?' He grinned, but it was more of a leer and my stomach heaved. 'You know the score, Holly,' he said. 'You know what I want.'

'Will this be the end of it then?'

'Why, are you not enjoying it?' He licked his slobbery lips and looked at me lasciviously.

'I don't like being unfaithful to Luke.'

He leaned in closer. I tried not to recoil. 'But I like you being unfaithful to Luke. That's part of the thrill.'

There was uproar from the crowd as the intensity of the match heightened. His gaze fixed on the television screen, Jay began shouting at the referee, along with half the fans in the pub. It was a good moment to go to the bar for more drinks, more of the same. Jay hardly noticed when I returned to the table, beyond picking up his fresh glass and downing half of it in one go.

Good. Any time from now on. There was bound to be plenty of drama in a Man United match, Luke had said. I just needed to be ready once Jay was drunk enough to be unsteady on his feet. Then everything happened in a split second, although it seemed to take a lifetime. The referee awarded United a penalty, and for the couple of minutes before it was taken there was huge anticipation among the pub crowd. Then finally, as the penalty-taker started his run-up, I glanced at Jay's phone and mentioned needing the bathroom. Jay was staring up at the screen. I slid down off the stool and, squeezing behind Jay, I swiped his phone.

It took him a minute to react, a precious minute that gave me time, a minute in which United scored. Fear gave me the rush of adrenaline needed to squeeze through the throng and head for the back door, just as the crowd erupted once more and rose in a staggering tidal wave of unrestrained joy, accompanied by shrilling whistles, stamping feet and raucous cheers. I glanced behind, through the jam of shifting bodies, and saw Jay, his face contorted with fury, caught up in a wall of fans, arms linked, roaring gustily at the top of their voices.

There would just be enough time, I guessed.

I hurried out through the back door, cold air and snowflakes hitting my face. I was in a short laneway at the back of the pub, littered with industrial refuse bins and wooden pallets. I shoved Jay's phone into my pocket and pulled up my hood, but I was so overcome with fear and anxiety that when I dashed to the end of the laneway, I hesitated. Left or right? I thought the plan had been to turn right, but hadn't Luke reminded me to turn left in those fraught moments when he'd said goodbye to me outside Arabella's?

I turned left. A fatal mistake.

I was supposed to have arrived back around to the front entrance of Arabella's, where Luke would be ready and waiting for me once he'd seen my dash to the back door. The plan was to pass the phone to him, then both of us, together, making a quick escape.

Instead, I found myself in a covered alleyway.

It was unlit, almost pitch black, so that I sensed rather than saw the long narrowness of it. A pale glow struggled through from the far end. Hearing a shout behind me, I hurried towards it, feeling the dank, clammy air and still, silent walls close in on me, tunnel-like, as I half-ran, half-jogged, my breath coming in gasps, my heart thudding, my eyes watering with a mixture of fear, fright and frustration, knowing that Jay was following me. I imagined hands coming out of the wall, clutching and grabbing at me as I hurried along.

And just as I neared the end of the alleyway, when I had to stop to catch my breath on account of the stitch in my side, he caught up with me, pulling at my hood, yanking me back against him.

'You bitch, where's my phone?' His voice was slurred with alcohol but not so much that I couldn't make out the words.

It seemed to burn a hole in my pocket. 'I threw it away,' I fibbed, shaking uncontrollably. 'In one of the big bins outside the pub. It's buried in the rubbish.'

He pushed me face-first against the wall and leaned into me. I caught the smell of his sour breath. Nausea rose in my throat.

'You think you're clever, getting rid of the evidence,' Jay snarled.

'Yeah right,' I babbled.

'You won't get away with this, Holly.'

'I already have. So that shook you.' Keep him talking, my head said, above the thump of my heartbeat in my ears. Luke will come. He'll know something has gone wrong. He'll come looking for me. He *will*.

'There are photos ...' Jay said. 'Big glossy ones. Sent to Luke. I'd love to see his face when he gets them.'

Photos. Vice-like panic gripped my chest.

'See, I didn't trust you, Holly, so I got that covered ...'

I sensed him teetering a little, relaxing his hold on me. It was all I needed. I made a dash for it, and once more I was half-running, half stumbling, down to the end of the alleyway, out of the stale claustrophobia and into open space, where falling snow hit my face like nails and the cold air caught my breath.

The snow shower shifted and rolled, and as it eddied in the wind, I saw glimpses of a long stretch of water tossing and heaving just in front of me. I stood for a moment, steadying my breathing and trying to get my bearings, dizzy with how close I'd come to the edge of the quay. There was no wall between me and the water, just a few well-spaced bollards. The wind screeched and moaned as it gusted. When my vision adjusted, I realised that I had arrived out onto a section of Grand Canal

Dock. It was black dark on this side, faint light filtering across from the far side of the dock and in the distance, over by the theatre, I saw the red gleam of the angled light sticks thrusting up from the ground and, snaking around below them, the green glow that formed part of the iconic street art of the area. Behind me loomed the high walls of an old building.

I heard him then. Jay Slater. Heard his heavy breathing, his uneven gait shuffling closer.

'Where are you, you fucking bitch,' I heard him mutter in a low, slurred voice. The rasp of his breath and thick voice plunged me back to a night I had tried to blank out, but I was there again, in the dense nightmare of it, being pinned to the bed by the weight of his slobbering body, trapped like a butterfly in a jar, wings flapping futilely against the glass.

Something tipped over inside me...

I'm not sure how much later it was – ten, fifteen minutes? – when the snow slowed to a drizzle. I stood flattened against the wall of the old building, frozen in fear, too petrified to move let alone go back up the darkened alleyway, never mind venturing further around the dock. I was fervently praying I'd wake up from this nightmare and be safely tucked up in my bed in Liffey Gate, when a dark figure emerged from the shadows and I jumped.

'Luke?'

'Holly? Are you okay?'

It wasn't Luke. It was Ronan.

CHAPTER 49

Holly, 2012

MY TEETH BEGAN TO RATTLE WITH A mixture of cold and confusion. Hard pellets of shock thumped into my chest. I had to grapple with my tongue to get words out.

'Ronan? What are you doing here?'

'Coming after you. To make sure you're safe.'

'Me? How come? Where were you?' My mouth felt rubbery, and my head was spinning.

'I saw you. Rushing out the back door of Arabella's.'

'What were you doing there?'

'Never mind that now. I saw Jay going out after you. Are you okay?' Ronan took out a mobile and an oblong of light reflected up against his face so that it looked ghostly. His thick auburn hair was plastered to his head. By now, the snow was beginning to thin.

'No. I'll never be okay again, thanks to him,' I said. It wasn't what I wanted to say to Ronan of all people but my brain had turned to jelly and the words slipped out.

'Why? What the hell is going on, Holly?'

'Nothing … I just wish I'd never laid eyes on him.' My voice sounded strangled. Knots of fear tightened painfully in my stomach – where had Ronan been? 'If you were following me what took you so long?'

'I'd only arrived into the pub when I saw you making a dash for the back door, Jay trying to go after you. I was trapped by the crowd myself and by the time I got out the door, there was no sign of you. I thought I saw someone at the end of the alleyway but Alice rang me and the signal was so bad I had to go back up to the laneway to talk to her. Where *is* Jay?'

'I don't know where he went.'

'Where's Luke? Was he with you?'

'Yes, but I don't know where he's got to either,' I said, knowing there was no way I could tell Ronan the truth.

'Fuck's sake. This is weird. I wouldn't have my wife wandering around on a night like this, let alone down here.'

No, he wouldn't. Then again, Ronan would have dealt with Jay all by himself.

'I just went out for fresh air, then when I heard Jay calling me, I took a wrong turn,' I said, unable to stop my voice from shaking.

'Christ. I'll have you home in a jiffy. And stay away from Jay – he seems like a piece of work.' He turned to go up the alleyway.

'I can't go back up there,' I said, immobilised, every impulse in my body screaming out against the thoughts of those dank walls pressing closer and suffocating me again.

'Holly,' Ronan said, a tinge of impatience in his voice, 'I'm not walking all around by the docks. The sooner we get to my car, the sooner I get you home, and the sooner *I* get home to your sister.'

His words eventually filtered past the paralysis in my body. Ronan's car, home, safety of some kind; it was good to be taken care of. I allowed him to hook my arm through his, needing his support as we went into the covered darkness of the alleyway, Ronan using the torch function on his phone so we had some kind of light. We came around by Arabella's. Sounds of revellers drifted on the air and I knew the party would go on for a while yet. Ronan's car was parked down a side road and I was never so relieved to get out of the cold and gloomy night. I collapsed into the passenger seat, the thunk of the door closing securely as Ronan shut it. The scent of new car wafted about me, reminding me of the magical day Luke had collected me from Victoria Row in his jeep. A crippling pain gripped my stomach when I thought of how carelessly we'd shattered those glittery lives.

'Is this new?' I asked, needing to get the memory of Jay Slater's leering face out of my head. As if. I knew already that his image would be branded there permanently.

'Yeah,' Ronan said. 'I wanted more space to make it easy to work a baby seat.'

Lucky, lucky Alice.

I couldn't imagine the luxury of living in financial security, of not having to worry about a roof over your head, let alone enough money for food. It seemed like a far-off dream. I thought of Ronan leaning in to kiss me on the night of his wedding. How terribly stupid I'd been. Alice could never know about that.

'How *is* Alice?' I asked. 'You said she phoned you. Is she okay?'

'She was heading to bed. She feels like a beached whale right now,' he said. 'Her blood pressure is still high, so they'll bring her in before her due date. I could be a daddy before the end of the week.'

I pictured my sister resting in her beautiful bedroom in Leopardstown. One part of me wanted to bawl my eyes out. In another life I would have been rejoicing with Alice that she was soon to bring new life into the world. I would have been a big part of it, looking forward to a tiny little niece or nephew, supporting the sister who'd always loved me, bringing grapes and magazines and fruit drinks to distract her and help pass the time. Instead I was conscious of a great wall of grief and anguish trapped inside me, thanks to my stupidity with Jay and the way I had wrecked everything.

It was a short journey back to Liffey Gate. The snow was turning to slush on the pavements. Some match supporters drifted along, waving bottles and cans of beer. I waited until we were close to Liffey Gate before I spoke again.

'How come you were in Arabella's?'

'I came in to check out my potential investment, I wanted to see for myself how busy it is on match nights. Lucky for you.' He threw me an odd glance. 'I could ask you the same question – what were you and Luke doing there with Jay?'

My head buzzed. 'What makes you think Luke was there?'

'You said Luke was with you.' I felt his sharp glance on my face. 'Are you sure you're okay, Holly?'

'I'm fine,' I said, struggling to keep the wobble out of my voice. Then I remembered Ronan had only seen me going for the back door. 'We weren't actually with Jay. I didn't know he was there until he followed me out.'

'Kind of careless of Luke, losing his precious wife like that.'

'He hasn't lost me,' I said. 'It was too hot in the pub and I felt sick. I bet he thinks I've gone home.'

'Yeah, right,' Ronan said.

The car turned out onto the quays. 'Here we go,' he said, as Liffey Gate came into view. 'Home safe and sound.'

We pulled up outside the apartment block. I was so shattered I didn't think I could get out of the car. I hoped Luke was at home. Ronan watched in silence as I unclipped my seat belt and opened the passenger door. The overhead light came on, and in the pale illuminated wash, his eyes were flat and inscrutable.

'See you soon,' he said.

'I doubt it,' I said.

'Oh? Aren't you going to visit Alice in hospital? Welcome our new arrival? Congratulate us?'

I blinked. 'Of course – yes, I'd forgotten for a moment.'

'I'll forgive you this time,' he said, his voice softened with a hint of warmth.

It almost broke me. I wanted to hang my head. I wanted to weep on his shoulder. I wanted to tell him everything that had happened. Instead I scrabbled together the last fragile crumbs of my composure. 'I'll be talking to Alice,' I said, stepping out of the car, the chill in the air hitting my face, thinking I'd never be warm again. Before I was halfway across the pavement, Ronan was gone, gunning away from the kerb and breaking the speed limit up along the quays.

CHAPTER 50

Holly, 2012

LUKE WASN'T HOME. I CALLED HIS MOBILE but it went to voicemail. I was too exhausted to care, too scarily empty. I hobbled into bed and when he finally arrived, almost an hour later, I was still there, trying in vain to warm my chilled limbs, images from the night playing and replaying in my head, burning into my frozen brain. Every part of Luke was damp and dishevelled, from his hair to his jacket to his shabby jeans. His face was deathly pale and his eyes looked as haunted as I felt.

'What the fuck happened, Holly? I waited and waited for you.'

I pressed my trembling knees together. 'I think I took the wrong turn, in the laneway outside the pub.'

His eyes widened. 'For God's sake, we went over and over it, you were supposed to turn right.'

'Was I? I was so nervous I got confused and I ended up down by the dock.'

'Jesus. You had me worried sick. Did Jay catch up with you?'

My hands gripped the underside of the duvet. 'No. I managed to get away from him.'

'Thank God for that.'

I let out a tiny breath. 'What took you so long to come home? Why didn't you answer my calls?'

'My mobile ran out of power. I've been looking for you all over the place. I even came back here and went out again. How long are you home?'

'A while. Ronan brought me.'

He flinched. '*Ronan?* How come?'

'He'd been in the pub,' I said, looking at his ashen face. 'He had some business there. One of his investments. He saw Jay following me out the back door, so he came after us.'

'Did you tell Ronan what we were doing?'

'I'm not that stupid.'

Luke took off his jacket and slung it over a chair. He took off his shoes, rubbed his face with his hands, then collapsed, fully clothed, on top of the duvet.

'I don't want to see or hear of that shithead again,' he said. His skin was clammy in the lamplight. 'Where is it? His phone? I don't want that trash in our apartment.'

'I threw it into the dock,' I said, my voice trembling as I allowed myself to recall the moment I'd lobbed it into the dark water. 'The photos, everything on it, is gone.'

The photos would never be gone. The images would always be spinning around in my head, mocking me, seared on my heart. Luke put his arms around me, wrapping me tighter in the warmth of the duvet. 'You don't have to worry about Jay's threats any more.'

'Don't I?' I recalled Jay's words in the alleyway about photos on the way to Luke, but I was too fraught to think it through right then.

'Forget about him. We'll be making a fresh start soon. This will all be in the past.'

Luke talked for a short while about moving to Rose Cottage, while I stared at the ceiling. I knew it was our only option. I wanted to get as far away from Dublin as I could. Remote suited me fine. The more remote, the better.

I hardly slept all night. The following morning, when Luke went out to the supermarket, I slipped downstairs and checked our post box in the foyer. There were two brown envelopes marked urgent addressed to Luke, and under them, another larger, slightly crumpled one. Postmarked the day before yesterday, it looked like the envelope was being recycled, the flap sealed with sellotape. It had a window where the intended recipient's name and address should have been visible from the correspondence underneath, but through the opaque paper, all I could make out was a sliver of crimson. Fear slammed into my chest. My fingers burned as I opened it and peeked in.

My eyes blurred. Photographs, four of them, Jay and me. Not only had he carried out his threat, but he had hand-delivered this sometime last evening, as it hadn't been there when Luke checked the post yesterday lunchtime.

Had Luke opened this, he would have got the shock of his life. Even though he knew what we had done, the sordid images of Jay and me, together like this, would have killed him altogether. I closed the box, leaving the urgent post behind, and, clutching the envelope to my chest, I stumbled across the foyer to the lifts. My mind racing, I found it impossible to think where I might conceal this from Luke. Surely not the apartment, which we were beginning to clear out prior to our departure. On impulse, I went down to the basement car park, with a hazy vision of tearing everything up and scattering the pieces into one of the green bins housed there. And then, halfway across, I recoiled. Three women in puffa jackets over gym gear were standing by the bins, deep in conversation about the dire economy, one of them leaning on her box of recyclables. My chest tightened as I skulked around, going across to our car, pretending to check the tyres, and clad in my jeans, jumper and slippers, getting colder and colder in the chilly morning. A few moments later, there was still no sign of them moving. I knew Luke would be home soon and I had to get back to the apartment before him – otherwise he'd be full of questions as to where I'd been.

And I wasn't capable just then of any more lies.

I edged slowly around a corner, swallowing back my dizziness, passing by the steel utility cabinet that was encased in the wall. I stood for a moment catching my breath. I heard the lift doors rattle open. Someone laughed. Footsteps approached. Then I spotted it – a long, narrow chink of space between the side of the cabinet and the surrounding wall. Even though my fingers were numb by now, I managed to slide the envelope and its inflammatory contents into the space until it was practically unnoticeable.

That would have to do for now. I'd retrieve it later and dispose of it properly.

I got back to the apartment seconds before Luke.

That afternoon Luke and I went through the inventory of the apartment, trying to figure out what was ours and what had been part of the rental pack – we had a week's grace before we moved out. I went through the hours in a daze, my fingers slithery with anxiety, my head pounding, struggling to breathe as images from the previous evening shrieked through my head. Then that night, twenty-four hours after he'd chased me down an alleyway, Tara rang, her voice hysterical with grief.

Jay was dead. His body had been found. In the water. In Grand Canal Dock.

I dropped the mug I'd been holding and it shattered on the floor, while a silent scream of fear coalesced inside me. Our television had been sold, so Luke brought up the late-night news on his laptop, and we stared at the images: the docks area shadowy and dark except for pockets illuminated by the glare of temporary arc lights where they glinted across the murky depths of the water; the reporter saying that a body of a male had been recovered from the water earlier that night – it could have been there for up to twenty-four hours and had been identified as Jarlath Slater, a thirty-year-old Dublin man. I stumbled out and stood on our small balcony, heedless of the cold as I hugged myself and stared at the slate-grey river flowing past.

Luke came out behind me. 'It'll be okay, we'll be fine.'

I leaned back against him. I knew it would never be fine again.

'It's my fault,' I said.

'Don't be ridiculous. It was an accident. You had nothing to do with it.'

Oh yes, I had, and the truth of what happened that night was lurking tightly inside me like an unspeakable, malignant poison. Luke knew I was distressed, although he didn't know the full reason why. He did his best to comfort me. He opened the last bottle of wine. In bed, he wrapped the duvet around me and enclosed the thick roll of it and me in his arms, holding me as tightly as he could. He told me over and over that I wasn't to upset myself, neither of us could have foreseen such a tragedy. He would always love me. I was his sweet Holly. I would be safe with him. From now on, he would always protect me.

The following day the police released a statement. According to information they had, Mr Slater had planned to be in Arabella's that evening. While it appeared to be a tragic accident, the police were appealing for anyone who might have been with Jay that day or evening, or anyone who was in the vicinity of Arabella's or the dock, and who might have seen him, to come forward and help with their enquiries. My throat and chest were sore, as if scoured raw.

'I hope you're not thinking of doing anything reckless like going to the police,' Luke said. He had dark circles under his eyes, emphasising his pale-grey skin.

'Why not?' I asked tonelessly, my insides gripped with anxiety.

'What difference will it make to Jay, or his family?' he said. 'Nothing whatsoever. We've nothing to say that would help with an enquiry. God knows what can of worms we'll open up if they start to question us about that evening. Or our relationship with him. What he did to you. It would be all over the media.'

'I might have been seen,' I said, dredging one of my fears out into the open, 'in the pub, with him.'

'Who's going to remember for sure? The crowd were all glued to the match, and they were soaked with drink. Like Jay himself. Anyway you were only with him for a short while.'

'What about the time I had the row with Jay? In the café? When he showed me the photos? I was really angry.'

'We'll just have to hope no-one remembers that.'

Then the knowledge that Ronan had seen me with Jay crashed into my head. He hadn't been drinking. He'd be what you could call a reliable witness: R.L. Russell, Solicitor. He must have heard the news about Jay, but he hadn't contacted me.

'What about Ronan?' I said.

'Shite. I'll talk to him,' Luke said. 'I'm sure he won't want his name involved in this.'

◆

On Sunday, we finished going through everything in the apartment. 'I want to get rid of as much as possible,' I said, 'cut away the past. And I want to make sure,' my voice broke, 'that Jay didn't leave anything else here, anything at all to link us to him.'

'Anything else?' Luke looked at me closely.

I bit my lip and felt heat rush across my face.

'Holly? What is it? What else could there be?'

Lots, I wanted to say. *If only you knew*. It all rose up inside me, the gut-twisting fear and alarm that had slowly been choking my head and my heart since Thursday night. The terrible silence that gripped my voice and held it hostage.

'Come on, spit it out,' Luke said.

I knew he'd keep pestering me so I told him about the photographs I'd hidden, reckoning it was the lesser of two evils. I'd already tried to retrieve them, when Luke had met his father and accountant to go through our mountain of debt, but my attempts had been unsuccessful. In coaxing out the envelope, I'd inadvertently pushed it in further, and it had slipped back somewhere into the dark recesses of the gap. Luke was furious but calmed down slightly when we went to the basement and I showed him the spot. Even he agreed that it would be impossible to guess anything was concealed in that narrow crevice.

But if I thought our financial worries had been a nightmare, I was wrong. The real torment was Jay's death, and that was never going to end.

You can come back from financial worries, but you cannot come back from the grave.

CHAPTER 51

Alice

SHE WOULD HAVE TO TALK TO DAMIEN, ALICE decided, no matter how difficult it was. When she'd texted him to ask if he could spare time to see her, his reply, in the affirmative, had been terse.

Now it was lunchtime on Friday, and they were sitting on a bench in Merrion Square Park, like two strangers, while the sun smiled benignly and red and yellow tulips exploded with colour in the shafts of light.

'So how come it's okay to talk to me now?' Damien's voice was neutral, his eyes devoid of expression.

'It's not okay for me,' Alice said, 'not after the stunt you pulled, pretending to be kind to me because you were interested in Holly and Ronan.'

'I wasn't pretending to be kind,' he said. 'Please don't think that of me. The names caught my attention in the beginning, then around the time we went to the Convention Centre, and you spoke of Holly living in Liffey Gate, I guessed she was the woman my cousin had been talking about in the pub that night. I tried to tell you once or twice, but I loved what was happening between us, Alice, and I didn't want anything to darken the connection I felt between us. As far as I was concerned it had no relevance to us anyway. So if it's not okay,' he faced her, 'why did you want to see me?'

'I'm concerned about Holly.'

Concerned? More like angry, furious, exasperated at the situation she was now in thanks to Holly's disappearing trick, and the way she'd been lying to her all these years, making out everything had been fine when, quite clearly, it hadn't. She hadn't wanted to see Damien – she could have done without this fresh reminder of all she had lost – but she was desperate for information of any kind.

'Are there any updates on the police investigation?' she asked. 'I accept Holly was … with your cousin, but I'm still trying to figure out what's going on.'

'So am I,' Damien said.

He looked at her, his soft hazel eyes almost stopping her breath. All she could think of right then was the curve of his smooth shoulders, the indent of his backbone, his touch on her bare skin, his limbs coiled around hers. She inhaled a thin stream of air. Meeting him in the park on a sunny Friday lunchtime had not been a good idea.

'What kind of person was your cousin?' she asked, her mouth grappling awkwardly with words. Had Holly been genuinely attracted to him, she'd been asking herself. Did Luke find out? Was he afraid Holly might have told Alice about it the day of the christening?

'I only knew Jarlath on the surface,' Damien said, 'saw him at family gatherings, that kind of thing. He was the mischievous one, always looking for a laugh, a messer, but you got the feeling he wasn't happy. His older sister, Joyce, was the intelligent one, star pupil, she could do no wrong. Jarlath was different …'

'In what way?'

'He wasn't academically inclined like Joyce. I thought it might be tough on him, living in his sister's shadow. He knew he disappointed his father, but Jarlath acted as if he didn't give a shite. Now I can't help thinking about what could have been going on underneath. But Holly was certainly with him. You see, Alice …' Damien gave her a look that cut her to the core.

'What?' she asked, supressing a shiver.

'Please keep this to yourself but the police have advised my uncle that the evidence found in Liffey Gate linking Holly and Jay are photographs of both of them together. They were found in an envelope. The police need to talk to Holly to rule certain things out on account of …'

'Account of what?'

'Look, Alice, I was hoping all this would come to nothing, it's a heap of tough shit.'

'Just tell me everything. Please. I need to know.'

Something in his eyes made her brace herself. 'The sexual content, the tawdry nature of them,' he said.

A dark dread squeezed her innards. Office workers strolled by, enjoying some sunshine on their lunch break, and Alice marvelled that they were innocent of all this. 'What do they need to rule out?'

'For example, was Holly a willing participant? Or exploited in some way?'

'Jesus.'

'The family are going through torture,' Damien said. 'Jarlath had been avoiding them for a couple of weeks before the accident, and he'd just broken up with his girlfriend. He'd been flat-sharing with some guys from Limerick, and they hadn't seen much of him either. He told Cormac, one of them, a couple of weeks before the accident, that he was going to do something he'd wanted to do for years, but it might upset some people and there could be consequences, not that he'd care.'

'God.'

'He'd been absolutely sozzled, and laughing about it – too wildly, Cormac thought. He even joked about who might turn up to his funeral if anything happened to him. Cormac thought it was just drunk talk. As well as that, Jarlath didn't appear in work that last week. When the family heard all this afterwards, they couldn't help wondering …' He swallowed.

'Couldn't help wondering what?'

'None of this has been released to the media, of course, and the case was ruled an accidental drowning, but the family always wondered if Jarlath might have planned to take his own life that night.'

'Oh gosh.' Alice felt tears pooling at the back of her eyes.

'You see,' Damien said, 'Cormac had sent Jarlath a text the day before to say he didn't know if he'd be around to watch the Man United match with him, but Jarlath said it was okay, he was meeting someone in Arabella's. But no one has come forward. The police checked activity on his mobile but there was nothing unaccountable on that. Mostly work stuff. Was he really meeting someone or was it just an excuse to put Cormac off? Had he planned to be alone that night? These were the questions the family were plaguing themselves with seven years ago. Now that the case has been reopened, it's like a scar being ripped apart again. And the sordid nature of the photos have raised more issues. Did Jarlath mean something completely different when he spoke to Cormac about his funeral? Was there any chance he was involved with prostitution or something else shady?'

Alice's mouth filled with the cold, hard taste of fear. She thought she'd hit rock bottom before, but it had been nothing like this; even the sight of the glowing flower beds was a painful assault on her senses.

'What consequences was he talking about?' Damien continued. 'Had he got himself into trouble? There was a date franked on the envelope, the day before Jarlath died.'

'Who was the envelope addressed to?' Alice asked tonelessly.

'They don't know. It was one of those window envelopes. The address would have been included on whatever document it originally held. It was stuck in beside a utility cabinet in the basement.'

'I wish I could get my hands on Holly.'

'Have you any idea where she might be?'

'She's not left the country, I know that much – her passport is still at home.' She told him about her calls to Rose Cottage and the note under the laptop cover. 'I keep imagining the worst,' she said. 'Maybe Luke caught Holly in bed with Jay, or something similar, and he was so enraged he –' She stopped, swallowed. 'It sounds mad. Luke seems an ordinary enough guy, kind of wishy-washy if anything, but I sometimes thought he was a little possessive with Holly ...' Alice paused. 'I shouldn't be telling you this.'

'I'm not going to go ratting to the police,' he said, so gently that it almost unravelled her. 'You won't know anything for sure until you talk to your sister. But, Alice, surely we can find some way around this, the two of us?'

'That's impossible. We're sitting on different sides of this ... this awful catastrophe. There might as well be a ten-foot barbed-wire fence between us.'

'There doesn't have to be.'

'But there is.'

'You're not your sister, Alice,' he said. 'You're *you*. You're not responsible for Holly. Are you going to walk away from what we could have together because of her?'

'Families come first and I'm on Holly's side.'

'I understand you're worried about her, but don't I mean anything to you?'

'Please don't ask me that, Damien. I've looked out for Holly from the moment she was born – I can hardly stop now.'

'At the expense of your own happiness? At the expense of us?'

'She's my sister,' Alice said, digging her fingernails into the palm of her hand. 'I could never be happy with you after ... the suggestion that she could be involved with your cousin's death. It would always come between us. Anyway,' she said, forcing a careless tone into her voice, 'what have we ever had? A night when I spilled my guts? Too many dates when I've bent your ears with my silly conversation? It was fun while it lasted but it was only a few weeks.'

She got to her feet, catching a glimpse of his wintry eyes. It was over, whatever there had been. Between them sat his cousin, and Holly, and a dark forest of pain and family heartache. Even if it transpired that Holly had nothing to do with Jay's death, she'd act as a constant reminder to Damien of his cousin, thanks to the photographs and the questions they had posed. Hardly able to breathe for the pain in her chest, she walked away from him as quickly as she could.

CHAPTER 52

Holly, 2012

JAY'S FUNERAL PASSED IN A BLUR: THE seagrass coffin at the top of the aisle, pews spilling over with people, the other side of Jay's life revealed, rounded and colourful. Gifts brought to the altar included his guitar, CDs, a notebook with handwritten songs and poetry. His clever sister, also musical, sang a verse of 'Forever Young', breaking down in tears. His father, in a quiet voice, paid tribute to the son who'd always followed his own star, sometimes his lone star, and who'd regularly visited his grandfather in a nursing home, playing his guitar for him. Then the cloying scent of incense, the heart-wrenching sight of Jay's family walking back down the aisle behind the coffin. Outside, in a day bursting with early February sunshine, straggling queues waited to pay respects to his family. I didn't dare join them.

Some of the old college gang were there. I'd been holding tightly to Luke's hand, but we were separated by the crowd, and that was when Ronan found me.

'What are you doing here?' I asked. I was facing the sun and I lifted my hand to my forehead to shade my eyes. He moved slightly to block out the sun from my face, his figure like a dark and powerful bulwark between me and the light.

'Same as you, I guess,' he said.

Nausea swelled in my belly and chest. It was beginning to become a permanent fixture in my life.

'He won't be pestering you again.' Ronan's face was impassive as he stared down at me.

'Shut up,' I said.

'I'll let that pass,' he said, 'I know you're bound to be feeling fragile. And I won't tell Alice about the other night. It would only upset her.'

'Not as much as some other incidents between you and me might upset her,' I retorted. 'But I won't tell her about those either.'

'All things considered, they're best forgotten about.'

'Congratulations, by the way. Chloe is beautiful.'

In the way that life can be hideously cruel in one breath, and in the next, breathtakingly beautiful, two days after Jay's death was confirmed, Alice was admitted to hospital and had given birth to Chloe. I'd been to visit, and had lifted the small weight of Chloe into my arms, but under the surface of my big, bright smile, my adoring voice and the joy with this perfect new life, my tattered emotions were jangled up in some kind of nameless, creeping dread. I hadn't seen Ronan then – he'd been in Dundrum Town Centre, buying up most of it for his beautiful new daughter.

'Thank you,' Ronan said evenly. 'I know. She's the image of me.'

'Does Alice know you're here?' I asked.

'No. Does she know you're here?' he countered.

'She does.' I'd mentioned to Alice that I was going to the funeral of an old college mate, who'd died suddenly.

'When the news broke, she didn't seem to think Jay had a connection to you.'

I looked him straight in the eye. 'What connection?'

He tipped his head in salute. 'No flies on you – eh, Holly?'

'What are you really doing here?' I asked.

'I guessed you'd be here. I told you, I like to make sure family are okay. I was talking to Luke and he said you weren't going to go to the police. Is that still the case?' His question was ultra-casual, but I knew it was the only reason he was talking to me.

'Yes. I've nothing to say to them.'

'Me neither. But what do you think,' he said, his voice silky, 'really happened to Jay?'

'What do you mean "really"?' I stared at Ronan. 'He was hammered. He went too close to the edge. It was a horrible night, an accident waiting to happen.'

'On that we're agreed. By the way, the CCTV in Arabella's was on the blink. They didn't think it was worthwhile forking out to have it fixed in case the place went into receivership. As well it might. I have no interest in that investment any more.'

I remained silent, absorbing that information.

'How are things with you and Luke?' He gave me a shrewd look, and I wondered how much he knew about our financial difficulties, considering all his connections.

'We're moving,' I said. 'Out of Dublin altogether. A fresh start, in a cottage belonging to Luke's family. I haven't told Alice yet. I'm sorry I'm moving so far away from her when she's just had Chloe, but –' I paused. There was nothing further I could bring myself to say.

'Alice will have her hands full with the baby,' Ronan said. 'A fresh start will be good for you both. It's probably for the best.'

Luke came over then to congratulate Ronan, and with the niceties taken care of, Ronan stalked off. We hung around chatting to Tara and Conor for a few minutes, then gradually people began to disperse.

'Right,' Luke said, 'let's get out of here.'

I stood still for a moment, unable to move. It seemed crazy that Luke and I had the ability to just walk away, go back to what was left of our lives and try and pick up the pieces. I was still alive and breathing, whereas Jay – it was all over for him. His cold, stiff body was about to be buried in a deep hole in the ground, to lie there forever more.

The jeep edged slowly out of the church grounds in the thick funeral traffic. I thought it was slightly ridiculous that drivers were drumming on steering wheels, impatient to get back into their busy lives, while the person they'd been here to pay their respects to was going nowhere except to a still graveyard adjacent to a traffic-snarled motorway. I repeated Luke's mantra silently. Going to the police would never bring Jay back. It would make no difference to him or what happened, make no difference to his family, but it would ruin the rest of our lives and sour Alice's happiness with her beautiful new baby. We'd already been through a hell of sorts, Luke and I. I don't think I could have taken any more and remained sane.

Then we accelerated out on to a sun-soaked dual carriageway, where the grass verge was bursting with early spring daffodils.

CHAPTER 53

Holly, 2012–now

AFTER JAY'S FUNERAL, WE HANDED BACK THE jeep, ridding ourselves of that symbol of our shiny new life, just as that shiny new life had dissolved. Luke's father transferred money into our bank account, and we sat down with his accountant, figuring out the best way forward. A friend of Luke's, who was Sydney-bound, sold us his twelve-year-old Fiat Punto at a knock-down price.

Nine months after Jay's death, a verdict of accidental death was delivered at the inquest. Toxicology reports showed a high level of alcohol in Jay's system. There was mention of CCTV footage on a camera outside a warehouse along by the docks, but it was too grainy to confirm if the person in it was Jay. No witnesses had come forward to confirm whether or not he'd been in Arabella's that night, and the pub had no CCTV available. The report didn't merit more than a paragraph in the newspaper – all that tragedy, heartbreak and grief reduced to a few lines of print – and once again I thought how fragile and inconsequential our lives can be.

It was only then that I woke up from the shocked limbo of fear that had encased me since the night of Jay's death. It was only then that the nightmares began in earnest, their frequency and terrifying intensity swamping me, and by then we were well ensconced in Rose Cottage. I secured freelance proofreading assignments, mainly tutorials and business publications, thanks to contacting two of my former managers who had left Clery Consulting before I'd been fired and were happy to recommend me. Luckily I had managed to hold onto my laptop and I was able to work from Rose Cottage. Luke also worked from home, picking up IT contract work. Occasionally he had to go to Dublin for meetings, but most of his business interactions happened through email or conference calls. Once a week, we drove into Kilkenny for groceries, preferring to shop in an anonymous shopping centre rather than locally. I didn't want to become friendly with the locals, who might start asking questions about where we'd come from – a life I didn't want to talk about. By degrees, as one year slid into the next, our debt began to reduce, and occasionally we went out for lunch or an early-evening meal.

We found our way back to each other in bed too, Luke sometimes bathing me beforehand, calling me his sweet Holly as he sponged my body slowly and carefully in the big claw-footed bath.

We surprised ourselves by developing green fingers. Great Aunt Nora had been a keen gardener, and when we had settled in a little, we took it upon ourselves to bring the acre of land around the cottage back to life, Luke tending the vegetables and cutting the grass, while I looked after the roses and flower beds. I found the physical work, even the act of getting soil under my fingernails, and watching the fall of rain, the slow bloom of flowers, immensely therapeutic. I didn't like leaving Rose Cottage. I was grateful for the remote peacefulness and slow rhythm of the days, going out into the garden every morning no matter the weather to take in great gulps of clean, fresh air, right down to my toes. I watched the changing seasons paint different colours across the landscape, sunshine and clouds in turn drifting over mountains and valleys. But while by day the peaceful surroundings of Rose Cottage and the quiet miracles of nature helped to soothe my spirit, my night-times were filled with anxiety and three-o'clock-in-the-morning horrors.

Often, I was still running down that alleyway, mocking skeletal hands reaching out to trap me. Only now there was no end to it, and Jay's face was everywhere, looming in the darkness, pale and swollen and running with water. I would wake up half-sobbing, half-breathless, but I never got out of bed because, outside, the country nights were filled with pitch black. I stayed under the covers, nuzzling as close to the warmth of Luke's body as I could, without disturbing him, until the break of light.

Two years after Jay's inquest, I heard from Tara that Jay's grandfather had died, then his parents and sister left their home and jobs and moved out to New Zealand, where his mother had family ties. I didn't see much of Tara – by now she and Conor had two daughters under two years of age and were busy juggling the crèche, the crazy commute from north County Meath into the city centre and their day jobs. We spoke on the phone occasionally, and she was envious of the peace and flexibility of our lives, and the freedom to come and go as we liked without fear of a baby going into meltdown mode while another one puked all over our clothes. I laughed, thinking how little she really knew, thinking of how different our conversations were to those on the long summery evenings we'd sat on the balcony in Liffey Gate, sipping pomegranate Bellinis, chatting about clothes and holidays, planning illustrious futures. Thinking of the time I'd once had a longing for a baby, but now I felt too broken inside to consider it.

We were three years in Rose Cottage when Alice came down for a weekend visit with Chloe, though she ended up staying only one night. She clearly wanted to talk to me in confidence, but Luke put paid to that, sticking to me like glue the whole time. I'd had a few bad nights in a row and he was afraid I'd let my guard down and blurt out something about Jay. I felt removed from Alice both physically and emotionally and I know she sensed it. I cried after she left, thinking of the hurt look on her face as she'd gone out the door, hating the distance between us. A distance I couldn't bridge.

The next few years slid past quietly, a chink of light appearing at the end of our debt-ridden tunnel. Then the past finally caught up with us when the police reopened the file on Jay. Getting away to west Cork, Luke said, would give us precious time and space away from media headlines and police appeals, when I might be tempted to do something silly.

He thought it might all blow over.

I didn't think any such thing.

CHAPTER 54

Holly

LUKE AND I HAD ALMOST THREE WEEKS IN our west Cork hideaway: a surreal capsule of time. We went for long walks on deserted beaches, we listened to CDs and read books, and made slow, tender love most nights, Luke telling me I was still as beautiful as ever. I pretended we were back in the early days of Liffey Gate before anything went wrong. We stared at each other, we inhaled each other's scent, tasted each other's skin, absorbing each other through every cell in our bodies, Luke at his slow and sensual best, as though every night was the first time. Or the last. Because I had the fateful sense I was storing up a mountain of love and precious memories against an unknown future.

I knew we were fooling ourselves if we thought we could hide there indefinitely. Running through the back of my mind on constant ticker tape were dark thoughts of Liffey Gate and Jay. On a practical level, our money would run out and my gut clenched at the thoughts of being in that penniless situation again, scrabbling for enough cents for a litre of milk. The reality was that the mobile park would soon open for the summer season.

Families would arrive who came year on year, friendly but inquisitive. Luke's parents would find out that we were there – and then what?

Luke knew our idyll was over when he saw he'd missed two calls from his father and a text to call him urgently. He hadn't been answering his phone, any more than I had, but he couldn't ignore those. According to his father, the local police had dropped in to the pub in Fermoy and were asking questions about him.

'Dad said it was all very casual,' Luke said. 'He thinks I ignored some parking fines or forgot to show my insurance. They were confirming that we're still a couple and our address in Rose Cottage. They asked if we were away, or had gone on holidays …'

'They've made a connection with us and Jay,' I said.

Luke's face was bleak. 'We don't know for sure.'

'They have. Alice has sent me messages that I've ignored. They've also called to her.'

He eyed me. 'I thought your phone was switched off.'

'I had it on silent,' I said, my throat dry. 'I saw her texts but I didn't answer them. If they release my photo, it might jog some memories, even the time I had the row with Jay in the café. We can't stay here forever.'

'I want to keep you safe.'

'You always have.'

He stroked my cheek. 'Soulmates. Don't ever forget.'

On Friday evening, I walked along the clifftop, my hair tugged in a wild, crazy dance. I gulped the salty, breeze-tattered air, watched the swooping down-dives of the raucous gulls and the crash of huge Atlantic rollers thundering onto the long curve of golden sand, just as they had been doing for aeons and would continue to do long after Luke and I had passed through this world. I felt like a tiny, inconsequential dot in the great immensity of the universe. I was infused with the energy of just being alive. I could see. I could feel. I could breathe. Right at that moment, I was whole and everything was okay.

And in the space of a breath, it all seemed so simple. I could tell Alice everything, from the beginning, right to the end. Unload my heavy burden and share it with her. Why had I run from her? Alice had always looked out for me, cared for me; always put my needs before her own. Alice had been my second mother and surrogate father, all through my childhood and beyond. Why had I turned from her in my time of greatest need? Why hadn't I unburdened myself and told her the horrible truth?

Alice had always loved me with perfect and unconditional love. She would soothe me and rub my back and tell me it was okay, as she'd done countless times in the bedroom in Victoria Row when I'd been disturbed in the night. Whatever dark secrets came out of my mouth, I knew beyond the shadow of a doubt that she'd be on my side.

Just as Luke had been, when I'd told him the truth about the night Jay Slater died.

CHAPTER 55

Holly, 2012

LIFFEY GATE; OUR LAST NIGHT. LUKE AND I sitting on the floor of the living area, propped up against the wall, the remnants of our lives strewn around us, bundled into black sacks and cardboard boxes. Outside, the surface of the river sparkled in the glowy night-time lights as it surged to the open sea. I knew I'd never feel the same lift in my heart whenever I looked at it from now on, because I knew that, underneath the glittering surface, the depths were full of murky blackness. Just like my life. I knocked back more of the wine Luke had bought as a farewell toast to ourselves, and I found myself unable to contain the malignant darkness in my head any more.

Luke was terribly silent as my jerky words echoed, while I tried to recount the exact sequence of events on the night Jay had died. As I spoke, I was back there on that cold, snowy night, hurrying out of the pub ahead of Jay, dashing down the long, dank alleyway, where he caught up with me momentarily until I ran again, out into space where freezing cold wind whipped up across the basin of the dock, and flurries of slanting snow tore at my face and froze my lungs.

Where, behind me, loomed the high walls of an old building.

Where I heard him coming towards me, Jay Slater, his heavy breathing, his uneven gait shuffling closer, calling me a fucking bitch.

Where something tipped over inside me.

I ran at him in the darkness, taking him by surprise, cannoning into him and pushing him backwards with such force that he banged his head off the wall. Yelping in pain, he slumped down. I kicked him. Once, twice, three times, not sure where my foot was connecting with his body. Trembling from head to toe, I stopped to catch my breath. From the sounds he was making, I sensed rather than saw him getting clumsily to his feet. I stepped away from him and as gingerly as I could, I moved out towards the glint of churning water. Clutching a bollard for safety, I took Jay's mobile out of my pocket and threw it into the dock. The sound of it hitting the water was scarcely discernible above the whine of the wind, the blanketing fall of snow, and the churning water splattering against the quay wall.

'I'll get you, you filthy cow.'

'I'm here,' I said, clinging to the bollard. 'Come and get me, you wanker. Come on, I dare you.' Whatever had tipped over inside me was pouring through my veins like an unstoppable flood. I didn't recognise myself.

'My head ... what d'you do that for, fuck's sake.'

I heard him groan, mutter an expletive, his footsteps coming towards me where I stood by the water's edge.

I could have warned him. I could have told him to go back. Instead, silently and slowly, I moved away to safety until I was standing once more against the wall of the building and I left him to his fate. The breeze gusted and the snow shower intensified. I strained to listen, but I couldn't hear anything above the roar of the wind and the rattle of snowflakes hitting windows up behind me. I stood flattened against the wall of the old building, frozen in fear. The snow thinned out.

And then Ronan came along.

Had Jay fallen into the dock by then? Had he slipped into the water, hammered drunk, disorientated by the crack to his head, never mind my sharp kicks, deliberately lured too close to the edge by the sound of my voice? Hadn't I sent him to his death? These were the questions I desperately asked Luke.

Why hadn't I told Ronan? We could have shouted out Jay's name, and if he hadn't responded we could have called for help there and then. But even had we done that, would it have been too late? The water would have been freezing and Jay, wasted, hardly standing a chance.

Or had Jay wandered off, further up the dock, before drifting too close to the edge and falling in? Either way, I was responsible.

When I finished talking, the echo of my words bounding off the apartment walls, Luke held both my hands in his, gripping them firmly.

'Listen carefully to me,' he said. 'You must never tell anyone about this. Put it out of your head altogether. If you mention one word to anyone, you could end up being cross-examined on a witness stand, and you wouldn't be able for it, Holly. You're too soft and gentle. You might say all sorts of things. Wrong things. Silly things. Words that could get you into trouble and ruin the rest of our lives.'

A mountain of tears was lodged in my chest, but I couldn't cry. 'I feel so guilty … if only I hadn't been there that night. If only I hadn't bashed his head off the wall. If only I'd warned him.'

'You can't risk saying one word about this to anyone,' Luke said. 'It will lead back to what happened between you and Jay – do you think you could stay silent about that? What would the media make of it? It humiliates both of us.'

'Luke – it wasn't like that.' Or was it?

'You agreed to have sex with Jay for money. How does that make me look? Don't tell me that's not humiliating. You might as well have sliced off my balls with a razor blade.'

My heart surged into my throat. 'So it's about you, now, and your pride. A man is *dead*, because of me.'

'It was an accident. That's all you have to say to yourself, Holly. Maybe that bang on his head didn't help but it's not as if you actually pushed him in.'

'No. But I must have made him fall in, and none of this would have happened if he hadn't been chasing me for his phone.'

'Which you wouldn't have had to take if he hadn't got those filthy pics. Which wouldn't be there if you hadn't tempted him in the first place.'

'Hang on Luke,' I cried, 'I did that for us, to help us out of a nightmare.'

He gathered me close. 'I didn't mean to upset you. I'm just explaining everything the way the police could see it,' he said, his voice gentle now, almost hypnotic. His love voice. 'It was an accident, Holly,' he repeated. 'You didn't do it on purpose. If you went to the police, what would they make of it? They have a way of twisting things.'

'But his family – surely they should know?'

'What about *your* family, Holly? Me, your husband, Alice with her new baby. And Ronan – he wouldn't take kindly to having Alice's family dragged into the courts. If you said the wrong thing you could end up in jail. Ronan might take it out on Alice. She wouldn't deserve that. Neither would you deserve that horrific experience. What you need to remember is, whatever you say or don't say, it won't change a thing. It'll never bring Jay back. Anyway, how do you know the police won't try to point the finger at me?'

'Why should they?' I said. 'It had nothing to do with you.'

'Jay's death might have nothing to do with you either, Holly. Maybe you lured him too close to the edge and with that head injury …' he paused. 'You'll never know for sure. After what he did to you, I wouldn't blame you. But the police could just as easily try to pin some of the blame on me.'

'You? Why?'

'Circumstantial evidence. Accessory to the case.'

The words hung there, dripping into the silence like blood. Then Luke spoke again, his voice soft, his words all the more alarming. 'Think of the case they could build against me,' he said. 'Me, out for revenge, feeling emasculated that the little wanker had fucked my beautiful wife having stalked her for years, taking disgusting photos that sickened me. They could suggest we set it up between us, that you lured him down to the docks and I followed.'

'But we didn't. You couldn't have. You're my Luke – you wouldn't hurt a fly.'

He put his hand on the nape of my neck, caressing it in slow circles as he spoke. 'You wouldn't hurt a fly either, my sweet Holly. But see how easy it is to do something irrational if you're pushed to the limits. I'd rather have subjected Jay to some long-drawn-out torture and watched his face while he suffered. Still, if the police checked my movements, it wouldn't look good. I wasn't home until well after you, was I? They might ask what I'd been doing all that time.'

'But you were looking for me.'

'I know, but I've no way of proving that. So promise me you'll forget everything you told me,' Luke said. 'Put it out of your head. Let me protect you from now on.'

I was glad to leave Liffey Gate and disappear into the depths of the country. I wanted to disappear into a tiny dot. I wanted to go asleep and never wake up.

◆

Seven years later, I still wanted to go asleep and never wake up. I took a final look along the length of the wild west Cork beach, a gulp of clean, fresh air and turned down the track to the mobile home.

'We have to go back,' I said to Luke. 'We can't live like this any more.'

Luke sank his head into his hands. 'We've had this conversation already. Nothing has changed.'

'Things *have* changed. The police are looking for us. They called to your dad. They've also called to Alice.'

Luke rubbed his face and sighed. 'I can't do this.'

'Jesus, Luke, we have to do something. We can't ignore the police.'

'If you say the wrong thing, we could both end up in trouble.'

'I'm already in trouble,' I said, facing him. 'This is destroying me. I have nightmares … I still see Jay … They've never gone away and it's wrecking my head. There are times when I feel like the worst person alive. Let me talk to Alice.'

'You can't tell Alice,' Luke said. 'You promised not to breathe a word.' He raised his head and looked at me with such a blank expression on his face that my breathing constricted.

I knew Luke would never agree to call to Victoria Row if he knew my real intentions. 'What if we see Alice first,' I said. 'We'll mention nothing about Jay until we find out what she knows and what kind of questions the police are asking. We can take it from there.'

I didn't tell Luke that I had decided to tell Alice the truth, exactly as I'd told him, and face the consequences. Even the consequences with Luke. Seven years of torture later, I needed to unload the anxieties that plagued me, disturbing my sleep, eating away at my peace of mind. I'd lived with them long enough; they had become my personal hell. I knew my sister better than Luke ever had. Alice would understand. Alice would know what to do.

Alice, with her kind, loving attention, her soft hug, would make me feel at peace again.

CHAPTER 56

Alice

ON FRIDAY EVENING, IN VICTORIA ROW, Chloe was full of chatter while she skipped around her bedroom.

'Guess what Ruby's having?' she said, ticking off items one by one on her fingers. 'A magician, a disco, a new movie, pizza … and Ruby's big sister is going to do our hair and our nails …'

Alice listened to her daughter's stream of conversation, relieved to be distracted while she packed Chloe's night things and a change of underwear into her Minnie Mouse wheelie case – far too big for a one-night sleepover for her friend Ruby's seventh birthday, but Chloe had insisted on it. And Chloe insisted on wrapping her friend's present and writing the card, while Alice supervised, and then Maeve collected her, Lucy waving from her booster seat in the back, Chloe giggling and laughing with excitement as she rushed down the garden path, Alice following, blinking at the blast of sunshine and fractures of silvery glimmer coming off the sea, the cool evening air kind and benign on her face.

Back in Victoria Row, she refused to think. Full of

anxious energy, she tackled all the jobs she'd been putting off, pouring her angst into scouring the bathroom, scrubbing every inch of the bath, the overhead shower and the tiles. In Chloe's bedroom, she changed the bedsheets and sorted through her clothes, putting half of them in the laundry basket. Down in the kitchen, she was just about to don a pair of rubber gloves and tackle the innards of the cooker when the doorbell chimed.

Damien.

She stared at him, feeling her insides collapse. 'What are you doing here?'

He had something in his hands. Something wrapped. For a moment she allowed herself to breathe in the sight of him; he was wearing jeans and a light jacket, and he looked beautiful and amazing, and the most wonderful sight on her doorstep. Then her shutter came down again.

'What do you want?' she asked.

'I have something for Chloe.'

'Chloe? You've just missed her. She's not here.'

'That's a pity. I wanted her to have this. I thought I'd drop it in now, before ...'

'Before what?'

He looked at her, his eyes soft. 'Before you forget about me altogether, before I become a guy relegated to your past, someone you used to know, once upon a time.'

Her heart contracted. 'What is it?'

'It's a Harry Potter book, signed. I picked it up years ago in London. It was sitting on my shelf back home. I'd like Chloe to have it.'

Alice shook her head, felt her eyes misting over, knew

what was going to happen next but couldn't stop, and then once more she was crying in front of him. She allowed him in, allowed him to take her into his arms and shut the door behind him with his foot. The warmth of his hug, his hands smoothing her hair, his fingers softly wiping away her tears washed over her like a calming balm and knit together the broken strands of her heart. She lifted her mouth to his, welcoming his kiss.

Eventually, Damien said, 'Can we just – um – suspend hostilities long enough to talk?' he asked. 'Without having a row? This is too important, Alice. *You* are too important to me.'

'No,' she said.

'No?'

'I don't want talk,' she said, putting the tips of her fingers to his face. 'I don't want you to talk about your cousin or Holly. Not tonight.' She was fed up with her thoughts and anxieties about Holly going around and around in circles. She wanted to step away from it all for just one night. He caught her hand and kissed it. The touch of his mouth sent an ache through her. Then she was in his arms and nothing else mattered.

'I have a free gaff,' she said when they were sprawled on the sofa, his arm curving around her, their clothes in disarray, the sky outside turning into streams of pink and gold.

'So I gathered.'

'I bet you came here on purpose to seduce me,' she said, snuggling closer to him. 'The book was just an excuse.'

'Yeah. I even have a toothbrush in my pocket.'

She drew back and stared at him. 'You don't.'

'Nah.' He grinned.

'Chloe's not due home until lunchtime tomorrow.'

She brought him upstairs to her bedroom. She'd never even had Ronan up here. It was her private sanctuary, the bedroom she'd had for most of her life, moving from childhood to adolescence to adulthood. It didn't seem strange having Damien in here. It seemed right. The room filled with new warmth, the familiar walls welcoming her, welcoming him, the lights on the Poolbeg chimneys outside winking happily for her in this dusky April evening.

'I don't have any vinyl on offer,' she said, turning to face him, suddenly shaking.

'I'll have to improvise,' he said, taking her hand, twirling her around, laughing softly when they both tumbled onto the bed.

◆

Much later, she awoke in the dark. Remembering. His heat. His touch. The electric warmth of both of them, together. He must have sensed her awaken because he gathered her close to him again, and she breathed his scent and absorbed the feel of his body in the bed beside hers, his limbs around her. She kept her eyes closed when they came together, half in sleep, savouring the beautiful joy of it.

When she awoke again, a sliver of dawn light was glowing above the curtain rail. She slipped out of bed, grabbed her robe, slid open the curtains and raised the blind. The orangey red gleam of dawn glowed on the horizon, tattered grey clouds latticed the eggshell-blue sky and, even though the tide was out, the rosy light refracted across pockets of sea-water caught in the expanse of the rippling strand.

Then Damien was behind her, his arms around her, and she relaxed back into the solid bulk of him, her head in the curve of his neck. They stood together silently for several moments, watching the rising sun break free of the horizon, and then they went back to bed. Alice stretched her limbs luxuriously, knowing they had most of this morning, and she wasn't going to leave this bed until she had to, then she smiled sleepily at him and curled into his body one more time, lost in a capsule of tenderness.

◆

Damien went downstairs at eleven o'clock and brought up tea and toast. Soon after that, the doorbell rang and Alice looked at him in surprise. 'Chloe? I'm not expecting her until one o'clock …' She slipped on her robe again and went to the window, staring outside for a long moment.

'What is it?' Damien asked. 'Do I need to hide in the wardrobe?'

'No,' she said, biting her lip as she turned and looked at him. 'That's Luke's car outside. I can see him sitting in the driver's seat. It must be Holly at the door. Holly! Oh, my God, Damien, she's here.'

All her anger, fear and exasperation melted away. Her sister had come home.

CHAPTER 57

Holly

WHEN I STEPPED INTO THE HALLWAY AT Victoria Row, the house seemed to embrace me with warmth. It was a sanctuary of love and comfort that I'd taken for granted, thanks to the unconditional care and attention lavished by Alice and Mum. I fell, weeping, into Alice's arms.

We both spoke at once.

'Holly, Holly,' she said, over and over as she clutched me.

'We need to talk …' I could hardly get the words out through my chattering teeth.

Luke came in and we moved into the living room, my head full of what I wanted to say. Then I realised she was still in her dressing-gown – at almost midday, this was unusual for early bird Alice. She eventually drew back from our embrace and grabbed a tissue from her pocket. She dabbed her eyes. 'Oh, Holly,' she said, 'I can't believe you're here. I've been so worried.'

'Sorry, I should have talked to you sooner.'

I heard footsteps coming down the stairs and a pleasant-looking man walked into the room, clad in jeans and a T-shirt. To my surprise, Alice took his hand and drew him forward.

'Holly, this is Damien,' she said, blushing slightly. 'Damien, meet Holly – finally.'

Alice's face was illuminated in a way I'd never seen it before; likewise, her cinnamon eyes were softer and warmer: my sister was in love. Possibly for the first time in her life. Damien had clearly stayed over the night before. I was envious of her glowing happiness and the realisation washed over me like a shower of ice-cold water. What was *wrong* with me? For a moment we stood there awkwardly, Damien looking at me guardedly, as though he didn't particularly like what he was seeing.

And Alice – there was something else besides the softness in her eyes, a flicker of unease. Her hand trembled when she smoothed the front of her dressing-gown. Still wearing his jacket, Luke threw himself into an armchair. He sat back, legs spread, one knee jiggling, the morose expression on his face telling me he wanted to be anywhere but here, his eyes watching me carefully.

Alice said, 'Holly, I guess you're here to talk about Jay Slater. Jarlath? You know the file on his accidental death has been reopened? The police have been looking for you.'

'I don't know where to start,' I said. 'Did the police say why they were looking for me?'

'I think you should know something first,' Alice said, glancing at Damien, who gave her a tiny, private nod. There was something united about them that made me feel excluded.

'Damien is related to Jay – Jarlath,' she said.

It took me a few seconds to absorb that piece of information. I heard my voice speak, sharp and tinny. 'What do you mean exactly?'

'They're first cousins,' Alice said. Damien's hand reached out and held Alice's in an interlaced grip. He looked at me steadily with a pair of hazel eyes that were neutral but watchful all at once. Then the full meaning of her words detonated like a bomb inside my head. I stared at my sister, my head spinning. Alice was in love with Damien; Damien was Jay Slater's *cousin*. This was unreal. This changed everything.

My mind spooled into reverse. I saw Alice's beaming smile encouraging me at every stage in my life: from the audience in the school nativity play; by the sidelines when I'd won the egg and spoon race in the sports day; the hard benches where she'd sat for hours at the gymnastics contest; the time I'd come back down the aisle having being conferred with my degree; smiling through her tears at the airport boarding gate just before I'd left for Ocean City. Other images poured in: Alice pulling me to the floor at Maeve's New Year's Eve party and twirling me around to the sound of 'Sisters Are Doing It for Themselves'; Alice soothing me during countless nights, the absolute security of being hugged by her, her light fragrance, her unconditional love; the Alice who'd insisted I hadn't done anything to cause my father's disappearance or my mother's death. The Alice I wanted more than anything to make me feel right again.

She'd taken on board all my worries and in doing so

had halved them. I wanted to tell her how scared I'd been when we had financial difficulties, how desperate I'd been to behave as I did with Jay, how ravaged I'd been in the aftermath of that night, and even more ravaged after his death. I wanted her to tell me I hadn't been responsible for that; I wanted her to take away the pain and make me feel better. But all my plans for unburdening myself and looking to Alice to soothe my conscience crashed into smithereens. I knew I didn't deserve her unconditional love. I was the disgraceful sister who'd flirted carelessly with her husband; who'd behaved utterly recklessly with Jay. I knew if I halved my burden with her, she'd carry her portion until the end of her life.

And Damien. My kind, loving Alice didn't deserve to have her relationship with Damien destroyed, thanks to my bombshell. Knowing Alice, if she thought for one moment that I'd been any way involved in the death of Damien's cousin, she'd let it come between them and ruin her chance of happiness.

It all came down to one hard fact: no way could I tell Alice the truth about that night. Not now. Not ever.

'I'm putting the kettle on,' Alice said, giving me a loaded glance. 'Will you give me a hand, Holly?'

I don't think Luke was too happy that I left him sitting there, but I had no choice.

As soon as we were in the kitchen, the questions poured out of Alice's mouth. 'Where have you been?'

'Luke and I were down in west Cork for a while.' I shook my head. 'Long story.'

'We're all so concerned,' Alice said. 'I was worried

sick when you went missing and wouldn't answer my calls. Jarlath's family are in bits. It's been a desperate time. I know you were both in college at the same time and I heard he seemed to be stalking you? Was that right? Then soon after he died, you and Luke moved out of Dublin. What's going on?'

'Luke and I had money problems,' I began hesitantly, sticking as closely to the truth as possible. 'We had to leave the apartment. That's why we moved to Rose Cottage.'

'You should have told me,' Alice said. 'I could have helped.'

'I was embarrassed about the whole thing.'

'A lack of money is nothing to be embarrassed about. It's the photos I don't understand.'

'What photos?'

'Photos of you and Jay, found in Liffey Gate.'

'Oh no,' I said, struggling to think.

'They were found in an envelope, stuck in beside a utility cabinet in the basement.'

I stayed silent.

'You were identified through your college photo. Was Jay Slater pestering you, Holly?' Alice asked gently. 'Did you know about these photos? Apparently, they're quite … I don't know how to put it.'

I couldn't answer her. She hadn't a clue. It was better that way.

'What about Luke?' she said. 'Did he know about you and Jay? Did he see the photos? He can't have been happy with them, to say the least.'

I saw in an instant where Alice's thoughts were leading. Never in a million years would she dream that I might have had anything to do with Jay's accident, but Luke, in a fit of jealousy, could have had a motive if he'd seen the photos.

'It's all a bit delicate, Alice,' I said, speaking slowly, trying to find a way out of this. 'It's mega embarrassing, for both of us. But you see, Luke couldn't have been annoyed: he knew.'

'Luke *knew*?'

'Yeah,' I said, thinking as fast as I could. Lying through my teeth one more time. 'We were really stressed, bored with having no money and unhappy with the way our lives had turned out. We were just fooling around with Jay one night. We saw him from time to time as part of the college gang. I don't know what made you think he might be stalking me,' I said, biting back a sob, turning it into a half-laugh. 'He used to joke about us getting together … He called over a few nights before … the accident. He knew we had money troubles and our jeep would have to go. He worked in that financial firm and wanted to see if he could help. With the paperwork. He brought bottles of wine … we drank too much … we started fooling around … one thing led to another … I don't expect you to understand …'

Alice's face collapsed with disappointment. I wanted to weep. I wanted to scream. 'Are you saying what I think you're saying? The three of you? Together?'

'Well, sort of,' I said. 'Luke took those photos. On his phone.'

In the space of a minute, my sister aged. My heart splintered, every molecule in my body silently weeping. My lovely Alice would never look at me in the same light again. I couldn't believe I was saying these horrible things. But I was fighting for Alice's future with Damien, and for me and Luke, for whatever kind of future we might have left. Not that we deserved one, but Alice certainly did.

'So. There was no question of you not being a willing participant?' she said, her voice dulled.

'No,' I said, hanging my head.

She sighed heavily. 'Damien has to know this. His family haven't a clue what went on. They've been imagining all sorts of horrible things.'

'God,' I said, wracked with anxiety.

We went back outside. It took Alice just a few words to relay what I'd said to Damien. Hearing them fall from her mouth, with the way I had lied to her, and then hid from her, I knew I didn't deserve her. I stared at Luke, shaking my head slightly, willing him to stay silent and not contradict the version of events I'd given Alice. Eventually his face cleared as he copped on to how I was trying to take him out of the frame for having any kind of motive for Jay's death.

'It this true?' Damien asked, turning to Luke.

Luke shrugged. 'Like Holly said, it just seemed like a bit of fun at the time.'

Damien leaned forward and stared at him, his eyes cold. 'Are you saying that you actually watched Holly have all that sex with my cousin? And took photographs?'

'Hey, man, look, it's not something I'm proud of. Any more than Holly is. We got carried away, we were hammered, it seemed good craic at the time.'

I couldn't bear to look at Alice, her face was so pained.

'How then,' Damien said, 'did photos end up in the basement?'

CHAPTER 58

Holly

LITTLE DID ALICE KNOW THAT LUKE AND I used that morning in Victoria Row as a practice run for talking to the police. We were making it up as we went along, sticking closely to the truth where possible. My lovely sister was oblivious to that. She was still stunned at our sudden reappearance, never mind our revelations. I'm not sure if Damien was fooled, however. He looked from me to Luke with active dislike.

'Yes,' Alice said, her eyes dull with disillusionment, 'how did your photos end up there?'

'That was my fault,' I said, thinking swiftly, holding Luke's gaze with my own. 'We were seeing Jay about the jeep in the basement the evening before we went to the pub. Luke had printed a few of the photos and I shoved them into a spare envelope and into my bag before we left the apartment. We were teasing Jay about showing them to him, but as soon as I took out the envelope, I got cold feet. Jay was messing with me, chasing me round the basement, trying to grab the envelope … and …' I gulped, hardly able to believe the lies out of my mouth.

'Don't tell me *you* hid them, Holly,' Alice said, shaking her head.

'I was teasing Jay, and I pushed them into the narrow gap beside the utility cabinet, knowing he wouldn't be able to reach them. You said no one would find them there, didn't you, Luke?' I lifted my chin and stared at my husband, hoping he'd help.

'We went looking for them afterwards,' Luke said, his voice suitably subdued, 'but Holly had shoved the envelope in so far that we could hardly see it. We were keeping our fingers crossed that no one would ever find the photos, they are a bit … much.'

'Jesus – I can't believe I'm hearing this,' Alice said, blinking hard.

'So you were in the pub the night Jay died,' Damien said.

I blinked, momentarily disconcerted. 'Did I say that?'

'You just said you saw him in the basement the evening before you went to the pub. Jay told his friend he was meeting someone there. Was that you?'

I felt hot and cold. Luke shook his head warningly. I tried to think, recalling everything about Arabella's that night, knowing I'd have to stick to the truth as closely as possible, not sure if Ronan had decided to talk and had mentioned seeing me that night. 'I'm not sure if he meant us.' I shrugged. 'We hardly got to talk to him. The pub was squished with people and very noisy. I think half the dockland inhabitants were in there that night. There was a match on.'

'But you did see him and talk to him?' Damien pressed.

'Just briefly,' I said. 'Have the police not seen the CCTV?' I said as innocently as possible, already knowing from Ronan that it hadn't been working that night.

'I don't think there was any CCTV of Arabella's,' Alice said. 'The only CCTV they mentioned was a camera down by the docks. They've been able to enhance the image and they have picked up someone else in the area around the same time as Jarlath. They still don't know who that was.'

Had I been anywhere except Victoria Row, I think I would have bent over and vomited on the spot. As it was, I drew some support from the security of the walls around me – or maybe, with my world crumbling I found a seam of strength inside me. I thought rapidly. The police would more than likely keep the file open until they identified this other person. Maybe further digital enhancements in time would help to identify who it was.

'That person could have been me,' I said.

'*You?*' Damien looked surprised.

'Holly?' Alice was startled.

Even Luke looked at me in shock.

'Yeah. The pub was so jammers and hot that I felt sick and needed some air. We were nearest the back door so we went out that way and down the alleyway – it was really dark, the breeze was ferocious, the snow was stinging –' I paused, gulping. I didn't need to act a part. Every time I thought of that alleyway, I got shivers down my spine.

Alice looked puzzled. 'But the CCTV only picked up one person, so where was Luke?'

'He was with me,' I said, 'probably outside the camera range.'

'Did you see Jay?'

'No, we didn't,' I said.

'So that image mightn't have been you at all,' Alice said, a tiny ray of hope in her eyes.

'Probably not,' I said casually. 'When we heard what had happened to Jay —' I stopped, shook my head, back there in that devastating moment '— we were gutted. It was unbelievable.'

'Why didn't you go to the police at the time?' Damien asked. 'They were appealing for anyone who'd seen him that night to come forward.'

I looked at my sister's lover, Jay's cousin, and I wanted to go through the floor. 'We didn't think there was any need to talk to the police — we weren't exactly proud of what we'd got up to with Jay and thought it was best forgotten. We'd nothing constructive to say, nothing to offer the investigation.'

He stared at me silently.

'I'm so, so sorry, Damien,' I went on. 'I can only imagine what you and Jay's family have been going through — it's a huge loss. We were upset enough ourselves.'

'You haven't a clue,' he said, a mixture of anger and sadness oozing from every syllable. 'You haven't a clue about the torture our family have been through, all the unanswered questions, the agony, the going around in circles. Apart from the huge loss, the absolute nightmare of not quite understanding how your loved one ended up as he did. You two could have been the last people to talk to Jarlath, the last people to see him alive – you were there that night, in the pub, along the dock – and you never once thought to talk to the police? Or his devastated family? He was a mate of yours – so you said. Hadn't you any basic respect for him and his broken family? I just can't get my head around this. I don't understand it.'

There was a long, ringing, horribly thick silence.

I noticed that Alice and Damien were now on opposite sides of the room, both of them stuck in some kind of separate, frozen misery. I hope I hadn't put a wrecking ball through their happiness. I'd never forgive myself for that either.

Well done, Holly.

'The other thing I don't understand,' Damien said, 'is why you disappeared just as the investigation was reopened?'

I decided to leave that one to Luke, staring at him pointedly.

'When we heard there were problems with the Liffey Gate demolition,' Luke said, 'I thought it was best to bring Holly to west Cork, away from all media and news coverage; she was upset enough about our time there and Jay's death and still has nightmares about it, don't you Holly?'

I nodded silently.

'We're really sorry for any concern we caused,' Luke went on, and I could see the effort he was making, trying to sound suitably apologetic. 'We'd no idea the police were looking for us until I heard from my father.'

'So now,' Damien said, his eyes hostile as he looked at Luke, 'I take it you are going to go to the police.'

Luke stared at me. 'Absolutely,' I said, glad that I managed to keep the fear out of my voice.

CHAPTER 59

Alice

BY THE TIME HOLLY AND LUKE LEFT Victoria Row, Alice knew that she and Damien were right back where they'd been at lunchtime Friday – on different sides of a ten-foot wall. Standing in the living room, she held onto the sofa for balance, staring at him in the ringing silence, the air around her exploding with the images her sister's words had painted. All the warmth and closeness of last night and earlier that morning had vanished like a snowflake on her hand.

'Well,' Damien spoke eventually, his hands in his jeans pockets. 'That was some story. I don't know what to make of it.'

'Neither do I,' she said, swallowing hard, unable to compute the pictures Holly had planted in her head.

'Do you believe your sister?'

'Of course,' she said stoutly, automatically defending Holly, even if she didn't like what she'd done. 'What other explanation could there be?'

'There could be any number of explanations. We only have their word for what happened.'

'In other words, you don't believe what Holly said.'

Silence.

'Just go, Damien.'

'Is that really what you want?'

'It's for the best.'

'Whose best? Yours or Holly's?'

'She's my sister. It's obvious you don't believe her. You're right to be angry with her for not talking to the police before now. I'm not condoning her behaviour, far from it, but I know it will always come between us.'

'It doesn't have to.'

'For God's sake, Damien,' she said, her voice a mixture of the fury and pain that was squeezing her heart, 'of course it will. Every time you see me you'll think of Holly. And what she did or didn't do.'

He shook his head. 'They're your thoughts, not mine. I'm upset with what happened to Jarlath – how could I not be? And I'm not convinced Holly and Luke are telling the truth. I'm saying this now, simply to put my honest opinion out into the open, but after this morning, I never want to talk about it again. I had hoped you and I were … separate from all this. That we could put it to one side and try and make a go of our relationship. Life will always throw us curve balls, Alice, but we can choose how we respond to them.'

Alice shook her head. But Damien wasn't finished.

'I don't think of your sister when I look at you,' he said. 'Every time I see you, I remember the night of your accident, how honest and beautiful and vulnerable you looked. I wanted to wrap you up in a big hug but I had to make do with a kiss on your forehead when you fell asleep. As time went on, and I got to know you, you began to take over my head and my heart with your smile and your laugh. I saw your warm brown eyes everywhere. The time we spent together was special to me. You said it was fun while it lasted – I wanted it to go on being fun and last forever. Even this thing with Holly, I've seen how wounded you've been. You've no idea how much I wanted to wipe it all away for you and kiss you better. It doesn't have to end now. Unless – maybe I'm wrong ...'

'Wrong about what?'

'Unless you're choosing to allow your sister to come between us because it's a convenient way out for you.'

'I've always put Holly first, from the time she was born.'

'Why, exactly?'

'I don't have to justify my relationship with my sister to you.'

'No, but Holly's an adult now and she seems well capable of making her own decisions. Isn't it about time you realised that your first responsibility is to yourself, and that includes your own happiness?' Damien went on, looking at her bleakly. 'You should be honouring your own life, your own feelings, Alice, whether or not they include me.'

Time rolled back and Alice was there again, bending over the Moses basket, staring in wonder at the perfect beauty of her baby sister, vowing to herself to always look after her, to make up for a father's absence. An absence that Alice had always felt deep down she might have been responsible for, until a moment of clarity earlier that month. She still loved Holly in spite of what she'd done, she always would, but did that mean Alice had to put her life in cold storage because of a course of action Holly had chosen to take? Something flickered inside her, a letting go, a recalibration, as faint as gossamer. Was it possible she could have a new beginning with Damien after all the dark things that had happened?

Then sounds of commotion came from the garden outside.

'You have visitors,' Damien said.

Alice looked out the window in time to see Maeve, along with Chloe and Lucy, coming up the garden path, the two girls laughing and chattering. When she opened the hall door they scrambled inside, Chloe and Lucy gabbling excitedly about the party, the sleepover, the magician. They paid little attention to Damien when she introduced him, stopping to say hello as swiftly as they could get away with in a mannerly way before rushing upstairs to Chloe's bedroom in a cascade of laughter and giggles.

But in one all-encompassing, appreciative look, Maeve's eyes flickered delightedly from Alice's attire to Damien's face, and behind his back she made exaggerated 'wow' faces and thumbs-up signals, until Damien said, in a tight voice, 'Lovely to meet you, Maeve, but if you'll excuse me, I was just leaving.'

He gave Alice a neutral glance. 'See you around.' Then he plucked his jumper off the back of the sofa. Out in the hall, he shrugged into his jacket and went out the door, closing it quietly behind him.

Maeve's eyes resembled saucers. 'Wow – what a gorgeous guy, but what did I say wrong?'

'Nothing, Maeve,' Alice said, silently crumpling under a wave of exhaustion.

'Did we interrupt something?'

'No, he was just leaving.'

Leaving; gone. She almost heard the sound of her heart plummeting to her toes.

CHAPTER 60

Holly

ON SUNDAY, IN A HORRIBLE, AIRLESS, CELL-like room that made me feel sick, one of first questions the police asked me was what we'd been doing in west Cork just as their fresh appeal for information issued.

Before we contacted the police, we prepared well, going over and over the version of the story we'd given Alice until we were happy we knew it by heart and had everything covered. Then Luke called the phone number that had been given out with the appeal.

I don't know how we came through those interviews unscathed. We were questioned separately. By running from Rose Cottage, together with the photos, we looked as though we'd something to hide. The police asked about our mobile phones at the time of the accident, but at least we could be truthful there. We'd had to get rid of our expensive phones before we'd left Liffey Gate, changing numbers and downgrading to basic pay-as-you-go models. Luke had already sussed that there was no way of retrieving his old phone records or files – otherwise our lies about him taking the photographs of me and Jay could have been uncovered. I felt sick, close to the end of the interview, when I was shown a blown-up map of the area where Arabella's had been and was asked to point out the alleyway down which I'd run in my quest for fresh air, and I showed them where I must have been standing when I'd been captured on CCTV.

At the end of a long, gruelling day, the police thanked us for our help and asked us to notify them should we decide to leave the country while the case was still open.

By the time we arrived home to Rose Cottage, I was beyond exhaustion.

I went out into the back garden and looked down at the valley stretching away into the distance. It seemed so peaceful and serene: folds of green and gold and gorse yellow, the silent forests and, in the near distance, undulations of the blue-rimmed slopes of the mountains. Luke's vegetable patch to the side of the garden, the flower beds that had somehow sustained me. The breeze riffling through the grass. I wanted to take off my shoes and walk on the soft earth, feel the clay with my bare feet, allow the grounding calm to seep up my limbs and ease my jangled heartstrings. A memory crashed through of summer days on Sandymount Strand, gritty sand curling between my bare toes, a laughing Alice silhouetted against the glimmering bay, Mum smiling happily as she splashed in foamy waves. A stab of pain; how precious those days had been, how perfect.

Luke came behind me and curved his arms around me, resting his chin on my shoulder. 'I think we did okay,' he said. 'But we'll never talk about this again, we'll leave well enough alone – promise me, Holly?'

'I promise.'

'As soon as the investigation is suspended, we'll move as far away as we can go – Sydney, maybe. I have friends out there, and some relatives. I'm sure someone will sponsor us.'

'Yeah, sure,' I said, unable to look at his face.

'We'll start again, away from all of this.'

'Yes.'

'We're soulmates, don't forget. Wherever you go, I go.'

'Yes.'

'It really is over, Holly.'

'Yes, Luke.'

We stood for a moment, until Luke went inside. I stayed outside, trying to centre myself in the calm evening air.

Moving to Sydney was the only solution, even if I'd miss Alice and didn't want to uproot myself yet again, because I knew that at any future point in time, in the right circumstances, I was likely to crumble and give her the true version of events, putting her in an intolerable situation.

And I'd have to destroy the account I'd made, detailing everything that had happened with Jay up to the time we'd left Liffey Gate. Here in Rose Cottage, it had been easy enough to type it up between proofing jobs. I'd done it for two reasons: the therapy of putting everything down on paper might have helped ease my nightmares, but I'd also wanted to have a record of events in case anything untoward happened to me, anything inexplicable – a shadowy fear I couldn't articulate even to myself, which had also prompted me to give Alice a key to Rose Cottage. Not that I'd saved the account on my laptop, where it could have been found. Instead I'd typed it using a small font to take up less space, printing each page as soon as it was full. The pages were folded and tucked in under the bottom tray of Mum's old jewellery box, a keepsake Luke would have paid no attention to, but a keepsake Alice was sure to be interested in.

I couldn't run the risk of anyone finding it now, especially Alice.

Even though the police seemed satisfied enough after our interviews, and we'd be moving to the other side of the world, I knew my mind would never cease churning around in vicious circles, that the 'what ifs' and 'if onlys' and 'maybes' would never stop plaguing me, and that images of Jay would always be twirling around, invading my consciousness and revisiting my dreams, as they had over the last seven years.

Had I really sent Jay to his death? How long had Ronan been there before he stepped out of the shadows? How much had he known about me and Jay? How far was Luke prepared to go, in his efforts to protect me? Had he really been late home because he'd been searching for me? I'd been so sure he'd said to turn left at the end of the laneway, just before we parted outside Arabella's that night. After I'd told him I'd thrown Jay's mobile into the water on that dark January night, he'd said I didn't have to worry about Jay's threats any more. But I realised later, when I had more time to think in the quiet of Rose Cottage, that if he hadn't died, Jay could easily have bought a new phone and, chances were, he could have had them backed up somewhere.

I strolled back up the garden, taking a final deep breath of the fresh evening air before I went inside. Luke turned on some music, and Lana Del Rey's 'Young and Beautiful' swirled around the cottage on full blast. When I met those heavily fringed grey eyes, I put a smile on my face. I told myself that innocent happenings could be twisted and contorted into whatever dark shape or form you wanted, but Luke had promised he would always take care of me and make sure I was safe.

Soulmates: bound to each other for the rest of our lives.

CHAPTER 61

Alice

'IF THIS IS ABOUT HOLLY GOING TO THE police,' Alice said, 'and you're afraid mud might stick, she seems to have got on okay.'

'I know,' Ronan said. 'I spoke to her, both before and afterwards.'

Alice had called him the previous Saturday evening, bringing him up to date with Holly and Luke's visit, skimming over the mention of Damien as a friend of hers who also happened to be Jay's cousin. She half-expected Ronan to vent acidic comments on Alice's wayward family, annoyed that something might reflect on his self-perceived upstanding citizenry, never mind have a go at her for having a male friend. Instead he'd listened quietly, immediately offered his services to Holly and said he'd call her himself. Then he'd phoned Alice on Tuesday evening and arranged to meet her for lunch the next day in the Merrion Hotel. It was far from a suitable venue if Ronan wanted to give her a piece of his mind, but she was ready for him.

Ronan, for once, seemed slightly subdued. He was drinking still water. Alice passed on his offer of wine, opting for water also.

'I asked you here to talk about us,' he said, 'but I want to say something first.' He leaned forward and looked at her earnestly. 'I want to apologise for messing around with Holly when I did, and for carrying on with other women behind your back. I was stupid and immature. You were right to give me the push. It was the least I deserved.'

'Wow – what brought this on?'

'Various things. Chloe activating my conscience, plus the realisation, finally, of what's important in life and what's just fluff. I've been thinking hard since we came back from Euro Disney, and not liking what I'm seeing or how stupidly I've behaved. It was wrong of me, and –'

'Is this about more access?'

Their main courses arrived, beef for Ronan and sea bass for Alice, and he waited until they'd been served before he said, 'Please let me talk, Alice. I'm sorry I've messed up with you. I've done some idiotic things in my lifetime, but I feel the worst failure in the world when I think of what I threw away with you, how selfishly I behaved, especially when my fantastic seven-year-old daughter asks me why I don't live with her mummy and be a proper dad.'

Something landed in Alice's heart with a thud. *Oh, Chloe.*

'Chloe means the world to me, always has,' Ronan went on. 'But it was only after we split, when she turned into a real little person who loved me unconditionally, that I realised what I was missing. The way she looked at me one day recently, when I was leaving her back to

Victoria Row, it kind of jolted me, but it also gave me a right kick up the arse. Being away with her for a whole week, seeing how adorable she looks first thing in the morning, was brilliant. The Disney part was good as well. And Amanda was there.'

'Is that what this is about? Amanda? You're looking for some kind of permission from me …?'

'Not just that. I'm trying to make a fresh start, Alice, and leave the past where it belongs. I'm deadly serious about this.'

Ronan was wearing the most contrite expression Alice had ever seen on his face. Nonetheless, she put down her knife and fork and eyeballed him. 'Talk is cheap, Ronan. What you're saying has to be backed up by some kind of action. You can't just wave a magic wand with your words and hope that all is forgiven.'

'I appreciate that. I know it'll take time for you to trust me again. If you ever do. I know this sounds corny but I feel as though I've only started to grow up a bit in the last few weeks.'

'It certainly does sound corny, coming from you. What happened to bring about such a transformation?'

'Partly Chloe. Being away with her, able to relax and enjoy her for a few days in a row, it felt so good and made me reflect on things. And …' He paused and looked at Alice, a hint of entreaty in his eyes. 'I'm seeing a lot of Amanda. She's good for me – she takes absolutely no crap – but I'm still on probation with her. I know she'll give me a run for my money. She loves Chloe. I'm more conscious than ever of what Chloe might think, now that she's growing up a little. I want her to have a father she's proud of. I've always felt bad that I couldn't make a go of us, even for Chloe's sake if not ours. And all that talk of full custody – I was mostly trying to rattle you.'

'It didn't feel like that to me, Ronan. There were times when you sounded quite threatening.'

'For which I humbly apologise.'

'Somehow the words humble and Ronan Russell don't go together in the same sentence. It sounds a bit like the fairy tales of Ireland.'

'I mean it. I know Chloe's happy, secure and contented with you. I'd never uproot her from that.'

If Ronan was being honest with her, the least she could do was be honest in return.

'I wasn't the right person for you,' she said. 'You didn't marry the real me, Ronan, but someone I was pretending to be, a souped-up version of what I thought I should be. I feel for Chloe when she talks about her mummy and daddy being together, and we'll have to work out a calm, united approach to that.'

'Thank you, you don't know how much I appreciate that.'

'For God's sake, Ronan, less of the grovelling. You're beginning to go over the top. I was the one who left you, and you've already agreed that I was right to do so because of your intolerable behaviour. Staying trapped in a loveless marriage was no example to pass on to Chloe. But whatever way we live, she needs lashings of love and security in her life. That has to come first.'

'You're right,' Ronan said. 'I think this is the first time

we've had such an honest conversation. We should do it more often. Chloe will always be part of us both, and I will always respect you as her mother.'

Alice raised an eyebrow. 'Really? You had a funny way of proving that up to now.'

'Certainly from now on I'll prove it to you. I'm sorry I was a bollocks over the years, but that came partly from guilt at not making a go of things and being unable to provide Chloe with a secure family background.'

'You do provide security,' Alice said. 'You care for her and love her. I know, and she knows, that you would come at the drop of a hat if there were any problems. Now, is that it, or have you anything else you want to get off your chest?'

'I didn't mean to be such a thorn in your side when it came to seeing other men.'

Alice gave an exaggerated sigh. She stared at him pointedly. 'Didn't you?'

'Well, I did and I didn't,' Ronan hedged. 'Leopardstown was horribly empty after you left. I couldn't believe how much I missed you both. I went a bit mad for a while. I was insanely jealous of the idea of you meeting someone else, another man getting to experience the ordinary things that I miss about Chloe, like homework and bedtime stories, giving her a kiss goodnight when she's sound asleep, spoiling her when she's sick. But I know I've no right to stand in your way should you meet someone. How can I, when I'm hoping that me and Amanda might make a go of things, if and when she eventually decides I pass muster, and only if

Chloe is happy with it. But with or without Amanda, I'd love to see more of Chloe, even at the weekends. Being away with her brought home to me just how much I'm missing.'

'This is all very interesting,' Alice said after a while. 'I never expected you to turn over a new leaf to this extent. The new, improved Ronan is on probation with me too, and will be for a while. But in time, if things work out, and if Chloe is happy with it, I might be willing to renegotiate access a little. At the weekends anyhow. And, yes, she does look adorable first thing in the morning.'

'I saw that in Euro Disney.' Ronan's face was soft.

They chatted for a while, comparing fond anecdotes about their daughter and her escapades. Then looking a little more serious, Ronan said, 'How about you? What's happening with you and Damien?'

Alice felt a painful constriction in her chest. She examined her fingernails before meeting Ronan's gaze. 'I don't know. It's messy, him being Jay Slater's cousin, with Holly and Luke in the mix. It's all come as an unpleasant shock.'

'I'd say so. Probably as much of a shock for Damien as for you.'

She thought she saw genuine empathy in Ronan's eyes. 'Yeah, but I don't see a way ahead for us,' she admitted, fiddling with her napkin. 'Holly told me when she rang on Monday night that she and Luke are planning to move to Sydney. I got a bit of a shock. In spite of what's happened, I hate the thoughts of her going that far away. At least in Kilkenny I wasn't a thousand miles away.'

'I'm sure you feel caught in the middle, Alice,' he said, 'but no matter what happens with Holly and Luke, you're entitled to make a life of your own. Holly said Damien seemed sound. I hereby decree that you deserve love and happiness.'

'Thanks,' Alice said. 'Holly didn't exactly endear herself to Damien. He can't understand why she didn't talk to the police at the time. It wouldn't have changed things, he said, but it would have showed some respect to Jay's family at a horrendous time for them.'

Ronan leaned forward, rested his elbows on the table and looked at Alice for a long moment. 'I can see where Damien is coming from,' he said. 'It must have been hell for the family, and it still is – there are loose ends all over the place and no satisfactory closure – but sometimes, through no fault of our own, we're simply in the wrong place at the wrong time,' he added, looking at her steadily. 'Something else I wanted to mention – I was in Arabella's that night, sussing it out for investment.'

'Jesus, Ronan, did you see Holly and Luke?'

'I saw Holly all right, and Jay, just briefly.'

'Why didn't you come forward? Or did you?'

'Luke asked me not to.'

'*Luke?*'

'He spoke to me just after Jay's death was announced and said he and Holly had been caught in a sensitive situation with Jay by pure chance, he didn't want her name to be dragged across the media, it would upset her too much. It would have upset you, also, he pointed out, especially with you due to give birth any day. Obviously

I didn't know then what exactly had transpired between the three of them.' He sighed. 'I understand how Holly might have panicked, given the nature of the relationship with Jay. What young woman would have risked having those details splashed all over the tabloids at the time of Jay's death? And what of Jay's family if those photos had been leaked? What kind of respect would that have shown him or his family? At least now, if any of those details get out, the passage of time and worse scandals over the years might dilute things a little.'

'I found it all a little shocking coming from Holly, to be honest,' Alice said. 'And this now, coming from you.'

'I'm sure you do. I probably should have spoken up at the time. I stayed quiet to safeguard both the family and my reputation. I made a judgement call, thinking it was best to leave well enough alone, especially if it wasn't going to fundamentally change the outcome of an incident. Call it self-preservation, self-care, minding the family, whatever you like. But we all do stupid things from time to time, we make mistakes, foolish decisions – at least that's how they appear to other people, even if they seem right to us at the time.'

'You could also call it selfishness, so I'm not sure I agree with you,' Alice said.

'Also, Alice,' Ronan said, 'you need to know there could be more repercussions for Holly and Luke.'

'Like what?'

'I heard from my source that the police found those photos in Liffey Gate as a result of a tip-off. Otherwise they'd never have been found where they were hidden.'

'A tip-off? I don't follow you … what does that mean?'

'That's what I'm trying to figure out,' Ronan said, frowning as he pushed away his plate.

'I can't think any more right now,' Alice said, a sudden tiredness sweeping over her.

'Whatever the outcome,' Ronan said, 'remember that you have to live your own life, and I'm here if you need me, both as a friend and in a professional capacity.' He ordered two coffees and asked for the bill. Outside the hotel, he saw Alice into a taxi. 'Thanks for meeting me, I appreciate it,' he said, holding open the passenger door.

She looked up at him. 'Apart from Holly and Luke, all this full-on politeness is making me nervous, Ronan,' she said. 'Your guilty conscience must have been troubling you big time. You're not only turning over a new leaf, you're writing a whole new script.'

'That's how determined I am to make a fresh start,' he said.

The bright daylight caused her to notice the deepening lines around his eyes and the increasing silvering of his hair. 'Better late than never,' she said. 'I suppose, in fairness, I'd better give the new you a trial run. But as I said, you're on strict probation,' she added, getting into the taxi.

'I guess I can live with that,' Ronan said, before he closed the door and waved her off.

CHAPTER 62

Holly

IN THE WEEK AFTER WE'D BEEN TO SEE THE police, when Luke and I began to pack up our lives again, I had the overpowering feeling I was living on fragile, borrowed time. Luke, however, seemed full of resolution, reminding me a little of the time he'd come home from Liverpool, determined to get our messy lives back on track again, only now he was far more impatient. Life in Rose Cottage must have stifled him, thanks to being anchored to me, thanks to him having to watch me like a hawk and monitor every word that came out of my mouth in case I spilled something about our time in Liffey Gate and Jay.

'You'll love it in Sydney, Hol,' he said. 'It'll be great to get away from all this. Why didn't we think of going before now? Our finances are well back on track.'

He emailed friends and family out there, determined to get the wheels in motion, even though it would be weeks before we'd be leaving. 'We'll be ready to go as soon as the police suspend the investigation,' he said.

'I don't think the police told us not to leave the country,' I said.

'Holly, dear – you're so innocent,' he said. 'They didn't tell us out straight, but that's what they meant. They'd take a dim view of us heading to the far side of the world while the investigation is still on.'

'So it's still on. Do you think they suspect me or saw through my story?' I asked, searching his face for the truth. He must have been really agitated when the police interviewed us separately and he wasn't able to supervise my replies. I wondered if he'd answered all their questions exactly as we'd pre-agreed. Or if he'd deviated in any way.

'If they did I'm sure they'd have arrested you by now, Holly. Don't worry, I'll soon have you whisked away from here.'

The far side of the world – Luke and I away from everything I'd once known. No Alice within driving distance. No meeting her for birthday lunches in convenient restaurants or garden centres, even if Luke had always accompanied me. I might not have seen her that often, but I'd always known she was there, ready to come running if ever I called her.

Then on Wednesday, Luke had to go to Dublin for a conference to do with the implementation of his recent project, the first time in weeks he'd left me alone like this. I went into the guest bedroom and over to the wardrobe, reaching for Mum's jewellery case. Today was the best opportunity I had to tear up that closely typed document outlining everything that had happened with Jay, a sort of confession in a way. I wasn't going to put anything into the recycling bin where it might be found and questioned. I planned to dig up a rose bush in the back garden, blending the torn fragments with compost, before burying the mix under the root ball. Luke would never notice. But when I lifted out the jewellery case and took out the document, something like a chill of premonition ruffled across the back of my mind and I found myself returning it to the wardrobe shelf. I observed Luke as quietly as possible after he came home that evening, feeling so unravelled that I was sure he'd pick up on it, but thankfully he didn't. The following day, when he was out cutting the grass, Alice phoned.

'I met Ronan yesterday,' she said, after she'd asked how I was. 'We'd a long talk, the best we'd had in years. I know about his chat with Luke after Jay's death, I have to say he surprised me with his safeguarding of our family. But Holly, he doesn't think it's over yet and I'm concerned for you.'

My sister. My safety net. Always there, warmth spilling out of her voice in spite of everything. How I loved her at that moment. I could tell her the truth and she'd come running in an instant, even if she couldn't forgive me. I could tell her the truth and she'd still love me, even if she hated what I'd done.

Alice was still talking. 'Ronan told me the police only found the photos in Liffey Gate as a result of a tip-off. But I was thinking afterwards ...' she paused, and I knew in a flash of ice-cold comprehension what she was about to say, 'surely the only people who knew about their whereabouts were you and Luke ...?'

My skin prickling, I looked out the kitchen window,

to where the figure of Luke was silhouetted darkly against the peace and serenity of the valley. Now he was turning the petrol lawnmower around and straightening it to come up the centre of the back garden. He saw me standing with the mobile in my hand and he paused. I assumed he'd paused because he was wondering who I was talking to, I wasn't supposed to take any calls unless he was within earshot, but then I heard it just after he must have – the sound of cars coming slowly up the lane and stopping outside the front of our house. There were footsteps on gravel and then the peal of the doorbell cut through the silence of the cottage. I turned around to where the kitchen door was open, giving me a view up through the hall. The shadows of two people against the glass were unmistakeable. I turned back to stare out the window at Luke. He was watching me steadily, his face shuttered, his expression unreadable.

I must have dropped my mobile, because it wasn't in my hand when I opened the door to the police.

But they hadn't come for me.

They'd come for Luke.

CHAPTER 63

Holly

THEY'D COME FOR LUKE, BUT I WAS INVITED up to the station, as there were discrepancies in my earlier statement that needed to be addressed. Once again I was back in a cell-like, airless room, this time with Detective Fitzpatrick sitting across the table and a Sergeant Lawlor. I'd phoned Alice earlier, telling her that Luke had been taken into custody and that the police needed me to give a further statement. She'd texted me back to say she'd phoned Ronan and they'd both be waiting for me in the station, no matter how long it took.

'Call me Trish,' Sergeant Lawlor said, giving me a sympathetic smile along with a glass of water. My body was trembling so much that my teeth chattered against the glass, my lips feeling loose as I tried to take a sip.

'This time, we need a full and honest statement from you,' Detective Fitzpatrick said.

'Where's Luke?' I asked.

'He's in another part of the station,' Trish said.

'Being questioned under caution,' Detective Fitzpatrick added.

409

'Caution? What does that mean? He hasn't done anything wrong, has he?' I said.

'That's what we're trying to establish,' the detective replied.

'I see,' I said, which was a ridiculous statement, because I didn't see at all and was failing to make sense of anything. Was Luke still trying to protect me?

Or had the shadowy fear that sat deep down inside me all along finally been substantiated?

'Holly, it would be in your best interests to co-operate fully,' Trish said.

'I know,' I said, a dull resignation to my fate sweeping over me. 'This might help.' I took out the written account I'd had tucked away for so long, and I explained exactly why I had tipped them off about the photos hidden in the basement.

Afterwards, I went outside to the waiting area, where Alice and Ronan were sitting on plastic seats in a draughty corridor. I was grateful there were no recriminations from Alice when I unburdened myself. She just hugged me tight and did her best to comfort and calm me while we waited for news of Luke.

'Ronan, can you find out what's happening now?' she asked when we were on our third cup of weak, tasteless coffee. Earlier, Ronan had called a solicitor colleague to represent Luke, and he went off to check for updates, but he didn't have good news when he returned.

The police had seen through the flimsy version of events I'd given them on Sunday, but thanks to that, they were better able to calculate Jay's movements. Indeed, the alleyway I had run down that night, the building outside which I'd indicated I'd been standing, plus the time I'd left Arabella's just after the penalty kick, were not compatible with the time and place where Jay had last been seen on CCTV, and where he'd been found in the water. I'd sensed something wasn't right when the police had shown me the map and I'd pointed out where I'd been standing that night. Crucially, it had put Luke in the frame, and a further examination of the CCTV taken from the general docklands area around the time of Jay's death had picked Luke up in a couple of locations consistent with him arriving in the same place, and at the same time, where that final image of Jay and the unidentified person had been caught.

The police were satisfied that having left the alleyway, Jay had wandered up around the dock area, where he'd been followed by Luke. They had ascertained that it was Luke, not me, whose figure appeared on the enhanced CCTV. He was still unable to account satisfactorily for his movements that night, and, according to Ronan, was on the point of cracking and confessing to pushing Jay into the water in a fit of rage. The police were preparing to arrest him and remand him in custody while a file was being prepared for the Director of Public Prosecutions.

Something hardened inside me as my shadowy fears were realised.

'I have to see him,' I said, feeling weirdly disconnected, as if someone had snapped off all my ties to the life I once knew. 'Please. I have to talk to him.'

'Ronan, can you arrange this?' Alice asked.

411

'I'll see what I can do,' said Ronan.

He set up a quick meeting for us in the corridor. Luke's eyes were red-rimmed, the rest of his face drained of colour. It reminded me of the night Jay died, when he'd come home so dishevelled, but this time fury swept through me. He'd known exactly what he'd done that night, yet allowed me to assume the blame, and live with nightmares thereafter.

I looked at him, not bothering to soften my stony face. 'All these years you let me believe I had caused Jay's death. You knew I was living in a nightmare.'

'Well, it did start with you,' he said, 'when you opened your legs to him.'

He was right in one sense. I had started the chain of events, a guilt I would never be able to get rid of.

'You know I did that for us,' I said, my voice shaking. 'I was desperate.'

He looked at me crookedly, the face that had looked at me with love – obsessive, devouring, all-consuming love. 'Bet you enjoyed it too.'

I recoiled. 'How dare you.'

'You deserved your nightmares, Holly. You gave me a nightmare, thinking of you and that prick, together. In our bed.'

I stared at him. 'All that time, you pretended to be looking after me, protecting me. Instead you were covering up for yourself. All those years you let me blame myself, warning me off going to the police, suggesting they might suspect "innocent" you? You set it all up, didn't you, that night? You intended things to happen exactly as they did, rehearsing it with me beforehand, telling me what drinks to get Jay, making me take the wrong turn outside Arabella's. You wanted me to lure Jay down to the docks. It must have been a great relief for you when I blamed myself.'

He looked at me, a muscle working in his jaw. 'I believe you tipped off the police, Holly. When did you manage that, exactly? Talk about an act of self-sabotage.'

My mind slewed back to the day we'd been in Kilkenny grocery shopping, sometime after the television programme about Liffey Gate: telling Luke I needed the bathroom urgently as we went out to the car with the trolley; nipping back into the shopping centre, but instead of going to the bathroom, I'd called the anonymous number I'd seen listed on the police website, my heart ricocheting around my chest.

'It was more like self-survival,' I said. 'I'd finally reached breaking point. I couldn't bear to live with the grief of it any longer, or what we'd done to Jay and his family, or the suffocating existence I had with you.'

'What?'

'You were constantly watching me, monitoring everything, controlling me. I was sick of pretending everything was fine in front of Alice. There were times when I might as well have been in jail. But then I found myself in recent years beginning to wonder about you and the night Jay died. What had you really been up to during that missing hour? Why there was no mention of a head injury in the coroner's report? Maybe it hadn't been as bad as I'd imagined. Why hadn't I heard some kind of splash or cry for help from Jay over the noise of the wind that night? Why were you always so afraid I might let something slip? It was your own skin you were trying to save all along, Luke, not mine.'

'I loved you Holly,' he said, 'I adored you, I did what I did because of you. I couldn't live with thoughts of that little wanker putting his dirty paws all over you and getting away with it. And this is how you repay me? Look what you've done to me, to us,' he said, his voice breaking.

'No, Luke, you did that to yourself by pushing Jay into the water.'

'I thought we were soulmates, Holly.'

For a moment, the dingy corridor with its faded grey paint and dog-eared posters dropped away as a stream of memories of our early days together exploded through me. I felt the thread of connection between us tighten, as if Luke was reeling me back in under the shadow of his control. My breath fluttered in my throat. I met his gaze, the gaze I had once loved until it had turned into something that had stifled me. Then I forced myself to turn around and walk off, and I didn't watch as he was led away.

CHAPTER 64

Alice

IN ABBEY LANE LIBRARY, ON FRIDAY MORNING, Sharon was late again.

Funny how the ordinary, everyday things in life kept going on, Alice decided, agreeing to cover desk duty until she appeared. Naturally, Sharon arrived in straight from her father's car, dressed to perfection in a cream midi dress and glittery ballerina shoes, smiling brightly at the creative writing group filing into the function room.

After morning break, Alice came out of the kitchen in time to hear Sharon say, with a hint of warm amusement in her voice, 'Here comes Alice now. I think she was hiding from you.'

Her gaze shot to the desk. Damien. In a crisp navy suit. He turned around to smile expectantly at her.

Time stopped.

Alice wished it could go back to that Thursday morning in February, when Damien had first appeared at the reception desk. The last thing she'd expected to see was him, here, now. Overcome with sudden emotion, she walked back through the staff area, into the bathroom.

Sharon followed her. 'What's up?' she asked. 'Don't you want to talk to him?'

'No.'

'Why not? He seems so nice, and you're perfect together. I thought you were all set for the great adventure of love.'

'You don't know what you're talking about,' Alice said. 'Adventures! Dreams! They're for the likes of you, with your life before you. Not for me, thank you.'

'Alice, you're lovely, but you're too … safe. You have to go out there and grab life with both hands. And with that gorgeous man.'

'So you're the expert, Sharon – you're half my age, and you know it all.' Alice was shaking, her voice quivering. 'You haven't a clue about life or my business.'

Sharon hadn't a clue that, in less than twenty-four hours, Luke Summers' arrest would break all over the media. Alice had dragged herself in to work for a few hours that morning, partly because they were short-staffed, but primarily because it was easier to talk to Finbarr about such confidential matters face to face rather than over the phone. She'd requested a period of leave without pay, starting that afternoon, until matters settled down a little. He'd agreed straight away, adding that she was to call him any time if there was anything at all he could do.

People were good, she thought, sometimes they didn't realise how much their kindness meant. Even Sharon, who was looking at her now, her blue eyes warm, meant well.

'That's the thing,' Sharon said, 'none of us knows what's really going on in anyone else's life. And we don't know what's around the corner either. You have years still ahead. Are you going to hide in a safe little box like a safe little mouse for the rest of your life? You deserve adventure and good things but you have to go out there and make them happen. Do something that scares you, Alice, it's totally exhilarating. And now,' she said, 'I'd better get back to the desk. I'll tell Damien you're on the way.'

Sharon gave her an encouraging smile, managing to look soft and wholesome, as though she'd stepped out of a Greek-yogurt ad shot on location in Crete, before she swirled out of the bathroom. Just like the way Holly used to look.

Alice's heart cracked. Was there any chance that her beautiful, effervescent sister was still there under the layers of deceit and distress and false smiles? Was there any chance Alice could reclaim her life? Only time would tell.

◆

When they'd left the police station late yesterday afternoon, Alice had invited Holly to stay in Victoria Row for a while but Holly insisted on going back to Rose Cottage. Maeve was minding Chloe overnight, so Alice accompanied Ronan when he drove Holly home, stopping in a service station en route for some provisions and wine. Rose Cottage and the surrounding countryside were basking in April sunshine, a sharp contrast to the oppression of the police station and the dark story Holly relived as they sat at the kitchen table, the two sisters sipping wine, Ronan sticking to water because he was driving.

'I wish you had told me of your money problems at the time,' Alice said, still overwhelmed by the terrible secrets Holly had been hiding. 'I could have helped you out financially. I could have done *something*.'

'I was too ashamed with the mess Luke and I had made.'

'No need for shame,' Alice said, silently weeping inside. She topped up Holly's wine. 'You made mistakes. We all do. We're only human.'

'Then after Jay ... how could I have told you? I would have spoiled your joy with baby Chloe. No way would I have done that to you.'

'Oh, Holly.' Alice sighed. 'I see now why you kept your distance, and there was me thinking you and Luke were joined at the hip.'

'We were, to all intents and purposes. I couldn't move without him,' Holly said, giving a shiver. She stared out the window, recovering herself, before looking back at Alice. 'Little did I know I was setting up Luke when I made that anonymous call,' she said, 'although, as time went on, whenever I thought about that night I began to find it all very peculiar. There were things about Luke that made me nervous – the way he spoke about that night, how he had set it all up, how he was so sure my problems with Jay were over before I knew he was dead, the way he was always watching me ...'

'I'll kill him,' Alice said, knocking back more wine before re-filling her glass. 'Ronan, open another bottle, please.'

'Going to jail will kill him,' Holly said, shivering. 'And me. Oh God, I was lying to the police ... perverting the course of justice in not coming forward. What does that mean, Ronan?'

'It means they'll be preparing a file on you, Holly,' he said. 'I'll put out a few calls tonight, make sure you have the best team looking after you. I think, in your case, taking everything into consideration, it's safe enough to say there are extenuating circumstances that will keep you out of jail.'

'Do you know,' Holly said, 'in a funny way, I already feel as though I'm just out of jail? Luke was ... always watching me, almost obsessively. The whole thing with Jay was like a thick black cloud that I couldn't see my way through. But now that's been lifted a little.'

In the hallway of Rose Cottage, before she and Ronan left, Alice turned to Holly and hugged her. 'Are you sure you're happy staying here?' she asked.

'Yes, I'll be fine,' Holly said. 'For the first time in my life I want to stand on my own two feet. I want to be me, just me for a while. And I need a little time alone to get my head around everything before it all breaks.'

'You'll come through it, and you'll have a life at the other end,' Alice said.

Holly managed a half-smile. 'I feel I can breathe now, instead of being scared by my own shadow. And I don't want to be under your feet, Alice. Apart from Jay, if there's only one thing I truly regret, it's the way I've messed things up for you and Damien.'

'Ah, but you're going by lily-livered Luke's standards,' Ronan said, curving a protective arm around Alice. 'I'd say, knowing Alice, that Damien is made of sterner stuff.'

◆

Last night, even though she'd been exhausted after the events of the day, Alice had texted Damien, asking him to contact her, knowing he and his family would have been fully updated by the police.

'*Life will always throw us curve balls, Alice,*' he'd said, '*but we can choose how we respond to them.*'

How would he respond to this latest curve ball? She'd waited up late but he hadn't replied. Then, this morning, in spite of everything that had happened and whatever the future might hold, here he was, choosing to arrive into Abbey Lane Library in person, smiling expectantly at Alice, much as he had that first morning. This time, the sight of him standing there, and all the possibilities it might mean for her, for them, had sent Alice's heart ricocheting so much that she'd fled into the bathroom.

I had hoped you and I were above all this.

Were they? Alice stared at herself in the mirror, her senses thrumming with a mixture of joy and uncertainty, love and trepidation, and a fresh understanding of the craziness and fragility of this amazing thing called life. *Do something that scares you, Alice.*

There was no more time to waste. With her heart taking flight and soaring through her mouth and something vibrant fizzing through her veins, she took a deep breath and harnessed her courage and walked out to where light drizzled through the stained-glass windows and sent kaleidoscope patterns glowing across walls.

To where the air rippled with warm expectation.

To where Damien waited.

ACKNOWLEDGEMENTS

I'd like to send a huge and heartfelt thank you to the wonderful people who continue to champion me and my writing, and offer encouragement and support every step of the way:

To my agent, the amazing Sheila Crowley, and the team at Curtis Brown, London, including the lovely Sabhbh Curran.

To the team at Hachette Books Ireland, including Breda, Jim, Ciara, Ruth, Siobhán, Bernard, for all the fantastic work on my behalf, and a very special acknowledgement to Joanna Smyth for her excellent and skilful editorial guidance, which has helped to raise this story to a new level. Also Emma Dunne, the copy-editor and Aonghus Meaney, the proofreader, who helped to polish the script and make it shine.

To the wonderful Irish writing community, to book-bloggers, and booksellers, and most especially to all my loyal readers, for helping to keep me in my dream job. Your kind messages and support mean everything to me and I am indebted to you all.

In writing this novel, it was a joy for me to have one of my main characters, Alice, working in a library. I'd like to pay tribute to the Irish library service, which is a remarkable and vital based resource, freely available to all. Libraries are wonderful places, bringing the world to your fingertips. In recent years, the extraordinary range of services and facilities available and the variety of experiences and events on offer have been enhanced and expanded to fully support the social, nurturing and learning needs of library users. I'd like to thank the staff of my local library in Ballyroan for the wonderful service they deliver with a friendly smile, and in particular Síle Coleman and Siobhan Feeley, who took time out of their busy days to answer some of my library-related queries.

Last but by no means least, a huge thank you to my family and friends, for always being there throughout the swings and roundabouts of life. You fill me up with love and kindness, friendship and inspiration. I wouldn't be where I am without your unstinting support.

I hope you all enjoy *The Perfect Sister*.

Zoë xxx

THE
VISITOR

Is he who he says he is?

ZOË
MILLER

Is he who he says he is?

Izzie Mallon is looking forward to celebrating Christmas
on a relaxing yoga retreat. At least, that is what she's
telling her mother and colleagues. In reality, she will
be shutting herself away from the festive season, and
the snowstorm that has brought the city to a standstill,
in her apartment on Henrietta Square — the beautiful
home she shared with her beloved husband Sam until his
tragic death a few months ago — with only her grief for
company.

Then, there's a knock at the door — a stranger,
stranded by the bad weather.

He tells Izzie that he's Eli Sanders, her husband's long-
time friend. Izzie has never met him in person, but feels
she owes it to Sam to welcome Eli into her home. Even
though her instincts say that she should do otherwise …

As Izzie tries to reminisce with Eli about her husband,
cracks in his story begin to show. But will she be able to
see clearly through her grief before it's too late?

Also available as an ebook

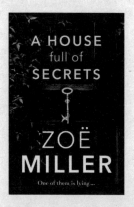

A HOUSE
full of
SECRETS

ZOË
MILLER

One of them is lying ...

All she sees is the perfect man –
but what is he hiding?

An invitation to visit Niall's childhood home is too good
an opportunity for Vikki to pass up. This is the chance
she's been waiting for to get closer to her friend, and to
meet the family he's always been so cryptic about.

But when Vikki arrives at the beautiful but remote
Lynes Glen on Ireland's west coast, and finally meets
Niall's estranged brother Alex and his overbearing
sister Lainey, she realises that this reunion will be far
from heart-warming.

As Vikki fails to convince any of them that she saw
a mysterious woman at the lake – off-limits since a
tragic accident – strange and sinister incidents begin to
happen at the Blake family home. What secrets are they
keeping? And why exactly did Niall ask Vikki to join
him for the weekend?

Also available as an ebook